THEATRE AND THE
Macabre

HORROR STUDIES

Series Editor
Xavier Aldana Reyes, Manchester Metropolitan University

Editorial Board
Stacey Abbott, Roehampton University
Linnie Blake, Manchester Metropolitan University
Harry M. Benshoff, University of North Texas
Fred Botting, Kingston University
Steven Bruhm, Western University
Steffen Hantke, Sogang University
Joan Hawkins, Indiana University
Alexandra Heller-Nicholas, Deakin University
Agnieszka Soltysik Monnet, University of Lausanne
Bernice M. Murphy, Trinity College Dublin
Johnny Walker, Northumbria University
Maisha Wester, Indiana University Bloomington

Preface

Horror Studies is the first book series exclusively dedicated to the study of the genre in its various manifestations – from fiction to cinema and television, magazines to comics, and extending to other forms of narrative texts such as video games and music. Horror Studies aims to raise the profile of Horror and to further its academic institutionalisation by providing a publishing home for cutting-edge research. As an exciting new venture within the established Cultural Studies and Literary Criticism programme, Horror Studies will expand the field in innovative and student-friendly ways.

THEATRE AND THE
Macabre

EDITED BY MEREDITH CONTI AND
KEVIN J. WETMORE, JR

UNIVERSITY OF WALES PRESS
2022

© The Contributors, 2022

All rights reserved. No part of this book may be reproduced in any material form (including photocopying or storing it in any medium by electronic means and whether or not transiently or incidentally to some other use of this publication) without the written permission of the copyright owner except in accordance with the provisions of the Copyright, Designs and Patents Act. Applications for the copyright owner's written permission to reproduce any part of this publication should be addressed to the University of Wales Press, University Registry, King Edward VII Avenue, Cardiff, CF10 3NS.

www.uwp.co.uk

British Library Cataloguing-in-Publication Data

A catalogue record for this book is available from the British Library.

ISBN   978-1-78683-845-2
eISBN 978-1-78683-846-9

The rights of The Contributors to be identified as authors of this work have been asserted in accordance with sections 77 and 79 of the Copyright, Designs and Patents Act 1988.

Typeset by Chris Bell, cbdesign

Printed by CPI Antony Rowe, Melksham, United Kingdom

For Ryan
and
For Lacy

Contents

Acknowledgements	ix
Contributors	xi
Introduction: I Made the Dance of Death Meredith Conti	1
Part One: Histories of the Macabre	**11**
1. The Mortification of Harvey Leach Humour and Horror in Nineteenth-Century Theatre of Disability Michael Mark Chemers	13
2. The Horrors of the Great War on the London Stage The Grand Guignol Season of 1915 Helen E. M. Brooks	29
3. Phantoms of the Stage The History and Practice of Uncanny Apparitions Richard J. Hand	45
Part Two: Dramaturgies of the Macabre	**61**
4. Time and Punishment Gothic Maternal Bodies on the Contemporary British Stage Kelly Jones	63
5. The Body Dismembered Allegory and Modernity in German *Trauerspiel* Magda Romanska	79
6. Macabre Children on the Australian Stage Angela Betzien's Cycle of Crime Plays Chris Hay and Stephen Carleton	95

7. **Martin McDonagh's** *Hangmen*
   Justice and Guilt in Public and Private Acts of Hanging   113
   Michelle C. Paull

8. **Fear of Death and Lyrical Flight**
   Mortality Salience Mediation in *Fun Home*   127
   Christopher J. Staley

Part Three: Staging the Macabre   143

9. **The Severed Head on Stage**   145
   Kevin J. Wetmore, Jr

10. **Dancing Haunted Legacies**
    Diana Szeinblum's *Alaska*   161
    Jeanmarie Higgins

11. **'To Die Over and Over Inside My Body'**
    Three Deaths in Hijikata Tatsumi's *Butoh*   175
    J. Hoay-Fern Ooi

Part Four: The Immersive Macabre   191

12. **'Black and Deep Desires'**
    Sleep No More and the Immersive Macabre   193
    Dan Venning

13. **The Dark Ride Immersive and the** *Danse Macabre*   207
    David Bisaha

14. **Liveness and Aliveness**
    Chasing the Uncanny in the Contemporary Haunt Industry   223
    David Norris

15. **American Hells**
    Hell Houses, Abortion Frames and Unsexed Women   237
    Robyn Lee Horn

16. **Haunting the Stage**
    Macabre Tourism, *Lieux de Mémoire* and the Immortal
    Death of Abraham Lincoln at Ford's Theatre   251
    Meredith Conti

Bibliography   267

Index   287

Acknowledgements

THE EDITORS would like to thank the University of Wales Press and especially Sarah Lewis and series editor Xavier Aldana Reyes. Thank you to the contributors to this collection, who created essays of boldness and perceptivity, and to Ian Downes for providing invaluable editorial support in the final months of this project. We remain grateful for the faculty, students and staff at our home institutions, the University at Buffalo, SUNY (UB) and Loyola Marymount University.

Meredith would like to thank three generous communities of scholars whose support and insights benefitted her research on macabre tourism and sites of gun violence: the University at Buffalo's Humanities Institute and her cohort of 2019–20 Faculty Fellows; the university's Gender Institute; and the American Society for Theatre Research's 'In Memoriam' working group convened by D. J. Hopkins, Shelley Orr and Alison Urban. She is grateful to UB colleagues Carrie Tirado Bramen, Becky Burke, Anne Burnidge, David Castillo, Lindsay Brandon Hunter, Eero Laine, Christina Milletti, Ariel Nereson, Danielle Rosvally, Maki Tanigaki and Hilary Vandenbark, as well as the graduate and undergraduate students in her 'Horror Theatre' course. Meredith would also like to thank Ryan, Milo, Vivian and Bo.

Kevin would like to thank his family (Lacy, Kevin III and Cordelia), the staff of the William H. Hannon Library, Samuel L. Leiter and the students in his 'Horror and Terror on Stage' seminar and 'Haunting of Hannon' performance series.

Contributors

David Bisaha is an assistant professor of theatre history and theory at Binghamton University, SUNY. His research on twentieth-century scenic design and the more recent history of immersive and participatory performance has been published in *Theatre Survey*, *Theatre and Performance Design* and *Theatre History Studies*.

Helen E. M. Brooks is reader in theatre and cultural history at the University of Kent. She is primary investigator on the community-research 'Great War Theatre' project and co-investigator on the Arts and Humanities Research Council projects 'Performing Centenaries' and 'Gateways to the First World War'. Prior to working on First World War theatre, she published widely on eighteenth-century theatre.

Stephen Carleton is an associate professor and the director of the Centre for Critical and Creative Writing at the University of Queensland. He also teaches on the drama major in the School of Communication and Arts. Carleton is a playwright and theatre scholar, with particular research interests in Australian theatre, Gothic drama, cultural landscapes and playwriting.

Michael Mark Chemers is professor of dramatic literature at the University of California, Santa Cruz. He is the author of several works on disability and monstrosity in performance, including *Staging Stigma: A Critical Examination of the American Freak Show* (Palgrave Macmillan, 2008) and *The Monster in Theatre History: This Thing of Darkness* (Routledge, 2018).

Meredith Conti is an associate professor of theatre at the University at Buffalo, SUNY and a historian of nineteenth-century performance and popular culture in the United States and Great Britain. She is the author of *Playing Sick: Performances of Illness in the Age of Victorian Medicine* (Routledge, 2019) and of published essays on medicine and theatre, the 1893 Chicago World's Fair, and gun violence on the US American stage.

Richard J. Hand is professor of media practice at the University of East Anglia. He has a special interest in popular performance culture, especially horror, using critical and practical research methodologies. He is the author of books on Grand Guignol horror theatre, horror radio drama, and horror and Gothic film.

Chris Hay is senior lecturer in drama and an Australian Research Council Discovery Early Career Research Award Fellow in the School of Communication and Arts at the University of Queensland. He is an Australian theatre and cultural historian whose research examines the history of arts subsidy in Australia and the impact of state funding on the nation's live-performance culture.

Jeanmarie Higgins is an associate professor in the School of Theatre at the Pennsylvania State University. A new works dramaturg in theatre and dance, Higgins publishes widely on the intersection of theory and practice. She is the editor of *Teaching Critical Performance Theory in Today's Theatre Classroom, Studio and Communities* (Routledge, 2020).

Robyn Lee Horn is a PhD candidate at the University at Buffalo, SUNY. Her research focuses on performance and religion in the United States. Ongoing projects explore embodiments of rhetoric, eschatological temporality and the biblical imaginary. She is the managing director of Alleyway Theatre in Buffalo, New York.

Kelly Jones is a senior lecturer in drama at the University of Lincoln, where her work focuses on staging the Gothic as well as theatrical realisations of the supernatural. She has co-edited *Contemporary Gothic Drama: Attraction, Consummation and Consumption on the Modern British Stage* (Palgrave Macmillan, 2017) and is currently working on a monograph, *The Ghost Story on the English Stage*.

David Norris has worked in the scare entertainment industry for over a decade as a performer, writer, director and producer. He is a lecturer at University Campus Oldham and a PhD candidate at the University of Birmingham. His research centres on immersive horror, with a particular emphasis on its relationship to identity.

J. Hoay-Fern Ooi is a PhD candidate in the English Department of the University of Malaya. Her thesis explores Georges Bataille's *l'informe* as literary operation. She was recently awarded the Monbukagakusho scholarship and will further her study of Hijikata Tatsumi's *butoh* choreographic notation while based at the University of Tokyo.

Michelle C. Paull is associate professor in drama at St Mary's University. She has published on Sean O'Casey, George Bernard Shaw and contemporary Irish drama, and researches contemporary theatre, new writing, adaptation studies and London theatre.

Magda Romanska is an associate professor of theatre studies at Emerson College. She is the author or editor of five critically acclaimed theatre books, including *The Post-traumatic Theatre of Grotowski and Kantor*, *Reader in Comedy: An Anthology of Theory and Criticism*, *The Routledge Companion to Dramaturgy* and *Theatermachine: Tadeusz Kantor in Context*.

Christopher J. Staley is an actor, director and teaching artist. He is currently a PhD candidate in theatre and performance studies at the University of Pittsburgh and holds an MFA in acting from the American Repertory Theatre/Moscow Art Theatre Institute for Advanced Theatre Training at Harvard University.

Dan Venning is an assistant professor of theatre and English at Union College, where he is also a core faculty member in the interdisciplinary programmes in gender, sexuality and women's studies and American studies. He holds a PhD in theatre from the CUNY Graduate Center.

Kevin J. Wetmore, Jr is professor of theatre and director of the MFA programme at Loyola Marymount University. He is the author, editor or co-editor of more than two dozen books, including *Post-9/11 Horror in American Cinema* and *Eaters of the Dead: Myths and Realities of Cannibal Monsters*, as well as numerous articles on horror theatre.

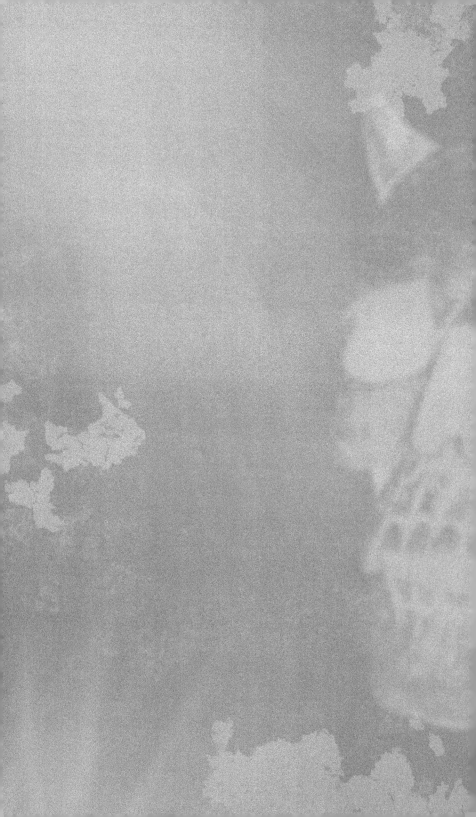

Introduction

I Made the Dance of Death

Meredith Conti

'LE RESPIT DE LA MORT', a 1376 poem by Jean le Fèvre, marks the first recorded use of the word 'macabre'. 'Je fis de macabre la dance', the didactic poem declares, or 'I made the dance of death', a phrase some scholars believe le Fèvre wrote while recovering from the plague. Twenty years later, notes R. C. Finucane, 'a dramatic performance of a *danse macabre* in a church in Normandy – an actual dance of death' is documented. However, as Sophie Oosterwijk suggests, the loss of medieval texts and the transient nature of performance leave open the possibility that le Fèvre's 'macabre la dance' was not the start of something new, but a reflection of something pre-existing: '["Le Respit de la Mort"] may have been referring to some now unknown form of "macabre" performance that he expected his readers to be familiar with . . . [or a] no longer extant poem that he himself wrote.'[1]

The emergence of an embodied *danse macabre* in fourteenth-century France is unsurprising, given that Normandians engaged in elaborate, seemingly interminable dances with death on battlefields both literal and figurative. English and French armies clashed in and around Normandy throughout the Hundred Years' War, while the Great Famine, the Black Death and high mortality rates for children, childbearing mothers and manual labourers made death a constant companion to medieval life in the region. Across a spectrum of artistic mediums – frescos and paintings, poems and music, court masques, folk dances and morality plays – the allegorical *danse macabre* depicts Death, normally in the form of a cavorting skeleton crew, leading the living in a processional dance towards the grave. In some instances, visual representations of the procession arrange the living figures by their social status, from pope to hermit, before the inevitable hands of Death 'equalise' them. In late-medieval renderings of the *danse macabre*, the faces of the living register a variety of responses to their circumstances, including revulsion, disbelief, placidity and acceptance. The dead clasp hands with the living or hold them by the wrists or shoulders, marking the futility of resisting or evading death. Repulsive yet beautiful, horrific yet humorous, the *danse macabre* dramatises the transformative, liminal moment between life and afterlife.

The 'macabre', as a process and product, has been haunting the theatre – and more broadly, performance – for thousands of years. In its embodied meditations on death and dying, its thematic and aesthetic grotesquerie, and its sensory-rich environments, macabre theatre invites artists and audiences to trace the stranger, darker contours of human existence. Scholars of theatre and popular culture, among them Analola Santana, Janet M. Davis, Kelly Jones, Benjamin Poore and Robert Dean, Catherine Wynne, Richard J. Hand and Michael Wilson, Beth A. Kattelman, John Fletcher, Soyica Diggs Colbert and Michael M. Chemers, have generated a rich catalogue of works on circuses, freak shows, Gothic dramas, the Grand Guignol, Evangelical hell houses, August Wilson's ghosts and William Shakespeare's monsters.[2] Yet the very nature of the macabre allows it to traverse sites, mediums and genres, making the task of reckoning with 'macabre performance' well-suited to a multi-authored, multidisciplinary collection. *Theatre and the Macabre* is the first scholarly volume to theorise on and illuminate theatre's intimate, productive and at times confounding relationship with the macabre. Across sixteen essays, scholars and practitioners of theatre, dance and performance studies scrutinise the texts, designs, choreographies, scores and habitats that create the macabre on stage. Together, these contributors argue that macabre theatre, as something that is performed and witnessed, does not just frighten or entertain; its cultural work both encompasses and exceeds such spontaneous reactions. Indeed, macabre performances have the potential to speak deeply and provocatively to shared social, cultural and political anxieties. They bring strange worlds into being and expose the peculiarities in our ordinary worlds. They exploit audiences' kinaesthetic empathy, staging graphic encounters that impel spectating bodies to respond. And, like Frankenstein and his creature, they often suture disparate parts together – genres, styles, forms – to make an affecting whole.

In this volume, we move from an understanding of macabre theatre as one that is disturbing, horrifying or provoking because of its involvement with death, injury, the gruesome or the grotesque. We acknowledge the challenge in this volume of distinguishing between the highly overlapping areas of macabre theatre and performance and theatre that directly engages death itself. Several significant texts on the latter have emerged in the last decade exploring the relationship between theatre and death itself. Karoline Gritzner edited *Eroticism and Death in Theatre and Performance* (2010), which contains essays linking eros and thanatos on stage. Mischa Twitchin's *The Theatre of Death – The Uncanny in Mimesis* (2016), as its title suggests, posits theatre as equally uncanny, as it is not only mimesis of life, but also of death. Most recently (as of this writing) Adrian Curtain's *Death in Modern Theatre: Stages of Mortality* (2019) explores how modern dramatists and theatre makers engage with and depict ideas about death and dying (shaped, for example, by the first and second world wars) in their works.[3] Although dramaturgies of this ductile performance approach vary greatly, macabre theatre commonly features at least several of the following: violations of bodies and the perception of 'bodily integrity'; manipulations of linear time; grim, unsettling or unpredictable atmospheres and environments; the inclusion of objects and symbols of death; a multi-sensory design aesthetic that deliberately moves beyond the visual; experimental staging practices that disrupt theatrical realism's actor-spectator divide; and the evocation of cultural myths and folklore. A study of the macabre in performance, then, could take a variety of theoretical or methodological approaches, and *Theatre and the Macabre*'s contributors do just that. What binds the collection's chapters together is a shared contemplation of the conditions and practices through which macabre theatre manifests.

The macabre is neither time-bound nor limited to a specific culture or cultures. Therefore, this volume offers essays that range across periods, geographic boundaries and sites of entertainment, inviting readers to consider how the macabre is simultaneously ubiquitous and idiosyncratic, global and site-specific. Nevertheless, scholars and practitioners of contemporary macabre performance must reckon with the enduring centrality of white European theatrical conventions and aesthetics, particularly as expressed in the genre of horror. (If represented in a Venn diagram, the formalised horror genre and the more diffuse notion of macabre theatre would overlap significantly. But while horror theatre is a frequent vehicle for the macabre, the macabre can materialise outside of horror's discrete boundaries.) As in some examples of the medieval and early Renaissance *danse macabre*, where skeletons first ushered the pope, lords and ladies to the grave before marshalling the unnamed commoners to Death (the great equaliser), performances of the macabre have historically prioritised the narratives, perspectives and tastes of the socially privileged. As film and literary theorists often remind us, horror conventionally fortifies white heteronormative values, representing human difference in problematic, limited or vexing ways.[4] Horror theatre is similarly culpable. Whether through the tragedies of Euripides and Webster, Parisian phantasmagoria, Victorian penny dreadfuls or 1980s slasher films, Western horror can obscure or under-interrogate the horrors of racism, ableism, homophobia, transphobia and misogyny, among others, while infantilising or villainising a spectrum of society's Others. Paratheatrical or non-narrative macabre entertainments, from the enfreaking scientific exhibitions of Sarah Baartman and Joseph Merrick to Halloween scare attractions, often reify such patterns.

Macabre forms of art-making have never been the sole purview of the dominant Western culture, however. Theatrical articulations of death and dying verge on the omnipresent; *día de los muertos* celebrations and the violent massacres staged in Iranian *ta'ziyeh* (meaning 'to comfort or console'), for example, invite communities to mourn and memorialise those who have passed. Furthermore, with few proscriptive rules governing its structures, language and effects, the macabre theatre is uniquely primed to critique white heteronormativity and the entrenched institutions that sustain it. In *Searching for Sycorax: Black Women's Hauntings in Contemporary Horror* (2017), Kinitra D. Brooks attends to the persistent 'absent presence' in literary and filmic horror of Black women characters, who she collectively names 'Sycorax' after *The Tempest*'s unseen islander, an Algerian witch and Caliban's mother. Despite centuries of erasure, marginalisation and violence, Brooks asserts, Sycorax 'rescues herself' through the restorative works of Black women horror writers.[5] Brooks's observations find support in the contemporary theatre, where Black women playwrights Kirsten Greenidge and Jackie Sibblies Drury leverage the horror genre to expose and interrogate gentrification, misogynoir and the ghosts of chattel slavery and Jim Crow. Similarly, as Tuscarora writer Alicia Elliott asserts, 'Indigenous writers know what it's like to live in a world where the horror never stops'.[6] On stage, the traumas of settler colonialism and Canada's murdered and missing Indigenous women inspire the macabre hauntings of Daniel David Moses's *Brébeuf's Ghost* (2000) and Tara Beagan's *Deer Woman* (2019). Just whose bodies, voices and stories find expression in and through the macabre continues to be a vital project for theatre and performance scholars, as chapters by Michael Mark Chemers, J. Hoay-Fern Ooi, Robyn Lee Horn, Kelly Jones, and Chris Hay and Stephen Carleton make clear.

Vital, too, is an assessment of the ways that theatre artists imagine, produce and stage the macabre, as well as how audiences witness and participate in these inventions. The four parts of *Theatre and the Macabre* coalesce around such topics of enquiry.

The three chapters of Part I, 'Histories of the Macabre', evaluate key manifestations of the macabre in performance – the exhibition of non-normative bodies, Grand Guignol horror and the staging of ghostly apparitions – as expressive of the curiosities, anxieties and values of their sociocultural moments. Michael Mark Chemers introduces readers to Harvey Leach, a nineteenth-century disabled actor who was publicly unmasked as a 'fraud' while performing as a snarling, wild and caged 'What Is It?' Chemers contends that Leach's mortification at the hands of audiences and the press exposes the undervalued 'aesthetic proximity' of horror and humour. Helen E. M. Brooks then evaluates the Grand Guignol's 1915 London residency, which staged graphic disfigurements and premature burials of the still living for British audiences who were watching the horrors of the Great War unfold from afar. While the famed Parisian company produced only one war play, Brooks asserts that the Grand Guignol's repertoire of fictional horrors invited wartime audiences to 'safely' witness and cognitively process World War I's grim realities. In Part I's final chapter, Richard J. Hand reanimates a transhistorical array of the theatre's most evocative visitors: ghosts. Attending to the written texts, cultural conditions and theatre technologies that manifest spectres on stage, Hand argues that what makes ghosts powerful figures in theatre history is also what allows theatre itself to exist: the magical fusion of real and not real, of presence and absence.

The contributors of Part II, 'Dramaturgies of the Macabre', analyse ways in which the theatre composes the macabre, be it textually, musically or aesthetically. Kelly Jones considers the live body of the monstrous mother as represented on the British stage, particularly through Robert Alan Evans's *The Woods*, Simon Stone's revisioning of Federico García Lorca's *Yerma* and

Selma Dimitrijevic's *Dr Frankenstein*. Jones argues that these plays borrow from the Gothic genre to complicate the monstrous spectacle of the subversive mother figure, rather than to reinforce it, allowing audiences to be co-present in the same interstitial space and non-linear time as the play's women characters. A puppet, according to Magda Romanska in the following chapter, is 'a corpse, an object that belongs neither to life nor to death, thus evading the laws of both'. And if the puppet itself arouses the terror of the unknown yet familiar, the puppet's dismembered torso is twice as terrifying. Building on Walter Benjamin's *Origin of the German Trauerspiel*, as well as Freud and Lacan, Romanska theorises on *Trauerspiel* through the dismembered effigy of a ruler, a puppet that becomes the very incarnation of allegorical destruction and deconstruction. Also considering allegory and incarnation, Chris Hay and Stephen Carleton use Australian playwright Angela Betzien's *The Dark Room*, *Mortido* and *The Hanging*, which together exploit the child as an avatar of the macabre in order to stage personal trauma as well as the national traumas that haunt contemporary Australia. Martin McDonagh is no stranger to the macabre in theatre, especially in such plays as *The Pillowman*, *A Skull in Connemara*, *A Behanding in Spokane* and *A Very Very Very Dark Matter*, which all contain elements designed to viscerally shock the audience. In her contribution to the volume, Michelle C. Paull examines McDonagh's 2015 play *Hangmen*, a discourse on capital punishment and the men who carry it out, leading to a debate about what constitutes a fair and just society. Given McDonagh's dramaturgical proclivities, this debate conveys the reality of execution via a stage death in real time. Proximity to death and its after-effects is also the topic of Christopher J. Staley's chapter, which finds the macabre in Lisa Kron and Jeanine Tesori's musical *Fun Home*. The title itself is a corruption of 'funeral home', where the protagonist and her family live. Staley uses terror management theory to explore how the creators evoke death and use flight imagery as provocations of the characters and the audience.

The chapters of Part III, 'Staging the Macabre', evaluate the publicly exhibited macabre body and explore, in one sense or another, the presentation of bodily trauma. Kevin J. Wetmore, Jr observes that while the stage privileges the skull as a symbol, the severed head represents a more macabre *memento mori* because, unlike a skull, it is the recognisable face of a character. Exploring the cultural differences between severed heads on the stages of Renaissance England, Tokugawa Japan and the Grand Guignol (after Revolutionary France), Wetmore concludes that severed heads signify differently within theatrical traditions, but the decollated body and disembodied head always function as greater symbols than the mere end of a human life. Jeanmarie Higgins and J. Hoay-Fern Ooi each explore the macabre body through dance. Higgins considers the performances that are danced conversations between death and the living, particularly in Diana Szeinblum's *Alaska*, a dance that stages the cultural trauma of Argentina's Dirty War, in which Higgins finds a deep embodiment of the literal *danse macabre* motif. Ooi examines the Japanese *ankoku butoh* ('Dance of Utter Darkness') of Hijikata Tastsumi, a traumatic evocation of the dead who return to inhabit the dancer's body. Both Higgins and Ooi consider how the dancing body becomes the site on which the traumas of war (both physical and psychological) can be made manifest through performance and serve to remember those gone and lost.

'[The English word] *space* slips between both a literal location and a metaphoric capacity to structure our perceptions of the world', notes Joanne Tompkins, scholar of theatre spatiality and site-specific performance.[7] Because macabre theatre operates both within and outside traditional performance venues, an analysis of this unwieldy genre must venture beyond the playhouse to include other sites of embodiment. In haunted houses, dark tourism locales, amusement parks, museums and even public execution grounds, the macabre expands and contorts to fit disparate parameters, technological capacities and audience expectations. The contributors to Part IV, 'The Immersive Macabre', together examine participatory, site-specific events that shape and are shaped by the macabre. In Part IV's first chapter, Dan Venning accesses the labyrinthine environs of Punchdrunk and Emursive's *Sleep No More*, the acclaimed adaptation of Shakespeare's *Macbeth* that has increased the mainstream visibility of immersive theatre on three continents. The production's signature elements – its dark aesthetics, sensual choreographies and anonymised participants, among others – together forge a carnivalesque 'immersive macabre' that Venning ties directly to *Sleep No More*'s capitalistic ambitions. In the next chapter, David Bisaha analyses the contemporary immersive theatre's spatial aesthetics and body-based storytelling. Bisaha detects in recent immersive productions a pair of macabre features that disorientate and affect audiences: the use of 'dark ride' structural and movement patterns (as in dark amusement-park rides) and evocations of the allegorical *danse macabre*. The haunt industry's scare attractions, and the monstrous embodiments and animatronics that they boast, are the subject of David Norris's essay on liveness and the macabre. In it, Norris presents the doll, brought 'to life' by the performer, as an uncanny figure that elicits exceptional affective responses. In the following chapter, Robyn Lee Horn examines one of the theatrical anchors of an Evangelical hell house: the abortion scene. As she articulates, such scenes are customarily gore-filled simulations of botched abortions performed by unemotional women doctors; however, recent deviations in staging abortion scenes suggest that wider trends in anti-abortion rhetoric have influenced how hell houses execute the ultimate 'sin'. Finally, Meredith Conti employs Pierre Nora's *lieu de mémoire* ('site of memory') alongside Marvin Carlson's notion of the 'haunted stage' to assess the dark touristic experiences at Ford's Theatre, the historic site of Abraham Lincoln's assassination. Conti argues that Ford's Theatre embraces the macabre as a theatrical and pedagogical tool, one that enhances – rather than detracts from – the site's mission to remember Lincoln and his legacy.

When author Stephen King penned a non-fiction book about the horror genre in 1981, he reached back in time to find its title: *Danse Macabre*. And when the Spanish edition of King's novel *The Stand* hit bookshelves, its cover read *La danza de la muerte*, or *The Dance of Death*. Clearly, the notion of 'dancing with Death' still fascinates, even centuries after it first appeared in poems and on church walls. In exploring the macabre theatre's dark dramaturgies, strange visitations, distressed bodies and unsettled spectators, *Theatre and the Macabre* perceives, and often honours, the indispensable figures of an embodied *danse macabre*: performers and audiences willing to join hands with (the concept of) Death.

Notes

1. R. C. Finuacane, *Ghosts: Appearances of the Dead and Cultural Transformation* (New York: Prometheus, 1996), p. 51; and S. Oosterwijk, '"Fro Paris to Inglond?": The *Danse Macabre* in Image and Text in Late-Medieval England' (unpublished PhD thesis: Leiden University, 2009), 12.
2. Analola Santana, *Freak Performances: Dissidence in Latin American Theater* (Ann Arbor MI: University of Michigan Press, 2018); Janet M. Davis, *Circus Age: Culture and Society Under the American Big Top* (Chapel Hill NC: University of North Carolina Press, 2002); Kelly Jones, Benjamin Poore and Robert Dean (eds), *Contemporary Gothic Drama: Attraction, Consummation and Consumption on the Modern British Stage* (Basingstoke: Palgrave Macmillan, 2018); Catherine Wynne, *Bram Stoker, Dracula and the Victorian Gothic Stage* (Basingstoke: Palgrave Macmillan, 2013); Richard J. Hand and Michael

Wilson, *Grand-Guignol: The French Theatre of Horror* (Exeter: University of Exeter Press, 2002); B. A. Kattelman, 'Magic, Monsters, and Movies: America's Midnight Ghost Shows', *Theatre Journal*, 62/1 (2010); John Fletcher, *Preaching to Convert: Evangelical Outreach and Performance Activism in a Secular Age* (Ann Arbor MI: University of Michigan Press, 2013); Soyica Diggs Colbert, *The African American Theatrical Body: Reception, Performance, and the Stage* (Cambridge: Cambridge University Press, 2011); and Michael M. Chemers, *The Monster in Theatre History: This Thing of Darkness* (London: Taylor and Francis, 2018).
3. Karoline Gritzner (ed.), *Eroticism and Death in Theatre and Performance* (Hatfield: University of Hertfordshire Press, 2010); Mischa Twitchin, *The Theatre of Death – The Uncanny in Mimesis* (New York: Palgrave Macmillan, 2016); and Adrian Curtain, *Death in Modern Theatre: Stages of Mortality* (Manchester: Manchester University Press, 2019).
4. See, among others, the published works of Carol J. Clover, Barbara Creed, Angela M. Smith, Tananarive Due, Justin D. Edwards and Ruth Bienstock Anolik.
5. Kinitra D. Brooks, *Searching for Sycorax: Black Women's Hauntings in Contemporary Horror* (New Brunswick NJ: Rutgers University Press, 2017), pp. 7, 15.
6. A. Elliott, 'The Rise of Indigenous Horror: How a Fiction Genre is Confronting a Monstrous Reality', *CBC*, 17 October 2019.
7. J. Tompkins, 'Space and the Geographies of Theatre: An Introduction', *Modern Drama*, 46/4 (2003), 538.

PART ONE

HISTORIES OF THE MACABRE

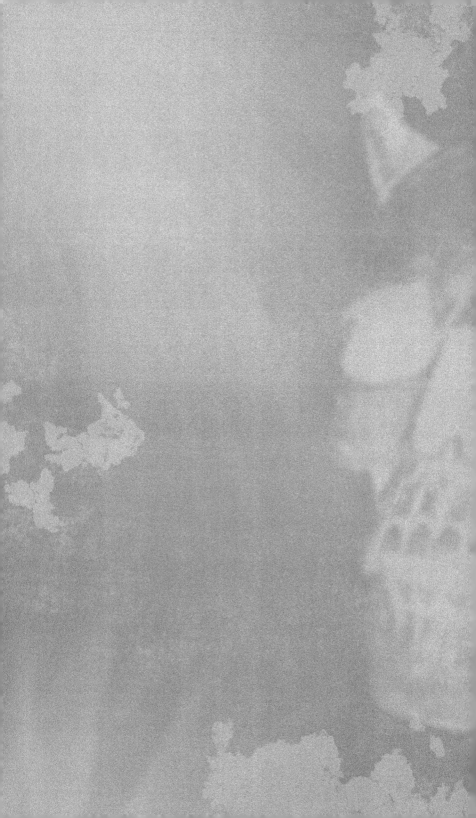

1

The Mortification of Harvey Leach

Humour and Horror in Nineteenth-Century Theatre of Disability

Michael Mark Chemers

THE MACABRE, AS A GENRE, is characterised not only by the presence of horror, but also of humour. Indeed, these two aesthetic states are often seen together in many genres, even as far back as the Greeks. In scholarly essays linking horror and humour, there is a recognition of a certain sympathy between the two. However, because of the revulsion of horror and the pleasure of humour, most theorists consider them to be diametrically opposed – two irreconcilable points of one of the binaries upon which Western thought stubbornly depends. But as is the case with most binaries, a careful examination reveals that these putatively oppositional poles are, in actuality, deeply imbricated. Using Noël Carroll's 1999 essay 'Horror and Humor' as a jumping-off point, I examine this overlap closely in a particular event that occurred during a nineteenth-century exhibition: the exposure and humiliation of an actor with a disability by the name of Harvey Leach.

It is not the purpose of this chapter to create a general theory of humour and horror. Indeed, this essay will demonstrate that the experience of horror and humour are *processes* (or, more often, the same process) which operate within dynamic systems of representation, shaping them in strange ways. As I have elsewhere demonstrated, it is more productive for the historian to recover specific case studies and apply those analytical methods that are most productive of useful enquiry.[1] Rather than generalise, this essay looks forensically into a single instant in 1846 that demonstrates the deeply systemic intersection of humour and horror.

The Mortification of Harvey Leach

On 29 August 1846, curiosity seekers attended a live human exhibit at London's Egyptian Hall of 'The Wild Man of the Prairies, or What Is It?'. They had been lured by a lurid image in *The Times* featuring a handsome-faced man with dark skin, long dirty hair and a hairy body proportioned as a strong man from the torso up but possessed of relatively short legs (see figure 1). The man is leaning against a wall, supported by a carved staff, looking around with intelligence and curiosity. His modesty is maintained by a pair of shorts. Behind him, incongruously, is a table set with a tea service. The text of the advertisement reads, in part:

> The exhibitors of this indescribable person or animal, do not pretend to assert what it is; they have named it THE WILD MAN OF THE PRAIRIES; or, 'WHAT IS IT,' because this is the universal exclamation of all who have seen it . . . 'WHAT IS IT' is decidedly the most extraordinary being that ever astonished the world.

When the exhibit opened, the creature, supposedly caught in California, was discovered in a cage, covered in thick hair, snarling, leaping and gnawing on raw meat. The audience must have been astonished – then, half an hour into the exhibition, one of the visitors suddenly recognised the What Is It? to be renowned American actor and aerialist Harvey Leach. The visitor opened the cage, entered it, and shook the creature's hand, saying something in the order of 'how are you, old fellow?'. Indeed, the wild man was Leach – the producers shut down the exhibition and the spectators got their money back. His reputation in tatters, Harvey Leach died some eight months later.

What to make of this occurrence, unusual even in the strange and convoluted history of disability and popular performance culture in the nineteenth century? Harvey Leach's career ran the gamut of the many kinds of performance that we would today call 'freak shows', which ranged

Figure 1. This image of Leach as Alnain the Gnome King is in the London Metropolitan Archives (Collage record no. 323406, Cat. SC_GL_ENT_018a), is mistitled as '"What Is It" attraction at the Egyptian Hall, appearing to be half human half animal' and is misdated.

from legitimate big-ticket performances featuring people with disabilities to these 'human exhibitions'. The student of such events must tread carefully, for the freak show of the nineteenth century was a cultural organism that fed mainly on lies – lies told usually to enhance and, paradoxically, relieve fear of the extraordinary body by exaggerating its apperception as inhuman, for purely mercenary reasons. But freak shows, and the exposure of Leach at the Egyptian Hall, are also exemplary of the aesthetic proximity of horror and humour. Investigating the mortification of Harvey Leach renders legible a strange phenomenon: that the mechanism by which audiences identify and process humour and horror are far more closely aligned than we might have previously supposed.

Who was Harvey Leach?

Born, according to what evidence exists, in Westchester County, New York, in 1804, Leach enjoyed a celebrated career as an aerialist, equestrian and acrobat. Sometimes erroneously described as 'the legless dwarf', Leach's ability to draw crowds seemed drawn from his feats of physical strength, performed entirely with his hands and arms, his facility as a clown and his conventional good looks.

On 31 January 1838, Leach began his most celebrated performance at London's Adelphi Theatre as the title character in a play called *The Gnome Fly* (see Figure 2). Leach, under his performing name 'Signor Hervio Nano', authored the play, which is described as an 'extravaganza' involving Alnain, the 'King of the Gnomes and Dives'. Directed by the Adelphi's manager Frederick H. Yates, the fairy-tale melodrama served as a vehicle for Leach's greatest feats as an acrobat and actor, as he also appeared as Sapajou, Baboon to the Prince of Tartary and as a magical bluebottle fly.

The reviewers of *The Times*, often sardonic when discussing exhibitions of extraordinary bodies, were amazed by Leach's acrobatics as the Gnome Fly. One review of opening night reads:

> He climbs . . . along the side of the theatre, gets into the upper circle in a moment, catches hold of the projection of the ornaments of the ceiling of the theatre, crosses to the opposite side, and descends along the vertical boarding of the proscenium . . . In a word, [he] performs some of the most astonishing feats ever exhibited within the walls of a theatre.[2]

Figure 2. Advertisement from *The Times*, 29 August 1846.

The Gnome Fly ran for forty-six performances between 31 January and 7 April 1838. Between *The Gnome Fly* and a companion piece, *The Major and the Monkey* (a burletta by Joseph S. Coyne starring the prominent character actor O. Smith, in which Leach played the 'Monkey'), Leach appeared at the Adelphi fifty-four times in the 1837–8 season.[3]

Leach had even better luck in the United States. *The Gnome Fly* enjoyed a wildly successful run at New York's Bowery and Chatham Theatres from 1840–1, which Leach supplemented by playing 'Jocko, the Brazilian Ape' at the Chatham and appearing in circuses as an equestrian and clown.[4] P. T. Barnum recorded a meeting with Leach in 1844 in his first autobiography, published in 1855:

> I was called upon by 'Hervio Nano', who was known to the public as the 'gnome fly', and was also celebrated for his representations as a monkey. His malformation caused him to appear much like that animal when properly dressed. He wished me to exhibit him in London, but having my hands already full, I declined . . . The exhibition opened Egyptian Hall, and as a matter of curiosity I attended the opening. Before half an hour had elapsed, one of the visitors, who knew 'Hervio Nano', recognized him through his disguise and exposed the imposition. The money was refunded to visitors, and that was the first and last appearance of 'What is it?' in that character. He soon afterward died in London.[5]

But this recollection seems at odds with a letter that Barnum wrote to his friend and fellow entrepreneur Moses Kimball in August 1846:

> The *animal* that I spoke to you & Hale about comes out at Egyptian Hall, London, next Monday, and I half fear that I will not only be exposed, but that *I* shall be *found out* in the matter. However, I go it, live or die. The thing is not to be called *anything* by his exhibitor. We know not & therefore do not assert whether it is human or animal. We leave all that to the sagacious public to decide.[6]

This letter seems to give the lie to Barnum's 1855 reconstruction of events; he *was* involved in this exhibition and had a significant hand in designing the ballyhoo of the event to avoid accusations of fraud (this is a characteristic of Barnum's promotional genius). That Barnum had a proprietary interest in the role of What Is It? is evinced by his resurrection of the character with the more famous William Henry Johnson, or 'Zip', around 1865.⁷ The exposure of Leach as a fraud was of great interest in the press throughout the following week:

> A correspondent of the *Times* – who characteristically signs himself 'Open-eye' – paid his shilling and was shown into the sanctum of the monster. He at once discovered the 'Wild Man of the Prairies' to be no other than the exceedingly tame dwarf Hervio Nano, otherwise Harvey Leach, who about ten years since performed the part of a blue-bottle at the Adelphi, Surrey, and other minor theatres.⁸

The identity of the man who exposed and mortified Leach may also be discernible from the historical record. In *Shows of London*, Richard Altick reports that the offending party was one Mr Carter, a lion tamer and possibly a rival of Leach, who held a grudge against Barnum for not allowing Tom Thumb to ride General Washington, a mammoth horse that belonged to Carter, during Carter's benefit night in the previous season at the Egyptian Hall.⁹ Altick reports that, oblivious to protestations from the What Is It?'s keepers, he entered the cage:

> Then, grabbing its forepaw, he 'drew the unresisting creature to the centre of the cage – with one strong tug tore the shaggy skin all down its back and sides' – and out, sheepishly no doubt, stepped the Gnome Fly. Carter's punchline was said to have been: 'And now, as you've been living on raw meat so long, come down to Craven street and have a broiled steak with me'.¹⁰

Even Altick allows that this account may have been 'apocryphal', but the next day, a letter signed 'Open-eye' did in fact appear in *The Times*, which read in part:

> Being a bit of a naturalist, and consequently anxious to see the 'what is it' at the Egyptian-hall in its first wildness, I arose two hours earlier than usual, proceeded thither in a kind of feverish excitement, paid my shilling magnanimously, and was shown into the sanctum of the 'wild man of the prairies' . . . Oh, the ghost of Buffon! What was my surprise when, at the first glance, I found 'what is it' to be an old acquaintance – Hervio Nano, alias Hervey Leech, himself! . . . I will

tell you how the 'wild man' . . . went to his kennel to argue with the proprietor on the propriety of returning my shilling.[11]

If Altick is right, it seems likely that Carter was allied with, or was indeed, 'Open-eye', and engineered the entire exposure by way of revenging himself on Barnum.

The death of Harvey Leach occurred in May 1847, eight months after the exposure of the What Is It?. James W. Cook, Jr, writing in 1996, finds an eyewitness account of Leach, his walking-on-the-ceiling trick, and his death in Henry Mayhew's 1851 *London Labour and the London Poor*. 'The Strong Man' relates:

> That 'What is It', at the Egyptian Hall killed him. They'd have made a heap of money at it if it hadn't been discovered. He was in a cage, and wonderfully got up. He looked awful. A friend of his comes in, and goes up to the cage, and says, 'How are you, old fellow?' The thing was blown up in a minute. The place was in an uproar. It killed Harvey Leach, for he took it to heart and died.[12]

It is impossible to know whether Leach died of embarrassment over this event, as the side-show strongman suggested. His mortification, however, emphasises the strange unification of horror and humour, and an analysis of this moment is revelatory of the deep imbrication of these aesthetic conditions.

Humour and Horror

Noël Carroll addresses this complex imbrication in his 1999 essay 'Horror and Humor'. Carroll begins by noting the apparent antagonism between the states. 'At least at first glance', he writes, 'horror and humor seem like opposite mental states. Being horrified seems as though it should preclude amusement. And what causes us to laugh does not appear as though it should also be capable of making us scream.'[13] But Carroll goes on to question a particular case, that of two portrayals of Frankenstein's monster (by the actor Glenn Strange) doing the same schtick in two films: *House of Frankenstein* (1944) and *Abbott and Costello Meet Frankenstein* (1948). In the first, the portrayal is met with horror, and in the second, humour.

What to make of this, especially in light of a trend among modernist cultural critics to associate the humour and horror reactions with similar stimuli? Carroll notes that in Freud's famous and influential 1919 essay 'The Uncanny', the feeling of uncanny horror is born when the percipient is unsure whether the subject of their gaze is living or mechanical, while Henri Bergson in his 1901 essay 'Laughter' considered that humour is triggered by exactly the same stimuli. Carroll posits a third position from which the comic and the horrific can be viewed as springing from similar inputs, which then begs the question of what exactly the difference is between these aesthetic responses.

Monsters are common if not completely indispensable elements of horror. Carroll defines monsters as creatures whose existence confounds widely held views of what is physically possible, inviting speculation into the inexplicable, occult or supernatural. This view of monsters accords well with the 'Seven Theses' of Jeffrey Jerome Cohen. In his essay, Cohen calls monsters 'harbingers of category crisis' not for a single category or set of categories, but for *any* category.[14] But Cohen's theory is more broadly useful than Bergson's, Freud's or Carroll's inasmuch as it recognises that the boundaries that a monster confounds can reside along *any* binary, not just that which separates the natural from the artificial. The vampire, for instance, confounds the separation between life and death; the ghost, between the present and the past; and the werewolf (and the wild man) between the civilised human and the feral beast.[15]

Seen from this perspective, it is clear that monstrous 'wild man' tropes have been applied to the performances of actors with unusual bodies for centuries in order to undergird racist ideologies that alleviate anxiety about the oppression of the colonial subject without or the ethnic minority within. In Leach's case, the performance of What Is It? included artificially darkened skin and a hairy costume, as well as a walking stick. When combined with the story that he had been 'discovered' on the American plains, the performance seems calculated to act as surrogate for, and thereby alleviate the anxiety of, the genocide of Indigenous Americans that was at that time in full, truly horrifying bloom. Configured as such, his true identity as a celebrated playwright, actor and aerialist disguised, Leach's unusual body becomes a site of titillating horror for the curious, worried, British audience.

But the confounding of binaries cannot be the only characteristic that distinguishes the monster from, say, the clown who imitates a bird or gets caught in the gears of a machine, since these also confound boundaries.

For Carroll, there must be the addition of fear and disgust: fear (or as I have elsewhere referred to it, 'fright'),[16] when the percipient understands that the subject of their gaze represents a clear and present threat of harm; and disgust, which is brought about by the offensiveness or odiousness of the dissolution of the binary. Carroll conjures by way of example the sudden appearance of a giant spider: 'Confronted by such a creature, our response would be to recoil, not only because of our fear that it might harm us, but also because it is an abominable, repugnant, impure thing – a dirty, filthy thing.'[17] It is therefore the impurity of the subject's category crisis that provides the necessary horrific stimulus: the violation of binaries that may be artificial but are nevertheless important to the percipient's state of mind regarding the nature of the universe and the percipient's own role in it. Thus, even a normal spider may be frightful, since it may present a threat of harm, whereas an unnaturally giant spider is properly horrific. The monster is that creature whose existence is, in Carroll's words, 'bound up with the violation, problematization, and transgression of our categories, norms, and concepts'.[18]

This notion of impurity as standing in not only category crisis, but also grotesquerie, has been before now attributed to the performance of Harvey Leach in his signature role. Jacob Smith, in his study of 'the human fly' character through the nineteenth and early twentieth centuries, writes of Leach that his effectiveness as the 'Gnome Fly' was his representation of a verminous, 'dirty' insect.[19] Horror, finally, is an emotional state of revulsion as much as fear, triggered not by a present fear of harm but of a profound, disgusting violation of some kind of social or natural binary (or most often both). But what is truly fascinating about all of this, Carroll goes on to observe, is that humour is predicated on exactly the same principles.

It seems possible to recognise that much of what is horrific and much of what is funny would be indistinguishable from one another without the conditioning of aesthetic distance, which is the result of contextual clues provided by the work of art. 'On the map of mental states', writes Carroll, 'horror and incongruity amusement are adjacent and partially overlapping regions . . . The impurities of horror can serve as the incongruities of humor'.[20] The totality of the performance (not just the interaction of the characters) must conspire to generate the proper lens through which it is to be viewed, and when this fails (as when a lion tamer with a chip on his shoulder ruins the show by giving the monster a hearty hello) the results are disastrous.[21]

Returning to the example of why Glenn Strange's Frankenstein's Monster is horrific in one film and funny in another, we must recognise the importance of incongruity. Abbot and Costello are clowns, well known to the audience before they bought their tickets. They react to the creature in a hyperbolised fashion because they are genuinely horrified; contrary to the expectations we have with Carroll's theory, this neither takes the threat out of the situation nor magnifies it – it merely contextualises it within a larger system of signification, one that is constantly changing. But we do know that clowns cannot really get hurt, or perhaps it is better to say that we have the *convention* that they are not going to really get hurt. This convention provides the context in which we view Strange's artistic choices and grants us the aesthetic distance so that we may laugh rather than scream.

The important observation is that while there are many kinds of humour, and many kinds of horror, and while the experiences of each are very personal and particular to each percipient, there is still a significant overlap in the kinds of stimulus that provoke either. That which is horrific may become humorous, and vice versa, with a flourish of the theatrical hand. This is exactly why clowns are so scary, and why humour and horror seem to walk hand in hand in so many cultural products. And it is for this reason, we may conclude, that the mortification of Harvey Leach, which contains elements of horror and humour, tragedy and comedy, is such a compelling tale to tell.

Disability Horror and Humour

Whether performing as the Gnome Fly or the What Is It?, Leach's unusual body was always a key component of his performativity. That he could transform himself from an aerialist and acrobat, which stunned crowds on both sides of the Atlantic, to a growling imitation savage is a testament, if not to his acting skills, then to the observation that disability (very much like race or gender) is a socially constructed identity, capable of different levels of, in Carroll's parlance, incongruity or impurity. What remained constant, and perhaps what enabled Carter to so easily 'recognise' Leach, was the extraordinariness of his body – what had been his unique performative features, in the end, were made to betray him.

Over the past three decades or so, disability studies has established itself as a site of vibrant intertextuality and interdisciplinarity, where it can work to identify and critique the social processes by which disability, as a social identity, is constructed and by which individuals with disabilities are then labelled for marginalisation. One of the chief concerns at this site is narrative tropes that fetishise disability, because these tropes rarely function to the benefit of the individual labelled as disabled. Performances of extraordinary-bodied actors in the nineteenth century, whether within the context of freak shows or big-ticket fairy-tale extravaganzas, are firmly within the realm of fetishisation. They are designed to magnify the 'otherness' of the unusual body for commercial advantage. Although I have argued that such discourses have vast potential for subversion and transgression, substituting a sense of wonder for a sense of disgust,[22] there can be no arguing that any narrative that questions the humanity of its subject contains the seeds of violence and violation, of exactly the kind that Leach experienced when Carter barged in on him at the Egyptian Hall.

But disability operates at the intersection of many discourses, some very different from those that impact upon discourses of race, gender, ethnicity, religion, class and other discourses of identity. For one thing, disability is (sometimes jokingly) understood as the only open-membership stigmatisation: anyone can become disabled at any time, for a variety of reasons that transcend and yet are specific to these other discourses. One may become disabled from exposure to drugs in utero or by falling off one's polo pony.[23] Unquestionably this anxiety is the true source of disability's efficacy at invoking horror. Confrontation with a disabled body can trigger fear and revulsion in a percipient who is not acculturated to look past the surface at the human beneath. Indeed, it seems easier (and more anxiety-relieving) to consider the disabled person *less than* human, and to treat them accordingly. But ironically (if not wholly unexpected), this is also the source of the humour of the disabled body.

Most of the world's comic traditions make use of disability, which plays well into discourses of inferiority as well as incongruity. 'Open-eye' invoked the 'ghost of Boufon' to characterise the moment that Carter literally and figuratively undisguised Leach, transforming him with a single action (i.e., entering the cage) from a creature of horror to a joke. How ironic, then, that those who laughed at him failed to demonstrate the very civilising process for which they were congratulating themselves a few moments earlier, when they were confronted by a dark and ravening savage.

Erving Goffman wrote in 1959 that death by embarrassment, or *mortification*, is possible when one's carefully constructed public image fails and exposes some qualities that one would have rather kept hidden.[24] It can be a crushing blow, capable of delivering real psychological damage and damage to one's physical health. It seems likely, from the recollections of Barnum and based on Leach's own highly creative competence in telling fanciful stories, that Leach himself was at least one of the architects of the What Is It?, that he would have developed the role painstakingly in preparation for exhibition at the Egyptian Hall. From what evidence exists, we may piece together a portrait of a great performer in decline, a one-time headliner forced to declare insolvency after his legal cases failed. What if the characteristic walking stick was not just a prop, but a device that he required as, entering his forties, his years of acrobatics had begun to exert their painful toll on his body? It is conceivable, is it not, that a man in such a state of being might receive a death blow from being thus exposed, ridiculed, humiliated and ultimately mortified?

Notes

1. See Michael M. Chemers, *The Monster in Theatre History: This Thing of Darkness* (Oxford: Routledge, 2018), pp. 2–5.
2. *Times*, 1 February 1838.
3. A. Koger (ed.), 'The Adelphi Theatre; Calendar for 1837–1838', *The Adelphi Calendar Project*, A. L. Nelson and G. B. Cross (general editors), www.umass.edu/AdelphiTheatreCalendar/m37d.htm.
4. Tom Picton, *Fun and Fancy in Old New York: Reminiscences of a Man About Town*, William L. Slout (ed.) (New York: Borgo, 2007), p. 239, n. 1.
5. Phineas Taylor Barnum, *The Life of P. T. Barnum, Written by Himself* (New York: Redfield, 1855), p. 346.
6. See A. H. Saxon, *Selected Letters of P. T. Barnum* (New York: Columbia University Press, 1983), pp. 37–8; see also James W. Cook, Jr, *The Art of Deception: Playing with Fraud in the Age of Barnum* (Cambridge MA: Harvard University Press, 2001), p. 134.
7. See J. W. Cook, Jr, 'Of Men, Missing Links, and Nondescripts: The Strange Career of P. T. Barnum's "What Is It?" Exhibition', in R. G. Thomson (ed.), *Freakery: The Cultural Spectacle of the Extraordinary Body* (New York: New York University Press, 1996), pp. 143–4; and Jane R. Goodall, *Performance and Evolution in the Age of Darwin: Out of the Natural Order*

(London: Routledge, 2002), pp. 73–4. Cook points out that Johnson appeared in a photograph staged in a remarkably similar manner to the drawing of Leach as the What Is It?, wearing a hairy costume and short trousers, and holding a long walking stick.
8. *Manchester Times and Gazette*, Saturday, 5 September 1846.
9. See Richard Altick, *The Shows of London: A Panoramic History of Exhibitions* (Cambridge MA: Harvard University Press, 1978), pp. 265–6; see also Michael M. Chemers, *Staging Stigma: A Critical Examination of the American Freak Show* (New York: Palgrave Macmillan, 2007), p. 76.
10. Altick, *Shows of London*, p. 265.
11. Altick, *Shows of London*, p. 266.
12. See Henry Mayhew, *London Labour and the London Poor*, 3 (1851), ebook at *Project Gutenberg* (2018), www.gutenberg.org/files/57060/57060-h/57060-h.htm; see also Cook, 'Of Men, Missing Links, and Nondescripts', p. 142. Altick confirms this version of events; see *Shows of London*, pp. 256–6.
13. N. Carroll, 'Horror and Humor', *The Journal of Aesthetics and Criticism*, 57/2 (Spring 1999), 145. Carroll goes to some pains to separate the aesthetic experience of horror (which he calls 'art-horror') from the kind of horror that we experience when, in his example, we read about 'urban violence'. I have no such qualms.
14. J. J. Cohen, 'Monster Culture: Seven Theses', in J. J. Cohen (ed.), *Monster Theory: Reading Culture* (Minneapolis MN: University of Minnesota Press, 1996), p. 7.
15. In *The Monster in Theatre History*, I apply Cohen's model to the 'surrogation' theory of performance by Joseph Roach as articulated in his *Cities of the Dead: Circum-Atlantic Performance* (New York: Columbia University Press, 1996), demonstrating that these depictions are employed to reduce social and psychological anxiety.
16. Chemers, *The Monster in Theatre History*, p. 12.
17. Carroll, 'Horror and Humor', p. 150.
18. Carroll, 'Horror and Humor', p. 152.
19. J. Smith, 'The Adventures of the Human Fly, 1830–1930', *Early Popular Visual Culture* 6 (2008), 66, n.1.
20. Carroll, 'Horror and Humor', p. 156.
21. Carroll notes 'of course, standardly, horror does not blend into humor, nor vice versa' (p. 157), which is an astonishing assertion. Anyone who has enjoyed, for instance, the hilarious antics of Una O'Connor in *Bride of Frankenstein* (1938) knows that humour and horror are the aesthetic equivalents of chocolate and peanut butter – two great tastes that taste great together.

22. Chemers, *Staging Stigma*, pp. 57–83.
23. R. L. Dawidoff, Foreword to *Why I Burned My Book and Other Essays on Disability* by Paul K. Longmore (Philadelphia PA: Temple University Press, 2003), p. vii.
24. See Chemers, *Staging Stigma*, p. 13.

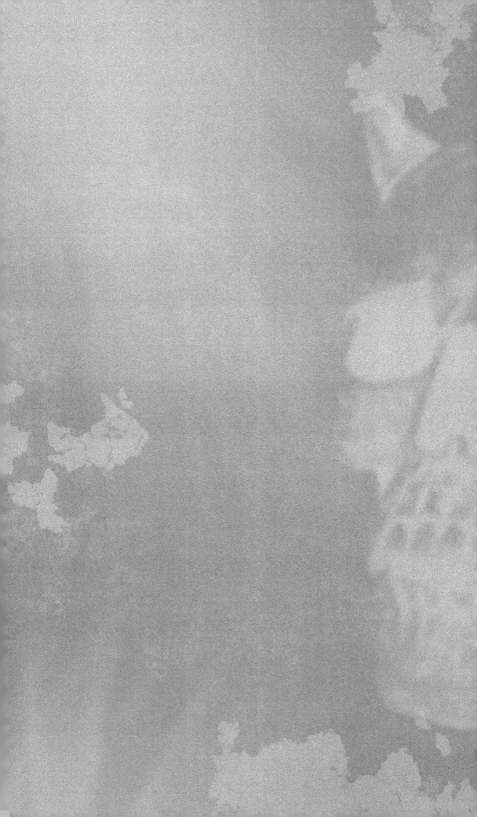

2

The Horrors of the Great War on the London Stage

The Grand Guignol Season of 1915

Helen E. M. Brooks

IN THE SUMMER OF 1915, just under a year into the Great War, the Parisian Grand Guignol theatre company, famous for its macabre, horrifying and thrilling dramas, arrived in London. Opening at the Coronet, Notting Hill on 14 June 1915, with a gala in aid of *La Croix Rouge Française*, the season of French-language plays was intended to last only four weeks. With audiences packing the 1,143-seat theatre, however, plans were soon made to transfer the company to the Garrick for a further five weeks.[1] With 1,250 seats the Garrick was only slightly larger than the Coronet, but it had the benefit of being a prominent West End theatre and accordingly the number of performances was increased from seven to nine each week.[2] The repertoire was also extended, with the addition of five translations given by a new English-language company that was put together especially for the Garrick residency. When the Grand Guignol season closed on 21 August 1915, the company had performed seventy-three times over nine weeks. In total, they had presented twenty-six French plays, almost half of which were thriller or horror pieces, and they had thrilled audiences of up to 88,000.[3]

That same summer, whilst audiences were flocking to see the fictional horrors of the Grand Guignol, men and women just over 160 miles away were experiencing the very real horrors of the Great War. When the Coronet season opened, less than three weeks had passed since the end of the Second Battle of Ypres: a battle known best for the first use of poison gas on 22 April 1915. Closer to home, civilians had been experiencing Zeppelin air raids since January 1915 and, with the first attack on the capital taking place on the evening of 31 May, Londoners had recently experienced the horrors of war too. By the time the season closed in late August, the Gallipoli campaign was well underway and the first anniversary of the Great War had passed with no end to the hostilities in sight.

For several cultural commentators, the disjoint between the horrific realities of war and the demand for the fictional horrors of the Grand Guignol was hard to reconcile. As 'F. G. B.' commented, after going to the Garrick in early August 1915, 'reminded as they must be every day of the ghastly realities of war, that there should be people in these times prepared to spend money so as to contemplate invented horrors in the playhouse seems strange and even troubling'.[4] This question of why anyone would want to be thrilled by fictional horrors, when a swift glance at a newspaper could bring the sharp reality home, underlay a number of critical responses to the Grand Guignol season. Yet, as I argue in this chapter, the macabre plays of the Grand Guignol appealed not in spite of the war, but because of it. By focusing new attention onto this long-forgotten season presented around the first anniversary of the war, moreover, we gain an important insight into an entirely ignored and fascinating aspect of wartime culture: the ways in which horror fictions might provide a safe space for audiences to confront the trauma of the war. Pre-war plays such as *Le Baiser dans la Nuit* and *Sous La Lumiére Rouge*, with their themes of facial disfigurement, bereavement and premature burial, I argue, took on new resonance when performed in the summer of 1915; mediating the fears and anxieties of the war, they provided a space in which audiences of British civilians, French and Belgian refugees, and men on leave from the fighting fronts could contemplate the all-too real horrors of war from the temporary safety of the theatre auditorium.

The Appeal of Wartime Horror

The standard formula for a Grand Guignol programme, as Richard J. Hand and Michael Wilson have shown, was a careful 'alternating of terror and laughter', with the actor negotiating 'the precarious journey between horror and comedy' across the four or five short plays presented in each bill.[5]

Reconstructing the programme from newspaper adverts reveals that this balance was carefully managed throughout the season, despite a somewhat tentative start in the first week, prompting Desmond MacCarthy to complain that there was only one 'play to make us shudder' and 'they would do better to give us more horrors'.[6] The draw for audiences, as MacCarthy's comment reveals, was rarely in the laughs. As another commentator noted, 'when the company turns to more ordinary plays they seem a little insipid. They are, in fact, not what we come to see'.[7] The particular appeal of the horror pieces is also evident in their life beyond the season. Both Jean Sartène's *La Griffe* (performed at the Garrick 2–7 August 1915) and Paul Autier and Paul Cloquemin's *Guardiens de Phare* (performed at the Coronet 28 June to 3 July 1915), the latter of which the *Manchester Courier* described as a twenty-minute piece of 'realistic horror . . . an onslaught on the nerves so painful that one shudders continuously and wishes it were all over', were soon 'snapped up by variety managers as being greatly to the taste of a public in search of a good thrill'.[8]

Whilst demand for tickets clearly spoke to the popularity of these macabre plays with audiences, commentators struggled to understand the appeal. For some, distance from the direct experience of war offered one explanation. With the Grand Guignol transferring from Paris to London in the summer of 1915, the *Bystander* concluded that in a city that was 'sadly up against the genuine article' and where 'the playfully extravagant horrors of the Grand Guignol Theatre have already been surpassed in real life' there was 'no use for cheap imitations'.[9] The *Tatler* drew a similar comparison between the two capitals, noting that whilst in Paris the 'atmosphere of death is too near to find a counterfeit of it at all amusing', in London, people were 'not being asked to face death bravely, but merely to "wake up"'.[10] Yet London audiences were not as detached from the reality of war as such commentators suggested. Only two weeks before the Coronet season opened, Londoners had experienced their first direct Zeppelin raid, with bombs being dropped in Whitechapel and Stoke Newington, only eight miles from the theatre. The presence of servicemen on leave and of 'French-speaking visitors' at the Coronet also reveals that the season appealed to those with direct experience – whether as combatants or refugees – of the horror of war.[11]

Taking a different approach to the commentators in the *Tatler* and *Bystander*, it was to these French-speaking 'visitors' that *The Sunday Times* turned in an attempt to explain the popularity of the Grand Guignol. The Garrick's programme 'leaves a good deal to be desired', reported their commentator in late July: 'Foreigners may not understand it, but it is a fact that at the present time we are not in a mood to be fed with horrors. If we want these, alas, there is enough and to spare in the daily press.'[12] In seeing the season as being primarily aimed at French-speaking audiences, whose different temperament might enable them to enjoy these fictional horrors, there was, however, little recognition of the evident appeal of the plays to both British audiences and to non-French speakers.[13]

Reflecting back on the Grand Guignol season at the end of August 1915, a commentator in the *Tatler* concluded that it could 'only be curiosity and a certain craving for the morbidly horrible' that could turn 'a season of such plays into a success at a time when the world is already drenched in blood sufficiently, and the blood, alas! is real'.[14] To an extent, it was an argument underpinned by the few critics who were vocal in supporting the season. As Desmond MacCarthy argued:

> The point is simply the thrill of horror . . . I would rather see [a play] which makes me feel something, even if it is only a thrill of horror. I would sooner be horrified than gently led to the fountain of easy tears, far rather be excruciated than look on at the travesties of heroism as the patriotic plays are at present exhibiting.[15]

For MacCarthy, there was more value in the macabre thrills of the Grand Guignol than there was in heart-warming romance or heroic melodrama; indeed such 'false sentiment', he went on to argue, 'hardens people more than shocks'. In being affected by these fictional horrors, MacCarthy suggested, audiences might even be prompted to reflect again on the heroism of those men and women who experienced such horrors in reality.

Ultimately, of course, the varied reasons why audiences flocked to the Coronet and Garrick to experience the horrors of the Grand Guignol are too broad to examine here. Rather than looking to philosophical explanations of the appeal of the Grand Guignol, however, my interest in the following section is in offering what Andrew Tudor describes as a 'particularistic account' of horror's appeal.[16] As such, I follow film scholar Brigid Cherry who argues that:

> What works as horror and the pleasures that horror cinema engenders can undoubtedly be explained in a number of ways but any explanation must also consider what works for particular social groups in particular cultures at particular times.[17]

Whilst Cherry is talking specifically about cinematic horror, the principal is equally relevant to live performance. The appeal of the macabre plays staged during the summer of 1915 can only fully be understood, I would argue, as the product of the specific historical and cultural context of the Great War. In a context in which death, violence and suffering were being taken to new extremes, the macabre horrors of the Grand Guignol provided, to draw on Joseph Grixti's theorisation, 'a safely distanced and stylised means of making sense of and coming to terms with phenomena and potentialities of experience which under normal . . . conditions would be found too threatening and disturbing'.[18] In analysing themes within two of the most celebrated works of the London season, *Le Baiser dans la Nuit* and *La Lumiére Rouge*, I will demonstrate the ways in which the Grand Guignol's pre-war plays spoke to and mediated the horrors of war.

Facing the Disfigured: *Le Baiser Dans La Nuit*

In the first week of the Grand Guignol season, only one play, as the *Athenaeum* put it, was 'of the special character associated with the Grand Guignol Theatre'.[19] Maurice Level's *Le Baiser dans la Nuit* had first been performed in Paris in December 1912, but made its British premiere at the Coronet and was performed there between 14 and 26 June 1915. The central character in this 'melodrama of vitriol-throwing' is Henri or, as he is known, *le Vitriolé*, (played in 1915 by M. Chaumont): a man who has been blinded and disfigured in an acid attack perpetrated by his jilted lover, Jeanne (played by Renée Gardès).[20] On the pretence of having forgiven her, but in fact seeking his revenge, *le Vitriolé* has lured Jeanne to his room in the middle of the night. The play climaxes in a terrifying acid attack, which was repeatedly described in reviews, such as this one from the *Stage*:

> Horrified when she turns the lights up, and sees his disfigured visage and bandaged eyes, the girl first allows him to pass her fingers over his mangled and indeed eaten-away flesh, and also consents to give him the farewell embrace that he requests. Then, with ferocious yells, the man seizes his victim, casts her down, and deliberately pours vitriol over the face of the shrieking woman, whose countenance is shown all red and scarred, by way of a final touch of horror, as the curtain falls.[21]

The horror of this final scene fulfilled every thrilling expectation of the Grand Guignol. 'The wonderful acting of Renée Gardès and M. Chaumont', the *Athenaeum* reported, gave 'the slightly artificial horror of the play an almost overwhelming effect of realism, which was too strong for some of the audience'. Indeed, on the evening that the *Sunday Mirror* reviewer attended there were two ladies who simply 'couldn't stand it'.[22] Other reviewers also celebrated the affective thrill of the play. *The Times*' critic considered it 'blood-curdling enough for the most jaded nerves'; the *Stage*'s reviewer concluded that it was 'quite likely to give one the horrors'; and *The Sunday Times*'s commentator found it 'harrowing and repellant'.[23] Beyond this, however, this latter reviewer refused to say more, noting that the performance was so 'horribly horrible in these times of war, when many hearts are bleeding' that they would 'refrain from comment'.[24] They did, however acknowledge the play's 'phenomenal success' with audiences.[25] So well-received was *Le Baiser* that Colin Messer, the season's producer, took the unusual step of retaining the piece in the repertoire for the following week, making it one of only five plays – and only two horror pieces – staged for longer than one week across the nine-week season.[26]

The play's exquisite tension, its origins in the late nineteenth-century French vogue for *vitriolage*, and the use of body horror make *Le Baiser*, as Richard J. Hand and Michael Wilson have argued, 'one of the definitive plays of the Grand-Guignol'.[27] Yet whilst the play firmly pre-dated the war, its popularity in 1915 should also be considered through the central figure of *le Vitrolé* and his particular resonance in a wartime context. At a time when men were returning from the front with severe facial injuries, the character of *le Vitrolé*, with his head wrapped in bandages and clearly suffering in the wake of horrific facial wounds, was not just a victim of an acid attack, but a figure that challenged audiences to confront their anxieties around veterans with facial disfigurements.

As Marjorie Gehrhardt has highlighted, facial injuries made up a significant proportion of wounds during the Great War, both because of the use of shells and machine guns combined with the lack of protective equipment, and also because of the 'nature of trench warfare in exposing the head'.[28] Yet, as Gehrhardt and others have emphasised, facial wounds remained the 'worst loss of all', being experienced as a loss of identity, masculinity and ultimately humanity.[29] Across numerous accounts, including the oft-cited 1918 memoir of Ward Muir, the facially disfigured were not only dehumanised, but figured as something almost monstrous. 'Hideous is the only word for these smashed faces' reflected Muir, an orderly at the 3rd London General Hospital in Wandsworth:

> the socket with some twisted, moist slit, with a lash or two adhering feebly . . . the skewed mouth . . . and worse, far the worst, the incredibly brutalising effects which are the consequence of wounds in the nose, and which reach a climax of mournful grotesquerie when the nose is missing altogether.[30]

Calling to mind an image of something monstrous rather than human, Muir's description speaks to the mix of pity, fear, disgust and revulsion that Suzannah Biernoff has argued was felt both by 'the men who suffered these injuries and . . . those who came into contact with them'.[31]

Understanding the mix of emotions provoked by facial injuries is key to appreciating the significance of *Le Baiser* during the Great War and its mediation of 'the complex nature of violence, suffering, and mortality' that Thomas Fahy argues is at the heart of horror's enjoyment.[32] In *le Vitriolé* audiences were confronted with a man who hads been transformed into a 'monster' by his facial injury. As such, this terrifying figure was the realisation of the fears and visceral responses that scholars such as Gehrhardt, Suzannah Biernoff, Joanna Bourke and Sophie Delaporte identify as being at the heart of responses to facial disfigurement. Yet, at the same time, and just like real-life victims of facial wounds, *le Vitriolé* also suffers as a result of a horrific experience and, as such, is a figure of pity. These tensions between *le Vitriolé*'s status as victim and monster, as the subject of both pity and terror, sit not only at the heart of the play, but at the heart of questions around and cultural attitudes towards victims of facial disfigurement.

In forcing audiences to confront their fears around facial injury *Le Baiser* was, for critics such as Desmond MacCarthy, 'more wholesome than those [plays] in which brutality is made unreal'.[33] It also contrasted with the collective 'looking away' that Suzannah Biernoff has identified within wider society.[34] Rather, in *Le Baiser*, the dramatic structure of the play, with *le Vitrolé* facing away from the audience with his 'hideously scarred face' masked by bandages, builds towards this ultimate, terrifying reveal.[35] As a letter in a Cornish newspaper in August 1915 reveals, it was this anticipation of horror that audiences loved. 'In some of the Grand Guignol plays' wrote C. King of Chapel Hill, Stratton, North Cornwall on 7 August 1915, 'the audiences are thrilled simply by looking at an open door'.[36] It 'hypnotises them', they added; 'they gaze at it with anticipatory shivers, and nothing that follows, no matter how terrible, is to be compared in horror with that silent suggestion'. In the Grand Guignol's staging of *Le Baiser*, of course, it was the imagined face beneath the mask that prompted such anticipatory shivers: a face, audiences may have reflected later, that was also far worse imagined than seen.

For C. King, the experience provided by the Grand Guignol, of waiting for the horror to come, was directly parallel to the experience of living through the war. As such, their comments provide a further insight into the particular pleasure of fictional horror in wartime. 'There are occasions', King wrote:

> when the daily newspaper exercises a similar hypnotic effect; blank days when a veil is carefully hung over military and naval movements. Then the mind is possessed by dread. People imagine that something terrible is happening, has happened, or that inertia has overtaken our leaders. The citizen's gaze is fixed upon the open door.[37]

In the finite and safe space of the darkened auditorium, King recognised, there would always be the final moment of what horror writer Stephen King described many years later as 'reintegration and safety': the moment when audiences faced their fears and realised that 'for now, the worst has been faced and it wasn't so bad after all'.[38] Yet the same could not be said of reality. In facing a world in which no one knew when that release would come, the pleasure of the Grand Guignol was, for some at least, in providing a safe and contained space in which the full cycle of 'anxiety, fear, relief and mastery' could be experienced, and in which the tension of wartime life might be temporarily relieved.[39]

Dealing with Death: *Sous La Lumière Rouge*

Whilst *La Baiser* was the first thriller to be staged at the Coronet, *Sous la Lumiére Rouge* (1911) was the last. Maurice Level and Étienne Ray's play features Philippe, a young man whose actress-lover has just died of influenza. Being a keen photographer, but only having photographs of her 'in character', Philippe wants to remember her as he knew her and takes a deathbed photo. After the funeral, however, when he develops the photograph, he discovers that her eyes are open. Fearing that she had simply been catatonic – the flash-bulb having momentarily roused her – Philippe immediately calls for an exhumation. But it is, of course, too late. With Philippe waiting in the next room, the coffin is opened revealing his lover's failed attempt to escape being buried alive. Philippe, however, is ultimately left in the dark: his friend, who had been present at the exhumation, lies to reassure Philippe that his lover had died peacefully in bed.

Whilst, like *Le Baiser*, *La Lumiére* was written before the Great War, the themes of grief, loss and being buried alive all spoke to the experience of war in ways that could not have been imagined four years earlier. 'The play has, apparently, been written with the object of securing greater precautions against accidents of the kind', the *Bystander*'s reviewer noted, 'but its production with such a wealth of morbid detail at the present time is, taking the most charitable view possible, a serious error of judgment'.[40] Examiner of Plays, George S. Street, who licensed the play for performance, concurred, commenting that 'this is another horrible play, and it is almost incredible that in such dreadful times as these there can be any demand for artificial horrors'.[41]

By July 1915, as such comments implicitly acknowledge, being buried alive was no longer just the subject of gruesome tales or terrible accidents; it was a real and deadly possibility. For civilians on the home front, increasing air raids brought with them the risk of being buried alive 'at home'.[42] At the same time, accounts in newspapers revealed the quotidian danger of being buried alive in shell bursts on the Western Front. Newspapers frequently published letters from men who had survived such deaths, such as the following from Corporal F. Robinson of the 1st Battalion West Kent Regiment, whose experience of being buried alive was published in the *Evening Dispatch* in early 1915:

> One day I was in a trench with three privates when a shell came on to the earthwork. I felt a great weight holding me down, and it was completely dark. I could not stir a muscle: my face was pressed into the earth, and I realised that I was buried alive, face downwards. I felt myself gasping for breath, and then gradually going to sleep. Luckily comrades were rapidly digging me and the others out . . . on four other occasions I have been buried, but usually I have got out with the aid of a pal. In any case it's better than being blown to bits.[43]

The light-hearted and reassuring tone of Corporal Robinson's account was echoed in other letters in the press but was a sharp contrast to accounts in uncensored diaries such as Arthur Graeme West's. West, a Captain in the 6th Battalion Oxford and Bucks Light Infantry, recorded his search for men buried in shell explosions in September 1916:

> Two men were buried, perhaps more you were told, certainly two. The trench was a mere undulation of newly turned earth, under it somewhere lay two men or more. You dug furiously. No sign. Perhaps you were standing on a couple of men now, pressing the life out of them, on their faces or chests . . . You dig and scratch and uncover a grey, dirty face, pitifully drab and ugly, the eyes closed, the whole thing limp and mean-looking: this is the devil of it, that a man is not only killed, but made to look so vile and filthy in death, so futile and meaningless that you hate the sight of him . . . here is the first, and God knows how many are not beneath him. At last you get them out, three dead, grey, muddy masses, and one more jabbering live one. Then another shell falls and more are buried . . . It is noticeable that only one man was wounded; six were buried alive.[44]

It is an account that vividly depicts the horror, as well as the ubiquity, of such a death: a horror that *La Lumiére* dramatises not only in its climactic, macabre moment when the body is disinterred, but throughout the whole play. The audience, after all, would have been all too aware of Philippe's lover slowly suffocating in her dark coffin throughout the action of the play, and ultimately share in the knowledge of her painful and horrifying death: a knowledge kept from Philippe in much the same way that families were often protected from the truth of their loved ones' deaths by the men who were with them when they died.

It is not hard to see how *La Lumiére* could have tapped into contemporary anxieties over the kinds of death that men faced in the trenches, both for those in the audience with loved ones at the Front and those who were on leave from the Front themselves. More fundamentally, however, *La Lumiére* was about the experience of loss and grief: an experience which, Adrian Gregory suggests, would touch virtually the entire population by the end of the war, with almost everyone having lost a cousin, friend or neighbour and around three million out of a population of fewer than forty-two million having lost a close relative, son or brother.[45] Throughout the play, the audience follows Philippe as he deals with his lover's death. 'You can't imagine how quickly the dead leave us', he reflects:

She's fading away . . . Fading away . . . her eyes . . . her mouth . . . her expression . . . it all eludes me. It's like being bereaved all over again . . . One minute she's there in front of me and then suddenly she's vanished! No, that's not what I want. This void, this darkness, it's horrible.[46]

Whilst the disinterring of the body was the climactic moment of horror in the play, it was in Philippe's articulation of his bereavement that the play tapped into the ultimate wartime anxiety: the shared and acute possibility of imminent bereavement. For those in the audience who had been bereaved, those who had seen friends killed on the battlefields, or those who feared that the photographs they held, like Philippe, would be the last image of their loved ones, these words would have resonated in ways unforeseen when the play was first performed in 1911.

Staging the Reality of War: *La Veillée de Jean Rémy*

Like *Sous la Lumiére Rouge* and *Le Baiser dans la Nuit*, most of the plays in the 1915 Grand Guignol season pre-dated the war. Only on one occasion, for the opening of the Garrick residency, was any attempt made to directly tackle the war within the Grand Guignol format. *La Veillée de Jean Rémy* by M. M. Yoria Walter and P. De Wattyne was performed during the week of 19 July 1915 and was more of a war melodrama than a Grand Guignol horror play. Depicting a 'Boche captain' killing a young French woman's children just before the slightly-too-late arrival of the English soldier, reviewers were split as to whether this was 'an awful war sketch, which even surpasses the atrocity pamphlets which are published from time to time' or 'disappointing because one felt that that brutal German Captain ought to have met a more horrible fate than that of being bayoneted by a British soldier'.[47] Speaking directly to the atrocities of the invasion of France and Belgium, it is no surprise that *La Veillée* was the only new horror play to be produced during the Grand Guignol season. In the Grand Guignol's pre-war macabre thrillers audiences could encounter their fears, but at one remove from the reality of the horrors of war. *La Veillée*, on the other hand, represented what many perceived as reality, particularly in the wake of the recent publication of the *Bryce Report on Alleged German Outrages* in May.[48] As the reviewer of the *Westminster Gazette* commented, *La Veillée* could be watched not as a dramatic fiction but rather 'as a perfectly realistic transcript of scenes such as we know on unimpeachable evidence to have actually occurred again and again'.[49]

La Veillée, and the other 'atrocity plays' that were produced in the first years of the war, demand fresh attention in the context of atrocity literature and propaganda. Yet, as I have argued here, the appeal of the Grand Guignol's horror in 1915 was not in its direct commentary on the war itself but in its reflection of the experience of war from a distance. These pre-war plays translated easily and gained new resonance in a world facing previously unimagined horrors, and in doing so provided audiences with the opportunity to 'encounter the dangerous and horrific in a safe context'.[50]

Finally, it is also important to recognise how the experience of the Grand Guignol itself provided a mirror for wartime life. As Hand and Wilson have argued, the skill of the Grand Guignol actor was to take audiences on a journey 'from bourgeois security to mortal danger, from the rational to the insane'.[51] In this journey from security to danger, from normality to the extraordinary, the wartime Grand Guignol mirrored and thereby mediated the experience of war, at both a personal and global level. Immersing themselves in a fictional world where 'action may or may not have meaning, where a monster may or may not be sympathetic, where evil people may or may not win out in the end', and coming out the other end audiences experienced for a brief moment the release from terror that they would have to wait more than three years to experience in reality.[52]

Notes

1. The popularity of the Coronet season was commented on in the press. The *Sheffield Daily Telegraph*, for example, noted on 1 July 1915 that 'Mr Colin Messer is attracting big audiences at the Coronet Theatre with his Grand Guignol Company from Paris'.
2. Matinees were given only on Saturdays at the Coronet; when the company moved to the Garrick they performed matinees on Wednesdays, Thursdays and Saturdays. The number of plays per programme was also increased to five at the Garrick, other than in the final week (week commencing 16 August) where four plays were given, as had been standard at the Coronet.
3. There is no firm evidence for audience numbers. This estimate is based on each theatre's capacity and the popularity of the season.
4. *The Sunday Times*, 8 August 1915.

5. Richard J. Hand and Michael Wilson, *Grand-Guignol: The French Theatre of Horror* (Exeter: Exeter University Press, 2000), p. 39.
6. The season opened with the comedies *Le Chauffeur* and *Une Femme Charmante*. A further light-hearted piece, *Le Triangle*, was added on the Tuesday. D. MacCarthy, 'The Grand Guignol Company', *The New Statesman*, 5/115 (19 June 1915), 256.
7. *Westminster Gazette*, 29 June 1915.
8. *Manchester Courier and Lancashire General Advertiser*, 30 June 1915; *Cheltenham Looker-On*, 14 August 1915.
9. '"The Grand Guignol" at the Coronet', *Bystander*, 14 July 1915.
10. *Tatler*, 28 July 1915.
11. On 17 June 1915 the *Stage* commented that there were 'a number of officers in the audience'. *Sheffield Daily Telegraph*, 1 July 1915.
12. *The Sunday Times*, 25 July 1915.
13. As the *Sheffield Daily Telegraph* noted on 1 July 1915, 'The audiences at the Coronet [were] not exclusively French and Belgian'.
14. *Tatler*, 25 August 1915.
15. D. MacCarthy, 'The Grand Guignol Company', 256.
16. A. Tudor, 'Why Horror? The Peculiar Pleasures of a Popular Genre', in M. Jancovich (ed.), *Horror: The Film Reader* (New York: Routledge, 2002), p. 50.
17. Brigid Cherry, *Horror* (London and New York: Routledge, 2009), p. 167.
18. Joseph Grixti, *Terrors of Uncertainty: The Cultural Contexts of Horror Fiction* (London and New York: Routledge, 1989), p. 164.
19. *Athenaeum*, 19 June 1915, no. 4573, 558.
20. *The Times*, 25 June 1915.
21. *Stage*, 17 June 1915.
22. *Sunday Mirror*, 27 June 1915.
23. *The Times*, 25 June 1915; *Stage*, 17 June 1915; *The Sunday Times*, 20 June 1915.
24. *The Sunday Times*, 20 June 1915.
25. *The Sunday Times*, 20 June 1915.
26. The normal pattern was for each week's performance to be made up of entirely new plays. *The Sunday Times*, 27 June 1915. Over the whole season, only four pieces were staged for more than one week: *Le Baiser* (weeks commencing 14 June and 21 June); the comedy *Rosalie* (weeks commencing 28 June and 5 July); the comedy *La Delnissée* (weeks commencing 19 July, 26 July and 2 August) and the English-language horror piece, *The Grip* (weeks commencing 2 August and 9 August).

27. Hand and Wilson, *Grand-Guignol*, p. 180.
28. M. Gehrhardt, '*Gueules Cassées*: The Men Behind the Masks', *Journal of War and Culture Studies*, 6/4 (2013), 267.
29. 'Worst Loss of All', *Manchester Evening Chronicle*, May to June 1918, quoted in Suzannah Biernoff, *Portraits of Violence: War and the Aesthetics of Disfigurement* (Ann Arbor MI: University of Michigan Press, 2017) p. 69. For further discussion of facial disfigurement, see S. Biernoff, 'The Rhetoric of Disfigurement in First World War Britain', *Social History of Medicine*, 24/3 (2011); Sophie Delaporte, *Les Gueles Cassées: Les blesses de la face de la Grande Guerre* (Paris: Éd. Noêsis,1996); Joanna Bourke, *Dismembering the Male: Men's Bodies, Britain and the Great War* (London: Reaktion, 1999); and A. Branach-Kallas, 'Faces', in A. Branach-Kallas and P. Sadkowski (eds), *Comparing Grief in French, British and Canadian Great War Fiction (1977–2014)* (Leiden: Brill, 2018), pp. 12–14.
30. Ward Muir, *The Happy Hospital* (London: Simkin Marshall, 1918), pp. 143–4.
31. Biernoff, 'Rhetoric of Disfigurement', p. 671.
32. Thomas Fahy, 'Introduction', in Thomas Fahy (ed.), *The Philosophy of Horror* (Lexington KY: University Press of Kentucky, 2010), p. 2.
33. MacCarthy, 'The Grand Guignol Company'.
34. Biernoff, 'Rhetoric of Disfigurement', p. 668.
35. *People*, 20 June 1915.
36. *Exeter and Plymouth Gazette*, 9 August 1915.
37. *Athenaeum*, 19 June 1915, no. 4573, 558.
38. Stephen King, *Danse Macabre* (New York: Simon & Schuster, Inc., 2010), p. 14.
39. Fahy, 'Introduction', p. 2.
40. '"The Grand Guignol" at the Coronet', p. 66.
41. George S. Street, 'Examiner's Summary' for *Sous La Lumiére Rouge*, British Library, Lord Chamberlain's Collection of Plays, 1915/17. Licensed for performance on 22 June 1915, *www.greatwartheatre.org.uk/db/script/501/*.
42. See, for example, 'Zeppelin Dangers', in *Broughty Ferry Guide and Advertiser*, 18 June 1915.
43. 'Buried Alive', in *Evening Dispatch*, 6 January 1915.
44. Arthur Graeme West, *The Diary of a Dead Officer, being the posthumous papers of Arthur Graeme West* (London: George Allen and Unwin, 1918), p. 67.
45. Adrian Gregory, *The Silence of Memory: Armistice Day, 1919–1946* (London and New York: Bloomsbury, 1994), p. 19.
46. Maurice Level and Étienne Ray, *Sous La Lumiére Rouge* (1911), in Hand and Wilson, *Grand-Guignol*, pp. 170–1.

47. *The Sunday Times*, 25 July 1915; *Sketch*, 28 July 1915.
48. The *Report of the Committee on Alleged German Outrages*, better known as the *Bryce Report* after the commission's chair, Viscount James Bryce, was published in May 1915 and documented accounts of German 'outrages' during the invasion. Whilst the accuracy of the report was challenged after the war, during the conflict it was seen as highly credible.
49. *Westminster Gazette*, 20 July 1915.
50. Fahy, 'Introduction', p. 2.
51. Hand and Wilson, *Grand-Guignol*, p. 269.
52. Cynthia A. Freeland, *The Naked and the Undead: Evil and the Appeal of Horror* (London and New York: Routledge, 2018), p. 274.

3

Phantoms of the Stage

The History and Practice of Uncanny Apparitions

Richard J. Hand

DURING THE GLOBAL coronavirus pandemic of 2020, thousands of theatres across the world closed. In a catastrophe for the cultural practice most antithetical to the convention of 'social distancing' – live theatre – creative teams were suddenly unemployed and venues padlocked shut. Millions of tickets were in limbo, booked for events that were postponed indefinitely or would never happen. The financial cataclysm meant that some theatres launched '#imagine you've seen it' campaigns, urging spectators to effectively donate money to the survival of the venue rather than be reimbursed for their unusable tickets. Beyond the ideal of myriad imagined shows, in thousands of physical venues the only sign of life that remained within the cavernous void of the auditorium was the 'ghost light', a single source of illumination (typically a lightbulb on a stand in the centre of the stage) used whenever a theatre is empty. Despite its importance as a health and safety device (dark theatres are perilous), the symbolism and name of the 'ghost light' immediately conjures up mystique and folklore. As Michael M. Chemers writes, one legend is that ghost lights were 'originally left onstage to propitiate (or abjure) the ghosts that were known to congregate in theaters where the metaphysical barriers between this world and the next are notoriously thin'.[1]

The ghost light is just one example of how the theatre is the most superstitious of cultural contexts, imbued with folklore, good-luck rituals, tall tales and 'walking shadows'. As Marvin Carlson stresses, theatre buildings are typically 'the most haunted of human cultural structures'.[2] We might argue this is because theatres respond to being jam-packed on one occasion and deserted the next. The stage space is a place of opulence in its materiality, regardless of how minimal the scenography or how small the ensemble. Yet, once the show is over, it is stripped bare and emptied, back into the state of a *tabula rasa*. For the spectator, theatres can be rich with nostalgia: remembrance of plays past; recalled social experiences; the 'oh, you should have been there!' recollection. The memory implicit within some examples of these buildings can be profound, whether a theatre chooses to present posters and photographs of past players and productions in the foyer or emblazon the names of benefactors and sponsors on walls, floors or seats. The evidence of spectral spectators may even abide in the wear, tear and creaks of the doorways and seating.

In the world of theatre, performers conjure up fantasy and imagination within the corporeal and tangible, making the world of dreams and nightmares *real*. Fictive characters are brought into physical being and historical characters are brought back from the dead. It is this practice, this summoning into existence, that is essential to the experience of theatre; it is the 'magic' of live performance. In writing about autobiographical performance art, Elyse Pineau states that 'Performance Studies . . . is hospitable to ghosts because the performer is the ghost's familiar',[3] thus making performers themselves the conjured daemon, the servant of the powerful spectre of the text. Furthermore, Jacques Derrida's concept of *hauntology*, which, as Colin Davis explains, replaces 'the priority of being and presence with the figure of the ghost as that which is neither present nor absent, neither dead nor alive',[4] can offer enormous potency in the study of performance, from the space itself to the processes of enacting and spectating. In exploring theatre, we witness ghosts that cannot possibly be 'real' yet live and breathe in front of us only to vanish when the play is over, leaving only memories that are, paradoxically, more meaningful than an empty, ghost-lit stage.

Some of the greatest characters in drama are ghosts. They were figures of great import in Elizabethan-Jacobean drama where they compelled revenge, aroused terror or signalled a political moral. These Renaissance spectres were immensely powerful and have never been exorcised from the stage. In exploring the popular genre of the ghost melodrama in the 1820s,

Diego Saglia argues that these sensationalistic, supernatural plays can be 'key cultural sites for understanding and constructing reality – especially one deformed by the revealing lens of the spectral – in 1820s Britain'.[5] In fact, this principle has never diminished, and the ghosts of the stage have remained key cultural sites for understanding reality. In other words, the spectral does not merely give the audience a frisson of escapism, it remains at the very heart of the meaning of theatre.

The meaning that the supernatural can give theatre is particularly striking when ghosts 'erupt' into realism. For example, August Wilson's play *The Piano Lesson* (1987) is a realist play set in the 1930s and yet the twentieth-century African-American family vividly portrayed in the play must confront the ghost of the owner of their enslaved ancestors as they negotiate their future aspirations. In Wilson's play, the (unseen but heard) supernatural presence frustrates and taunts the living until they find defiance. In this way, *The Piano Lesson*'s confrontation between the real and the spectral gives the audience a cultural site in which to understand the present. A similar eruption of the supernatural took place in Punchdrunk's site-specific *Clod and Pebble* (2008), a one performer, one spectator 'immersive' show that blurred the 'lines between the real and imagined' in such a way that 'you can't quite tell the point at which the show has begun'.[6] In this production, the experience was partly a self-directed promenade performance, the lone spectator needing to decipher a riddle to locate a shop in London. Entering what seemed to be an eclectic antique shop with nothing for sale, the proprietor – Robert – made small talk before gaining the spectator's trust and taking them into the basement. As things began to become uncanny through sound and a calculated shift in performance style, the spectator gradually realised they were in the company of a spectre: the ghost of William Blake's dead brother. Robert (Hector Harkness) was friendly, compassionate, wholly flesh and blood and yet emphatically 'not of this world'. The emergence of the supernatural is an unexpected, even arresting, device within the realism of *The Piano Lesson* and the journey from literal real world into ghost realm in *Clod and Pebble*. A similar, yet perhaps more premeditatedly terrifying process happens in some notable examples of French and Irish theatre.

The Théâtre du Grand-Guignol (1897–1962) in Paris prided itself on being the unique 'Theatre of Horror'. Its extraordinary venue – a deconsecrated chapel – was a Gothic space and the company developed horror effects and illusions that were as gruesome as they were ingenious. However, the theatre emerged from the ethos of Zola-inspired realism, meaning that its horrors were emphatically possible and rational rather than supernatural. Nevertheless, just as the venue itself was a 'sacrilegious' space, the plays it showcased exploited the signifiers and structure of the Gothic and popular horror culture. For example, in Marc Bonis-Charancle's *La Maison hantée* (*The Haunted House*, 1902), a group of thrill-seekers break into a reputedly haunted house. The play constructs a narrative of the spectral, with Gothic performative tropes such as flickering candles, distant noises and doors slowly creaking open. However, this is the Grand Guignol and the horrific presence that 'haunts' the house is nothing supernatural. As the play develops, we discover that a man is hiding in the house and tormenting his estranged wife, reducing her to an enslaved wretch. The play is a precursor to the 'torture porn' genre of popular horror, reminding us that the worst monsters lie in the human capacity for cruelty. The brutality is such that one wishes for the uncanniness of a phantom rather than the brutality of a flesh and blood man.

In another example of the Grand Guignol, Maurice Renard's *L'Amant de la mort* (*The Lover of Death*, 1925), we seem to witness the supernatural at the climax of the play, albeit manipulated through the psychological perspective of a desperately guilty character. In the play, a hypnotist, Robert, seduces his friend's wife Simone. Having brainwashed her to leave her husband, Simone is killed in a train crash. Robert becomes tortured by guilt and receives his comeuppance: the play culminates in a shocking apparition of the dead woman before Robert kills himself. In the staging of the denouement, Robert – and the audience – hear the voice of the deceased Simone. After this, Robert and the spectators become witnesses: 'Suddenly in the darkness, the audience can see what Robert has seen' and the mangled body of Simone lurches behind him eventually 'touching him with hands stripped of flesh'. In this climax, the audience judges Robert yet shares the vision of his guilty perspective. In some ways this is a 'jump scare' that we might expect at the end of a contemporary horror movie, but at the same time there is a process of implicated witnessing that goes beyond an adrenaline burst. The psychological ghost of guilt and abjection that haunts and horrifies Robert can also horrify and haunt us: after all, we were complicit witnesses in Robert's initial manipulation of Simone. What is interesting is that this is a Grand Guignol play that strays into the *unreal*, but this ghost is *real* in the mind of the guilty man and reified for the spectator.

Interestingly, Renard's Grand Guignol play ramifies in a contemporary Irish play: Conor McPherson's *Shining City* (2004). In this play, John visits a therapist, Ian, recounting how he keeps hearing and seeing his late wife Mari (killed in a car crash) in their home. Again, this is a ghost that can only be real in the mind of the guilty man. However, in the final sequence of the play, the audience briefly beholds this spectacle:

> In the darkening gloom of the afternoon, we see that Mari's ghost has appeared behind the door. She is looking at Ian, just as John described her; she wears her red coat, which is filthy, her hair is wet. She looks beaten up. She looks terrifying.[7]

The spectre of Mari that tormented John has now come to haunt Ian – and the spectator. The impact on audiences was evident, with the *New York Times* (10 May 2006) describing it as 'the most shocking ending on Broadway' through which 'McPherson has found an inspired alternative to those inadequate tools of communication called words'. In other words, the guilt, trauma and rationalism that the play tangles with are shockingly challenged in a visceral image of a ghost. For Benedict Nightingale, reviewing the premiere at London's Royal Court Theatre in *The Times* (11 June 2004), *Shining City* demonstrated 'acting and writing at its most riveting' but he had reservations about the finale, which he discussed without any 'spoilers':

> At this point I'd better reveal that there is a Grand-Guignol ending that is either cheap or deep but, either way, doesn't make clear what we are finally meant to think of Ian or John. Let's just say that it's a powerful if confusing image of suffering womanhood. But before this there is genuine excellence.

The shock finale may have proved too excessive for Nightingale and other spectators. However, this crossing of the line from realism into the supernatural is core to McPherson's ethos in plays such as *Shining City* and probably his most celebrated play *The Weir* (1997), as Christopher Murray elucidates:

> McPherson thinks allusively and analogically. He knows that ghost stories are and are not hokum: that they both hold the audience rapt – of *The Weir* (1997) for example – and at the same time offer entrance to the dark world of the Jungian unconscious and its disguised truths.[8]

In both McPherson's *Shining City* and Renard's *The Lover of Death*, we experience realist plays that offer a detailed analysis of male psychology, but in their final moments reify dead women from the depths of guilt, trauma and psychological horror. As the audience, we are given entrance to a dark world of the unconscious by being privy to these moments of horror: what paradoxically may or may not be 'hokum' comprises careful storytelling and realist acting, leading us to appalling spectacles of the (un)real and the (un)dead.

One of the most successful mid-twentieth century plays, which establishes realism then challenges it with the supernatural, is William Archibald's *The Innocents* (1950), an adaptation of Henry James' novella *The Turn of the Screw* (1898). The play establishes itself within realism but gradually shifts into the style and structure of Victorian ghost melodrama. As such, the play establishes a significant precedent for later plays, such as *The Woman in Black* (1987), Stephen Mallatratt's long-running stage adaptation of Susan Hill's 1983 novel. James' short novel is usually regarded as a psychological tale that explores, frequently with irony, the language and conventions of the Gothic: a naïve governess arrives in a rural mansion to look after two orphaned children and gradually detects what she believes to be an evil influence over the children from beyond the grave. The young heroine, the vulnerable children, the magnificent but eerie house, uncanny occurrences, the sense of suspense, secrets and revelation, are all characteristics of the Gothic narrative that James adopts but adapts with subtle but incisive irony. James frames the narrative through the testimony of the unnamed Governess, which places the reader in a quandary of reception: are the ghosts real or are they a figment of the Governess's imagination? In doing this, James sustains an exquisite balance that may even implicate the reader: do *we* believe in ghosts? Do *we* subscribe to Freudian or Jungian psychology? In contrast, however, William Archibald's play places us in a different position, insofar as the audience does *see ghosts*. This may seem to challenge fundamentally the deliberate opaqueness of James's narrative, but it may, as we shall see, create its own theatrical ambiguity.

With the stage adaptation of the story, Archibald steers the tale towards the tangible. In a live performance of the play, James's anonymous Governess is a flesh and blood woman made even 'more real' by being named as 'Miss Giddens'. The ghosts are characters in the script, appearing to Miss Giddens and to the audience, with even Mrs Grose the housekeeper acknowledging what 'I have seen'.[9] Nevertheless, the introductory note in the acting edition of Archibald's script mentions Peter Quint and Miss Jessel, the 'couple of seamy servants' who begin to haunt the house:

> Though both of these have died, their evil examples survive. They reappear as ghosts, but when you have left the theatre there is still the question of whether they were literal ghosts or figments of the mind. That you will have to determine for yourself.[10]

Archibald's note makes it clear that the audience will see the ghosts but still argues for the adaptation's ambiguity. It is very telling that he emphasises how we may doubt the ghosts' existence when we 'have left the theatre': up to that point, everything is done to place us in affinity with the Governess, seeing, hearing, jumping and screaming at horrors from beyond the tomb. Yet, once the play is over, we are meant to question if we saw them at all.

Throughout the script, Archibald signals how sound and light/darkness is to be used in conveying the tale. For example, we have stage directions such as this:

> Immediately, as Miss Giddens says 'Miles,' a thin vibration comes from far away – more of trembling of all inanimate things than of sound itself – and with this vibration, the Shadow again appears at the window, filling the window, blocking out the moonlight, almost as though about to enter the room.[11]

We have an abstract description of uncanny sound, the shadowy apparition (of Peter Quint's ghost) emerging then growing until it blocks out any natural light. This is almost an expressionistic moment, realism bending into the abstract and uncanny. Throughout the script there are detailed descriptions of candles, shadows, slowness, silences, screams, moans, heartbeats, throbs, vibrations and other eerie sounds, all with a calculated awareness of intended effect.

The Innocents was a huge success, first on Broadway in 1950 and then in the West End in 1952, and contemporary reviews signal the power of the production. When it premiered in London, Maurice Wiltshire reviewed the play for the *Daily Mail* (4 July 1952) in an article called 'Triumph in Horror – But You Need Tough Nerves', signalling that 'one of the finest pieces of fabricated horror to appear on the London stage for many a year' works on its audience in a way that 'tautens the nerves to an almost unbearable pitch'. Similarly praiseworthy, the prominent critic J. C. Trewin in the *Illustrated London News* (19 July 1952) reviewed the production (which was staged in the large Her Majesty's Theatre in London), describing it as a tale of 'daemonic possession in a lonely English country house':

> It is a broadening of the original tale . . . fitted to a big stage and managing to chill not by suggestion, but by unabashed treatment of the theme as a 'thriller' (for want of a better word), aided by décor and lighting markedly imaginative. The imagination is in these, and in the acting . . . rather than in the script.

It is noteworthy that Trewin praises the design, technology and acting rather than the 'script' *per se*: in fact, he perhaps means 'dialogue', as the script is highly detailed in spelling out the desired staging and effect. The reification of James's ghosts had caused Trewin some concern, but he concludes that the play can turn us 'almost to jelly with the act of fear'.

The Innocents was evidently a production that had an impact on its 1950s audiences in the United States and Britain and it remains an effective ghost play, albeit rarely performed. Archibald's careful description of sound and lighting effects turns the realism awry, and within this the effective performance practice of ideal actors – the Governess, the children, the housekeeper and the two ghosts – can lead the spectator into the realm of a haunted house and, once we leave the theatre, possess us with a haunted, doubting mind. That said, in some respects, Archibald's play of a single-set location (a Victorian drawing room), seen ghosts and mannered dialogue can feel like a simple throwback to Victorian melodrama. The play has been eclipsed by the celebrated film adaptation *The Innocents* (Jack Clayton, 1961) and the rise of *The Woman in Black* (1987) as the dominant 'ghost play' on the English stage. Moreover, there have been numerous subsequent versions of *The Turn of the Screw* including Rebecca Lenkiewicz's inventive adaptation in 2013; Tim Luscombe's adaptation in 2018; and Box Tale Soup's Fringe theatre version (2018), in which the children are puppets, making the psyche of the flesh-and-blood Governess the focus of attention and scrutiny. In 1999, Nick Dear wrote a television adaptation of *The Turn of the Screw* that was later adapted to the stage. Dear's intention in the play was to expose 'the degree of violence to which a Christian is prepared to go to preserve religious orthodoxy'.[12] The screenplay was reworked into a stage play which premiered in Bristol in 2005. The reviews were not entirely generous, with Lyn Gardner in *The Guardian* (12 April 2005) appalled by the first glance of what appeared to be a 'giant erect penis' (in fact, the enormous image of a lily stamen) and taking this as a warning about a production 'that transforms Henry James's delicate flower of a novella into a blunt instrument that hits the audience over the head with its blatant sexual and religious imagery and its penny dreadful horror'. Furthermore, Gardner argues that the production lost the story's ambiguity:

> The ghosts are the white-faced horrors of Victorian melodrama, the unconscious is made all too conscious and instead of multiple meanings, the story is given just one reading: the tale of a young woman who becomes sexually fixated on her unattainable employer and goes completely bonkers.

It seems that James's ironic take on Gothic horror can be problematic when adapted with an agenda and an interpretative 'answer'. Perhaps Archibald's dramatisation, for all its own manners and melodrama still has something to offer in its realism-turned-awry that makes us doubt not just Miss Giddens but ourselves once we have left the theatre.

The 'ghosts' we have seen in the plays that we have looked at so far, from the Grand Guignol and contemporary Irish drama to the adaptation of Victorian ghost fiction, do not require technological effects beyond makeup, costume, lighting, sound (and perhaps puppetry) to make a shocking impact. However, if we turn to Victorian melodrama and/or spectacle itself, we find popular productions that have used innovative technological effects to make its audiences 'see' the supernatural. For example, the first British production of Dion Boucicault's *The Corsican Brothers* (1852), based on a French dramatisation of Alexandre Dumas' 1844 novel, invented an elaborate sliding trapdoor called the 'ghost slide' or 'Corsican trap' to create its ghostly illusion of emerging ghosts. The effect caused a sensation as Geraint D'Arcy explains:

> It is easy to imagine that it once amazed audiences in the western world by behaving unlike any other stage device, producing a ghost like no other and guaranteeing the success of an otherwise unremarkable melodrama.[13]

In other examples of Victorian theatre, technology helped audiences witness the uncanny. Leopold Lewis's *The Bells* (1871), an adaptation of Erckmann-Chatrian's *Le Juif polonais* (1862), was a hugely successful melodrama that remains synonymous with the actor Henry Irving. Assessing Irving's significance, Valerie C. Rudolph writes:

[Irving] was a proponent of pictorial realism. It was Irving who, in 1881, removed the grooves that had been used to shift scenery, thus opening the way for increased use of three-dimensional sets. He also extended historical accuracy of costume to include those of the minor characters, who had previously been neglected in favor of the major characters. Stage lighting received the same care, and Irving experimented with color as well as with intensity of lighting.[14]

Although these revolutions in theatricality enhanced pictorial realism on the stage, Irving's most famous production, *The Bells*, used this realism as a springboard into the uncanny. In this play, Mathias, the seemingly respectable burgomaster, is haunted by guilt over his murder of a merchant fifteen years before. In Irving's production, a gauze backdrop was illuminated, revealing an enaction of Mathias's dreadful crime. The depths of guilt and memory become a vivid reality for the audience and the murderer himself. This simple but highly effective scenographic technology continues to be used in plays such as *The Woman in Black* (1987), in which superficial reality yields up its secrets from behind a gauze, drawing the protagonist – like Mathias a century before – into a deeper, spectral truth.

For another contemporary example, we shall look at Shaun McKenna and Peter James's 2019 adaptation of Peter James's novel *The House on Cold Hill* (2016). James is a prolific writer who has achieved success with bestselling novels, including (since 2005) a large number of crime thrillers featuring Detective Superintendent Roy Grace as hero. Despite being best known for his crime fiction, James has explored the supernatural in his output. In *The House on Cold Hill*, a married couple Ollie (a web designer) and Caro (a lawyer) move into a dilapidated Georgian mansion with their adolescent daughter, Jade. What they hope will be an escape into a wholesome, rural idyll rapidly becomes less than blissful. The house proves to be a money-pit, the locals are somewhat mysterious, and the disturbing history of the house is revealed. Gradually, the family become aware of a supernatural presence which manifests in different ways (from glimpsed entities to interference in the house's Wi-Fi). The confidence and privilege of this middle-class family is worn away by the attrition of financial woes, ill-health and a cursed house to the point of destruction. As a novel, *The House on Cold Hill* melds the classic Gothic tropes of haunted houses, spectral manifestations, eccentric natives and mental anxiety with the contemporary exploration of digital culture, the modern bourgeoisie and the descent into financial crisis. In 2019, McKenna worked with James on an adaptation of *The House on Cold Hill*, their fourth collaboration on dramatising James's fiction since 2014 but the first to take a supernatural theme.

The stage play of *The House on Cold Hill* follows the novel closely, albeit with Jade reworked into an older teenager. The first production permitted a strongly Gothic stage design, with the play taking place entirely within the ominous, faded grandeur of the House. The detailed, realist stage design of this production was reminiscent of the typical staging of the dark thriller or supernatural worlds of Agatha Christie's *The Mousetrap* (1952), Archibald's *The Innocents* and other plays. Moreover, the stage design was by Michael Holt who also created the staging for *The Woman in Black* in the West End and on tour. The stage adaptation was effective in using the live environment. The twists and turns of the plot, as well as some jump scares, could create audible reactions from the audience. The production made use of the traditional stage effects that made shadows loom large at the window, things move by themselves or ghostly figures appear within mirrors and so on. At the same time, the production brought terror playfully up to date with the family's Alexa device becoming possessed and uttering ominous messages. Although James's novel follows the formula of a classic ghost story, the use of multiple uncanny effects in James/McKenna's stage version was designed not merely to reify the supernatural, it was also designed to be a unifying thrill, as James makes clear in an interview:

> There's a kind of comfort in it because you've got the shared thrill and you're surrounded by hundreds of others so everybody jumps at the same time, then everyone laughs . . . I think the world is a scary place and part of the reason people love reading a good thriller or going to a thriller play is because they can be scared but in a controlled environment.[15]

The aforementioned mirror effect in *The House on Cold Hill* was effectively a modernised version of a famous Victorian effect: 'Pepper's Ghost'. John Henry Pepper's scientific experiments in optics led to a phenomenon that could only be practically used for entertainment. This famous illusion used sheet glass, lighting and reflection, creating a see-through, life-sized ghost that was like an early hologram. The first theatrical showcase for the effect was Pepper's staged reading of one of Charles Dickens' ghost stories, *The Haunted Man and the Ghost's Bargain* (1848). As Russell Burdekin writes, the 'device created quite a stir and chimed in well with the Victorian obsession with ghosts'.[16]

Pepper's Ghost remains a key illusion in the experience of the performed uncanny, notably Disney theme parks rides such as *The Haunted Mansion* and *The Twilight Zone Tower of Terror*. The technology has also been used for a range of 'resurrectional' performances of deceased singers. Although often popularly described as 'holograms', these productions are in fact contemporary versions of Pepper's Ghost. Most notable amongst these is the appearance of Tupac Shakur (1971–96) at the Coachella concerts in April 2012 to sing solo and in duet with Snoop Dogg. The hauntological concept of being 'neither present nor absent, neither dead nor alive' was never more apt than in these Tupac appearances. Critics from diverse disciplines have been fascinated by Tupac's 'ghost' and its theoretical ramifications. For Matthew Harris, 'Tupac at Coachella bears some similarity to the cult of saints in late antiquity',[17] an adored figure no longer on this earth but still conscious. Michael Ralph et al. are similarly hagiographic, arguing that the 'Tupac hologram' [sic] represented 'the spiritual power of his resurrection as an apotheosis, or divine ascendency toward sainthood'.[18] However, they go further in drawing on multiple Afrodiasporic logics such as the '*palo monte* practice of enslaving dead spirits for economic gain in the form of a spiritual cauldron (*nganga*)'.[19] The result is dualistic, with Tupac being resurrected for financial gain but also 'the rebel spirit of this murdered rapper continues the fight against systematic oppression'.[20] Ultimately, however, the experience signals a distinctly hauntological paradox: 'Ironically, Tupac's holographic Coachella performance reinforces the idea that he is dead.'[21]

For Danielle Lavendier, the spectacle of a reanimated Tupac is less than sanguine with the dead performer becoming a 'modernized Victorian ghost',[22] not just in terms of technology but also the Victorian obsession with death (from funereal photography to spiritualism) and what we might call fetishised *momento mori*. More troublingly, Lavendier argues that the performative apparition revealed a long American tradition of being obsessed with 'physically and financially exploiting black bodies'.[23] Ultimately, for Lavendier, the spectacle was something profoundly abject as Tupac had 'no say': 'The appropriation and display of Tupac's "body" brings to mind dreadful images of slave auctions and lynchings from this country's past and the ghoulishness of it conjures a séance.'[24] The phenomenal interest in Tupac's technologically created 'phantom' echoes the Victorian fervour for ghost traps, gauze effects and Pepper's Ghost. In this recent manifestation, we can detect the potency of staged ghosts: they can be fantastic and hagiographic experiences, but they can also be politically and ethically disturbing.

We began this chapter looking at the impact of COVID-19 on the contemporary stage. In 2020, the vivacious world of live theatre became a shadow of its former self. Ghost lights became the most prolific performers on the empty stage, and we were reminded of the prevalence of ghosts throughout the history of theatre, from the vengeful spirits of the Renaissance stage to Victorian spectres and their progeny or the shocking spectacle of reified psychological guilt and trauma. Although clumsy when overstated or mishandled, the paradoxical 'neither present nor absent, neither dead nor alive' of the theatre ghost can wield immense power. Assessing the multitudinous phantoms of the stage, perhaps some futures for a new world of theatre began to creep like uncanny truths into what we assumed to be concrete reality, from the self-directed, promenade journey of an immersive show, the chilling voice of a possessed Alexa, or the multiple ghosts of Pepper.

Notes

1. Michael M. Chemers, *Ghost Light: An Introductory Handbook for Dramaturgy* (Carbondale IL: Southern Illinois University Press, 2010), p. 9.
2. Marvin Carlson, *The Haunted Stage: The Theatre as Memory Machine* (Ann Arbor MI: University of Michigan Press, 2003), p. 2.
3. E. Pineau, 'Haunted by Ghosts: Collaborating with Absent Others', *International Review of Qualitative Research*, 5/4 (2012), 463.
4. C. Davis, 'Hauntology, spectres and phantoms', *French Studies*, 59/3 (2005), 373.
5. D. Saglia, '"The frighted stage": the sensational proliferation of ghost melodrama in the 1820s', *Studies in Romanticism*, 54/2 (2015), 290.
6. Josephine Machon with Punchdrunk, *The Punchdrunk Encyclopaedia* (London: Routledge, 2019), pp. 62–3.
7. Conor McPherson, *Plays: Three* (London: Nick Hern Books, 2013), p. 56.
8. C. Murray, 'The Supernatural in Conor McPherson's *The Seafarer* and *The Birds*', in L. Chambers and E. Jordan (eds), *The Theatre of Conor McPherson: Right Beside the Beyond* (Dublin: Carysfort Press, 2012), p. 198.
9. William Archibald, *The Innocents: A New Play* (London: Samuel French, 1950), p. 69.
10. Archibald, *The Innocents*, p. 3.
11. Archibald, *The Innocents*, pp. 20–1.
12. Nick Dear, *Plays 1* (London: Faber and Faber, 1999), pp. 1–2.

13. G. D'Arcy, 'The Corsican trap: its mechanism and reception', *Theatre Notebook*, 65/1 (2011), *https://tinyurl.com/y7pa2str*.
14. Valerie C. Rudolph, *Nineteenth-Century British Drama, Encyclopedia of Literature* (Amenia NY: Salem Press, 2019), *https://tinyurl.com/y6vx54lt*.
15. P. James, 'Interview: Author Peter James talks *The House on Cold Hill*', *Frankly My Dear* (18 April 2019), *https://tinyurl.com/y8s7dhrs*.
16. R. Burdekin, 'Pepper's Ghost at the Opera', *Theatre Notebook: A Journal of the History and Technique of the British Theatre*, 69/3 (2015), 154.
17. M. Harris, 'The Hologram of Tupac at Coachella and saints: the value of relics for devotees', *Celebrity Studies*, 4/2 (2013), 239.
18. M. Ralph, A. Beliso-De Jesús and S. Palmié, 'SAINT TUPAC', *Transforming Anthropology*, 25/2, 90.
19. Ralph et al., 'SAINT TUPAC', 90.
20. Ralph et al., 'SAINT TUPAC', 90.
21. Ralph et al., 'SAINT TUPAC', 92.
22. D. Lavendier, 'The More Things Change, the More They Stay the Same: Tupac Shakur's "Hologram," Victorian Death Customs, and American Voyeurism', *Relevant Rhetoric: A New Journal of Rhetorical Studies*, 11 (2020), 5.
23. Lavendier, 'The More Things Change', 2.
24. Lavendier, 'The More Things Change', 8.

PART TWO

DRAMATURGIES OF THE MACABRE

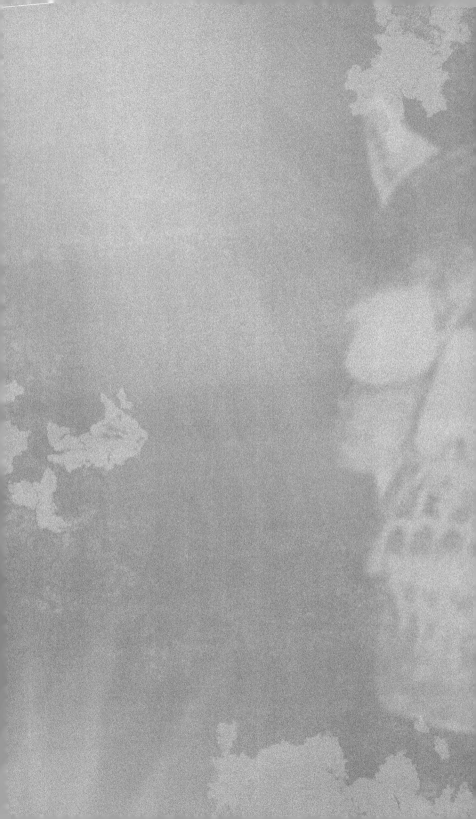

4

Time and Punishment

Gothic Maternal Bodies on the Contemporary British Stage

Kelly Jones

THIS CHAPTER ANALYSES the representation of the maternal body and its relationship with the monstrous in a series of plays that have recently appeared on the British stage. With a specific focus on Robert Alan Evans's *The Woods* (2018), Simon Stone's revisioning of Federico García Lorca's *Yerma* (2017) and Selma Dimitrijevic's *Dr Frankenstein* (2017), this chapter interrogates how such dramas have inherited elements of Gothic horror to explore representations of motherhood. Moreover, it questions how the theatrical medium, as it draws upon live bodies in a shared time and space with its audience, can offer a distinct and resonant platform to consider the horrors attached to the monstrous maternal, particularly in its complicated relationship with patriarchal and neoliberal constructions of time and place.

Our Gothic Mothers

From tales of jealous stepmothers in fairy tales to the domineering harridans of Hitchcock's *Psycho* (1960) and Stephen King's *Carrie* (1974), the maternal has frequently provided a locus of horror. Marilyn Francus argues that 'the gothic is a particularly fertile ground for maternal monstrosity', as she suggests that the subversive maternal figure may be seen as a response to the emergence of an idealisation of motherhood that surfaced in the eighteenth century, the 'golden age' of Gothic literature.[1] She aligns these representations of monstrous mothers to nascent delineations of bourgeois spaces allocated to the private female domestic sphere. She writes that as maternal bodies became increasingly seen as objects of spectacle and surveillance to be policed, the anarchic maternal body appeared as an object of aberration as:

> Eighteenth-century British narratives of mothers veered toward deviance and sensationalism, as wicked mothers, abandoning mothers, infanticidal mothers, pushy mothers, and evil stepmothers dominated the cultural landscape in ballads, fables, novels, plays, and court records.[2]

Conversely, writes Francus, the emergence of stories in which the mother figure does not materialise in any physical form foregrounds the trope of the spectral mother who provides an unattainable ideal as one who 'could be inscribed upon endlessly . . . displa[cing] the flaws of real mothers and experiments with emotionally and socially satisfying possibilities of motherhood'.[3] The spectral mother is as pliable as wax upon which to impress the lofty ideals of motherhood, distanced from the distasteful reality of the maternal body. It was the grotesqueness of the maternal body that became an inspiration for horror in the twentieth century with the advent of cinema, as Barbara Creed notes in her allusion to the 'monstrous-feminine' in horror films; the maternal body is frequently and explicitly staged as a gory and scatological spectacle of unruly abjection.[4]

Scholarship has long focused upon the threat of the maternal body as represented in literature and on screen, but despite the promise of theatre to offer a live encounter with depictions of these unruly bodies, remarkably sparse critical attention has been directed to this medium and its engagement with the monstrous maternal. This neglect is even more striking given that there is a long-reaching history of the representation of this relationship between mothers and the monstrous on the British stage. Certainly, some of the earliest precedents for the theatrical Gothic introduce the subversive mother as agent of horror. Tamora in Shakespeare's *Titus Andronicus* (c. 1591) offers a perverted maternal love as she enlists her sons to avenge the death of their brother by raping the daughter of her sworn enemy; she is duly punished by feeding unwittingly upon the flesh 'that she herself hath bred' (V.v.62). Another Shakespearean tragedy stages a son's revulsion at being forced to confront his mother's sexuality, whilst the central female character of *Macbeth* (c. 1606) boasts of her steely resolve to incite her husband to regicide: 'I have given suck, and know / how tender 'tis to love the babe that milks me: / I would, while it was smiling in my face, / have plucked my nipple from his boneless gums, / and dashed the brains out' (I.vii.54–8).

The first 'Gothic' drama to be recognised as such emerged in the mid-eighteenth century. Horace Walpole's *The Mysterious Mother* (1768) scandalised its readers with a tale of maternal incest. Grieving for her husband, who was killed in a hunting accident, the Countess of Narbonne plays the 'bed-trick' on her son, Edmund. Edmund emerges from years of subsequent banishment to fall in love and marry Adeliza who, unbeknown to Edmund, is the resulting offspring from this illicit tryst. The play seems to court the primal fears of the maternal abject as son and daughter are punished, not for their inability to break free from the mother, but from her inability to detach herself from her children. Almost half a century later, tormented mother Imogine of Charles Maturin's *Bertram* (1816) is punished for her 'monstrous' extra-marital transgressions with the loss of her infant to the Dark Knight of the Forest. Such dramas emphasised the destabilisation of patriarchal authority and the threat to the law of male primogeniture that the subversive mother presents as part of her Gothic menace. Elsewhere, the much safer figure of the spectral mother proliferated as in Henry Siddons's 1794 production of Ann Radcliffe's novel, *The Sicilian Romance; or the Apparition of the Cliffs*, in which the long-lost mother figure appears as a ghost to save her daughter. Whilst the mother figure here is not a supernatural entity but a long-held captive at the hands of a bigamist husband, she paves the way for the staging of other absent mother figures, victimised by tyrannical male villains, such as, most famously, the Lady Evelina in Matthew Lewis's *The Castle Spectre* (1797).

The monstrous mother figure in the twentieth century seemed to become an archaic Gothic trope, replaced by the idea of child cruelty as the product not solely of parental agency but of society more widely. For example, despite the unspeakable horror of the stoning of the baby in Edward Bond's *Saved* (1965), the play that paved the way for the abolition of the Lord Chamberlain's censorship of plays, the audience is not invited to lay the blame squarely at the feet of Pam, the child's mother, as she abandons the baby, leaving it in the purview of its killers. Caryl Churchill's

Top Girls (1982) explores motherhood through the businesswoman Marlene, as she abandons her daughter to pursue a lucrative career. Again, Gothic horror here is averted, replaced by a cold Darwinian pragmatism as the monstrous maternal is redirected towards a grisly depiction of the neoliberal feminism that women such as Marlene embrace to survive. Nevertheless, the Gothic impulse that aligns subversive maternal bodies with the monstrous continues to stalk the contemporary British stage. Stephen Mallatratt's theatrical adaptation of Susan Hill's novella *The Woman in Black* (1989), for example, hearkens to a brand of Gothic Victoriana with its staging of a retributive mother, Jennet Humphries, who practises vengeance for the death of her illegitimate son. More recently, Polly Stenham's *That Face* (2007) presents a mother caught in the fog of a manic-depressive state, struggling to adjust to life abandoned by her husband, overwhelmed by the challenges of her wayward teenage daughter, and erotically fascinated by her son's blossoming heterosexuality.

Responding to recent critical interest in cultural representations of motherhood, Jozefina Komporaly pursues a reading of a series of plays that reveal how 'the representation of mothering and of the desire for motherhood is often located in a discourse that spectacularizes the maternal body'.[5] In doing so, Komporaly argues how such plays illustrate 'the loss of agency that comes with being looked at', but how they also offer 'the celebration of the maternal subject's desire to unleash its performative potential as a platform for consolidating or reclaiming agency'.[6] As this present essay explores the maternal body and its relationship to the monstrous as a residual Gothic trope on the modern British stage, it follows Komporaly's example in questioning how the theatrical medium complicates the objectification of this body. The argument presented here is that the theatrical medium itself renders the monstrous maternal subject complex, because of its own potent misalignments with hegemonic strictures of 'productive' time and space.

Time, Space and the Aberrant Maternal

Komporaly contemplates the convoluted effects of time-scape in her reading of the plays of Anna Furse, Lisa Evans and Laura Wade and she reflects upon, 'the treatment of the maternal in terms of the Butlerian performative – considering the maternal as "a kind of doing, an incessant activity performed"'.[7] Similarly conscious of the abstruse effects of time connected to the performance of the maternal, Lena Šimić and Emily Underwood

Lee write that 'mothering is revealed as a social contract, as a social activity, and as a responsibility. It seems it is not possible to move on from motherhood. The cycle is repeated. A mother's work is never done!'.[8] The Sisyphean sprawl of the practice of motherhood brazenly complicates the linear patriarchal notion of time that aligns the temporal, under neoliberal capitalism, with productivity. Motherhood continues to occupy an ambiguous position in the neoliberal consciousness: it is not viewed as work, in that, in contemporary Britain at least, it is not rewarded with concrete financial remuneration. The bourgeois domestic sphere that, according to Francus, women were to adhere to in the eighteenth century has been rendered indistinct and permeable through contemporary working practices, soaring childcare costs and the rise of single-parent families. Media propaganda incites the guilt associated with motherhood and its choices: stay-at-home mothers are criticised for their perceived failure to return to the workplace, whilst mothers who return to work either full or part-time are often faced with a self-reproach that accompanies their decision, as well as potential limitations in their career progression.[9] In a culture that continues to privilege heterosexual child-rearing, cautionary tales proliferate of career-driven women, having failed to reproduce at the same time as being economically productive, who are punished by their fast-expiring biological clocks. Whilst modern technologies such as IVF and egg-freezing have appeared to liberate women, they concurrently confirm patriarchal notions of time, as costs associated with such treatments demand complicity with a system that privileges capital accumulation through workplace labour. Motherhood possesses an ambiguous relationship to neoliberal notions of time because the female experience, whether biological or psychological, does not always obey its strictures. Somewhat poignantly, Jay Griffiths draws upon the work of chemists Ilya Prigogine and Isabelle Stengers and their research into complex, often chaotic 'dissipative structures' that conjoin seemingly opposite forces, characterised by shape and flux, stability and instability, the non-linear and the linear. Griffiths writes that 'time's character, as revealed in the model of dissipative structures, has all the qualities which patriarchy has attributed to *women*, and has therefore devalued for so long'.[10]

The disorder associated with the maternal and its threat to productive time carries echoes of Gothic dissonance. David Wiles, writing of the time-scapes that seem at odds with each other in Christopher Marlowe's *Doctor Faustus*, traces this alignment between time and productivity to the Protestant ethos that emerged in the sixteenth century, that:

the striking of the clock at the eleventh hour marks, in Marlowe's play, the convergence of two configurations of time: Catholic time, which concentrates on the rhythm of life and death and on the insignificance of life before eternity, and Protestant time, which demands that time be used profitably, for good works.[11]

Echoing Faustus's horror, as he is caught between a fascination for old beliefs and a desire for science and enlightenment, part of the paranoia of the Gothic lies in its obsession with the structures and spaces of the past that it struggles to free itself from. The past refuses to stay buried; the ancient regime continues to burst its tenements and supernatural figures such as the vampire and the ghost refuse to respect linear progressive time. The Gothic is characterised by its obsession with dust: matter out of its respective place and time that refuses to honour borders and boundaries, uncontainable, excessive labyrinthine sprawl. As Emma McEvoy writes, the characteristic attached to many Gothic texts of the Romantic Period is 'their experiments with time – featuring moments that stretch to eternity, years that are often traversed in seconds – and their radical dislocation of chronology'.[12]

Theatrical performance is the most potent medium for this experience of Gothic ambivalence of time and space. Theatrical time itself possesses a potentially abject proclivity in its relationship to time that David Ian Rabey notes with reference to Barbara Adam's work on time-scapes. He writes that:

> theatre raises questions of value: of what should be communicated, endured and changed over time. From a neoliberal economic perspective that conceives of power in exclusively monetary terms, theatre might be condemned or dismissed as a 'waste of time', without immediately visible or predictable consequences in terms of exchange or investment (according to the presumption that 'any time that is not translatable into money tends to be associated with a lack of power'. . .).[13]

Significantly, for the argument advanced here, according to Rabey (and Dylan Trigg), 'theatre's phenomenological aspect might thus be identified as how it not only depicts but also demonstrates "appearances at being resistant to enclosed borders and fixed points"'.[14] The ambivalence that characterises theatre's depiction of and resistance to agents of containment suggests a distinctly Gothic resonance.

This chapter will now use Robert Alan Evan's *The Woods*, Simon Stone's adaptation of Lorca's *Yerma*, and Selma Dimitrijevic's *Dr Frankenstein* to explore the representation of the relationship between the maternal body and the monstrous. As it does so, it subsequently investigates the ways in which all three plays use the theatrical medium itself to displace notions of linear, 'productive' time and place to challenge the idea of the mother as monstrous spectacle.

Robert Alan Evans's *The Woods*

The Woods, in a production directed by Lucy Morrison, opened at London's Royal Court Theatre in September 2018. It centres upon the experiences of the Woman, lost in the woods, as she endeavours to rescue a boy she finds buried in the snow. As she does so, she is unrelentingly pursued by the Wolf, a protean figure who veers between cruel taunts and desperate pleas for her affection. Despite the play's suggestion of her infanticide, the play resists casting the Woman as monster. Instead, it is the Wolf who, playing on the cunning ascribed to the beast in folkloric tales, embodies the monstrous as he attempts, and eventually fails, to summon the maternal abject body to the surface. Fergus Morgan, in *The Stage*, described the play as 'a haunting meditation on what society expects from women, and on how giving birth doesn't necessarily make you a mother', whilst similarly joining a range of critics who decried the play's lack of clarity and 'wilfully obtuse' narrative in 'a heavy portrait of a mother's emotional trauma but one that pours its focus into atmosphere and image'.[15] Narrative seems to give way to experiential effect as the audience are plunged into the density of the Woman's psychological dislocation: the theatrical medium insists that they share this confusion as they navigate between the two worlds, the darkness and the light, and attempt to make sense of this terrain.

As she stands stranded in snowdrifts in the dark woods, the Woman catches occasional glimpses of her past life, symbolised by a kitchen seen suspended above the stage in a glass box. Throughout, the play foregrounds the boundaries between kitchen and forest, the latter something easy to slip into but not to escape from. The stage directions at the outset of the play reveal that 'something has happened', and the two spaces of the kitchen's ordered world and the forest's unruly gloom come to be defined by their temporal relationship to this event.[16] There are anaemic suggestions of linear time. Time ravages Woman and Wolf as both visibly age between scenes. The shack in the woods where the Woman nurses the boy has, according to the stage directions, 'been here a long time'.[17] The Woman wears a shabby summer dress in the depths of winter, the detritus of another, presumably much sunnier, world. The woods too are littered with the debris of the motherhood experience prior to the 'something' that has happened: a discarded baby monitor, a cardigan, a child's broken nightlight, a deflated helium balloon. But, 'there's no clock in the forest', so says Orlando in Shakespeare's *As You Like It* (III.ii.271), and linear time is confounded. Her memory is in disarray. 'You been here forever', gibes the Wolf, 'You know how long that is? Since always.'[18] As the woods become darker, the semantics of light and sound that give shape to time disappear:

> **Woman:** . . . they take all the sound away, those trees.
> That's what they do.
> They're so thick your voice just gets sucked up by them.
> . . .
> You just walk and walk.
> And eventually you can't tell night from day.
> Or up from down.[19]

When she locates the shack, she experiences a feeling of homecoming, a place she feels she knows and can hold the Boy. As soon as she does so, she spies her strewn baby relics and follows them to slip through the walled glass of the kitchen and recall her devastating past. Divided from herself, the Woman is simultaneously in the kitchen and the forest 'watching herself' as she relives the painful moment when she reaches in and through the kitchen cupboard, to touch the border of this arboreal netherworld and retreats, tainted with a dark stain that spreads across her clothes and skin.[20] A baby cries and, alarmed by the unfurling tarnish, the Woman attempts to soothe the child seconds before the Woman in the forest watching emits a cry 'of grief' and the infant's sobs are suddenly smothered.

The audience, also plunged into this frightening world where concrete time and place are suspended, are invited to see the Woman as a victim rather than as a spectacle of monstrosity and this passage from patriarchal 'linear' time, a portal opened by motherhood, as not liberation but a prison. In the final scene, she describes to the Boy the early days following his birth, the spectacle that she became to 'people' who mutter elliptical niceties, and those who are jealous, and those too 'feeling the same. Like . . . "What's happening to me?" "Why don't I feel . . ." Day. And night. And day. Milk. And radiators on. And all these people. And all these nights when I'm just . . . I get further away.'[21] Her unwillingness to embrace this confusion counters her monstrosity. She disowns her abject maternal body. She has, reluctantly, strayed from the pathway, pursued by the Big, Bad Wolf, to whom she eventually surrenders the Boy, and walks towards the light. The audience, by contrast, are swallowed up by the darkness.

Simon Stone's *Yerma*

Unlike Evans's play, Stone's 2017 adaptation of Lorca's *Yerma* chronicles the pursuit of motherhood rather than the repercussions of its realisation. Like the Woman in *The Woods*, the nameless protagonist here is given simply an anonymous cipher, 'Her'. She is both an Everywoman and a nod to an archetype of the hysterical mad woman, frustrated by her inability to fall pregnant, haunted by her deepest fear of becoming 'irrelevant' as 'small insignificant marks someone will rub out as soon as we're gone'.[22] For Her, having a child is the ultimate act of self-assertion, a riposte to the impermanence of time.

Under Stone's direction at London's Young Vic Theatre, captured for a National Theatre Live recording, black glass encases the stage action so that the audience can peer into the play world that the characters cannot see out of. In this glass box, she is a spectacle, caged in a life in which she strives to embody the urban myth of the woman who 'has it all'. The audience watch Her attempt to market her subjective experience of fertility struggles for her online blog. Unlike the rural community of Lorca's original play, the online community here is faceless, churlish and hungry for *schadenfreude*. She succumbs to the temptation of pursuing the rules of the marketplace as she transgresses the boundaries between the public and the private. Dee, her younger colleague, reminds her that in journalism it is the taboo, 'the dark secret brought into the light', that sells, as Her confronts the guilt of having marketed her sister's miscarriage agony.[23] In doing so, she turns herself into a clickbait exhibition of the monstrous feminine to satisfy the hunger for 'the ugly stuff. The regrets. The night-time horrors'.[24]

Her's desperation contrasts with the detachment of Helen, her academic mother, who struggles to own the maternal body and to express a motherly affection for her daughters. She describes her own experience of pregnancy in overly Gothic tones: 'being colonised by someone's sperm' and cites the film *Alien* as a 'very accurate representation of what my pregnancies felt like. Waiting, horrified, feeling this creature growing inside me, until the day where it forced itself out of me, screaming demandingly, expecting me to satisfy its every whim, a parasitic succubus.'[25] Her's pursuit of motherhood is thrown into stark relief too by her sister who reveals her 'monstrous' postnatal struggle to bond with her son, her fantasies about jumping from the tube-station platform, and her wry jokes of child abandonment. Her, by contrast, is haunted by her biological urges: 'You're not getting the messages I'm getting', she tells her husband, John, 'Every single second of every single day'.[26] Enslaved by the calendar, obsessed with her fertile days, her age, yearning nostalgically for 'The Old Days' with her fecund former lover, she imprisons herself within a suffocating impression of linear time and its ravages upon her reproductive system. Notably, in Stone's production, Billie Piper's Her is the only character consistently shackled by a wristwatch. Time in the production is measured chaotically as the stage action is divided into nominal chapters, each chapter framed by a statement that references time, sometimes arbitrarily, 'Months pass', and at other times with exact precision, 'That Wednesday'. Audience experience of time is alloyed to Her's as the time-scape shifts wildly between stasis and fluidity. Finally, linear temporality is suspended entirely as, at a festival, intoxicated, she immerses herself in a nightmarish montage of scenes in which she encounters doppelgangers of her husband, her former lover and her mother, and attempts to make-believe the reality she would live if she had the agency. The Gothic intensity of these festival scenes as she wanders the stage, clad in a white sundress, accompanied by dissonant music and the pathetic fallacy of a rainstorm, plunges the audience into a shared sense of disorientation as the doppelgangers are played by the same actors as their counterparts.

The final scene opens on an empty apartment, stripped of all its promise, in a poignant cyclical return to the first scene. Confronted with John's confession that he did not share her dreams for a child, we hear the snarl of her fury and see the flash of the knife, before the final spectacle of the blade having ruptured Her's abdomen, billows of scarlet spreading across the shabby vestal sundress. In a twist on Lorca's original tale, in which Yerma stabs her apathetic husband, it becomes clear that Her has gored herself as she sinks down with her final words to her imagined child, 'Maybe I'll be coming to you'.[27]

The audience witness Her's descent into monstrous spectacle, ravaged by her obsession with the ticking clock. She loses her subjectivity, fettered by the expectations of the gaze of a virtual world, both in her head and online. But the audience are not encouraged to share in this creation of the monstrous feminine as spectacle as, from a respective distance, they have followed her journey into despair. They might not share Her's frustration, but they are encouraged to sympathise with its emergence and its effects.

Selma Dimitrijevic's *Dr Frankenstein*

In charting their struggle, Her and the Woman are to be seen as victims, unable to circumnavigate time and place in ways that they would choose. The Woman is displaced in the unruliness of maternal time, having slipped through the domestic space of motherhood – 'the kitchen' – into the dark forest, and Her is barred by her infertility from moving into this maternal sprawl, into this idyllic domestic sphere. In the final case study here, Dr Victoria Frankenstein in Dimitrijevic's play brazenly flouts any external perception that she should confine herself to this sphere of domesticity; instead, she brings the business of maternal creation into the scientist's laboratory. In changing the gender of the creator, *Dr Frankenstein* rewrites the narrative of the mother figure, using Mary Shelley's tale to foreground how a resistance to linear time can challenge the way the monster (either Creator or Creation) is held up as a spectacle, enabling their reclamation of their subjective agency over the external gaze.

There have been many adaptations of Shelley's Gothic novel for both stage and screen, but Dimitrijevic's appears to be distinctive in gender-reversing the creator. Despite this progressive depiction of woman as scientist, the protagonist continues to operate as an anomaly for the historical moments in which the play is set, England and Germany in 1831 and 1832, some thirteen years after Shelley's publication of the story. In a play that echoes the novel's original themes – parental responsibility, the effects of nature and nurture, lost and surrogate mothers – Dr Victoria Frankenstein is a woman tormented by societal expectations of the duties of matrimony and daughterhood that she avowedly abjures in pursuit of a career in science. The play, then, in another marked distinction to Shelley's novel, shifts the focus to the subjectivity of the female characters.

In Dimitrijevic's play, the potential to create life is returned to the woman. Notably, unlike the original Frankenstein, her progeny is the dead revivified rather than various corpses stitched together and reanimated in a vain attempt to create a 'masterpiece'. Moreover, rather than fleeing in horror like her male counterpart as the Creature awakens and reaches for her, Victoria approaches her charge with a mixture of scientific fascination and an attempt at performing maternal tenderness. She struggles to marry cold rationalism to her emotional warmth and excitement, attempting to gently reassure her progeny as she prods his flesh with a surgeon's knife. The Creature escapes as he unwittingly knocks his 'mother' unconscious, frightened of her experiments with the scalpel. Later, he denies any physical pain he felt at her hands, and remembers her tenderness, the warmth with which she spoke to him and her refusal to look away, 'She never did. Just like a child. Looking straight into my eyes. Ready for anything'.[28]

Reunited at the play's close, as the Creature disaffirms his monstrosity and proclaims his innocence from the murder of William, Frankenstein's young brother, they work together. The Creature, dying, rotting from within, relates to his mother-scientist what he remembers from his experience of life so that it might be 'useful' for 'next time'.[29] Together, the Creature and his maker work to attempt to undo the oppression of linear time, with the hope that they can remake what is subject to decay.

Despite the subject matter's repeated affront to the ethics of 'playing God', the play refuses to cast either scientist or Creature as monster. Instead, it is the linear progressive march of life towards death that becomes monstrous. 'I was talking to one of the doctors a while ago, to Professor Waldman. He said something very interesting, he said "if only we could stop time, to give us a moment to think, a moment to act"', Frankenstein tells her family friend, 'It's a revolutionary thought, Henry, "if only we could stop time"'.[30] In the ultimate act of daring, she enters the masculine space of the laboratory where she seeks to undo patriarchal notions of linear time through the creation of new life.

That it was a theatrical medium used to present this gender-subversive retelling of Shelley's story is important. Theatrical time, with its 'monstrous' capacity to undo stable perspectives of linear time, to provide the audience with a collective space and moment to 'think' and the performers 'to act' outside the neoliberal strictures of 'productive' moment and place, enabled the play more readily to challenge preconceived ideas of the monster as a spectacular abomination of place and time.

Conclusion

Dr Frankenstein presents an innovative attempt to rewrite the narrative of the relationship between mothers and monsters. Yet, all three plays borrow from the Gothic genre to complicate the monstrous spectacle of the subversive mother figure, rather than to reinforce it, choosing to do so via a medium that enables audiences to share the confused experiences of these dislocated female protagonists as they stand in interstitial spaces and non-linear time-scapes that do not accord with the neoliberal construction of either time or place. Nor can these women enter, with any confidence, a welcoming domestic sphere that allows for the chaotic sprawl of time. The extent to which these women are held up as spectacles of the monstrous-feminine who transgress rules is problematised by a medium that itself refuses to honour boundaries as it tells and retells stories of mothers, and the monsters that society tries to make of them, when they are not quite able to live up to what it demands them to be.

Notes

1. Marilyn Francus, *Monstrous Motherhood: Eighteenth-Century Culture and the Ideology of Domesticity* (Baltimore MD: Johns Hopkins Press, 2012), p. 180.
2. Francus, *Monstrous Motherhood*, p. 10.
3. Francus, *Monstrous Motherhood*, p. 17.
4. Barbara Creed, *The Monstrous-Feminine: Film, Feminism, Psychoanalysis* (London: Routledge, 2007), p. 8.
5. J. Komporaly, 'Making a Spectacle: Motherhood in Contemporary British Theatre and Performance', *Theatre History Studies*, 35 (2016), 162.
6. Komporaly, 'Making a Spectacle', p. 162.
7. Komporaly, 'Making a Spectacle', p. 162; Judith Butler, *Undoing Gender* (London: Routledge, 2004), p. 1.
8. L. Šimić and E. U. Lee, 'Editorial', *Performance Research*, 22 (June 2017), 3.
9. For a short sample of the recent plethora of media attention, research and journalistic opinion that surrounds debates of stay-at-home or working mothers in the United Kingdom alone, and the financial penalties associated with being a working parent, see: *www.theguardian.com/commentisfree/2016/nov/18/stay-at-home-mum-job-parent-pressure-women-mother; www.telegraph.co.uk/science/2016/11/16/kids-better-off-at-nursery-rather-than-staying-at-home-with-mum/; www.dailymail.co.uk/debate/article-2895620/PETER-HITCHENS-*

s-absolute-proof-mothers-better-staying-home; www.theguardian.com/money/2015/mar/28/childcare-costs-uk-ireland-worst-on-price; and www.bbc.co.uk/news/education-39566746.

10. Jay Griffiths, *Pip Pip: A Sideways Look at Time* (London: Flamingo, 1999), p. 135; see also David Ian Rabey, *Theatre, Time and Temporality: Melting Clocks and Snapped Elastics* (Bristol: Intellect, 2016), p. 56.
11. David Wiles, *Theatre and Time* (Basingstoke: Palgrave, 2014), p. 56.
12. E. McEvoy, 'Gothic and the Romantics', in C. Spooner and E. McEvoy (eds), *The Routledge Companion to Gothic* (Abingdon: Routledge, 2007), p. 22.
13. Rabey, *Theatre, Time and Temporality*, p. 14; Rabey cites Barbara Adam, *Timescapes of Modernity* (London: Routledge, 1998), p. 68.
14. Rabey, *Theatre, Time and Temporality*, p. 17; Rabey cites Dylan Trigg, *The Memory of Place: The Phenomenology of the Uncanny* (Athens OH: Ohio University Press, 2012), p. 47.
15. Morgan, F., 'Review: *The Woods*', *The Stage*, 13 September 2018, www.thestage.co.uk/reviews/the-woods-review-at-royal-court-london--harrowing-and-hallucinatory.
16. Robert Alan Evans, *The Woods* (London: Faber and Faber, 2018), p. 7.
17. Evans, *The Woods*, p. 8.
18. Evans, *The Woods*, p. 15.
19. Evans, *The Woods*, p. 39.
20. Evans, *The Woods*, p. 42.
21. Evans, *The Woods*, pp. 79–80.
22. Stone (after Federico García Lorca), *Yerma* (London: Oberon, 2017), p. 77.
23. Stone, *Yerma*, p. 22.
24. Stone, *Yerma*, p. 31.
25. Stone, *Yerma*, p. 33.
26. Stone, *Yerma*, p. 54.
27. Stone, *Yerma*, p. 88.
28. Selma Dimitrijevic, *Dr Frankenstein* (London: Oberon, 2017), p. 58.
29. Dimitrijevic, *Dr Frankenstein*, p. 94.
30. Dimitrijevic, *Dr Frankenstein*, p. 23.

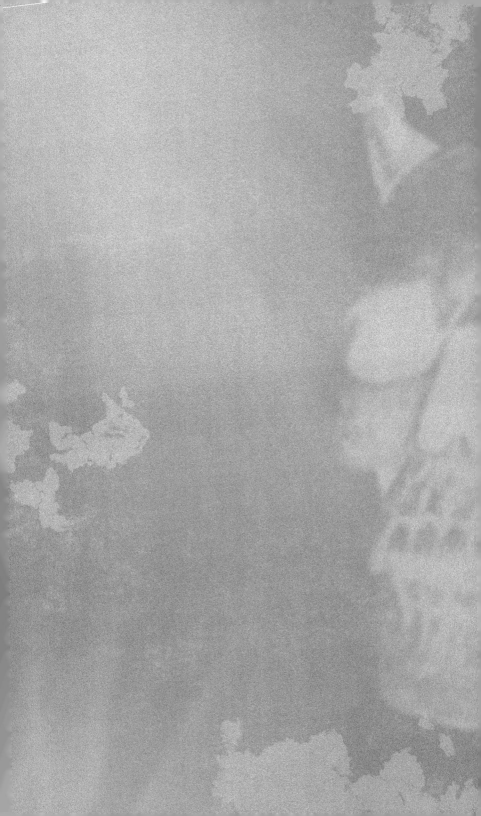

5

The Body Dismembered
Allegory and Modernity in German *Trauerspiel*

Magda Romanska

> These fragments I have shored against my ruins...
> T. S. Elliot, *The Waste Land*[1]

IN LIGHT OF THE RADICAL Marxist critique of modernity launched by the Frankfurt Institute for Social Research (eventually known as the Frankfurt School), with which Walter Benjamin remained in a somewhat cautious but nonetheless direct relationship, a book on German Baroque theatre might seem extraneous and obsolete. What connection, if any, did Benjamin see between the Baroque *Trauerspiel* and modernity?

Although Benjamin had just began to study Marxism, and although *The Origin of German Tragic Drama* (1928) appears to focus only on the question of theatre, his analysis of Baroque allegory encompasses a far more radical discourse on modernity than perhaps even he himself realised at the time. Drawing a distinction between the Greek theatre, based on the tragic inevitability of fate and the futility of individual choice, and the Baroque theatre's open and despondent disdain for the world and its affairs, Benjamin inaugurated a dramatic conceptual shift in the notion of modern subjectivity, at the centre of which he located the dismembered body of a puppet (effigy of the king). As Eli Friedlander notes, Benjamin juxtaposed tragedy with *Trauerspiel* ('mourning play') while confronting

Nietzsche's *The Birth of Tragedy* and its focus on Wagnerism: 'Benjamin's critique of the mythical elements inherent in Nietzsche's Wagnerism also bear on his preoccupation with the problematic face of modernity.'[2] Was Benjamin's book a commentary on the implications of Wagnerism? In his book *Polish Theatre of the Holocaust*, Grzegorz Niziołek, quoting Adam Lipszyc, notes that Benjamin foreshadowed the Holocaust in the macabre of the Baroque drama:

> Reconstructing Benjamin's vision of the theatre created in the 1920s, Adam Lipszyc endows it – consciously or not – with after-images of the Holocaust; in Benjamin's book on German tragic drama, Lipszyc read an outline of 'future' catastrophe. The baroque theatre of 'fallen history' is gory and slapdash, painfully material and makeshift, while the destruction mechanism of history turn people into puppets; 'In his world, death contains nothing noble, life is merely a production line of corpses, which lasts in perpetuity along with the cutting of hair and nails, and does not end, at least not in any definitive way, with the moment of death, just as . . . hair and nails did not stop growing'.[3]

Contrary to the prevailing conviction about the seeming remoteness of modernity from Baroque sensibility, it is in Baroque's *Trauerspiel* and the mournful melancholy of form expressed in its allegory of the sovereign/puppet that Benjamin locates the origins of modernity and its horrors.[4]

The modern notion of allegory, according to Benjamin, originates with Baudelaire's *Les Fleurs du mal* (1857) and 'the notion of the *correspondences*, a concept that in Baudelaire stands side by side and unconnected with the notion of "modern beauty"'.[5] Baudelaire (and Proust) perceive *correspondence* as a ritualistic experience of memory, a reminiscence instigated by sensation and transcended into the unity of 'spleen and idea' – the idea supplying 'the power of remembrance', and the spleen 'the multitude of seconds against it'. The Platonic split between object and idea that Benjamin sees in Baudelaire is significant, as it marks the distinction between symbolic and allegorical representation. For Baudelaire, *correspondence* entails more than a simple symbolic parallel between signifier and signified. What is at stake in its structure is the historically bounded ontological cohesion of the subject whose 'power of remembrance' opens up the microcosmic realm of *le temps perdu* – memories lost and regained via a 'consciousness ready to intercept [their] shock'.[6] What follows is the abyss between memory and the self, 'between signifier and signified' – an abyss that indicates a radical shift in the conceptualisation of the modern subject: '[s]omething about subjectivity seems to be at stake in allegory, and [Baudelaire's] "return to allegory" indicates a "turning away from [hitherto prevailing notions of] subjectivism"'.[7]

Prior to Goethe, allegory and symbol were treated interchangeably. In a letter to Schiller from 1797, Goethe provides a first rudimentary distinction between the two, describing symbol as belonging to the 'sensual' and allegory to an 'inner vision'. Thus, symbolism 'transforms appearance into an idea, the idea into an image in such a way that the idea remains always infinitely effective and unreachable', while 'allegory transforms appearance into a concept, the concept into an image, but in such a way that the concept can be grasped . . . as something delimited in [and by] the image'.[8] In allegory, according to Goethe, 'the particular serves only as an instance or example of the general . . . Whoever grasps the particular in all its vitality also grasps the general, without being aware of it, or only becoming aware of it at a late stage'.[9] Opening up the space between the singular and the general, allegory masks its own mediation in 'order to reconcile sense and senses in an appearance of immediacy of vision and intuition'.[10] Looking for the particular in the general, allegorical representation 'appears as a form that is excluded from the fullness of meaning. It must look for meaning, and in searching for it, it constantly defers [it]'.[11]

Following Goethe's definition, Friedrich Creuzer defines allegory as 'the very incarnation and embodiment of the idea'.[12] Through its very form and content, allegory 'is both: convention *and* expression; and both are inherently contradictory'.[13] As an embodiment of an idea, the particular that represents the general, allegory is inherently ambiguous: 'always the opposite of clarity and unity of meaning'.[14] In Goethe's definition, the appearance is transcribed into the *concept*, a term classified by Kant as the product of analytical reason. To analyse means to dismember, to deconstruct; and the process of allegorical transcription is in itself a dismembering of the body, of signs (of signifier from signified), of the unity of the Hegelian *Gestalt*, ridden with anxiety and melancholic longing for the relinquished (sacrificed, perhaps) and lost parts (of body, memory and language). Its analytic sterility and deathlike aura set allegory 'in the realm of thoughts, what ruins are in the realm of things'.[15] 'Allegory is the dissolution of the speculative synthesis of subject and object, visible in the dismembered body and in the ruin',[16] and as such it articulates the threat to the symbolic totality of the modern psyche and the terror that confronts it in the face of its own degeneration.

The motive of tyrannicide is a focal point of the Baroque *Trauerspiel*. The dismembered effigy of the ruler, who is both tyrant and martyr sacrificed on the altar of communal unity, becomes the very incarnation of allegorical destruction and deconstruction. The effigy is both grotesque and subtle, material and sublime, dead and alive. Tadeusz Kantor describes the mannequin in his theatre as 'a MODEL through which passes a strong sense of DEATH and the conditions of the DEAD'.[17] Devoid of essence, the marionette epitomises the body as a condition of non-being. '[It] is a "human" thing . . . a "non-thing"'.[18] Made in the image of man, the puppet both negates existence and suggests it. Looking at the wax face of the marionette, frozen eternally in a grimace shaped by someone else, one cannot avoid the uncanny feeling of life caught in death's mummifying grip. For Ernst Jentsch, the puppet evokes the feeling of the 'uncanny', of terror, precisely because it makes one 'doubt whether an apparently animate being is really alive; or conversely, whether a lifeless object might not be in fact "animate"'.[19] On the border between life and death, between the body in its materiality and the psyche that it lacks, the puppet 'confronts us with that larger than life silence that tinged us later from the great space when we stepped somewhere at the limit of our existence', writes Rainer Maria Rilke.[20] By reducing the human body to a material thing, the puppet, 'the essence of materiality devoid of any traces of psyche', as Bruno Schulz put it,[21] forces the viewer to confront the corporeality of his own body. It is a corpse, an object that belongs neither to life nor to death, thus evading the laws of both.

The puppet's liminal position between life and death embodies the allegorical dialectic of the extremes. The sovereign, Benjamin argues, whose marionette body is offered 'to the unknown gods as the first fruits of a new harvest of humanity',[22] is both tyrant and martyr. His death too has a double significance; it is:

> at once a first and a final sacrifice: a final sacrifice in the sense of an atonement to gods who are upholding an ancient right; a first sacrifice in the sense of a representative action, in which new aspects of the life of the nation become manifest.[23]

It is a tragic death on the altar of communal unity and nationhood. Benjamin sees in the Baroque drama what René Girard defines as a collective sacrifice: a sacrifice during which the community washes off its sins by projecting them onto the figure of a lone victim.[24] As Benjamin reads it, '[His] death thereby becomes salvation'.[25] For Foucault, the Baroque's spectacular executions fulfilled a didactic function as well: 'The criminal was asked to consecrate his punishment by proclaiming the blackness of his crimes.'[26] His role was to re-solidify the law and, in doing so, to reinstate the communal unity: 'A convicted criminal could become after his death a sort of saint, his memory honoured and his grave respected.'[27]

Translated into the language of *Trauerspiel*, the Foucauldian 'spectacle of the scaffold' gives rise to a martyr drama in the tradition of the Christian passion play, in which the body of the condemned tyrant becomes an arena of dialectical negotiation between transcendence and immanence. By virtue of its very materiality, the puppet's cavity renders despair over death's 'immanent reality',[28] while the sacrificial nature of death it represents attests to the eternal:

> Baroque knows no eschatology . . . The hereafter is emptied of everything which contains the slightest breath of this world. [That is why, like] a vacuum, [it is to] one day destroy the world with catastrophic violence.[29]

It is the role of the monarch to forestall the impending catastrophe by whatever means necessary, including his self-sacrifice. 'The Baroque work of art [is a response to the imminence of a Judgement Day, and as such it] wants only to endure, and clings with all its senses to the eternal.'[30] In this apocalyptic vision of the world, the puppet's body represents the space between what Lacan calls the two deaths – to quote Slavoj Žižek explaining Lacan's concepts: the 'natural death, which is a part of the natural cycle of generation and corruption . . . and absolute death – the destruction, the eradication of the cycle itself'.[31] 'This place "between the two deaths," a place of sublime beauty as well as terrifying monsters, is the site of *das Ding*, of the real-traumatic kernel in the midst of symbolic order.'[32] This space of in-betweenness is also the space occupied by allegory. It is from the dialectic of beauty and monstrosity that allegory derives its ambiguity, its 'richness of meaning',[33] and it is from the space in between the two deaths that it brings about the proliferation of signifiers and 'the crisis of meaning'.[34] It is also from here that it brings forth the dual nature of the sovereign: he can be both tyrant and martyr; he commits his crime as an act of sacrifice, in the name of a higher ideal, 'the redemption of mankind',[35] and he is sanctified for his commitment. 'The tyrant and the martyr are but two faces of the monarch. They are the necessarily extreme incarnations of [the] princely essence.'[36]

The same 'movement between extremes',[37] and 'crossing of the borders'[38] between transcendence and immanence, inscribed in the sacrificial execution of the monarch, pervades the process of sublimating his effigy. For Plato, ideas are the inventions of God, and objects are the embodiments of ideas – their copies – insofar as they are based on their internal, 'spiritual' resemblance to the ideas from which they derive. The visual (or poetic) representation of an object is not its copy but its simulacra, its imitation, a false image based on a superficial external resemblance to an object it represents; it is a mere appearance of reality. The *truth* thus lies in the realm of ideas, not of objects or their representations. One who makes objects 'does not make that which exists [and] he cannot make true existence, but only some semblance of existence'.[39] The representation (imitation) is therefore twice removed from the *truth* of the idea:

> The real artist, who knew what he was imitating, would be interested in realities and not in imitations . . . the imitator has no knowledge worth mentioning of what he imitates. Imitation is only a kind of play or sport, and the tragic poets, whether they write in iambic or in Heroic verse, are imitators in the highest degree.[40]

Our perception of reality is that of an artist; all we see are shadows of the objects on the walls of the Platonic cave, 'like the screen which marionette players have in front of them, over which they show the puppets'.[41] To the Platonic-ontological-epistemological triad of idea, copy and simulacrum, St Augustine adds a fourth dimension. Before the fall, man is a copy of God, but after having sinned, man loses his status as God's image and becomes God's simulacrum. Hence any representation of man is a simulacrum of a simulacrum, or, as Baudrillard calls it, a remainder, a simulacrum of simulation. If in the model of Platonic-ontological monotheism man is thus twice removed from the perfection of God, what is the place of the marionette in relationship to God?

It is the puppet's meta-status, between life and death, between transcendence and immanence, that constitutes (for Rilke) its allegorical alienation:

> The doll embodies a paradoxical duality as anthropomorphous dead thing. Although its anthropomorphous figure invites dialogue and dialectic self-experience in the apparent likeness of another, the dead shell of the stuffed body blocks and displaces identification . . . The

puppets can no longer be grasped through the transference and
empathy that they have outgrown and escaped, but yet they have
grown out of this transference and empathy. They are a determinate
negation of transference and empathy, their negative embodiment.
It accounts for 'their horrible dense forgetfulness'. It is the horrible
density of something the subject does not want to remember, 'the
hatred that, unconsciously, certainly was always part of our relations
to it [the puppet]'.[42]

What is the horrible, forgotten, yet known secret of the puppet that Rilke
speaks of? The death of the tyrant/martyr represented in his dismembered
effigy arouses both fear and pity. 'Fear is aroused by the death of the villain,
pity by that of the pious hero. For Birken even this definition [of *Trauerspiel*]
is too classical, and he replaces fear and pity with the glorification of
God . . . as the purpose of *Trauerspiel*'.[43] And yet, the glorification of God
in allegorical representation is, as Michel Steinberg notes, 'rooted in the
absence of God'.[44] It is 'an early spectacle of God's infamous absence'.[45]
The dialectical tension between presence and absence that gives allegory
its ambivalence comes from the fact that 'in [its] context, the [allegorical]
image is only a signature, only the monogram of essence, not the essence
itself in a mask'.[46] Thus, allegory conceals its own lack, veiling it in the
language of its own internal contradictions.

In Lacan's vocabulary, allegory is that which can be approached but
never fully grasped. It represents the gap within the symbolic and imaginary
and stands for the unimaginable and the unspeakable; it is the 'impossible'
Lacanian Real, in which the tyrant's effigy, sublimated in *Das Ding* – an
interior void and the embodiment of the death drive[47] – performs the lack
it conceals. Thus, the identification with the puppet is always a misidentification
(*méconnaissance*). At the mirror stage, the subject's self-recognition
advances from the internalised realm of the imaginary to the realm of the
symbolic,[48] but 'the puppet . . . becomes the scene of an early subject formation
different from the formations and identifications before the mirror
and with living persons'.[49] What constitutes the failure of identification is
the allegorical void between signifier and the signified.

For Freud, the puppet embodies all the qualities of the 'uncanny': 'the
terrifying which leads back to something long known to us, once familiar
[but] now frightening precisely because it is *not* known and familiar'.[50]
In Julia Kristeva's words, the puppet epitomises the stranger within, the
alien Thing unrecognised by cogito yet integral to it. The empty 'dead-like'

beauty of the marionette, the shell devoid of consciousness, personifies the inability of cogito to conceptualise itself as a totality. The puppet stands in direct opposition to 'the voice of the will to symbolic totality venerated by humanism in the human figure . . . [It] is as something incomplete and imperfect that objects stare out from the allegorical structure'.[51] In allegory, 'the whole nature is personalized, not as to be made more inward, but, on the contrary – so as to be deprived of soul'.[52] Allegorical representation verbalises the act of consciousness becoming conscious of itself: the impossibility of framing into language the act of its being and *non-being*. Allegory brings forth the failure of language to circumscribe the meaning and silence of cogito faced with the horror of its non-existence: '[The tragic hero] shrinks before death as before power that is familiar, personal, and inherent in him . . . The idea of death fills [him] with profound terror.'[53] Thus, in *Trauerspiel*, 'the spoken word makes no pretense to be dialogue; it is only commentary on the images, spoken by the images themselves'.[54]

In Kristeva's words, allegory 'speaks the unspeakable'. The puppet contains that which cannot be spoken, all that is terrible – all that arouses 'dread and creeping horror'.[55] As Rainer Nägele put it: 'To avoid death and taboo, we need the puppet'.[56] But there is more to allegorical representation than 'a question of reflection about the end of life'.[57] The puppet's dialectic of melancholy for language, the soul and God is an integral element in the construction of the notion of the modern subject. As Michael Steinberg notes, 'Benjamin analyzes the Baroque lamentation play as a crucible for early-modern cultural fragmentation'.[58] What, then, is at stake in the process of Baroque melancholic disintegration?

In *Mourning and Melancholia*, Freud defines melancholia as a 'morbid pathological disposition' resulting from the loss of a love object, a loved one or an abstraction with which the libido entered into the bond of identification. What distinguishes mourning from melancholia is that the melancholic forecloses any possibility of replacing the lost love object, even though he is often able neither to discern nor to define that which has been lost. What characterises the relationship between the melancholic and the lost love object is an ambivalence of emotions: a loss or fear of loss inspires hate; identification inspires love. The contradictory feelings of love and hate find their outlet in depreciation of the love object (or its substitute, which can be the ego itself caught in narcissistic self-identification). Freud writes, 'Depreciating it [the lost object], making it suffer and deriving sadistic gratification from its suffering', becomes a part of the melancholic's sadomasochistic cycle of emotional and physical economy of pain.[59]

In *Trauerspiel*'s melancholy dialectic, the tyrant is both condemned and revered to the point that the ambiguity of emotions towards him 'create a fundamental uncertainty as to whether this is a drama of tyranny or a history of martyrdom'.[60] 'What is the significance', Benjamin asks, 'of those scenes of cruelty and anguish in which the Baroque drama revels?'.[61] The spectacle of tyrannicide itself is 'not so much concerned with the deeds of the hero as with his suffering, and frequently not so much with his spiritual torment as with the agony of the physical adversity which befalls him'.[62] In the scene of execution, the body of a victim is dismembered 'part by part and limb by limb'.[63] If a spectacle like Damiens' death as described by Foucault[64] were to be represented on the stage, the actor himself could not portray it without actually undergoing torture. Thus, the puppet comes to replace the living body. For Freud, 'dismembered limbs, a severed head, a hand cut off at the wrist – all have something uncanny about them'.[65] And if the puppet itself arouses the terror of the unknown yet familiar, the puppet's dismembered torso is twice as terrifying. It is here that the dialectic of the puppet's 'divine beauty' and horrifying monstrosity becomes the terrain for a melancholic recapitulation of death, God and the self. It is here that 'the presentation and representation, *Darstellung* and *Vorstellung*, intersect in the actor as a paradigm for the strange oscillation of the body between physical entity and imaginary subject/object'.[66] For in Baroque *Trauerspiel* the effigy not only represents the dismembered body of an actor, and 'the body of the actor does not merely represent something but shows and presents itself, the Self as body'.[67] The puppet hosts the lost object – God, Self, language – and as such it must suffer sadistic tortures. Therefore, the reason for substituting the body of the actor with the puppet is not purely logistical. The puppet is a liminal object in which contradictions burst open the tensions within the illusory totality.

Rainer Nägele suggests that the *Trauerspiel* is foremost a drama of mourning for the lost object – God, Self, immortality: 'Theatrically and ostentatiously the lost object, or rather its loss, is staged in mourning.'[68] But Benjamin says, it would be too simple to perceive Baroque drama as a mere play of mourning in which the function of allegorical obsession with a *memento mori* merely lies in its literal reconfiguration of loss. Epistemologically and phenomenologically, the Baroque violence to the body is an expression of reclaiming a symbolic signification over a lost totality. If the allegory dismembers, it is only to refurbish that which was fragmented through 'the violence of the dialectic movement within [its] depth'.[69]

Written in the norms of emblematic representation, the Baroque dismembered body of the puppet 'frees the spirit' in order to enter 'into the homeland of allegory'.[70] The central norm of an emblematic representation with regard to the human body necessarily leads to the dismembered:

> The whole human body cannot enter a symbolic icon, but it is inappropriate for part of the body to constitute it . . . [T]he human body could be no exception to the commandment which ordered the destruction of the organic so that the true meaning, as it was written and ordained, might be picked up from its fragments.[71]

For Lacan, the 'abstract thing' that the melancholic cannot define, yet whose loss he cannot stop to mourn, becomes a lost object that was never lost but instead never existed in the first place. As a monument to the never-existing lost object, the puppet masks and exposes its own void in the allegorical dance macabre of object and subject, of the subject's 'profound inner emptiness'.[72] 'Mourning is the state of mind in which feeling revives the empty world in the form of a mask [creating] the distance between the self and the surrounding world to the point of alienation from the body'.[73] 'The self knows of nothing other than itself; its loneliness is absolute.'[74] But the self itself is a lack, and it is the lack that the allegory conceals and venerates; it remains 'obscure to itself'[75] via its own abyss of signification. Thus, as the tyrant's body and the self, the allegorical language 'is only afflicted by meaning . . . as if by an inescapable disease; it breaks off in the middle of the process of resounding, and damming up of the feeling, which was ready to pour forth, provokes mourning'.[76] For Lacan, language signifies the death of the Thing; language, like allegory, veils that which is unspeakable, and that is perhaps why the only language 'that is completely proper' to the tragic hero is that of silence.[77]

Hence the dialectic of allegorical representation is not only the melancholic acting-out of the pleasure of mourning, but also the systematic recapitulation of the fundamental absence. The fragmentation is a process of symbolic purification: if the totality masks its own void, deconstructing the totality unveils the absence of the lost object. It is only in the form of the corpse, a symbolic totality, that the Baroque hero could reclaim lost meaning, and 'it is not for the sake of immortality that [he] meets his end, but for the sake of the corpse'.[78] The Baroque corpse/effigy thus becomes a site of the contestation of meaning: it performs the lack of a lost object, but it also performs the loss itself. The limbs and flesh that fall off the

Baroque body of the puppet become a substitute for the non-existent lost object, allowing the subject's mourning to gain symbolic validity. The role of the puppet amplifies the dialectic of loss and absence as the puppet itself is devoid of the consciousness that its form suggests. It is its 'divine beauty' and the monstrosity of the unspeakable terror it hides that constitute the core of Baroque's violent excavation of meaning from the abyss of the sacred and the profane. The allegorical ambiguity is at the heart of the cathartic sacrifice that brings forth the meaning scattered among the ruins of modern thoughts.

Meaning is derived from the disintegration of ruins via the dialectical violence of object/subject, life/death, sacred/profane, immanence/transcendence oppositions that constitute the modern model of subjectivity. As Max Pensky notes:

> In the allegorical mode of seeing, devaluation is followed by fragmentation . . . Together, devaluation and fragmentation are the propadeutics to allegorical *Konstruktion*, the third productive moment of allegory. Only through the gaze that sees the homogeneity and repetition . . . can the allegorist come to construct meaning of his own, by assigning subjective meanings to the fragments.[79]

In allegorical representation, 'any person, any object, any relationship can mean absolutely anything else'.[80] Thus, 'allegory leads to intensification of the subjective – hence arbitrary – creation of meaning'.[81] It is this arbitrariness that Saussure saw in the relationship of the signifier and signified that Benjamin locates at the core of the modern subject. What is mourned in the process of Baroque and modern melancholia is the loss of an object that never was – 'me'[82] – the self that never existed beyond its language. And the 'dismemberment and cutting to pieces . . . [erects] the explosive vision of a body [Self] delivered to "symbolic wounds"' of its loss.[83]

Susan Buck-Morss notes that by drawing a parallel between the macabre of the Baroque *Trauerspiel* and the macabre of the turn of the century European culture, Benjamin was trying to comment, in a meta-fashion, on the unspeakable:

> And just as the Baroque dramatists saw in the ruin not only the 'highly meaningful fragment,' but also the objective determinate for their own poetic construction, the elements of which were never unified into a seamless whole, so Benjamin employed the most modern

method of montage in order to construct out of the decaying fragments of nineteenth century culture images that made visible the 'jagged line of demarcation between physical nature and meaning'.[84]

Was Benjamin trying to capture the sense of the impending doom of the Holocaust, a prospect beyond one's imagination? At that time, in 1928, the murmurs of the catastrophe must have been palpable, but also perhaps beyond language. Allegory, with its process of deconstruction and reconstruction, veiling and unveiling, would capture that which escaped language. The puppet, with its sense of the uncanny, both commented on and illustrated the relationship between the sovereign and the subjects: the sovereign channels communal murmurs into action, but the desires of the community are so unspeakable that he too must be destroyed as the witness to the horrors he helped perpetuate. It is perhaps this sense of impending doom that appears simultaneously both inevitable and too terrible to actually happen that *Trauerspiel* shared with tragedy, after all, and what perhaps Benjamin believed, it shared with the Germany of the late 1920s.

Notes

1. T. S. Eliot, *The Wasteland*, www.poetryfoundation.org/poems/47311/the-waste-land.
2. E. Friedlander, 'On the Musical Gathering of Echoes of the Voice: Walter Benjamin on Opera and the *Trauerspiel*', *The Opera Quarterly*, 21/4 (Autumn 2005), 631.
3. Grzegorz Niziołek, *The Polish Theatre of the Holocaust*, translated by Ursula Phillips (London: Methuen Drama, 2019), p. 66.
4. Rainer Nägele, *Theatre, Theory, Speculation* (Baltimore MD: Johns Hopkins University Press, 1991), p. 78.
5. W. Benjamin, 'On Some Motifs in Baudelaire', in M. W. Jennings (ed.), *The Writer of Modern Life: Essays on Charles Baudelaire* (Cambridge MA: Harvard University Press, 2006), p. 161.
6. Benjamin, 'On Some Motifs', p. 184.
7. Nägele, *Theatre, Theory, Speculation*, p. 82.
8. Quoted in Nägele, *Theatre, Theory, Speculation*, p. 88.
9. Quoted in Walter Benjamin, *The Origin of German Tragic Drama* (New York: Verso, 1998), p. 161.

10. Nägele, *Theatre, Theory, Speculation*, p. 87.
11. Nägele, *Theatre, Theory, Speculation*, p. 87.
12. Quoted in Benjamin, *Origin*, p. 164.
13. Benjamin, *Origin*, p. 175.
14. Benjamin, *Origin*, p. 177.
15. Benjamin, *Origin*, p. 178.
16. Nägele, *Theatre, Theory, Speculation*, p. 92.
17. Tadeusz Kantor, quoted in Krzysztof Miklaszewski's *Encounters with Tadeusz Kantor*, translated by George M. Hyde (New York: Routledge, 2002), p. 39.
18. Nägele, *Theatre, Theory, Speculation*, p. 18.
19. Quoted in S. Freud, 'The Uncanny' (first published in *Imago*, 1919, reprinted in Norton's *Collected Works of Sigmund Freud*), p. 347.
20. Quoted in Nägele, *Theatre, Theory, Speculation*, p. 19.
21. Quoted in Wiesław Borowski, *Tadeusz Kantor* (Warszawa: Wydawnictwa Artystyczne I Filmowe, 1982).
22. Benjamin, *Origin*, p. 107.
23. Benjamin, *Origin*, p. 107.
24. René Girard, *Scapegoat* (Baltimore MD: Johns Hopkins University Press, 1985).
25. Benjamin, *Origin*, p. 107.
26. Michel Foucault, *Discipline and Punish: The Birth of the Prison* (New York: Vintage, 1995), p. 66.
27. Foucault, *Discipline and Punish*, p. 67.
28. Benjamin, *Origin*, p. 136.
29. Foucault, *Discipline and Punish*, p. 66.
30. Benjamin, *Origin*, p. 181.
31. Slavoj Žižek, *The Sublime Object of Ideology* (London: Verso, 1989), p. 135.
32. Žižek, *Sublime Object*, p. 135.
33. Benjamin, *Origin*, p. 177.
34. Max Pensky, *Melancholy Dialectics: Walter Benjamin and the Play of Mourning* (Amherst MA: University of Massachusetts Press, 1993), p. 116.
35. Benjamin, *Origin*, p. 79.
36. Foucault, *Discipline and Punish*, p. 69.
37. Pensky, *Melancholy Dialectics*, p. 114.
38. Benjamin, *Origin*, p. 177.
39. Plato, *The Republic* (New York: Quality Paperback Books, 1999), p. 378.
40. Plato, *The Republic*, pp. 378, 416.
41. Plato, *The Republic*, p. 265.
42. Rilke quoted in Nägele, *Theatre, Theory, Speculation*, p. 17.

43. Benjamin, *Origin*, p. 61.
44. M. Steinberg, 'Benjamin and the Critique of Allegorical Reason', *Walter Benjamin and the Demands of History* (Ithaca NY: Cornell University Press, 1996), p. 10.
45. Pensky, *Melancholy Dialectics*, p.107.
46. Benjamin, *Origin*, p. 214.
47. Jacques Lacan, *The Ethics of Psychoanalysis, Seminar VII* (New York: Norton, 1992).
48. Jacques Lacan, 'The Mirror Stage', in *Écrits: A Selection* (New York: Norton, 1977).
49. Nägele, *Theatre, Theory, Speculation*, p. 17.
50. Freud, 'Uncanny', p. 370.
51. Benjamin, *Origin*, p. 186.
52. Benjamin, *Origin*, p. 187.
53. Benjamin, *Origin*, p. 114.
54. Benjamin, *Origin*, p. 195.
55. Freud, 'Uncanny', p. 369.
56. Nägele, *Theatre, Theory, Speculation*, p. 19.
57. Benjamin, *Origin*, p. 218.
58. Steinberg, 'Allegorical Reason', p. 16.
59. Sigmund Freud, *Mourning and Melancholia* (New York: Norton, 1978), pp. 161–2.
60. Benjamin, *Origin*, p. 73.
61. Benjamin, *Origin*, p. 216.
62. Benjamin, *Origin*, p. 72.
63. Benjamin, *Origin*, p. 176.
64. 'On the scaffold . . . the flesh will be torn from his breasts, arms, thighs and calves . . . his right hand . . . burnt with sulphur, and, on those places where the flesh will be torn away, poured molten lead, boiling oil, burning resin, wax and sulphur melted together and then his body drawn and quartered by four horses and his limbs and body consumed by fire, reduced to ashes and his ashes thrown to the winds.' (Foucault, *Discipline and Punish*, p. 3).
65. Freud, 'The Uncanny', p. 397.
66. Nägele, *Theatre, Theory, Speculation*, p. 6.
67. Nägele, *Theatre, Theory, Speculation*, p. 3.
68. Nägele, *Theatre, Theory, Speculation*, p. 10.
69. Benjamin, *Origin*, p. 166.
70. Benjamin, *Origin*, p. 217.
71. Benjamin, *Origin*, p. 217.

72. Benjamin, *Origin*, p. 114.
73. Benjamin, *Origin*, p. 141.
74. Benjamin, *Origin*, p. 108.
75. Benjamin, *Origin*, p. 158.
76. Benjamin, *Origin*, p. 209.
77. Benjamin, *Origin*, p. 108.
78. Benjamin, *Origin*, p. 218.
79. Pensky, *Melancholy Dialectics*, p. 117.
80. Benjamin, *Origin*, p. 175.
81. Pensky, *Melancholy Dialectics*, p. 110.
82. M. Torok and N. Abraham, 'The Illness of Mourning and the Fantasy of the Exquisite Corpse', in Nicholas T. Rand (ed.), *The Shell and the Kernel: Renewals of Psychoanalysis* (Chicago IL: University of Chicago Press, 1994); '"The Lost Object – Me": Notes on Endocryptic Identification', *The Shell and the Kernel*.
83. Jean Baudrillard, *Simulacra and Simulation* (Ann Arbor MI: University of Michigan Press, 1994), p. 111.
84. Susan Buck-Morss, *The Dialectics of Seeing: Walter Benjamin and the Arcades Project* (Cambridge MA: The MIT Press, 1989), p. 164.

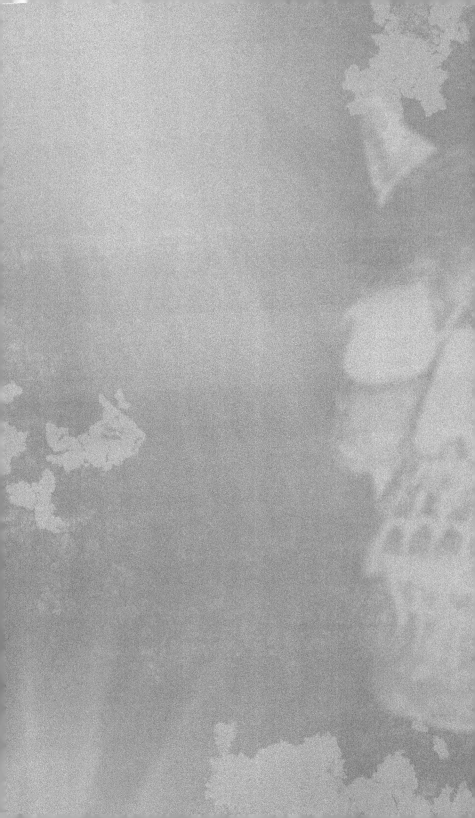

6

Macabre Children on the Australian Stage

Angela Betzien's Cycle of Crime Plays

Chris Hay and Stephen Carleton

> We're becoming used to content warnings posted in theatre foyers and company websites. Belvoir's new production has one longer than most: *Mortido*, a story about drug trafficking, contains smoking, theatrical haze, strobe effects, adult content, violence, strong language, nudity, live gunshots, and loud sounds and music. But what concerned some audience members during *Mortido*'s Adelaide season wasn't explicit violence or strong language; it was the presence of a child.[1]
>
> Elissa Blake, *Sydney Morning Herald*

IN THIS PROFILE, written to accompany the 2015 season of Angela Betzien's play *Mortido* at Sydney's Belvoir Street Theatre, the figure of the child on stage is introduced as a locus of anxiety in the production. The profile goes on to detail the changes to the script that were required by the New South Wales Office of the Children's Guardian, and reveals that 'during the season, when backstage, the boys wear headphones to insulate them from the play's content, all of which would usually be audible via the backstage sound system'.[2] Quite apart from their fate within the fiction, these children are marked from the outset as in need of protection and care – the article is accompanied by a smiling photograph of the two boys (Toby Challenor and Otis Jai Dhanji) who alternated the role of the child, alongside *Mortido*'s star Colin Friels. Of course, on one level, the producing company is going on the front foot here and acknowledging the inevitability of anxiety linked to the child (which had, as the article notes, accompanied the production's premiere in Adelaide). On another level, promoting the play through this anecdote is an acknowledgement of the power of the child to disrupt and transcend the narrative and thematic concerns of the work.

As in the other plays that we consider in this chapter, the figure of the child in *Mortido* 'disquiets the mind and degrades the art'.[3] A child on stage, like the animals and laughing actors of Nicholas Ridout's study, is always *first* a child, and only thereafter a character in a fiction, and therefore capable of invoking in the audience, through anxiety, an ethics of care and compassion. By provoking this sense of anxiety – for the child's ability, comprehension and safety – the figure of the child on stage has the potential to transcend the fictional frame and provoke a sense of 'uncanny alterity'[4] that we argue below is a hallmark of the macabre. The words from the *Sydney Morning Herald*, with which this chapter begins, respond to this same sense: despite the many graphic sensory intrusions that *Mortido* promises, it is the figure of the child who is most disquieting. These affective qualities of the macabre child on stage are also key to the efficacy of each of the works that we discuss here. We take as our case study the work of Australian playwright Angela Betzien, particularly the plays that director Sarah Goodes names Betzien's 'cycle of crime plays': *The Dark Room* (2009), *Mortido* (2015) and *The Hanging* (2016).[5] Betzien has a deep engagement with children on stage, especially through her celebrated work as a playwright for and with young people. We focus here on her most recent plays for adult audiences, while acknowledging this work is informed by her long history of creative engagement with children onstage and offstage.

In this chapter, we argue that the child also carries an especial valency in the Australian context, both in the popular and the literary imagination. After all, this is the land in which dingoes make off with babies, and small blond boys disappear from country gardens.[6] Literary critic Peter Pierce writes in *The Country of Lost Children: An Australian Anxiety* that:

> Australia is the place where the innocent young are most in jeopardy. Standing for girls and boys of European origin who strayed into the Australian bush, the lost child is an arresting figure in the history and

folklore of colonial Australia. More profoundly though, the lost child is the symbol of essential if never fully resolved anxieties within the white settler communities of this country.[7]

When a child appears on stage in Australia, particularly when that child is lost, abandoned or otherwise imperilled, that child carries with them deep-seated national anxieties and stands in for traumas that may at first seem distant from the fictional context in which they appear. We extend Pierce's argument into the twenty-first century, and align Betzien's work with Pierce's reading of Patrick White's plays (one of the few theatrical examples that appear in *The Country of Lost Children*): 'neglected, aborted or murdered as they so often are, these children are emblems of those adult fears of the self and the future that the plays so vividly dramatize.'[8] We also build upon Helen Strube's association of Betzien's earlier work with Pierce's,[9] by considering her recent texts for adult audiences.

This imbrication of the child with the anxiety of the adult, both the fictional adult on stage and the real adult in the audience, also aligns Betzien's children with theoretical constructions of Gothic children. Kelly Jones, for example, argues that the 'alignment of children with the monstrous presents the young as the ideal conduits of horror for an expressly adult audience';[10] Jennifer Balanzategui argues that 'childhood is positioned as the site of traumatic, imperfectly recalled pasts that haunt the adult's present in obfuscated ways'.[11] Across this body of theoretical work, the child's uncanniness functions in part as 'a blank canvas onto which societies may project ideas, and ideals of innocence'.[12] We argue that this effect is heightened in the theatre, where the all-too-real body of the child appears before our very eyes, provoking an embodied confrontation with the ethical compact that we introduced above. Throughout our work here, we will follow Balanzategui by interrogating the ways in which the child is simultaneously:

1. Tasked with embodying futurity and teleological progress.
2. Entwined with the adult's origins and personal past.
3. Externally situated as adulthood's inferior binary opposite.
4. Associated with a buried, enigmatic realm still lurking within the depths of the adult unconsciousness.[13]

These concerns are united by the same 'both/and modality' (or 'liminality') identified by Jones,[14] which is at the heart of the experience of uncanniness.

We aim to superimpose the tripartite reading developed by Jones, Benjamin Poore and Robert Dean over the top of Balanzategui's formulation of the child as incipient adult, to position Betzien's macabre children as particular markers of millennial cultural anxieties in the Australian context. Jones, Poore and Dean draw on Jeffrey Cox's seminal study of eighteenth-century Gothic drama (via Diego Saglia) to offer this reading of the symbolic representations that underpin the uncanny theatrical language of the Gothic:

> Saglia explicitly builds upon Cox's thinking when he offers a 'tentative definition' of stage Gothic as 'a theatrical language of "the extreme" combined with sensationalism of a supernatural, psychological and political nature'.[15]

We begin, then, by exploring the ways in which children in the three plays can be read according to Balanzategui's symbolic scaffolding – either as embodying futurity and teleological progress, as a stand-in for the future adult, as the adult's inferior binary opposite, or as a marker of the return of the repressed within the adult consciousness – and in so doing, align this with Cox's supernatural and psychological layers of interpretation. In the second part of the chapter, we examine the ways in which Balanzategui's and Jones's uncanny child can be interpreted through the political layer of meaning in Cox's equation. Here, we bring this analysis together with our earlier reading of Pierce to argue that, in the twenty-first century, Betzien's macabre children can operate as agents of political anxieties – as 'lost children' – tapping into very specific cultural traumas pertaining to Australia's status as both a postcolonial settler/invader society (explored particularly in *The Dark Room*), and as a global capitalist/consumer society (in *Mortido*).

One final frame that brings these theoretical concerns into conversation is the macabre, which we acknowledge by naming Betzien's characters as macabre children. There is some slippage in vocabulary here, especially between the Gothic and the macabre, and the precise distinction between them interests us less than the macabre's explicit association with death and dying. The 'brutalising of the young'[16] that takes place in Betzien's crime-cycle plays is linked directly to the death of the child, either their literal death (in *The Dark Room*) or the prospect thereof (in *Mortido*). This is also another instance of liminality – between life and death – a space in which *The Hanging* operates for the majority of its narrative. In the sections that follow, we offer a reading of the three plays, focusing on how the figure of the macabre child advances the thematic and political concerns of the work, as outlined above. We do so to demonstrate the resonance of the figure of the macabre child across Betzien's crime cycle, and the wider functions of macabre children on the contemporary Australian stage.

Macabre Children as Incipient Adults

Three schoolgirls have disappeared; only one has returned. In *The Hanging*, Betzien stages the interrogation of the returned girl, Iris, by a police inspector, Flint, as witnessed by Iris's chosen 'support person'[17] – the girls' English teacher, Ms Corrossi. The one-act, single-location play unfolds as a procedural crime drama, framed by Iris's visions of the Australian bush into which her friends have disappeared. Shot through with literary allusion, most notably to Joan Lindsay's seminal Australian novel *Picnic at Hanging Rock*, the play is interested in liminality and in-betweenness. In her introduction to the published script of *The Hanging*, director Sarah Goodes identifies that 'it explores things and people on the cusp, when things stop being one thing and become another'.[18] *The Hanging* was commissioned by the Sydney Theatre Company, on whose Wharf One stage it premiered in August 2016. Notably, the role of Iris in this production was played by the then-twenty-three-year-old actor Ashleigh Cummings, and so the body of the actor on stage did not carry the same significations of incipient adulthood that are present in the text.

The girls of *The Hanging*, as represented by Iris, aspire to a state of permanent stasis. Not only do the three who disappeared each bear a tattoo of a circle, which Iris explains is because 'they go on for eternity. No beginnings no endings. They can't be broken',[19] but also the girls act in ways that deliberately seek to arrest their development. Iris speaks about the competitive eating disorders amongst the young women of her school and suggests that Hannah 'won' because her period stopped: 'Hannah stopped time'.[20] As she begins to reveal the truth of what happened in the bush, Iris wonders if perhaps she will never escape this circle, asking 'what if my memory is like a clock that has stopped and it can't go forward and it can't go back and I'm caught inside a dream?'.[21] This image of circularity plays out in the dramaturgy of the script itself too: *The Hanging* opens and closes with the description of Flint alone in the bush, an impression solidified by Goodes's production, which added a detailed video and sound design that overtook the stage and linked the two moments visually.

There is a sense throughout *The Hanging* that the narrative is simultaneously urgent and taking place out of time. Flint's interrogation is time-sensitive – the two girls who remain missing have been gone for 'one hundred and forty-four hours and counting'[22] – and his questions build to a crescendo of urgency. Against this, however, is the sense that this story could be taking place at any time: Iris's opening monologue, describing Flint's search in the bush, wonders 'perhaps a minute or was it millennia that passed'.[23] The girls could be millennia old; they could be the girls of Lindsay's *Picnic at Hanging Rock*,[24] set in 1900; they could even be, as Corrossi suggests, sisters of Lindy Chamberlain whose baby was infamously taken by a dingo in 1980 – 'and didn't she pay for it'.[25] The Diderot quotation repeated by the students and their teacher, 'it assures me of eternity in you and with you',[26] haunts *The Hanging*.

They are, in other words, prototypical of Pierce's lost Australian children. The desire of these young women to remain forever in-between is identified by Corrossi as a kind of national malaise, drawing on a common reading of Australia as a nation still in development:

> **Corrossi** In theory, given proper guidance teenagers will in time grow out of their awful aching adolescence and into mature, marginally decent human beings. In theory. Increasingly, in this country at least, they remain juveniles their entire lives. We are a terminally pubescent nation.[27]

To return to Balanzategui's assertion that the child may represent futurity, then the insistence of the children in *The Hanging* that they do not wish to move forward, combined with this characterisation of Australia as 'terminally pubescent', makes Iris a subversive figure. Far from being a binary, the adults and the children in the play resemble more closely the circle tattooed on the girls' wrists, part of a single continuum that is moving neither forwards nor backwards but instead becomes an uncanny timelessness. This impression is heightened by Betzien's decision to keep the other girls, Hannah and Ava, offstage, and as a result, Iris must stand in for all three – indeed, for all of the schoolgirls haunting the play across time.

Finally, Betzien also depicts Iris as the return of what might have been repressed by Corrossi, with the younger girl's actions reflecting the older woman's anxieties about her own unruly sexual and social desire. 'It is interesting to note the parallels between Iris and Corrossi's situations: both are outsiders . . . they recognise and resent their own weaknesses in each other and attack each other accordingly',[28] and these parallels are even acknowledged by the characters in the dialogue:

> Corrossi   You're like me. I love food. And cake, I could eat cake until the cows come home.
> Iris   I'm not like you.
> Corrossi   You're not like them.[29]

Corrossi's insistence here that Iris has more in common with her than she does with her friends is later accepted by the younger girl, and the play's final moment offers a staging of their inevitable imbrication. As Iris narrates Flint's discovery of the missing schoolgirls' bodies and speaks the play's final line 'are we doomed?',[30] the stage directions read simply: 'Corrossi falls into darkness'.[31] The repressed has returned, and it has destroyed – just as it does in Betzien's earlier play *Mortido*, named after the death-drive that Corrossi has embodied at the end of *The Hanging*.

The circular dramaturgy of *The Hanging* also appears in Betzien's *Mortido*, which similarly opens and closes with a single actor on stage narrating a macabre tale – in this case, a much darker one. Indeed, that character, Grubbe, reaches for the circle as metaphor when explaining the psychoanalytic concept that gives the play its name: 'existence is an endless circle of life and death, life and death. But ultimately, the aim of all life is self-destruction. That's *mortido*.'[32] *Mortido*, the development of which was supported by Playwriting Australia before its premiere as a co-production between the State Theatre Company of South Australia and Belvoir (Sydney) in October 2015, is an attempt to give the global drug drama dramatic form. Although the play moves swiftly between time and place, its narrative spine follows the attempts of Detective Grubbe to bring down the nascent cocaine trading partnership of Monte and Jimmy, who are striking out on their own to try to fill a void in Sydney's cocaine trade. Their globe-trotting drug business is contrasted with domestic scenes featuring Scarlet (Monte's wife and Jimmy's sister) and her son Oliver, whose dreams have started to feature the sinister figure of El Gallito.

The function of children as a locus of anxiety and the macabre in *Mortido* is telegraphed from the first line of the play: 'there once was a boy'.[33] By the end of Grubbe's monologue this boy has been killed and resurrected, but he 'was no longer a sweet *angelito*. Instead he was filled with a rage like a young cock . . . and so began a war that would have no end'.[34] The child as the motivation for violent acts recurs throughout *Mortido*.

It is later revealed that Grubbe's work as police detective in his final months before retirement is driven by the guilt that he feels towards his deceased daughter. Although his daughter's fate in the play is unclear, it is heavily implied that she was a victim of the drugs whose traffickers he is chasing.[35] The sense that parents have wronged their children in ways they cannot always name haunts *Mortido*.

As introduced above, *Mortido* demands a child actor for the doubled role of Oliver and Alvaro, two seven-year-old boys, one Australian and one Bolivian. On one level, the doubling is doubtless a practical concern – having a single child backstage was challenging enough – but on another, the doubling dramatises an argument about the far-reaching effects of the drug trade. As *Mortido* continues, the two boys begin to merge: the first hint of this is Alvaro's first introduction, where 'he wears the dirty shoes that Oliver was wearing earlier'.[36] The slippage of costume pieces continues, and the stage directions suggest that Oliver is slowly being infected by Alvaro (and thus taking on macabre characteristics): first 'Oliver enters from the darkness, wearing pyjamas and a dirty Bolivian beanie. He is sick and has a fever';[37] then shortly thereafter, 'Oliver enters in his pyjamas. He's wearing Alvaro's shoes, beanie and jumper. He is deathly pale and his hands are covered in red'.[37] These descriptions suggest that these young boys function as macabre irruptions of Jimmy's guilt over his involvement in the drug trade, the red on Oliver's hands standing in for the metaphorical blood on Jimmy's, and signalling the child's association with 'a buried, enigmatic realm still lurking within the depths of the adult unconsciousness'.[39]

By the time the play reaches its final act, the two boys are indistinguishable, especially to Jimmy; but also for the first time, the stage directions reflect this slippage. This exchange is the last time that Oliver is invoked on stage, although the stage directions specify that it is Alvaro who appears:

> *Alvaro enters carrying a blood-stained hessian bag.*
>
> **Scarlet**   Oli, say goodbye to Uncle Jimmy.
> **Jimmy**   What's in the bag?
>
> *Alvaro is silent.*
>
> **Scarlet**   We have to go.
> **Jimmy**   Wait. (*To Alvaro*) What's in the bag? (*Alvaro is silent*). Show me. (*Jimmy draws his gun. It's real*).[40]

The two boys have now become one in the world of the play, and so in the following scene when Jimmy force-feeds Alvaro packets of cocaine, the figure on stage is indistinguishable from his nephew; indistinguishable, too, from the boy of Grubbe's opening monologue who was eviscerated and packed with 'small white packages'.[41] The privileged Oliver, who has otherwise been living a life of luxury in Sydney, thus becomes yet another child victim of the drug trade, of 'the war that would have no end'.[42] The futurity that the child embodies in *Mortido* is thus the mutually assured destruction of the contemporary drug trade.

Finally, across both *Mortido* and *The Hanging*, Betzien suggests that her male protagonists are childlike, expressed as a kind of softness. This is particularly the case with Jimmy – the closest in age to the children of the plays – who is explicitly treated as a child by both Monte[43] and Grubbe,[44] when they try to feed him via the 'aeroplane game'. (As the previous paragraph suggests, this is in itself an echo of the force-feeding of child drug mules). There is also a repeated incantation across *Mortido* from both the men and the boys of the phrase 'don't forget that I am soft', which immediately recalls this exchange in *The Hanging*:

Corrossi	You seem a bit soft to me –
Flint	Soft?
Corrossi	– more like a preschool teacher than a policeman.
Flint	I've a background in child protection.
Corrossi	They're not children.
Flint	They're not adults either.[45]

This softness of the adult men in Betzien's plays lends them a child-like quality, but also carries with them traces of the children they once were and the children they have tried to protect. The notion of protection is also central to the political efficacy of the plays, which we discuss below.

Macabre Children as Political Symbols

> In Australia, we have a long and dark history of neglecting, abusing and forgetting the most vulnerable in our communities, our children. Justice will only come when we as a society acknowledge what the dead have suffered and what the living continue to endure, when we cease repeating the mistakes of the past, when we take action to truly protect all children, not just our own.[46]
> Angela Betzien, Foreword to *The Dark Room*

Whilst it can be argued that all Betzien's plays are 'political' in their repeated focus on abused, neglected and/or marginalised children, she has aligned this focus much more actively to external national and global concerns in her more recent body work for adult audiences.

Writing of 'the political child' in her broader study on the representation of children in Gothic literature and drama, Margarita Georgieva observes that in many eighteenth- and early nineteenth-century texts, the child operates as a 'building block' of a Gothic family that stands in for symbols of 'politics, the state and Empire'.[47] It is often the role of the child, within this equation, to 'recover, restore and preserve collective memory'[48] pertaining to this imperial agenda, thereby becoming an 'heir' and 'a vehicle for political ideas, in which the British Empire, British identities, colonial conflicts and rebellions are bonded into an ideal of a sublimated child who is a future ruler'.[49] In the postcolonial Australian context in which Betzien writes, it therefore makes perfect sense to invert this representation and to view children as the symbolic vectors of the *effects* of the imperial project. Betzien's own Foreword to the published version of *The Dark Room* makes this postcolonial political agenda explicit, as she describes how she links the neglected and abused children in that play to the 1991 Royal Commission into Deaths in Custody, and the 2007 Little Children Are Sacred report by Pat Anderson and Rex Wild.[50]

The Dark Room premiered at the Perth Institute of Contemporary Arts in 2009, before a second production at Sydney's Belvoir in 2011. The play is set wholly within one hotel room in a three-star motel in the Northern Territory. No particular town is mentioned, but diegetic markers referencing nightclubs, fast-food outlets, proximity to town camps and other cultural indicators would plausibly locate this fictional town as Alice Springs, in the very centre of contemporary Australia. Betzien's Foreword sets up a reading of the play that suggests the children in it may be Aboriginal, although this is not stated as a casting requirement for one of the characters; and indeed, in Belvoir's 2011 production, it is the case worker, Anni, rather than the ward in her care, Grace, who is played by an Indigenous actor (Leah Purcell). Three interlocked narratives are played out simultaneously in the one room. Child protection worker Anni has brought a clearly disturbed teenage child, Grace, into the motel to provide temporary sanctuary from violence at home. Meanwhile a policeman, Stephen, and his pregnant wife, schoolteacher Emma, also appear in the room – it could be another room in the same hotel, but the action is played out synchronously in the same space. It is the wedding night of another policeman, Craig, a colleague of Stephen's who we learn is likely responsible for the death in custody of an Aboriginal boy, Joseph. In the third narrative strand, this dead boy appears as a ghost in the wardrobe of the motel room.

As in both *The Hanging* and *Mortido*, we are witnessing uncanny disruptions in time and space, and it is Grace who senses this supernatural disjunction when she enters the room:

> **Grace**   Someone in here.
> **Anni**   It's just you and me.
>   Two's company hey.[51]

Grace has had Anni as her case worker before, and clearly feels she has failed to protect her from domestic violence and abuse. She 'acts out', accusing Anni (groundlessly) of paedophilia and wanting to 'perve' on her in the shower,[52] hinting at a historical knowledge or awareness of sexual abuse. Grace unsettles the viewing audience as she transgresses the boundaries between carer and ward, and also of child and adult, as she tells Anni she wants to masturbate,[53] that she is menstruating,[54] that she got raped at 'the res' – the official child protection facility that Anni took her to last time[55] – and that she has a sadomasochistic sexual relationship with her trans friend, who we have to assume is the now-ghostly Joseph:

> **Grace**   There's a boy I know.
>   He's a faggot.
>   Wears dresses and that
>   make up.
>   Wants to be a girl.
>   Wants me to call him a she.
>   He stays over at my place sometimes.
>   I can make him do whatever I want.
>   I put him on the chain under the house.
>   Once I gave him dog food on toast and he ate it.
>   I made him lick me.[56]

Grace is wearing a pillowcase over her head with the eyes cut out – a dog mask – and refuses to take it off. She names her 'oppositional defiance disorder', and repeatedly transgresses Anni's personal space:

> **Grace**   What's that?
> **Anni**   Scar. Twenty-three stitches.
>
> *... Grace kisses Anni on the scar.*
> *Grace tries to kiss Anni on the lips.*
> *Anni pushes Grace away.*[57]

Grace is at the same 'threshold' age of fourteen that Betzien's girls in *The Hanging* are, but she oscillates between demonstrating adult sexual behaviours, and resorting to little-girl behaviours, such as repeating everything that Anni says to annoy her and goad her into hostility.[58] It is clear to Anni that the sexual transgressions that Grace is initiating are bluffs, and are manifestations of sexual abuse that Grace has either experienced or witnessed.

The Dark Room leaps from the uncanny to the macabre when Joseph's ghost manifests. Grace is the only one to see it. She internalises the vision, perhaps viewing it as a manifestation of her own guilt for abuses she thinks she's perpetrated, which includes confessing to having had an abortion as a result of what we assume to be rape,[59] quite possibly at the hands of the man who Grace witnessed axing her own mother to death. As Joseph's frightening appearances increase towards the play's end, the revelations of endemic community violence escalate. We learn that Joseph's assailant, Craig, has been investigated and exonerated of the boy's death in custody. Grace knocks Anni out as we learn that Joseph seduced Craig, which triggered the internalised homophobic assault that killed the boy. His ghostly avatar seeks revenge by turning into a dog and attacking Craig on the bed. We learn in the play's final moments that tonight – in the here and now – is Anni's birthday. She's coming back to the scene of the crime; Grace stabbed herself to death while Anni was unconscious at the end of the sequence we have just witnessed and had previously presumed to be the present. Both children have effectively been ghosts throughout. We are invited to read their manifestations as the macabre return of the uncanny repressed, as avenging victims of systemic (post/colonial) violence, abuse and injustice.

Pierce's study of lost children also maps this postcolonial turn, citing the Aboriginal and Torres Strait Islander children lost to their birth parents as part of the Stolen Generation:

> Where once the land indifferently took lost Australian children of European origin, now Aboriginal children were systematically taken away from their land. If these bodies of suffering and story can be

connected, then the process of reconciliation between European and Aboriginal Australians, which can be glimpsed at times in the colonial tales of lost children, might be advanced in ways that do not allow regression to an age that once we thought of as less enlightened than this.[60]

Conclusion

Betzien's political concerns turn from the postcolonial to the global in *Mortido*, where, as discussed earlier, Sydney boy Oliver, Bolivian boy Alvaro, and the Mexican boy of fable, El Gallito, become symbols of inheritance and ingestion – a literal internalising – of the international drug trade. Betzien offers Coca-Cola and cocaine as interchangeable commodities of addiction and capitalism, as grotesque symbols of consumption at its most macabre. When Oliver enters the room in the first scene, for instance, his uncle Jimmy is drinking a can of Coca-Cola, and, after being 'shot' by Jimmy in a play gun fight – foreshadowing the merging of the crime worlds connecting contemporary Sydney and Central and South America – Oliver 'takes the opportunity to take a sip from Jimmy's Coke while prodding Jimmy's body with his foot'.[61] It is an image that Betzien returns to in the play's final moments. Jimmy's Sydney and Bolivian worlds morph and merge. They play out on stage synchronously as his drug lord/suppliers from both locations watch him feed Alvaro 'several small white balls':

> *First, Jimmy dips the ball in Coca-Cola. Alvaro opens his mouth. Barbie counts.*
>
> **Barbie**   *Cuatro.*
>
> *Jimmy feeds another ball to Alvaro. He swallows.*
>
> *Cinco.*
>
> *And another.*
>
> *Seis.*[62]

The children we have interrogated as incipient, uncanny vectors of adult addiction in this chapter embody Betzien's broadening political themes, aligning them with the children in *The Dark Room*, who the author suggests we have a societal duty of care to protect from neglect and abuse.

The macabre children in *Mortido* are not the avenging ghosts of *The Dark Room*; they are vessels and carriers – both figurative and literal consumers – of global capitalism at its most evil. Betzien's 'Writer's Note' for the play offers an account for the reasons she has turned to the crime genre in the suite of work we have discussed here:

> Playwright Simon Stephens said, 'I have this intuitive and completely unresearched notion that crime fiction is the narrative form that has defined the last ten years, in the way that the western defined the '50s. I wonder if we are operating in a culture with a sense that something awful has been done, and we want to find who did it?' What if that 'something awful' is global capitalism? What if it's the cruel and destructive pursuit of profit over people?[63]

It is a compelling theorem, and one that Betzien continues to connect spiritually, psychologically and politically with the macabre children that haunt her body of work.

Notes

1. E. Blake, 'Belvoir braces for controversy over child actors in Colin Friels' drug drama *Mortido*', *Sydney Morning Herald*, 11 November 2015.
2. Blake, 'Belvoir braces for controversy'.
3. Nicholas Ridout, *Stage Fright, Animals, and Other Theatrical Problems* (Cambridge: Cambridge University Press, 2006), p. 29.
4. K. Jones, 'Little Monsters: Gothic Children and Contemporary Theatrical Performance', in K. Jones, B. Poore and R. Dean (eds), *Contemporary Gothic Drama: Attraction, Consummation and Consumption on the Modern British Stage* (London: Palgrave Macmillan, 2018), p. 106.
5. S. Goodes, 'Introduction', in Angela Betzien, *The Hanging* (Sydney: Currency Press, 2016), p. 6.
6. The Lindy Chamberlain case will be familiar to international readers (if only through the film *A Cry in the Dark* or the many pop-culture references to 'a dingo ate my baby'); the second reference is to toddler William Tyrell, who disappeared from his grandmother's garden in September 2014, while dressed in a Spider-Man costume.
7. Peter Pierce, *The Country of Lost Children: An Australian Anxiety* (Cambridge: Cambridge University Press, 1999), p. xi.

8. Pierce, *The Country of Lost Children*, p. 113.
9. H. Strube, 'White Crocodile, Black Skirt: Theatre for Young People and Cultural Memory', *Australasian Drama Studies*, 47 (October 2005).
10. Jones, 'Little Monsters', p. 104.
11. Jennifer Balanzategui, *The Uncanny Child in Transnational Cinema: Ghosts of Futurity at the Turn of the Twenty-First Century* (Amsterdam: Amsterdam University Press, 2018), p. 12.
12. Jones, 'Little Monsters', p. 103.
13. Balanzategui, *The Uncanny Child*, p. 17.
14. Jones, 'Little Monsters', p. 103.
15. K. Jones, B. Poore and R. Dean, 'Introduction', in *Contemporary Gothic Drama*, p. 3.
16. Pierce, *The Country of Lost Children*, p. xiv.
17. Betzien, *The Hanging*, p. 21.
18. Goodes, 'Introduction', p. 6.
19. Betzien, *The Hanging*, p. 16.
20. Betzien, *The Hanging*, p. 36.
21. Betzien, *The Hanging*, p. 55.
22. Betzien, *The Hanging*, p. 26.
23. Betzien, *The Hanging*, p. 12.
24. Joan Lindsay, *Picnic at Hanging Rock* (Melbourne: F. W. Cheshire, 1967).
25. Betzien, *The Hanging*, p. 31.
26. Betzien, *The Hanging*, p. 42.
27. Betzien, *The Hanging*, p. 23.
28. Goodes, 'Introduction', p. 7.
29. Betzien, *The Hanging*, p. 44.
30. Betzien, *The Hanging*, p. 59.
31. Betzien, *The Hanging*, p. 59.
32. Angela Betzien, *Mortido* (Sydney: Currency Press, 2015), p. 29.
33. Betzien, *Mortido*, p. 1.
34. Betzien, *Mortido*, p. 3–4.
35. Betzien, *Mortido*, p. 77–8.
36. Betzien, *Mortido*, p. 35.
37. Betzien, *Mortido*, p. 54.
38. Betzien, *Mortido*, p. 59.
39. Balanzategui, *The Uncanny Child*, p. 17.
40. Betzien, *Mortido*, p. 82.
41. Betzien, *Mortido*, p. 2.
42. Betzien, *Mortido*, p. 4.

43. Betzien, *Mortido*, p. 40.
44. Betzien, *Mortido*, p. 64.
45. Betzien, *The Hanging*, p. 27.
46. Angela Betzien, *The Dark Room* (Brisbane: Playlab, 2009), p. 5.
47. M. Georgieva, 'The Political Child', in *The Gothic Child* (London: Palgrave Macmillan, 2013), p. 121.
48. Georgieva, 'The Political Child', p. 122.
49. Georgieva, 'The Political Child', p. 123.
50. These were federal Australian government investigations into the systemic maltreatment of Aboriginal and Torres Strait Islander people in state care, the latter focusing specifically on the sexual, physical and psychological abuse of children in the Northern Territory.
51. Betzien, *The Dark Room*, p. 15.
52. Betzien, *The Dark Room*, p. 16.
53. Betzien, *The Dark Room*, p. 17.
54. Betzien, *The Dark Room*, p. 17.
55. Betzien, *The Dark Room*, p. 21.
56. Betzien, *The Dark Room*, p. 26.
57. Betzien, *The Dark Room*, p. 29.
58. Betzien, *The Dark Room*, p. 47.
59. Betzien, *The Dark Room*, p. 63.
60. Pierce, *The Country of Lost Children*, p. xiv.
61. Betzien, *Mortido*, p. 5.
62. Betzien, *Mortido*, p. 86.
63. Stephens quoted in Betzien, 'Writer's Note', in *Mortido*, n.p.

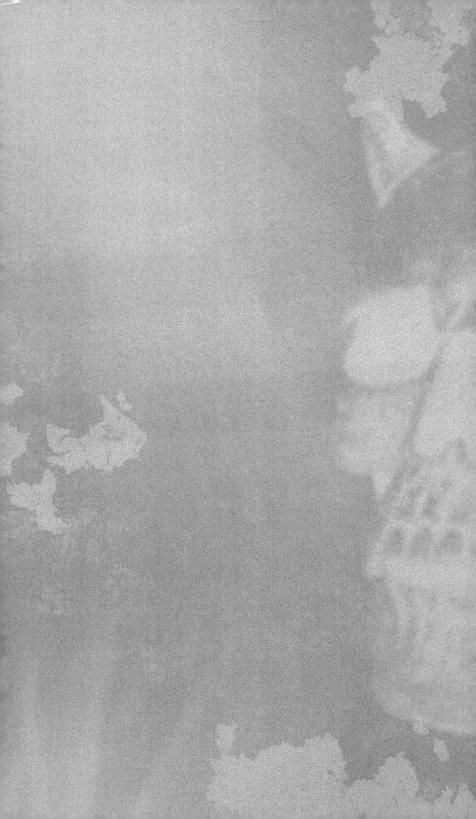

7

Martin McDonagh's *Hangmen*
Justice and Guilt in Public and Private Acts of Hanging

Michelle C. Paull

Hangmen (2015) was Martin McDonagh's first play in a decade, and the playwright's decision to return to the stage for this foray into the macabre is intriguing. As Joan Dean notes, 'In 2006 McDonagh revealed that he drafted all of his plays in the 1990s and suggested he was finished with theatre'.[1] McDonagh's own account of writing *Hangmen* fits with this timeline; he began the play in 2001 and took fourteen years to complete the script.[2] Yet this absence from the stage is not simply because McDonagh felt he had already written all his stage work, but also because he thought theatre 'the worst of all art forms'.[3] Theatre presented limitations for McDonagh and he was resigned to 'the fact that theatre is never going to be edgy in the way I want it to be'.[4] Theatre was not capable of creating the *frisson* that McDonagh wanted for an audience, so he turned to film, playing out themes of justice and retribution via *In Burges* (2008), *Seven Psychopaths* (2012) and *Three Billboards in Ebbing, Missouri* (2018).

Hangmen was one of the few plays McDonagh has set outside of his usual chosen environment of the west of Ireland, and this decision might be in part to distance himself from his reputation as a playwright who deconstructs pastoral myths of the rural west. Instead, *Hangmen* is the play that fulfils Ondřej Pilný's desire for McDonagh 'to prove his worth on non-Irish themes',[5] and follows the tradition of McDonagh's earlier plays including *The Pillowman* and even *A Behanding in Spokane*, which avoid a detailed focus on specificity of location to concentrate instead on a pan-national theme of injustice. As Patrick Lonergan notes 'by moving beyond the vexed and vexing questions of national identity, McDonagh allows other features of his work to emerge more clearly: to show us how he is using dramatic form and how his attitude to authorial intention has developed'.[6]

It is as if McDonagh is drawn back to the theatre because only the macabre in live theatre can provide the visceral shock and heart-in-mouth moments that he requires to engage an audience in an embodied recognition of the play's topics of capital punishment and injustice, since the macabre provides theatrical licence to convey the reality of execution via a staged death in real time. *Hangmen* creates the opportunity to examine 'capital punishment and miscarriages of justice'[7] in an unusual and disturbing way through the 'shocking juxtaposition of gruesome violence with an utterly blasé attitude towards the same'.[8] The theatre of the macabre prohibits audiences from escaping the horror of the subject; there is no distance, as in cinema, and no media off-switch. Theatre's corporeality, the live closeness of the characters in the same space and time, who you could reach out and touch if you were close enough, is the most frightening and shocking medium in which to represent a deeper exploration of social and personal culpability when faced with injustice. Through the play's use of the macabre motif of repeated hanging, the audience will be drawn into a kind of live complicity in the murder of two innocent characters. This evocation of communal involvement in dubious decision-making, over an issue as serious as a man's life, allows the play to question the specific process of just decision-making in the courts and much wider concepts of social and political injustices that frame these legal decisions.

Revisiting capital punishment in *Hangmen* in an English context might seem a choice that is more than fifty years too late for a UK audience, since hanging ended for all crime in England in 1969, six years after Scotland, eleven years behind Wales, and four years before Northern Ireland. There are still more than forty countries where capital punishment continues, and the United Kingdom seems to resurrect the subject whenever there is a call to bring back hanging for 'heinous' crimes such as terrorism, the murder of children or significant sexual offences. The visceral representation of two hangings in McDonagh's play reminds us that we have not seen a public hanging in England for more than 150 years. When public hangings were abolished in 1868, Samuel Johnson argued against the decision, commenting in a letter to Sir Walter Scott, 'Executions are intended to draw spectators. If they do not draw spectators, they don't answer their purpose'.[9] The 'purpose' for Johnson was one of warning, and the tone and style of *Hangmen* suggests that McDonagh shares this anxiety, fearing that contemporary audiences are now too detached from the sense of the physicality of death and are in danger of becoming inured to its horror and finality. It is as if McDonagh wants to revive that awareness of the actuality of death through the use of the macabre in *Hangmen*. By drawing on the macabre, a live 'hanging' in a theatre makes us psychologically re-engage with this moment of *schadenfreude* on a completely different emotional level.

As late as 1864 'you could catch the underground to see a hanging' with crowds of 100,000 people arriving for the most notorious cases at London's Tyburn gallows.[10] But contemporary awareness of the live, physical reality of capital punishment is no longer part of our culture. *Hangmen* works to reconnect us with the contradictory power and repulsion of the spectacle of death that Freud highlighted in 'The Uncanny'. As an audience to a public spectacle, or to a theatrical event, we are attracted and repulsed by that which we regard as disturbing, unknown or unfamiliar (the '*unheimlich*',[11] as Freud had it), which draws us towards the event, despite its strangeness. As Freud suggests, 'the "uncanny" is that class of the terrifying which leads back to something long known to us, once very familiar';[12] similarly, we are drawn in by our experience of watching the play to explore our eerie fascination with what we fear. In McDonagh's work, the audience can find themselves drawn in by what Philip Brophy calls 'Horrality', a blend of fear and humour, which Eamonn Jordan shows has an affinity with McDonagh's style, since it provides a kind of liminal emotional space for the audience, located between enjoyment and disgust. Brophy's definition of this tension between terror and bliss is more pithy than Freud's, but as Jordan's quotation from Brophy notes, he demonstrates the juxtaposition unequivocally: 'The pleasure of the text is in fact getting the shit scared out of you – and loving it: an exchange mediated by adrenaline.'[13] Brophy's sense of the joyful fear that the audience could feel through 'Horrality' is clearly in synch with the effect of the theatrical style of *Hangmen*, which works to re-familiarise the viewer with emotions and critical awareness that the play posits as dangerous to forget.

José Lanters links McDonagh's attempts to refresh the experience of these contradictory feelings with the diversity of approaches to emotional experience offered to us by postmodern culture. As Lanters points out 'postmodern culture is defined by images',[14] and the use of the macabre image of the hanged man creates a strong psychic draw for a postmodern audience, connecting them both with historical hangings and with the contemporary continuation of hanging as a means of capital punishment internationally. Eamonn Jordan points out that both McDonagh's postmodernity and his links to the theatre of the Grand Guignol are part of the strange allure of the violent and the fantastical in his work. McDonagh's plays use:

> the violent excesses of an anarchic postmodern and popular cultural susceptibilities, where distinctions between fantasy and reality, truth and illusion, pleasure and pain and fear and exhilaration do not easily hold.[15]

By drawing on such contradictions, especially the interrelated nature of pleasure, pain and fear, McDonagh blends the unique physical and psychological closeness built between the actor and the live theatre audience so that *Hangmen* creates a visceral experience of an intellectual contradiction for the audience. *Hangmen* is an attempt to theatricalise the paradox at the core of capital punishment. As Patrick Lonergan says, 'at the heart of our positive attitudes to the death penalty lies a fundamental incoherence: killing someone, we're told, is so severe a crime against our society that the only way to avenge it is . . . by killing someone'.[16] The use of the macabre in *Hangmen* provides a means for us to experience the faulty logic suggested by Lonergan's premise. Two men 'die' in front of us during the play, one at the beginning and another at the end, and that Beckettian circularity is unnerving, suggesting no resolution or change, only the disturbing continuation of muddied injustice.

McDonagh's theatrical style encourages his audience to bond with his characters, recognise their flaws and laugh at their silliness. But then we are required to experience what removing that connection means, and the play gives the audience this sense of finality through the characters' 'death' in real time. We do not know whether the first victim of hanging, James Hennessy, is guilty or not, but we see 'reasonable doubt' raised by the prisoner's protestations of his own innocence. But the relevance of his guilt or innocence is also somehow beside the point, because the play is raising much larger questions about the validity of capital punishment.

Hangmen is asking two separate questions: first, whether killing another human being can ever be justified – can we as a society condone the killing of one of our number under *any* circumstances? Second, is there ever a crime where there is not 'reasonable doubt' about some aspect of the evidence or the accused's role in the event? Hennessy points out specific flaws in the case against him: 'I've never even *been* to Norfolk',[17] denying even his geographical presence in the county where the crime was committed. Using Eamonn Jordan's phrase, this example demonstrates McDonagh's theme of the 'susceptibility of justice'.[18] In *Hangmen*, justice is seen to be vulnerable to failure whether as a result of court action, as in Hennessy's case, or via personal decisions in a pub, as in Mooney's case in Act 2. As Jordan points out, in McDonagh's work:

> the concept of justice is clearly not equated with fairness, rights, duties or equality, instead it is deviant and devious, primitive, dangerous, allusive, disavowed, in abeyance. This is not to undermine the credibility of justice, but to galvanise its significance.

Hangmen presents this very postmodern plurality contained in the concept of justice and draws attention to the necessity of making sure the right decision is made, rather than to arrive at a result that is convenient or timely for all involved. *Hangmen*'s presentation of a shared experience of the moment of death reminds us in stark terms that capital punishment produces a result that cannot be reversed. A life is lost, which is replicated in live theatre by the removal of the actor as character from the stage in front of us, reminding us what capital punishment means, even in an age when we might no longer feel that we need to be reminded. If it is true that 'All that justice needs is to be consequence-aware',[20] then there is no consequence more finite than the ersatz experience of death itself in McDonagh's play.

The First Hanging

McDonagh sets *Hangmen* in 1963, two years before hanging was suspended as the sentence for murder in England, although six years before it was finally abolished in 1969. As the play opens, the first hanging is about to take place. The prisoner, James Hennessy, has his head facing to the front on the table centre stage, with two guards either side of him, and he looks – as the stage directions note – '*terrified*'.[21] Harry Wade, McDonagh's fictional

British hangman, enters the death cell with his assistant Syd Armfield, and prompts Hennessy's opening comment 'Oh, you punctual bastards!',[22] setting the tone for the mordant, ironic humour throughout the play, and allowing the audience to balance the horror alongside humour to help them to cope with the tension of this theatrical experience. The sense of the macabre immediately underpins the scene as the audience is shown the 'duties' involved in the process of hanging a prisoner, and we have to face this process in the theatre, which had previously been hidden from public view in real life. The dialogue's arch wit, with Harry's platitudes carefully balancing Hennessy's sharp retorts, keep the audience's focus on the grim process of the execution. The audience must watch the macabre details of the prisoner's physical treatment as he resists his own execution. When Harry instructs Syd to 'get the strap', Hennessy asks the question the audience might also be wondering: 'What's the strap for?' The horror of what happens to a man facing death cannot be evaded and the audience helplessly witnesses this baroque throwback to a different time. Hennessy is presented literally clinging on to his life; in a perverse inversion of foetal safety, the stage directions note that he 'grabs on to his metal bedstead for dear life, curled up on the floor', while throughout the rest of the scene 'the men try to prise him off'. This hanging scene is relentless in its disturbing horror. A man fights with all his might to stay alive, and while this is inflected with McDonagh's sardonic humour, the reality of Hennessy's impending demise is inescapable. The stage directions note that Harry and Syd 'peel some fingers off the bedstead'. Syd's laconic comment to assure Hennessy that cooperation is the best policy ironically reminds his prisoner of the brutal fact: 'If you'd just tried to relax you could've been dead by now'. Harry 'thwacks Hennessy across the head. Groggy but still conscious, he [Hennessy] slumps and releases his grip on the bed', we realise that we are being made 'consequence-aware', we are seeing the graphic practicalities of capital punishment that we have been shielded from in the past.

Yet this awareness also suggests the play's critique of the audience, since the morality of our decision to see a play called *Hangmen* underlines our personal voyeurism. It is as if McDonagh is in dialogue with his audience, asking them to reflect upon their own desire to see graphic and brutal events. For example, for one terrifying moment it looks as if we are back in those days of public hangings and Hennessy will be hanged on stage in front of us when 'a noose appears on stage, downstage of the cell'. McDonagh is threatening to enact a graphic Grand Guignol-style death; and yet, the play seems to ask its audience, is that not why you are here? The name of the play is

Hangmen; have you not come to see a man be hanged? We are caught in the Freudian bind; there is something atavistic in our desire to see a hanging take place, even though we know what we will witness may appal us. McDonagh takes the audience through every step of the hanging as we watch Hennessy walked to the trap door, still protesting his innocence, and see Harry put the hood and noose over Hennessy's head while Syd straps up his legs. While Hennessy pleads with them to stop, the trap door opens with 'the rope pulling taut, breaking his neck, hanging him there out of sight'. The 'consequence' of going to see a McDonagh play about hangmen is that you see the men at work; McDonagh both engages with an audience's desire to see and their recognition of this desire's repulsive nature. The Wyndham's Theatre production of *Hangmen* in London ended this scene not with blackout as the script designates, but by lifting the cell set upwards and allowing the audience's gaze to be directed 'downwards' towards the emerging set for the basement of the cell. We knew that Hennessy's body should be in that space below and it was if we were about to see his hanging corpse on display for us, emphasising McDonagh's implicit query in the play: isn't this also what you wanted to see?

Hennessy has died and so the actor playing him must leave the stage, yet the actor's absence conversely reminds the audience of the finality of his character's fate. The actor will be back at the end of the show to take his bow, but within the play his execution has no such resurrection. Hanging might be all in a day's work for Harry and Syd, but McDonagh's dialogue prevents the audience from evading their communal responsibility. Harry's recourse to the responsibility of the state for his actions sounds like cant; his sanctimonious tone suggests his desire to avoid personal responsibility for his own forthcoming actions as the public hangman, and potentially speaks to our own attempts of a similar evasion of responsibility as an audience 'It's the courts that's hanging ya not us'. The state decrees the punishment, but society supports the underpinning grand narrative of this punishment to fit the crime. We are all culpable.

The Second Hanging: 'Private' Justice

McDonagh's critique of our morbid curiosities and obsession with horror is deepened through the play's second hanging. The subsequent scenes take place on the second anniversary of Hennessy's death in 1965, when the United Kingdom had stopped hanging accused murderers (but before such punishments were finally abolished in 1969). Harry is now running a pub in Oldham, with his wife Alice and teenage daughter Shirley. Syd Armfield arrives to warn Harry that a man, matching his customer Mooney's description, has contacted him, offering to sell him photos of the girl who was killed in Norfolk, the crime Hennessy was hanged for in the play's opening scene. But Syd is secretly working with Mooney to make Harry feel guilty over Hennessy's death. After an argument, Shirley leaves the pub and does not return. When Syd asks Mooney privately if he knows anything about the disappearance of Shirley, Mooney says he has her locked up in a garage. Eventually, Mooney tries to dispel his connection with Shirley's disappearance, but his unnerving manner persists, and his guilt is presumed by all in the pub. The representation of Mooney's private hanging questions what constitutes valid evidence and points out that projecting guilt often assuages communal anxiety rather than secures an accurate conviction. Through Mooney, the play demonstrates a desperation to convict 'someone' as hysteria builds. As Marianka Swain says, 'it becomes clear that truth is less important than how [Mooney's] perceived, and what kind of response that warrants'.[23] Shirley is missing, someone must be responsible, and Mooney, the outsider from London, looks like the nearest available candidate. *Hangmen* works to remind us of the danger of justice simply being 'seen to be done',[24] rather than reflecting an actual incidence of guilt. In this second execution, McDonagh subtly echoes the same dubious justice meted out to Hennessy when Harry strikes Mooney on the back of the head 'with the same billyclub he had used on Hennessy'. This Gothic re-enactment of the beginning of Hennessy's hanging layers the horror and revulsion of both deaths in the play; the vile circularity lures the audience into the inescapable repetition as baroque as it is absurd.

But the play complicates this narrative, because criminal injustice is not presented simply as a singular problem about individual guilt or innocence, but instead is part of a global overarching network of identifiable injustices:

> Criminal justice speaks to the larger injustices, associated with imperialism, class, gender and race inequalities, discriminations and subjugations. Encounters with and occurrences within the criminal justice system are indicative of widespread inequalities. The rights, obligations and practices around justice we associate with participative democracies are fundamentally breached on an ongoing basis in McDonagh's works.[25]

Hangmen raises these narratives of injustice as part of a reflection upon the conceptual injustices that underpin our national and international political cultures. Injustice is not restricted to the court; it is personal at the level of gender, class and race, inscribing all the discrimination, objectification, sexism, exclusion and bias that underpins culture and politics internationally. McDonagh's macabre style in *Hangmen* keeps the audience focused on the specifics of the 'personal' hanging of each character, but the surrounding issues of other injustices, cultural inequalities and political inadequacies also resonate as part of this examination of individual cases, suggesting a bleak dystopian anxiety about the varieties of injustice underpinning politics and society. The play suggests that once we accept that justice is unstable, the edifice on which that legal system is built is also destabilised. As Jordan points out, it is not that McDonagh is saying anything very different about the nature of injustice to many other writers, but he presents the case differently since he 'refuse[s] to make the case through rationality, impartiality and debate'.[26] Instead, the macabre is one of McDonagh's key means in *Hangmen* of foregrounding injustice.

The audience is not spared the gory practicalities of Mooney's death – any more than we were Hennessy's – as the macabre continues even into the second act. Harry sets about the logistics of hanging Mooney is his pub. He creates a makeshift noose from barrel rope and 'twists the noose tight around Mooney's neck, choking him'. Mooney's arms are strapped behind his back and, as with the hanging of Hennessy, there is the sense of a situation rapidly running out of control. As Mooney is hanging, the local police inspector remonstrates with Harry, who is dismissive of his misgivings: 'So it's alright to do this down the cop shop but int alright down the pub, is that right?' This central question about the nature of justice is posed for the audience in the middle of this grisly scene: who has the right to decide to hang a man, on what grounds, and with what evidence? The play points to the distinctions of context in justice here, and Harry's comments remind the audience to consider who makes the decisions of guilt and innocence in the legal system. While Hennessy's death shows us the flaws in the official legal system, the kangaroo court established for Mooney is no more successful at administering justice. In this way the play suggests that authentic justice is not simply about replacing one system of judgment with another, but about completely reconfiguring the concept of what we regard as just and fair. 'Widespread inequalities' must be addressed, rather than simply re-evaluating the specifics of the court and criminal justice system.

McDonagh's final dose of the macabre is administered as we partially witness Mooney's onstage death. Harry's acquaintance, the 'real' historical public hangman, Albert Pierrepoint, calls to see Harry at the pub and the partially hanging Mooney has to be hidden from him behind a curtain. A rag is put in Mooney's mouth to muffle him as he is left on tiptoes, 'so that only the chair he is standing on can be seen from the entrance side of the stage' as the stage directions dictate. Throughout the scene, the chair, just visible beneath the curtain, functions to represents Mooney himself, who remains out of sight. As Pierrepoint argues with Harry, he moves Mooney's chair completely out from under him. The audience knows that Mooney is now silently strangling to death, and it is a moment of pure macabre horror, which no one on stage does anything about. There is a bleak irony that Pierrepoint, the legitimate public hangman, has illegitimately hanged Mooney. McDonagh mercifully spares the audience the actual sight of Mooney's body swinging from the rope. When Pierrepoint leaves, Mooney is taken down behind the curtain and brought out to lie dead on the pub floor. At the same moment Harry's missing daughter Shirley returns safely to the pub and Harry's customer Arthur says to him, 'It would have been awful if she was dead',[27] a sentiment denied to Mooney.

Mark Lawson, reviewing *Hangmen* for the New Statesman suggests 'the debate about capital punishment is confined to five lines at the end of the play, but it is devastating when it comes'.[28] These lines are the final conversation between Syd and Harry, conducted over Mooney's corpse, noting their arbitrary conclusions of whether or not Hennessy and Mooney deserved their punishment. McDonagh's dialogue carefully delineates the casual and callous nature of their conversational tone as Harry philosophically concludes, 'I suppose that's just the way it goes, int it? With justice (*Pause*.)'.[29] This pause functions to highlight the throwaway quality of Harry's remark, allowing a moment of reflection on this chilling 'you win some, you lose some' logic. The audience has watched two men be killed; one of them, Mooney, had not been found guilty of murder, yet Harry appears to feel no guilt, sorrow or remorse for his death. Instead, the hangman acknowledges his taste for his former job: 'I'll miss it. (*Pause*.). I will. (*Pause*.). I'll miss it.'[30] This sense of becoming accustomed to injustice sounds a note of warning. The cyclical repetition of death has entrapped Harry because he has become used to it; the play suggests there is a danger that we, too, have grown accustomed to injustice and no longer feel guilt from it, whether in court, culture or politics.

The use of the macabre in *Hangmen* stimulates debate about the nature of a just and fair society. The repeated use of hanging as a motif allows both individual concepts of justice to be explored, while also drawing attention to other social, political and cultural injustices that frame our legal decisions. As Steven Connor notes, 'By setting different sorts of repetition in play against each other, art . . . can highlight the principle of pure difference'.[31] Hennessy and Mooney repeat the figure of the hanged man because each case, and each criminal, is different and distinct. Shirley's death would have been 'terrible', Hennessy's death was agreed by the court, while Mooney's death was, well, just one of those things. The play's use of the macabre works to forestall just such a dispassionate or detached response; when you have watched a human being, whom you believe to be innocent, die in front of you, twice, you are drawn to reflect upon religious, philosophical and societal concepts of justice and retribution that underpin such decisions. As Harry says, when the prison doctor confirms that Hennessy is 'quite dead' after the hanging: 'Course he's quite dead. What else would he be?'[32] McDonagh's use of the macabre allows the audience to experience that very finality in its most graphic, disturbing form.

Notes

1. J. Dean, 'Review of *The Theatre of Martin McDonagh: A World of Savage Stories* by Eamonn Jordan and Lilian Chambers', *New Theatre Quarterly*, 23/3 (2007), 287.
2. S. O'Hagan, 'Martin McDonagh Interview: 'Theatre is never going to be edgy the way I want it to be'', *Guardian*, 13 September 2015, www.theguardian.com/culture/2015/sep/11/martin-mcdonagh-theatre-never-going-to-be-edgy-hangmen-interview.
3. O'Hagan, 'Martin McDonagh Interview', online.
4. O'Hagan, 'Martin McDonagh Interview', online.
5. O. Pilný, 'Martin McDonagh: Parody? Satire? Complacency?', *Irish Studies Review*, 12/2 (2004), 239.
6. Patrick Lonergan, *The Theatre and Films of Martin McDonagh* (London: Bloomsbury Methuen Drama, 2013), p. 100.
7. O'Hagan, 'Martin McDonagh Interview', online.
8. K. Smith, 'Daggers Drawn', *The New Criterion*, 36/7 (2018), 37.
9. A. I. Borowitz, 'Under Sentence of Death', *American Bar Association Journal*, 64/8 (1978), 1261, www.jstor.org/stable/20744747.

10. M. Brown, 'When you could catch the underground to see a hanging', *The Londonist*, 6 September 2018, *https://londonist.com/london/underground toapublichanging*.
11. S. Freud, 'The Uncanny' (1919), *https://web.mit.edu/allanmc/www/freud1.pdf*, p. 2.
12. Freud, 'The Uncanny', p. 2.
13. E. Jordan, 'A Grand-Guignol legacy: Martin McDonagh's *A Behanding in Spokane*', *Irish Studies Review*, 20/4 (2012), 449.
14. J. Lanters, 'Like Tottenham': Martin McDonagh's postmodern morality tales', in Lonergan, *The Theatre and Films of Martin McDonagh*, p. 165.
15. Jordan, 'A Grand Guignol Legacy', p. 449.
16. P. Lonergan, *Hangmen* programme, London, Wyndhams Theatre, March 2016, 19.
17. Martin McDonagh, *Hangmen* (London: Faber and Faber, 2015), p. 12.
18. Jordan, *Justice in the Plays and Films of Martin McDonagh*, p. 135.
19. Jordan, *Justice in the Plays and Films of Martin McDonagh*, p. 135.
20. Jordan, *Justice in the Plays and Films of Martin McDonagh*, p. 135.
21. McDonagh, *Hangmen*, p. 11.
22. All notes on the first hanging are from pages 11–16 of McDonagh, *Hangmen*.
23. M. Swain, 'Tar-black gallows humour galore in Martin McDonagh's triumphant return', *Arts Desk.com*, 8 December 2015, *https://theartsdesk.com/theatre/hangmen-wyndhams-theatre*.
24. Jordan, *Justice in the Plays and Films of Martin McDonagh*, p. 135.
25. Jordan, *Justice in the Plays and Films of Martin McDonagh*, p. 137.
26. Jordan, *Justice in the Plays and Films of Martin McDonagh*, p. 136.
27. McDonagh, *Hangmen*, pp. 104–5.
28. M. Lawson, 'Killing Jokes', Review of *Hangmen*, *New Statesman*, 25 September–1 October 2015, p. 85.
29. McDonagh, *Hangmen*, p. 107.
30. McDonagh, *Hangmen*, p. 107.
31. Steven Connor, *Samuel Beckett: Repetition, Theory and Text* (Oxford: Oxford University Press, 1988), p. 33.
32. McDonagh, *Hangmen*, p. 16.

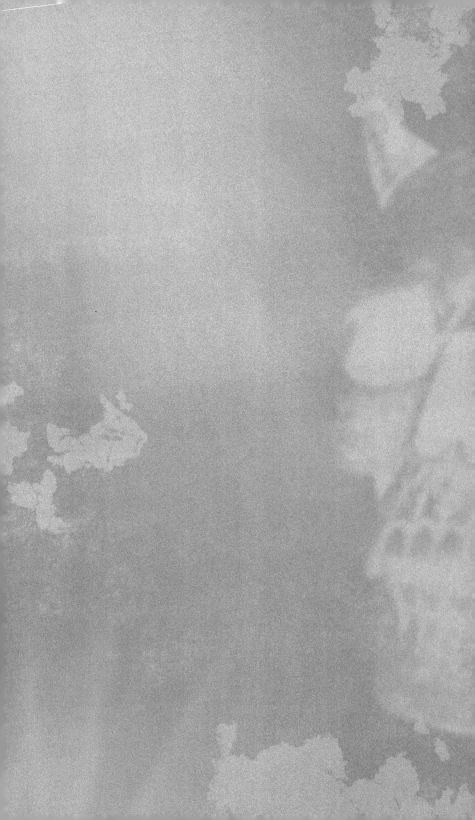

8

Fear of Death and Lyrical Flight

Mortality Salience Mediation in *Fun Home*

Christopher J. Staley

THE MUSICAL *FUN HOME* comprises an autobiographical and meta-theatrical narrative based on Alison Bechdel's graphic memoir *Fun Home: A Family Tragicomic*.[1] Bechdel garnered critical acclaim for the memoir's content and form, such as Best Book of the Year in more than ten major periodicals, along with a finalist position for the National Book Critics Circle Award. The stage production won the 2015 Tony Awards for Best Musical, Best Score (Jeanine Tesori and Lisa Kron), Best Book, as well as a clutch of nominations including a finalist position for the Pulitzer Prize for Drama. Now licensing across the United States within regional circuits, many later versions have operated in a manner generally consistent with the Broadway run (about which my perspective is written).[2] Clearly there is something compelling and enduring about this material despite its highly idiosyncratic origins.[3]

For those unfamiliar with the story, Bechdel recounts both her coming-of-age and coming-out stories, which are themselves interwoven with her father's demons around his own homosexuality. The character of 'Alison' appears in child, adolescent and adult forms, through which she accretes layers of vicarious objective and subjective witnessing iteratively and intermedially (i.e., from 'real life' to graphic memoir to musical book to film script). Pervasive reminders of death are explicitly outlined from the exposition: Alison's father dies by a grisly suicide and, as the title suggests, the family lives in a funeral home. Set mostly in the 'fun home', the play trades thematically in mortality. In triggering this existential awareness, it then surveys far-reaching themes including generational memory and nostalgia, forgiveness, parent-child dynamics, creative responses to trauma, sexuality and love, and the search for meaning and authenticity. As Bechdel cites Wallace Stevens's *Sunday Morning*, we learn that this dynamic is not necessarily causative, but can be progenitive: 'Death is the Mother of Beauty'.[4] How, in the face of such trauma, was Bechdel able to craft such a funny, heroic and beautiful ('No. I mean . . ., handsome') vehicle for self-sublimation?[5]

The current chapter explores this type of resiliency towards the macabre as a critical site of exploration. One aspect of Bechdel's creative response to trauma is metaphorised as flight imagery, or what I have 'captioned' herein as lyrical flight. Such *lyrical flight* threads throughout the play, and we know from the graphic memoir that this autobiographic metaphor of life-as-flying stems in part from Kate Millett's 1974 'heroic' memoir of the same name.[6] How does Alison 'fly away' to gain such perspectives while keeping her feet on the ground? How might we as audiences do the same? Research from terror management theory gives credence to the notion that the death content and flight imagery prevalent in *Fun Home* can induce the overall material to resonate and interplay with audiences more deeply – and the production to thus execute its artistic aims more effectively – than if death reminders were absent.[7] Such an implication not only informs dramaturgy, but also exposes the experimental stage ethics of this real-world material currently reaching a wide audience. The following introduces some central tenets of terror management theory, especially drawing on studies dealing with performance and narrative-based depictions of death, flight, humour, creativity and prosociality. In doing so, I argue that this research provokes us to treat this story with the renewed humility and seriousness, as well as the levity it requires. The below 'captioned' headings are signposts for an introduction, application and conclusion, evoking Bechdel's own use of the comic frame on the page and on the stage.[8]

Caption: Laughing in the Face of Death: Mortality Salience
On and Off the Page

Largely inspired by Ernest Becker's *The Denial of Death*, terror management theory is a theoretical framework of existential and motivational psychology.[9] More than 1,000 studies show that reminders of death elicit unique psychological effects across broad spectra of behaviours and belief systems including ingroup/outgroup dynamics and biases, self-esteem striving, or perceptions of sex, bodily activities, creativity, health, the appeal of fame, and more.[10] In a nutshell, the theory holds that, like all animals, human motivation stems from the base drive for self-preservation; however, unlike other animals, the uniquely human capacities for self-awareness and forethought (i.e., symbolisation) engender the unavoidable realisation that death is inevitable. The weight of such an understanding is more profound than the human cognitive apparatus can grip, and it therefore carries the potential for crippling existential anxiety: terror. As symbolic beings, people employ myriad pre-emptive and reactive strategies to keep existential terror at bay. These terror management strategies are bifurcated into a dual-process model of proximal and distal defences: proximal defences are literal, such as rationalisation or suppression of such thoughts out of consciousness (not me, not here, not now); while distal defences are more symbolic in nature, structuring the world and our role therein with purpose and order using cultural worldviews that provide the illusion of meaning and immortality (e.g., religion, family, nationality, among others). They act as cognitive 'buffers' against existential anxiety. Such defences form societal standards, and the subscription and achievement of these standards results in a type of 'psychosocial congruence', which is the terror management operational definition of self-esteem. The literature largely substantiates the mortality salience hypothesis, which holds that if worldview defences and self-esteem serve to buffer against existential anxiety, then people will rely on and defend these mechanisms especially after their mortality is made salient.[11]

What does this have to do with *Fun Home*? If you are in on the joke, then the words 'fun home' equate to death. As mentioned, death reminders – such as the titular setting of a funeral home and foregrounded suicide – immediately prime readers and audiences. Importantly, while terror management theory researchers have demonstrated controlled inductions of mortality salience in the laboratory, like supraliminal and subliminal priming of words such as *death*, *coffin* or *dead*, they have also shown that mortality salience effects are obtainable in more natural scenarios as well as performance/narrative media.[12] The most relevant are several studies that have used *proximity to a funeral home* as the induction variable. In one study, Pyszczynski et al. observed real-world effects by using nearness of a funeral home to induce mortality salience: German participants who were interviewed directly in front of a funeral home estimated that a higher percentage of other Germans would share their opinions on immigration, relative to control groups who were interviewed a short distance away.[13] A re-instantiation was done in Colorado Springs in the United States: in this case, interviewees were asked for their opinions on teaching Christian values in publicly administered schools. Again, participants interviewed in front of a funeral home – even those holding minority opinions – still enhanced their estimates on the amount of people they thought would agree. Other studies used the same paradigm and found mortality salience participants (compared to controls) showed enhanced favourability towards charities supporting their culture; similarly, death-related scenes (e.g., graveyards) can enhance worldview defence via justice sensitivity in contrast to less reactivity when encountering environmental images of neutral stimuli.[14] Put another way, real-life scenarios that revolve around death, such as walking through a cemetery as opposed to a community garden, might elicit greater potential for people to seek out justice-affirming behaviours and other defence strategies when those options are available in their environments.

These studies lend plausibility to the idea that mortality salience may be induced in the experience of *Fun Home* from the sheer fact that it takes place in the/a 'fun home'. Moreover, this modality of performance as a resonant experimental track is supported by a range of other studies that induced mortality salience effects within theatrical and fictional paradigms. For example, in one 2012 study, individuals primed with death ideation preferred television programmes with law and justice themes (e.g., *Law and Order*) more so than control groups primed with pain.[15] Insofar as beliefs of law and justice can serve to buffer anxiety, displaying such content can mitigate mortality salience effects. This was especially effective in a subsequent study, in which law and justice media were found to reduce self-enhancing biases, which are negative responses known to arise after mortality salience.[16] Thus, not only was appreciation of the material affected by death primes, but also psychosocial perspectives in the participants (audience) 'post-show'.

In line with this alteration to appreciation of tragic content, a prior study looked at the 'appeal of tragedy' using material from Ernest Hemingway novels, and reported that participants for whom mortality was made salient responded more emotionally to – and were more touched by – a tragic excerpt; they also found a non-tragic excerpt less enjoyable and cared less for a protagonist in the non-tragic passage.[17] Key to this study was its investigation into affect. Many terror management theory studies, in dealing with such troubling subject matter as death, surprisingly do not elicit valence changes in participant affect. Goldenberg et al.'s findings were the first to explain:

> Although reminders of death may not produce any explicit affective response, they may produce a nonconscious implicit affective reaction . . . Although this emotion does not usually manifest itself, when provided with an emotion-specific stimulus, individuals respond with an increased affective response to that stimulus.[18]

It is theoretically in line with a terror management model that *Fun Home*'s emotional accessibility – and clear audience appreciation – might in some way be attributable to these same tragic cathartics.

Using media much more relevant to *Fun Home*, Charles Hackney's 2011 study tested the hypothesis that mortality salience manipulations would impact on participants' appreciation of comic strips using death-related content.[19] The presented jokes were codified by the issues they depicted in graded applicability to target existential concerns. Hackney found that mortality salience priming enhanced the evaluation of humorous material in line with its relative centrality to death themes: mortality salience-primed participants gave the highest scores for jokes that had the most direct connection to death-relevant concerns. Put another way, for those primed with death compared to controls, the less relevant a joke was to existential matters, the less they appreciated the humorous material in that moment. This is especially provocative given Bechdel's originary medium and its theatricalisation via 'captioned' tableaus explicit in the musical's lyrics and direction.

The tragicomic humour in *Fun Home* is about as death-specific and macabre as it gets. One representative scene starts with Bruce, Alison's father, working with a client, Pete; his uncle has passed away in a horrific accident, and he is at the Bechdel Funeral Home to make arrangements. Pete moves towards the model-coffin on the floor, from which Bruce tactfully guides him away. After ushering Pete out of the door, Bruce suddenly says, 'Kids, get out of there', and Young Alison and her two brothers then pop out of the coffin.[20] This moment bleeds into perhaps the most overtly humorous song of the play, 'Come to the Fun Home', The children rehearse a commercial they wrote for the family business, and they sing such innocent lyrics as:

> Come to the Fun Home
> Ample parking down the street
> Here at the Fun Home
> Body prep that can't be beat
> You'll like the Fun Home
> In our hearse there's a backwards seat
> That's why we made up this poem
> We're the Bechdel Funeral Home.[21]

Such a song may act to prime the audience with death reminders, and then incorporate death-specific humour as a way to 'down regulate' the possible negative emotional experiences presented, a process outlined by Christopher Long and Dara Greenwood who studied humour *production* rather than evaluation. Their paradigm – in which participants were asked to caption cartoons in a humorous way after a mortality salience or control manipulation – was 'the first to investigate the impact of death reminders on the creative task of humour production'.[22] They showed that death reminders can at times facilitate creativity and open-mindedness: participants who were subliminally primed with mortality salience wrote funnier captions than control participants (when judged by outside raters). The findings expand the breadth of terror management theory's ramifications; whereas many studies have shown that death primes result in a 'perspective narrowing' of the psychosocial aperture, such experiments show that death primes can also, thankfully, elicit pro-social and creative behaviour under the right circumstances.[23] In lay terms, while most studies into terror management are cautionary tales revealing unsavoury levels of rigidity and attachment to one's worldviews, studies like these show the potential for death reminders to provoke a 'beautiful' and flexible behavioural profile. This is especially interesting when in vantage of (the real) Alison Bechdel's creative and pro-social blossoming despite, or in existential spite of, her father's suicide. It also offers a *heroic* model for the role of theatre and performance as a vehicle to find the 'perfect balance' for self and societal congruence.[24]

This type of heroic dramaturgy has been referred to by some psychologists as a 'Beckerian Reading'. For example, Daniel Sullivan, Jeff Greenberg and Mark Landau applied a terror management theory analysis to the films *Rosemary's Baby* (1968) and *Straw Dogs* (1971), classifying character motivation in existential goal-striving terminology, along with showcasing the power and presence of death imagery in narrative forms.[25] Jeff Zinn recently described such dramaturgical applications in *The Existential Actor: Life and Death Onstage and Off*, centring Becker's premise of the *causa sui* project ('the cause of oneself'). Zinn explains the *causa sui* project is a 'vital lie that we construct to provide some illusion of purpose in a random and oblivious universe'.[26] It is the illusory identity upon which we anchor ourselves in order to function stably amidst the random chaos of our lives, knowing that death can come at any moment. And it is a healthy lie, for without it we would be frozen in fear.

In *Fun Home*, Alison's *causa sui* project is to sublimate and free her bound creative, emotional and erotic energies, thus transcending her troubled past and creating a meaningful legacy for her future self via art and sexual authenticity. She succeeds in building a healthy terror management system of self-esteem striving and worldview buffering, and she processes reconciliation with her past and with her father. She pours herself into her graphic novels, and for that she garners critical accolades, leading to her life depicted in a Broadway musical. Such a recapitulation of reality back in her art (and vice versa) creates another means for transcending the perpetual death reminders and events of her childhood: an achievable/achieved congruence of her and her self's ability to requite societal standards, as well as to buck them.

Alternately, her father pines for such freedom as well, but is unable to confront the truth of his homosexuality. As Bechdel says in the graphic memoir, 'Sexual shame is in itself a kind of death'.[27] Bruce manifests a stunted and self-defeating *causa sui* project: to manage pretence, to invalidate authenticity, to display a false front. This is reflected in his compulsive restoration and obsessive caring for the funeral home, which of course masks personal and familial turmoil. Towards the end of the play – and his life – he purchases an abandoned and irremediable house on the outskirts of town that he intends to somehow repair. This project is the subject of his final song, 'The Edges of the World', and the conceit is that Bruce is standing on the side of the highway where we know he inevitably will walk into traffic. Such comparisons of the house as 'something cracking, something rotting, piles of ruin and debris' reflect his fractured and death-aimed mental states.[28] These images are potent primes for the audience as well.[29] The design of the play also shows such architectural variability then available for audience discernment; intact one moment, and later taking on the 'bad foundation' and 'gaping holes' as various platforms descend into the floor to create literal, dangerous pits.

Bruce manically switches gears several more times, psychically travelling back and forth from the rotting house to the road ahead where he stood for hours making his final decision. His life ends with words that seem to come straight out of Becker:

> I'm scared.
> I had a life I thought I understood.
> I took it and I squeezed out every bit of life I could.
> But the edges of the world that held me up have gone away,
> And I'm falling into nothingness
> Or flying into something so sublime.
> And I'm
> A man I don't know.
> Who am I now?
> Where do I go?
> I can't go back.
> I can't find my way through . . .[30]

Terror management theory is built on the idea that cultural worldviews and self-esteem help to structure the world around us into manageable and meaningful cognitive patterning. They give symbolic forms – or edges – to the chaos. If the 'edges of the world' are interpreted as these worldview defences and self-esteem buffers, then Bruce's final song provides a powerful theatrical frame within which audiences may witness and experience a failing of these mental systems and their sequelae. Rather than flying – if not just remaining – above ground, Bruce gives way and falls – apart.

Caption: Lyrical Flight and Existential Resilience

The play soon culminates after Bruce's death with another song, 'Flying Away (Finale)'. The score and libretto are circular, for 'It All Comes Back (Opening)' begins with the same lyrics. Alison commands her father to lift her up in the air, 'to play airplane . . . like Superman, up in the sky'.[31] Here the three Alisons come together to sing this finale and imagine themselves flying high enough to 'see all of Pennsylvania', an allusion to an earlier scene about gaining a 'bird's eye view' in the song 'Maps'. The meta-course of the play suggests we are witnessing a heroic reconciliation, and *witnessing Alison witness* and in turn reconcile her own heroism. This wraps with the final lines by adult Alison: 'Every so often there was a rare moment of perfect balance when I soared above him.'

The 'Opening/Finale' aspects of these songs are crucial; the relative positioning – in this case *before/after* such death reminders – is a key feature in terror management theory's cognitive functional model for flight imagery as cognitive buffer. As Sheldon Solomon has elucidated, flight fantasy, in which a person defies gravity and flies unaided, is completely in breach of natural laws *even in the imagination*.[32] Anthropological evidence validates the pervasive universality of flight imagery, wherein the conceptual metaphor of *upwardness* links with positive outcomes, action and vitality, whereas *downwardness* suggests negative outcomes, stasis and rot.[33] Supernatural/flight imagery buffers existential anxiety by (creating the illusion of) denying the limits of our animal bodies. Our minds embody such defiance into a symbolic denial of death, which is the ultimate limit to corporeality. This type of imaginative embodiment has an unconscious mitigating effect on distal defences, and in laboratory settings, death reminders have increased flight fantasies and the desire to fly.[34] While it is speculative to presume that the flight imagery opening and closing the play operates in such a pattern, the syntax of events, especially at the 'finale', does iterate similar temporal progressions in these experimental methodologies: a death reminder (Bruce's death), followed by distraction (Alison re-tracing childhood moments, literally), followed by flight fantasy (the final song), followed by dissipation (applause).

It is important to draw attention to the fact that the content/lyrics of these songs cannot be decoupled from the vehicular nature of the music itself. This is especially so when thinking through how one might engage in lyrical flight. In her article, 'Mitigating Death Anxiety: Identifying Music's Role in Terror Management', Audrey Berger Cardany emphasises the 'transcendant' nature of music and, quoting Daniel Barenboim, how it 'gives [us] the possibility to transcend physical, human limitations'.[35] Again, this type of speculative dramaturgy in music lends support to the argument that lyrical flight in *Fun Home* may provide a buffering function in order to handle and cathart the robust mortality salience that the show re-triggers. I agree that this 'raises the possibility that when mortality is salient we avoid songs that are reminders of our bodies – our *creatureliness*' and further add, per Solomon and others, that we then approach songs of flight, fantasy and bodily ambivalence.[36] It is significant that Berger Cardany bemoans the 'neglect' towards music in terror management theory research, to which she lists all of the visual arts in past literature reviews noting music's disciplinary lack. In the intervention, however, theatre's explicit status is unaddressed, save for a suggestion that 'death-related music works (e.g., requiem, tragic opera, wailing songs, funeral processions [be reassessed] through the lens of Becker's ideas'.[37] Despite noting the pervasiveness of music within all other arts and ritual spheres, this otherwise encompassing review compounds the problem at which this current paper begins to scratch: the significant paucity of research on the terror managing functions of theatre, dance and other live performance practices.

Caption: Limitations and Conclusions

The synthesis of flight in lyric, melody, rhythm, gesture and liveness makes *Fun Home* – and the musical form itself – a pluripotent site of research into the possible death-denial cognitions that this play might provoke. The same might be said for the way that it functions as a source of death-acceptance on an affiliative social level. Berger Cardany's review nodded at Julia Kneer and Diana Rieger's 2015 study in which participants who aligned themselves as members of heavy-metal subculture found the music of that form to be more meaningful in its buffering capacity than others. This 'further suggest[s] that anyone's favorite music[al] could serve as a buffer to mortality salience'.[38] One interesting approach might therefore look at the self-asserted affiliations of (non)devout musical theatre fans in their engagement and re-engagement with this material over time.

It would be unsurprising to find worldview defences in audiences given the macabre primes laden in *Fun Home*. However, it may be equally informative if they were *not* present, given not only confounding real-world variables, but as seen, the possibility to attenuate and pre-empt worldview defences. In this regard, experiencing the play within an experimentally controlled setting would not and could not mimic real-world variables fully. This is especially relevant in terms of the repertoire of meta-theatrical affects/effects which *Fun Home* traffics. Also, a number of recent research arms around terror management theory explicitly call attention to the confounding effects of theatrical conventions themselves, which again, is of interest insofar as null effects are still themselves results with interpretable, if disappointing, significance. Specifically, a clutch of studies have explored relevant trait/state (measures versus manipulations of) mindfulness and presence-of-mind, or humility and eco-centrism, and collective experiences of awe, to name a few.[39] These prosocial qualities or inductions have been shown to mitigate and/or pre-empt the rigidifying effects of mortality salience; with that, they present as highly complex confounders related to audience and spectator positionalities and their potential responses individually and statistically. Similarly, while outside the bounds of this chapter to provide a full treatment of music psychology and the macabre intersections to terror management mitigation, the (de)coupled nature of music and lyrics warrants considerable investigation into how music and melody might be further vehicles for 'flight *from* physical sensation' itself, or further 'ambivalence *towards* the body'.[40] Given the role and value of each of these phenomenal measures under the lenses of theatre and performance studies, this line of questioning is undertheorised and provides a rich opportunity to platform future research methods and sites, if not 'just' speculative dramaturgies.

Taken together, these questions show that the application of terror management theory in script analysis reveals *Fun Home* to be wildly multifaceted in its macabre underpinnings, and fruitful material for experimental paradigms. Most of the terror management corpus deals with small bits of information in research settings. Studies looking at *Fun Home* might delineate the production as a whole or investigate smaller bits in scene and image-specific analysis. The almost triumphant humour with which the narrative and performers (and audience) heroically diffuse such horrific circumstances is striking and warrants much longer discussion on its own *vis-à-vis* the few aforementioned studies. The same could be said with each of these terror management inductions, especially in the abstraction or literalisation of a theatrical event: verbal, visual and aural percepts directly dealing with death, as well as any imagery that calls into question the validity of subscribed worldviews. Given the death-reminding potential of verbal primes and/or proximity to a funeral home, could the large ads with 'FUN HOME' emblazoned on buses, subways and digital screens also have the potential to stir up mortality salience? Why, or why not? As the play's impressions continue to spread, this paper demonstrates *Fun Home* to be an even more apt opportunity for scholars to look at such terror management manipulations and defences on and off the stage.

What might we make of a more recent star-studded take on the play, seen in a one-night-only reading in an actual funeral home in New York City in 2019?[41] Billed as a 'site specific reading of *Fun Home* at a funeral home', Quintessence of Dust's staging itself did little more than call attention to the graciousness of the Plaza Jewish Community Chapel's generosity as host of the event. However, given the above ideas, perhaps nothing more was 'needed' in their theatrical ploy except real-world proximity. This generates an urgent enquiry for producers, directors, dramaturgs, actors, scholars and audiences encountering such death-relevant material. In this new existential spotlight, we might ask how, if at all, do such 'versions' transcend themselves as marketing gimmicks to become powerful frames reflexive of their own ethical considerations? One answer to this question is to engender more mindfulness of the humility and eco-centrism required of us by this story. This allows the focus of our work as scholars and practitioners to resist the lure of celebrity and profits at the expense of artistic discretion and integrity. A terror management approach can better inform our dramaturgical kitestrings and footholds, keeping us responsibly grounded in the moment while we continue to soar through these plays in lyrical flight.

Notes

1. Alison Bechdel, *Fun Home: A Family Tragicomic* (New York: First Mariner Books, 2004).
2. After premiering at The Public Theater on 22 October 2013, it opened on Broadway in April 2015 and closed in September 2016 after 583 performances. Lisa Kron and Jeanine Tesori, *Fun Home*, directed by Sam Gold (Circle in the Square Theatre, New York: 19 April 2015).
3. At time of writing, the rights for the film adaptation have been given to Jake Gyllenhaal as 'Bruce' and producer.
4. Bechdel, *Fun Home*, pp. 82–4. See Chapter 3, 'That Old Catastrophe'. My thanks to Sheldon Solomon for introducing me to this poem in the context of terror management theory in 2007, personal correspondence.
5. Tesori and Kron, *Fun Home* (New York: Samuel French, 2014), p. 57. The character of Small Alison corrects herself when describing a person that Adult Alison refers to as 'an old-school butch' in the ballad 'Ring of Keys'.
6. Kate Millet, *Flying* (New American Library, 1974). See the in-text citation of Millett's notion of 'heroism [a]s suspect' or 'deluded' in Bechdel, *Fun Home*, pp. 217–19.

7. For an accessible primer on terror management theory, see Sheldon Solomon, Jeff Greenberg and Tom Pyszczynski, *The Worm at the Core: On the Role of Death in Life* (New York: Random House, 2015).
8. Throughout the musical, certain scenes and phrases are literally 'captioned' so that the lyrics call to mind the comic/graphic frame explicitly via the musical book and score. This of course is evocative of Alison's own self-reflexivity as she plots her thoughts and memories into comic bits for the memoir.
9. Ernest Becker, *The Denial of Death* (New York: Free Press, 1973).
10. Current data range derived from S. Solomon, lecture for Ernest Becker Society, New York: (September 2016); S. Solomon, Webinar for Ernest Becker Society: 17 July 2020.
11. For reviews and meta-analyses, see J. Arndt and M. Vess, 'Tales From Existential Oceans: Terror Management Theory', *Social and Personality Psychology Compass*, 2 (2008); B. Burke et al., 'Two Decades of Terror Management Theory: A Meta-Analysis of Mortality Salience Research', *Personality and Social Psychology Review*, 14 (2010).
12. J. Arndt et al., 'Traces of Terror: Subliminal Death Primes and Facial Electromyographic Indices of Affect', *Motivation and Emotion*, 25 (2001).
13. T. Pyszczynski et al., 'Whistling in the Dark: Exaggerated Consensus Estimates in Response to Incidental Reminders of Mortality', *Psychological Science*, 7 (1996). See also S. Vedantam, 'Reminders of Mortality Bring Out the Charitable Side', *Washington Post*, 24 December 2007.
14. E. Jonas et al., 'The Scrooge Effect: Evidence that Mortality Salience Increases Prosocial Attitudes and Behavior', *Personality and Social Psychology Bulletin*, 28 (2002); A. Kastenmuller et al. 'Disaster Threat and Justice Sensitivity: A Terror Management Perspective', *Journal of Applied Social Psychology*, 43/10 (2013).
15. L. Taylor, 'Death and Television: Terror Management Theory and Themes of Law and Justice on Television', *Death Studies*, 36 (2012).
16. Taylor, 'Death and Television', 354.
17. J. Goldenberg et al., 'The Appeal of Tragedy: A Terror Management Perspective', *Media Psychology*, 1 (1999).
18. Goldenberg et al., 'The Appeal of Tragedy', 324.
19. C. Hackney, 'The Effect of Mortality Salience on the Evaluation of Humorous Material', *The Journal of Social Psychology*, 151/1 (2011).
20. Tesori and Kron, *Fun Home*, p. 20.
21. Tesori and Kron, *Fun Home*, p. 24.
22. C. Long and D. Greenwood, 'Joking in the face of death: a terror management approach to humor production', *International Journal of Humor Research* (2013).

23. C. Routledge et al., 'The Life and Death of Creativity: The Effects of Mortality Salience on Self Versus Social-Directed Creative Expression', *Motivation and Emotion*, 32 (2008).
24. See endnote 28 for use of 'perfect balance'.
25. D. Sullivan et al., 'Toward a New Understanding of Two Films from the Dark Side: Terror Management Theory Applied to *Rosemary's Baby* and *Straw Dogs*', *Journal of Popular Film and Television*, 37 (2010). See also S. Solomon and M. J. Landau, 'Little Murders: Cultural Animals in an Existential Age', in D. Sullivan and J. Greenberg (eds), *Death in Classic and Contemporary Film* (New York: Palgrave Macmillan, 2013).
26. Jeff Zinn, *The Existential Actor: Life and Death Onstage and Off* (Hanover: Smith and Kraus, 2015), p. 20.
27. Bechdel, *Fun Home*, p. 228.
28. Tesori and Kron, *Fun Home*, p. 72.
29. K. E. Vail et al., 'The Aftermath of Destruction: Images of Destroyed Buildings Increase Support for War, Dogmatism, and Death Thought Accessibility', *Journal of Experimental Social Psychology*, 48 (2012).
30. Tesori and Kron, *Fun Home*, p. 72–3.
31. Tesori and Kron, *Fun Home*, p. 73–7.
32. S. Solomon et al., 'Teach These Souls to Fly: Supernatural as Human Adaptation', in M. Schaller et al. (eds), *Evolution, Culture and the Human Mind* (New York: Taylor and Francis Group LLC, 2012).
33. George Lakoff and Mark Johnson, *Metaphors We Live By* (Chicago IL: University of Chicago Press, 1980), p. 25; Ellen Dissanayake, *Homo Aestheticus: Where Art Comes From and Why* (Seattle WA: University of Washington Press, 1992), p. 176.
34. F. Cohen et al., 'Finding Ever-land: Flight Fantasies and the Desire to Transcend Mortality', *Journal of Experimental Social Psychology*, 47 (2009).
35. A. Berger Cardany, 'Mitigating Death Anxiety: Identifying Music's Role in Terror Management', *Psychology of Music*, 46/1 (2018).
36. Berger Cardany, 'Mitigating Death Anxiety', 12–13.
37. Berger Cardany, 'Mitigating Death Anxiety, 13.
38. Berger Cardany, 'Mitigating Death Anxiety', 13. See also J. Kneer and D. Rieger, 'The Memory Remains: How Heavy Metal Fans Buffer Against the Fear of Death', *Psychology of Popular Media Culture*, (2015).
39. Y. Bai et al., 'Awe, the Diminished Self, and Collective Engagement: Universals and Cultural Variations in the Small Self', *Attitudes and Social Cognition*, 113/2 (2017); P. Kesebir, 'A Quiet Ego Quiets Death Anxiety: Humility as an Existential Anxiety Buffer', *Journal of Personality and Social*

Psychology, 104/4 (2014); C. Niemec et al., 'Being Present in the Face of Existential Threat: The Role of Trait Mindfulness in Reducing Defensive Responses to Mortality Salience', *Journal of Personality and Social Psychology*, 99/2 (2010). My endless thanks and 'awe' go to Sheldon Solomon for his insights in person and in correspondence about these particular studies, and his caution as well as excitement on applying such ideas of experimental settings to and from the stage.

40. As Berger Cardany cites J. L. Goldenberg, 'Ambivalence Toward the Body: Death, Neuroticism, and the Flight from Physical Sensation', *Personality and Social Psychology Bulletin*, 32 (2006). My italics.

41. Lisa Kron and Jeanine Tesori, *Fun Home*, directed by Rachel Kunstadt (Quintessence of Dust: Plaza Jewish Community Chapel, New York, 19 December 2019).

PART THREE

STAGING THE MACABRE

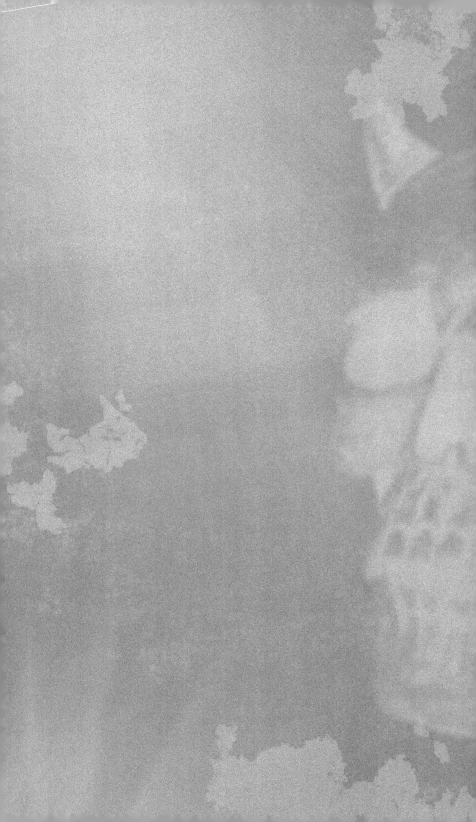

9

The Severed Head on Stage

Kevin J. Wetmore, Jr

> Like the wild Irish, I'll not think thee dead
> Till I can play at football with thy head.
> Francisco de Medici
> *The White Devil*, John Webster (1612)

IN HIS SEMINAL STUDY *The Stage Life of Props*, Andrew Sofer identifies the skull as one of the five more significant stage props throughout the history of drama.[1] Featured in a number of plays around the world, skulls are important in the history of theatre. One of the most famous (and most visually represented moments) in *Hamlet* is of the Danish prince and a skull, a philosophical contemplation of mortality after the gravedigger informs him, 'This same skull, sir, was, sir, Yorick's skull, the King's jester' (V.i.180–1). What is remarkable, if unremarked on, is that Hamlet did not know the skull was Yorick until he was told by the gravedigger. Despite the popular image of Hamlet as a young man studying Yorick's skull, the actual moment reveals Hamlet's disgust at the difference between memory of the living man and the actual object he is holding, with Hamlet proclaiming, 'how abhorr'd in my imagination it is! / My gorge rises at it' (V.i.188–9), (the English Renaissance equivalent of 'I just threw up in my mouth a little'). Hamlet, seemingly fine with a generic skull as an anonymous symbol, does not care much for *Yorick's* skull, despite the popular imagination thinking he does.

Sofer reminds us that, 'Skulls fascinate because of their sheer uncanniness, their disturbing ability to oscillate between subject and object. Unlike virtually any other prop, the skull is the remains of the deceased human subject'.[2] The skull is an uncanny object, but it is also an abstraction. In *Hamlet*, it is the naming of the skull that transforms symbolic object and *memento mori* into the remains of an actual person.[3] A mere skull is a symbol; Yorick's skull is a part of Yorick's specific physical body. The step beyond merely naming the skull is presenting a severed head to an audience. More than a skull, a severed head is far more uncanny, macabre and abject – more familiar and yet more terrifying because it evokes a much messier end. A skull is dry and clean, with no reminders of life, whereas a head is a reminder of an actual human being. A severed head has a recognisable face (indeed, facial recognition is the primary means by which we identify each other); even within hours of birth, humans can recognise and prefer the shape of faces. A skull is a *memento mori* – a reminder of death. A severed head is a reminder of a specific death – Yorick, or John the Baptist, or Macbeth, or Marie Antoinette is dead now.

Julia Kristeva's *The Severed Head: Capital Visions* (2012) surveys the severed head in art and literature, with a focus on Medusa and John the Baptist, among others. Kristeva asserts the head as symbol and metaphor, as religious object and physical fact.[4] Interestingly, she deals only with literature and visual art, and thus the severed head is never actually a 'physical fact' for Kristeva, since she ignores the dramatic arts in the volume. Unlike severed heads evoked through words or images, the presence on stage of a severed head takes the form of a physical object, a prop one holds in one's hands, that serves as metaphor and symbol as well as the thing itself. This is further complicated by how the head itself is manifested on stage. A severed head is abject, in Kristeva's sense (indeed, Kristeva refers to decapitation as a form of 'revolting abjection', filling the viewer with disgust and fascination more than other abjected body parts),[5] but also the most recognisable part of us and where we locate ourselves. The brain contains the mind and personality; all but one of the sensory organs are located in the head. We are head-centred beings. Our head is ourselves, more than any other body part.

The head and face are particularly important on stage; we might note an actor's photo is called a 'headshot', separating the face from the rest of the body. Kristeva observes that all portraits in a sense are thus a beheading, a severing of the face from the rest.[6] When one's head is removed, it matters more, it signifies more, it terrifies more than any other part of the body.

The fear of and cultural practice of beheading are almost universal. However, as Regina Janes argues, 'Beheading always signifies, but always signifies differently within specific codes supplied by culture'.[7] In this chapter, I will consider three theatrical cultures that presented severed heads on stage – the theatre of the English Renaissance, the *kabuki* theatre of Tokugawa, Japan and the Grand Guignol in twentieth-century France – in order to identify the similarities and differences in how severed heads can be presented on stage.[8]

Janes lists five types of beheadings: 'the ancestral head', in which the head is removed, respectfully, post-mortem; 'the trophy head', taken in battle; 'the sacrificial head', taken as part of a religious ritual; 'the presentation head', 'taken as part of a political struggle'; and 'the public execution', in which the head is removed as punishment arising from a legal decision.[9] The western stage is dominated by the presentation and publicly executed heads, while in Japan trophy heads are prominent devices. The stage head becomes a symbol of horror, but also a reminder of the real removal of heads occurring in the societies that put the severed head on stage. All three cultures that featured severed heads on stage are also cultures that displayed severed heads as part of the performance of justice and authority, from the heads on Tower Bridge to the samurai's *bundori* ('head trophy'), to the display (both in the immediate aftermath of decollation and then later again in a more formal, even artistic, presentation) of the victims of the guillotine from the French Revolution through to the Second World War.

Richard J. Hand and Michael Wilson observe, 'Historically, the power of decapitation has been exploited by those who have wanted to demonstrate, most unequivocally, the destruction of their enemies', whether in the form of the headsman, the guillotine or internet videos by Al-Qaeda, Daesh/Isis and Mexican cartels.[10] Severed heads still carry weight in public performance, even when obviously not real. In the present political moment, the display of a severed head indeed demonstrates the desired destruction of one's (political) enemies. The public display of the bloodied severed heads of George W. Bush, Donald Trump and Boris Johnson in separate settings in the past decade was the cause of considerable outcry. In 2012, the showrunners for HBO's *Game of Thrones* revealed that one of the severed heads on display in a scene was that of George W. Bush, causing tremendous objection among conservatives and media pundits that such a display was morally wrong and disrespectful. The simple use of a prop head in a background was deemed abusive and provocative, despite no actual harm being done to anyone. Similarly, on 30 May 2017, comedienne Kathy Griffin posted a video on social media of herself holding the bloody severed head of Donald Trump. The outcry was large and significant damage was done to Griffin's career, causing cancelled appearances and performances. Lastly, rapper Slowthai held up a mock severed head of Boris Johnson in September 2019 at the Mercury Prize ceremony to considerable hue and cry, again predominantly from conservatives and media pundits. In all three cases, a conservative political figure was presented as mock-decapitated, the severed head held up in public by a pike in the case of *Game of Thrones* and elevated by a performer holding the head in a style similar to the public displays of heads during the French Revolution, and the result was offence due not only to the implied disrespect, but to the threat of destruction behind it.

Ironically, therefore, the severed head performed in public becomes not a physical fact, but the embodiment of the power of authority figures (not just the state) to destroy the enemy (or in the case of Japan, to pretend to have done so, as will be examined below). The severed head on stage is 'physical fact' that therefore must be represented physically. Among the commonalities of these three theatrical eras, we might note that all three feature two types of severed head on stage: onstage decapitations, and the reveal of a severed head. In the former, the illusion of a head being separated from a body must be achieved; in the latter a head is shown to the audience, suggesting time since decollation. Furthermore, all three theatrical eras seemed to explore how best to achieve representing the severed head, be it suggestive or realistic.

The Severed Head on the English Renaissance Stage

The medieval English decapitated enemies on the battlefield to garner trophy and political heads, although the practice vanished with the growing importance of gunpowder and firearms. As Regina Janes observes, however, 'Under the Tudors, the ad hoc battlefield decollations of the Middle Ages were restaged as great public scaffold dramas'.[11] Two of the wives of Henry VIII, Robert Devereux, second Earl of Essex, Rodrigo Lopez (Queen Elizabeth I's physician accused of conspiring to poison her), and dozens of others were beheaded on scaffolds at Tower Green or nearby locales. According to long-standing practice, the executioner or one of his assistants would hold the newly severed head up before the gathered crowd and shout, 'Behold the head of a traitor!' (or, in the case of the Earl of Essex, 'God save the Queen!').[12] 'Held up by the hair and presented to the people, the decollated head models the sovereign's power over the living . . . Yet that head held up also gestures towards the realm "justice."'[13] The former, we should note, is the view of Michel Foucault; the latter of the state.[14] These heads would then be placed in public locations, most notably the London Bridge's Southwark Gate, which in 1598 had more than thirty severed heads displayed upon it.[15] The public severing of the head and its post-decapitation display are thus performative; they play out as a public performance denoting power of the state, justice, but also the end of the narrative of the human life extinguished by decollation.

The English Renaissance audience was familiar with the sight of a severed head and thus their presence on stage must be passable for audiences. Michael J. Hirrel asks were the prop heads pumpkins or did the theatre of the English Renaissance use 'realistic representations of the actors themselves?'[16] He concludes that they must have been fairly realistic representations, and that companies must have had multiple heads, particularly ones resembling the major performers with the company. Shakespeare's plays feature numerous severed heads, almost exclusively of the executed type. Exceptions include Cloten in *Cymbeline*, Barnadine in *Measure for Measure* (although Barnadine's head is substituted as Claudio's executed head after the pirate dies of natural causes) and Macbeth, whose off-stage decapitation in battle is followed by Macduff's re-entry bearing Macbeth's severed head (V.vii). This last example is a point in Hirrel's favour, as the severed head must have resembled Richard Burbage on some level to pass as the man who just left the stage.

Henry VI, Part Two has at least four severed heads on stage: Lord Saye, Sir James Cromer, Jack Cade and Suffolk, whose head is delivered to Margaret, who then carries it around court for the last two acts of the play. Cade has Saye's and Cromer's heads put on pikes and made to kiss each other. After his rebellion is crushed, Cade's head is brought to the king. Hirrel argues that the sheer amount of heads on stage argues for realistic props and not one or two general heads, so to speak. Margaret, he notes, never identifies Suffolk's head as she carries it around, suggesting that the audience must have recognised the object in and of itself.[17]

In *Cymbeline*, Cloten, wearing the clothing of Posthumus, is beheaded in combat by Guiderius. Cloten tells him, 'When I have slain thee with my proper hand, / I'll follow those that even now fled hence: / And on the gates of Lud's town set your heads', the last a reminder of the tradition of setting heads on Tower Bridge as noted above (IV.ii.97–9). They exit fighting as Belarius and Arviragus enter. The stage direction reads, 'Re-enter Guiderius with Cloten's head' (IV.ii.sd 113).

> **Bel.** What has thou done?
> **Gui.** I am perfect what: cut off one Cloten's head,
> Son to the queen (after his own report),
> Who call'd me traitor, mountaineer, and swore,
> With his own single hand he'ld take us in,
> Displace our heads where (thank the gods!) they grow,
> And set them on Lud's town. (IV.ii.113–23)

Belarius suggests that they get rid of the head so that no one will know they killed the Queen's son. Guiderius exits the stage with the head, stating, 'I have ta'en / His head from him, I'll throw't into the creek / Behind our rock and let it to the sea' (IV.ii.150–2). And he does so, leaving the decapitated body to be found by Imogen, who, seeing the clothing, believes it to be that of her husband. As with *Macbeth*, onstage combat leads to an offstage decapitation and a re-entry with a recognisable severed head. The actors need not work how to remove a head in view of the audience, but the performance seems to require a realistic head being brought on stage.

While Shakespeare only presents severed heads and never head-severing, Fiona Martin, after Margaret Owens, identifies four English Renaissance plays in which a character is beheaded on stage: John Marston's *The Insatiate Countess* (1613), John Fletcher and Philip Massinger's *Sir John Van Olden Barnavelt* (1619), Thomas Dekker and Massinger's *The Virgin Martyr* (1620) and Geruase Markham and William Sampson's *Herod and Antipater* (1622).[18] In all these cases, an effect is required to simulate the head's removal, but the head that falls need not resemble the actor, as the effect is focused on a head coming off, not the presentation of the head to the audience. Severed heads on the Jacobean stage were a matter of special effect, not props. George Peele's *The Battle of Alcazar* (1588) features a scene in which, during a pageant presented by death foreshadowing the end of the play, the villain Mahamet is shown his own head placed in a dish carried by a Fury.[19] Mahamet was played by Edward Alleyn, who Hirrel surmises was thus on stage, in character, looking at his own head in the form of a prop which resembled him.[20] The same severed head would be brought on stage at the conclusion of the play, when Mahamet is killed. It strikes me that Peele's play, as much as *Hamlet*, concerns the relationship of one to one's mortality. Hamlet is presented with the skull of Yorick; whereas Mahamet is presented with his own severed head, resembling the actor. A skull is a *memento mori*; your own head is a reminder of your specific death.

The Severed Head on the *Kabuki* and *Bunraku* Stages

In the *bunraku* ('puppet') and *kabuki* theatres of Japan, the severed head is also an important prop, and indeed there even exists a handful of plays in which characters are decollated on stage by the sword-wielding hero.[21] According to prop master Eric Hart, 'among the most difficult props to make are the decapitated heads, known as kubi or kirikubi' (note: kirikubi literally means 'cut head', translation mine).[22] The prop heads are divided into two types, determined by social class: *dakubi* ('lower-class head') and *jōkubi* ('high-class head'). The lower-class head is made of cotton cloth, stuffed with wood shavings and painted with a face. A piece of red cloth may be attached the neck to signify the blood from the stump. The high-class head is carved of wood or made of papier-mâché over wood and designed to resemble the actor whose head it represents.[23]

As in England, Japan features two types of heads. The first is for decapitation scenes and is thus non-realistic. The second is for head-examination scenes and, as Hart observes, they tend towards the realistic. *Kabuki* features decapitation scenes in *tachimawari* ('*kabuki* stage combat'). Samuel L. Leiter observes:

> the severing of a head is usually done in a manner quite as symbolical as other deaths inflicted by a sword slash in Kabuki; that is, the blade need not come anywhere near the intended victim, and a simple stroke suffices to convince the audience of the act's artistic validity. Generally, the actor playing the victim lies so that his head is hidden from the audience's view by another character of the play or a property. A red cloth is thrown over the 'decapitated' head.[24]

No attempt is made to make either the decapitation or the head left behind realistic. Instead, the combat is highly stylised and symbolic. In plays such as *Ichijō Ōkura Monogatari* ('*The Tale of Ichijo Okura*', 1731) and *Benkei Jōshi* ('*Benkei the Emissary*', 1737), Leiter reports, fake heads wrapped in a red cloth are passed to the hero (who has severed the head) to hold aloft, as the beheaded actor throws a red cloth over his head and runs offstage.[25] Similarly, in *Shibaraku* ('*Just a Moment!*', 1697), one of the *Kabuki Jūhachiban* ('*Eighteen Great Plays*'), Gongoro, the hero, is attacked by a dozen of the villain's henchmen and, drawing his oversized *katana*, decapitates them all with a single blow. In this case, the severed heads are large red cotton balls on a string. This moment is designed to show the character's heroic strength, and its comic exaggeration requires no realistic heads.

Conversely, in *kubi jikken*, head inspection scenes in *kabuki/bunraku*, the tradition calls for fairly realistic prop heads to be used, as the characters inspect a severed head in full view of the audience. The first major example of this dramaturgy can be found in *Sugawara Denju Tenarai Kagami* ('*Sugawara and the Secrets of Calligraphy*' by Takeda Izumo I,[26] Miyoshi Shôraku, Namiki Senryû I and Takeda Koizumo I, 1746). Act IV's final scene is known as 'Terakoya' and is a *kubi jikken* scene.[27] In brief, the evil and power-hungry Shihei conspires against his rival, Kan Shōjō, and denounces him to the emperor. Kan Shōjō sends his young son, Kan Shūsai, to a provincial school far from the capital run by the noble Genzō in order to protect him. Shihei sends his retainer Matsuōmaru to kill the boy and return with his head. Unwilling to advance Shihei's goals and seeking to atone for his own failings as a samurai, Matsuōmaru substitutes and sacrifices his own son, Kotarō. Matsuōmaru stands on stage with Tonami, Genzō's wife, as Kotarō is taken outside. The narrator relates:

> In this room they stand
> On the threshold
> Between life and death
> From within is heard
> The sickening sound
> Of the beheading.
> (*A sound from offstage*)[28]

Matsuōmaru drops his sword when he hears his son executed. Genzō returns with the 'head casket' and shows Matsuōmaru the head within. As Shihei's agents watch, Matsuōmaru must identify the severed head as that of Kan Shūsai or all at the school will be executed. Matsuōmaru takes a piece of ricepaper from his *kimono* and cleans the face of his dead son, and then pronounces the severed head Kan Shūsai's.[29]

The level of horror found in the play is different from both the playful severed heads found in *tachimawari* scenes or in English heads brought back on stage after combat. The protagonist does not merely bring in the enemy's head, but must confront the head of his or her child and pretend it is an enemy's head. The severed head in this case is the head of a loved one; identifying it as someone else is part of the character's duty, but the emotional content of the scene is what horrifies onlookers: not that there is a severed head, but whose head was severed.

A very similar event occurs in the famous *Kumagai Jinya* ('*Kumagai's Battle Camp*'), the final scene from Act III from *Ichi-no-Tani Futaba Gunki* ('*The Chronicle of the Battle of Ichi-no-Tani*' by Namiki Sôsuke, Asada Icchô, Namioka Geiji, Namiki Shôzô I, Naniwa Sanzô and Toyotake Jinroku, 1751). Because of a debt owed, the samurai Kumagai cannot kill young Atsumori, a boy on the other side during Japan's civil war. Ordered to bring Atsumori's head to his superiors, Kumagai opts to sacrifice his own son, Kojirô, and offer his head as Atsumori's. The play's climactic scene involves the presentation of Kojirô's severed head to the gathered company at Kumagai's battle camp, including the mothers of both Atsumori and Kojirô. Part of the effect of the scene for the audience is in viewing the mothers on stage, side by side, realising whose head is actually being displayed, and then having to hide their reactions in order to fool General Yoshitsune, the leader of the shogun's forces. While Yoshitsune is not fooled (indeed, he helps smuggle Atsumori out of the camp), he publicly declares the head to be Atsumori's, honouring Kumagai and Kojirô's sacrifice. A similar variation can also be found in the *Moritsuna Jinya* ('*Moritsuna's Battle Camp*') scene from *Ômi Genji Senjin Yakata* ('*The Castle of the Genji Advance Guard at Ômi*' by Chikamatsu Hanji, Miyoshi Shôraku, Matsuda Saiji, Takeda Shinshô and Chikamatsu Tônan, 1769), in which a samurai claims a severed head is his brother when it is not.

In all three of these *kubi jikken*, a head is brought on stage in a head casket and then revealed. The scenes' horror comes not from the severed head but from the reaction of the characters who discover in that moment that the head viewed is a different one than they expected. This phenomenon does not occur in any other national dramas with severed heads, but rather is unique to *kabuki/bunraku*. We might perceive it as being unique and integral to Japanese culture, as Janes argued. *Kabuki* heads signify differently than English or French ones.

Echoes of the Guillotine: the Severed Head on the Late-Nineteenth and Twentieth-Century French Stage

The French Revolution began a tradition in France of displaying heads as public performance. The disembodied head and the decollated body both became literal props for performance during the Terror. As Mel Gordon reports, 'Around the Place de la Nation during the French Revolution's Reign of Terror, freshly-guillotined corpses were manipulated like oversized puppets in grotesque comedies', often with the wrong heads purposely placed on other bodies, thus using a real head as a prop.[30]

The English would coat heads in pitch and display them in public at the gates. The revolutionary French took a different approach: rather than preserve the severed head, it would be recreated for public display in order to have a trophy of individual's destruction that paradoxically kept them both alive in the public memory and in a form that would not decay. The preservation of the specific head became very important in the French Revolution. At the beginning of the White Terror, the Convention summoned both Madame Marie Tussaud and German-speaking Swiss physician and wax-model maker Phillipe Curtius to measure and model the severed heads of the guillotined 'for the purposes of both propaganda and record keeping'.[31] In the words of Emma McEvoy, 'Tussaud's bleeding heads were spectacles of mortality, records of a very bloody, and very recent history'.[32] The enemies of France were destroyed by the guillotine, and yet preserved in wax to celebrate that destruction, destroying them, in a sense, over and over again.

The display of heads was a history and a narrative in and of itself. In her biography of Marie Tussaud-cum-history of Madame Tussaud's, Pamela Pilbeam reports that the wax replicas of Louis XVI and Marie Antionette's severed heads were placed on display opposite the wax replica heads of the revolutionaries: Carrier, Fouquier-Tinvelle, Robespierre and Hérbert.[33] Pilbeam writes:

> All participants to the mass guillotinings of the Terror were deeply conscious that they were taking part in a public performance... People compared the ritual and ceremonial to a theatre, with agreed rules on how to die. Next day's victims practised their role in the prison.[34]

Madame Roland, a leader of the Girondist faction, as executioner Charles-Henri Sanson cut her hair before guillotining her, remarked,

'At least leave me enough for you to hold up my head and show it to the people, if they wish to see it!'[35] Danton, as well, awaiting execution, instructed Sanson that, 'It's worth the trouble' to display his severed head to the crowd.[36] Even the victims of the 'National Razor' promoted the display of their own severed heads as part of the performance. As a result, France may have been predisposed to the presentation of the severed head on stage.

By the end of the nineteenth century the guillotine was still active in public, although not to the extent of the Revolution. It did, however, contribute to the *fin de siècle* French embrace of Salomania. Salome, best known for demanding John the Baptist's head after dancing for Herod, became among the most popular figures in art and literature, being evoked by Gustav Flaubert, Aubrey Beardsley, Odilon Redon and Gustave Moreau, among dozens of others, and showing up most famously in Oscar Wilde's *Salome* (1891, published 1893). In Wilde's play, the eponymous character asks for the head of Jokanaan (John the Baptist), and an executioner climbs down into the cistern where he is being held prisoner by Herod. The stage direction reads, '[A huge black arm, the arm of the Executioner, comes forth from the cistern, bearing on a silver shield the head of Jokanaan. Salomé seizes it . . .]'.[37] She kisses it. She is still attracted to the man, but also angry at his severed head:

> Ah! thou wouldst not suffer me to kiss thy mouth, Jokanaan. Well! I will kiss it now. I will bite it with my teeth as one bites a ripe fruit. Yes, I will kiss thy mouth, Jokanaan. I said it; did I not say it? I said it. Ah! I will kiss it now . . . But, wherefore dost thou not look at me, Jokanaan? Thine eyes that were so terrible, so full of rage and scorn, are shut now. Wherefore are they shut? Open thine eyes! Lift up thine eyelids, Jokanaan! Wherefore dost thou not look at me? Art thou afraid of me, Jokanaan, that thou wilt not look at me?[38]

Herod calls her 'monstrous' and orders his soldiers to kill Salome.[39] The play ends with the death of her and her mother. And yet it is Salome's interaction with John the Baptist's head that is the play's climactic moment.

The legacy of the guillotine and Salomania was made manifest in the Théâtre du Grand-Guignol (1897–1962). The small theatre in a converted chapel in Paris's Pigalle neighbourhood specialised in explicit violence and psychological horror that grew out of the naturalist tradition. Hand and

Wilson identify a 'subgenre of guillotine plays' within the Grand Guignol, including *La Veuve* (*'The Widow'*, 1906), *Au Petit jour* (*'At Daybreak'*, 1921), *Vers l'au-delà* (*'To the Beyond'*, 1921) and *L'Homme qui a tué la mort* (*'The Man Who Killed Death'*, 1928), all of which feature severed heads on stage.[40]

Interestingly, the first appearance of a Grand Guignol guillotine occurred in a 1906 sex comedy. Eugène Héros and Léon Abric's *La Veuve* is a farce in which the lover of a museum curator's wife is subjected to an elaborate mock execution, but the guillotine blade is revealed to be made of cardboard.[41] The public deemed the fabricated guillotine's onstage presence acceptable. The first dramatic play to feature a working guillotine – Andre de Lorde and Jean Barnac's *Au petit jour* – on the other hand, caused a public outcry as 'to show a functioning guillotine was considered an act of sacrilege towards a national icon'.[42] The play ended with a murderer's onstage beheading; after a police enquiry, the theatre was forced to end the play before the convict mounted the scaffold.[43]

Arguably the most extreme of the Grand Guignol guillotine plays involved a severed head brought back to life. René Berton's *L'Homme qui a tué la mort* begins with execution preparations for the convicted murderer Morales, who insists upon his own innocence. Professor Fargus has invented a machine to keep severed heads alive and is given permission by the governor to experiment on Morales. The audience only hears, not sees, the execution. The sound of the blade falling cuts off Morales' final words in mid-sentence. A prison warden enters with the wrapped up severed head; Berton's stage directions indicate that the actors use their bodies to block the substitution of the prop head for the actor's head sticking through a hole in the table. Professor Fargus states the larynx is intact, attaching the head to a machine. After a pause, in which it seems the experiment is a failure, Morales' eyes open and (to the horror of all but Fargus) the head speaks, proclaiming its innocence. Fargus labels the experiment a success as the lawyer Gauvin goes mad, imagining himself back in the courtroom sentencing Morales.[44] Berton's play not only explores the horror of decapitation, but also the potential horror that a severed head might retain consciousness for a period after separation from the body. In a final bid for macabre realism (perhaps like the French Revolutionaries who made marionettes out of corpses), the play uses the actor's real head as a prop: no realistic facsimile was needed.

The three periods examined here all presented severed heads on stage, be they realistic, symbolic or utilitarian, for the purpose of thrilling and horrifying the audience. In the West, the severed head represented the utter destruction of the person and the triumph of the hero and/or state. In Japan, on the other hand, the severed head often was part of a larger narrative in which the head of a loved one was substituted for the head of an enemy, rendering the severed head less horrific than tragic. As the examples of the severed heads of Bush, Trump and Johnson remind us, severed head props still have tremendous power over us, not just for what they represent, but for how they are representing. Even the head of an enemy can become a horrific thing.

Notes

1. Andrew Sofer, *The Stage Life of Props* (Ann Arbor MI: University of Michigan Press, 2003).
2. Sofer, *The Stage Life of Props*, p. 90.
3. Sofer, *The Stage Life of Props*, p. 98.
4. Julia Kristeva, *The Severed Head: Capital Visions* (New York: Columbia University Press, 2012).
5. Kristeva, *The Severed Head*, p. 91.
6. Kristeva, *The Severed Head*, p. 121.
7. Regina Janes, *Losing Our Heads: Beheadings in Literature and Culture* (New York: New York University Press, 2005), p. 12.
8. This essay is not meant to be an exhaustive examination of the severed head on stage. Notable examples, such as the head of Pentheus in *The Bacchae* are not considered. Instead, I have chosen to focus on three cultures in which severed heads were presented in public performance more frequently.
9. Janes, *Losing Our Heads*, p. 14.
10. Richard J. Hand and Michael Wilson, *Performing Grand-Guignol: Playing the Theatre of Horror* (Exeter: University of Exeter Press, 2016), p. 198.
11. Janes, *Losing Our Heads*, p. 41.
12. Howard Engel, *Lord High Executioner: An Unashamed Look at Hangmen, Headsmen, and Their Kind* (Buffalo NY: Firefly, 1996), p. 113.
13. Janes, *Losing Our Heads*, p. 18.
14. See Michel Foucault, *Discipline and Punish: The Birth of the Prison* (New York: Vintage Books, 1995).
15. M. J. Hirrel, 'Severed heads on the Elizabethan stage', *The Review of English Studies* (15 March 2015), https://blog.oup.com/2015/03/severed-heads-elizabethan-plays/.

16. Hirrel, 'Severed heads'.
17. Hirrel, 'Severed heads'.
18. F. Martin, '"O die a rare example": Beheading the Body on the Jacobean Stage', *Early Modern Literary Studies*, 19 (2009), 1.
19. George Peele, *The Battle of Alcazar*, in C. Edelman (ed.), *The Stukeley Plays* (Manchester: Manchester University Press, 2005).
20. Hirrel, 'Severed heads'.
21. *Bunraku* and *kabuki* share a dramatic repertory, which is why these plays are presented as being both puppet plays and plays for the live *kabuki* performers as well.
22. E. Hart, 'Education: Kabuki Props', *Props* (21 February 2011), *www.props. eric-hart.com/Education/kabuki-props/*.
23. Hart, 'Education: Kabuki Props'.
24. S. L. Leiter, 'The Depiction of Violence on the Kabuki Stage', *Educational Theatre Journal*, 21/2 (May 1969), 151.
25. Leiter, 'The Depiction of Violence', 151.
26. Please note all Japanese names are given Japanese style, with surname first, followed by the given name.
27. The entire play, including 'Terakoya' has been translated into English by Stanleigh H. Jones, Jr: *Sugawara and the Secrets of Calligraphy* (New York: Columbia University Press, 1985).
28. Jones, *Sugawara and the Secrets*, p. 239.
29. Jones, *Sugawara and the Secrets*, pp. 241–2.
30. Mel Gordon, *Theatre of Fear and Horror: The Grisly Spectacle of the Grand Guignol of Paris, 1897–1962* (Port Townsend WA: Feral House, 2016), p. 10.
31. Emma McEvoy, *Gothic Tourism* (London: Palgrave McMillan, 2016), pp. 58–9.
32. McEvoy, *Gothic Tourism*, p. 60.
33. Pamela Pilbeam, *Madame Tussaud and the History of Waxworks* (London: Hambledon Continuum, 2003), pp. 53–9.
34. Pilbeam, *Madame Tussaud*, p. 57.
35. Engel, *Lord High Executioner*, p. 127.
36. Engel, *Lord High Executioner*, p. 127.
37. Oscar Wilde, *Salome*, in *The Plays of Oscar Wilde* (New York: Vintage, 1988), p. 122.
38. Wilde, *Salome*, p. 122.
39. Wilde, *Salome*, p. 124.
40. Hand and Wilson, *Performing Grand-Guignol*, pp. 196–7.

41. Richard J. Hand and Michael Wilson, *Grand-Guignol: The French Theatre of Horror* (Exeter: University of Exeter Press, 2002), p. 138.
42. Hand and Wilson, *Grand-Guignol*, p. 123.
43. Hand and Wilson, *Performing Grand-Guignol*, p. 197.
44. Hand and Wilson, *Performing Grand-Guignol*, pp. 272–5.

10

Dancing Haunted Legacies
Diana Szeinblum's *Alaska*

Jeanmarie Higgins

'Death and the Maiden', *Danse Macabre*

ROMAN POLANSKI'S 1995 film adaptation of Chilean playwright Ariel Dorfman's 1990 play, *Death and the Maiden*, opens as Paulina makes dinner for two in her charming seaside hilltop cottage on a stormy night in 'a country in South America after the fall of the dictatorship'. The phone service and electricity have cut out. She plates up her food, bringing it into a small interior room fitted out like an emergency bunker. There she eats her dinner by candlelight. Her lawyer husband Gerardo finally arrives home, explaining that he got a flat tyre, but a stranger had stopped to help him. Paulina is angry, not for his lateness, but for his failure to tell her that the president has appointed him to head a commission to try war crimes, news she heard on the radio earlier that day. Later that night, a man knocks at the door. The visitor is Dr Miranda, the stranger who drove Gerardo home; he is here to return Gerardo's spare tyre. While the men have a friendly drink, Paulina steals Miranda's car, drives it away, ransacks it and pushes it over a cliff into the sea.

Later, Paulina and Gerardo will come close to pushing the doctor himself over this cliff. We learn that while she was a student working for the revolution, Paulina was kidnapped, tortured, then released.[1] Certain that Miranda is her torturer from fifteen years ago, she walks back home to find the doctor asleep on her couch. She knocks him out with the butt of a gun, ties him onto a dining room chair, and recruits Gerardo into helping her get his confession on tape. What she found in the doctor's car that led to her destroying it was a cassette tape of Schubert's 1824 quartet, 'Death and the Maiden'. She explains to the men how much she had once loved the piece, but that hearing it now is a source of pain: 'Once I had to run out of a dinner party just to get away'. But, she adds, 'It's time for me to reclaim my Schubert'.[2] Paulina lists the tortures Dr Miranda meted out in 1977, which involved electrocution and confinement and – as Gerardo learns for the first time – raping her fourteen separate times, each time playing the Schubert quartet in order to, as the doctor said, 'soothe' her.

Schubert's 'Death and the Maiden' traces its lineage back to the late medieval visual and textual ideas collectively understood as the *danse macabre*. As Sophie Oosterwijk and Stefanie Knöll point out, *danse macabre* usually conjures up the image of the 1493 woodcut, 'Imago Mortis', that depicts Death in a graveyard playing a recorder as several skeletons dance along, but that *danse macabre* takes many forms: text, 'image, a superstition, a rite or enactment', and that 'in the course of its long recorded history from the fourteenth century to the present day it diversified yet further'.[3] Despite their diversity, two iterations emerge as particularly well known – the erotic Renaissance paintings of death and the maiden, and Schubert's eponymous quartet. Its multiplicity of forms notwithstanding, Oosterwijk and Knöll say, 'Its meaning is clear . . . Death comes to us all, irrespective of age or rank'.[4] Dorfman similarly uses this image of Death playing music while an innocent young woman is led to her death. As I will show, Oosterwijk and Knöll uncover a deeper dimension of the *danse macabre* motif that applies particularly to the performance under consideration in this chapter; that is, performances that are danced conversations between Death and the living. Of the various artistic forms the *danse macabre* takes, Oosterwijk and Knöll note: 'Most textual examples consist . . . of a dialogue between the living and Death, with little or no reference to dancing', and in art we may find 'an encounter like an arrest with the victims being marched away, irrespective of their status'.[5]

This chapter applies semiotic performance analysis to performance texts as responses to the Dirty War, the series of nationalist government actions beginning with the Argentine military's overthrow of the Peronist government in March 1976 through to the despotic government's defeat in the Falklands War that inevitably led to a democratically elected government in October 1983. Although I focus on contemporary Argentine choreographer Diana Szeinblum's 2008 play *Alaska*, I begin with a brief discussion of Griselda Gambaro's 1974 play-text *Information for Foreigners*.[6] As will become clear, Dorfman's Paulina can be seen as a character who might have escaped from Gambaro's nightmarish play world, living to tell the tale of her torture where others could not. Interestingly, both provide a range of uses of domestic *mises-en-scène* – from Gambaro's call for artists to perform her play in an actual house, to Szeinblum's insistence that *Alaska*'s performers 'inhabit' the dance space. No matter how directly these artists engage domestic spaces, their use of the domestic assigns value to private sphere places as sites of trauma and healing in response to the public sphere events of war. This value extends to the experiences of the women, children and men who inhabited these private, domestic spaces, and whose presence at home points to the disappearance from home of so many who were kidnapped and disappeared during the war. By valuing the experiences of those who are traditionally at home – and who were, perhaps, 'at home' during the Dirty War; that is to say, *not* soldiers or revolutionaries – these performance texts open a conversation about the legacies of the Dirty War on those who came of age after 1983.

Semiotics as a Critical Practice

To analyse the uses of domestic space in these texts, and to communicate in particular how Szeinblum's work stages a 'dialogue between the living and Death', or a *danse macabre*, I use a semiotic analysis informed by both historical and contemporary critical practices. It is sometimes argued that semiotic performance analysis exists more vibrantly in the history of dramatic criticism than in the present. For example, in the *Cambridge Introduction to Theatre Studies*, Christopher Balme writes, 'In its optimistic excesses, semiotics tended towards over-systemization and to the creation of a metaphorical vocabulary that was continually making a transfer from linguistic terms to non-verbal phenomena'.[7] Here Balme alludes to the early work of theatre semioticians Erika Fischer-Lichte and Patrice Pavis, who, proceeding from Tadeusz Kowzan's 1968 essay 'The Sign in the Theatre', employ taxonomies of stage languages that suggest a mathematical rigour to the practice of analysing performance, which leaves out crucial elements such as audience response. Nonetheless, Balme continues, poststructuralist revisions to semiotic practice, particularly through the work of Roland Barthes, have rescued semiotics from its place in the history of performance analysis as a quaint tool.

Still, semiotics remains a key tool for writers of criticism to organise thoughts about performance so that they may be written and shared. Thus, a second goal of this chapter is to explore classical semiotic theory as a critical practice. Just as I hope to show how domestic space organises these works, I also hope to demonstrate how semiotic practice can coax sign systems to the surface so that the critical writer can work with them. To do this, I follow Pavis's more recent articulation of an expanded notion of *mise-en-scène*, a term he reframes as encompassing a world beyond the scenic design and staging of any given performance.[8] Pavis's re-historicisation of *mise-en-scène* holds that performers, playwrights and audiences are equally responsible for creating meaning as are scenic, lighting and costume designers. Pavis opens the door for discussing the critic's role in meaning-making as well, especially in the context of semiotic analysis as a common language that nonetheless hosts a multiplicity of uses.

In the case of this chapter, by looking at performance responses to national trauma using domestic space as an analytic, I use a variety of semiotic lenses – from stark cataloguing of signs under categories used to articulate sign systems, to early theories of offstage (versus onstage) signifying processes, to contemporary theorists' uses of a semiotics of absence. All three of these ways of looking at these performances contribute to a common theme running through the texts under consideration here; that is, that the presence or absence of home and the things of home marks a common legacy of trauma on first and second-generation survivors of Argentina's Dirty War. Further, taking my inspiration from Gaston Bachelard, I connect home as a 'symbolic world' to performances as symbolic worlds, and as such connect the practice of semiotics – with all its attendant concern with signs such as symbols – to the uses of domestic spaces in performance.

Transgenerational Trauma

Holocaust literature and trauma studies scholar Gabriele Schwab links second-generation trauma to the shaping of art. In *Haunting Legacies: Violent Histories and Transgenerational Trauma*, Schwab contends that trauma is passed from generation to generation, and that trauma shapes narrative strategies in the writings of second-generation survivors:

> What I call 'haunting legacies' are things hard to recount or even to remember, the results of a violence that holds an unrelenting grip on memory yet is deemed unspeakable. The psychic core of violent histories includes what has been repressed or buried in the unreachable psychic recesses. The legacies of violence not only haunt the actual victims but also are passed on through generations.[9]

Schwab's objects of analysis are second-generation novels, poetry and non-fiction writing authored by children of Holocaust survivors. Schwab's analytic may be used to understand how dramatic texts and performed narratives are shaped by trauma. For this we may turn to contemporary performance theories of time and space such as Andrew Sofer's useful idea that theatre rehearses trauma's effect, producing 'an inaccessible history that can't be owned'.[10] I show how a contemporary dance/theatre piece authored by an Argentine artist one generation removed from the Dirty War, Diana Szeinblum's *Alaska*, is an instance of history-telling that stems from national transgenerational trauma.

Information for Foreigners

The most well-known twentieth-century Argentinian play is likely to be Gambaro's *Information for Foreigners*. The 1974 play is meant to be performed in an actual house. *Foreigners* stages a tour where several audience groups follow guides through a house with individual rooms that contain or promise to contain various theatrical scenes. The play's connection to Argentina's Dirty War is likewise clear. Its *mise-en-scène* is a metaphor for the placelessness of the *desaparecida*, citizens that disappeared during the Dirty War; the stage space signifies a place where political prisoners are being kept – those who have been captured, detained and sometimes killed by the government – presumably while the war itself is being fought elsewhere. Because audience members are positioned as tourists who have been promised entertainment, the play indicts the silent compliance of audience/bystanders as well. Most of the entertainment that the audience is promised – which includes grotesque adaptations of scenes from Lorca and Shakespeare, 'backstage' tableaux of brutalities such as rape and torture, and a reenactment of the Milgram Experiment – happens in hallways and stairways that are on the way to supposedly better, more complete scenes. In this way, the tour staged in *Information for Foreigners* is constantly deferred, and along the way people are tortured, killed and mourned.

Information for Foreigners predates and thus predicts the Dirty War. As is now well known, a dominant strategy of those in power was to kidnap dissidents and suspected dissidents, as the Chilean character of Paulina was in *Death and the Maiden*. Many of these captured people were never seen again. Gambaro's domestic setting reinforces the contradictory ideas that the Dirty War is happening behind closed doors in private spaces, but that these spaces are also homelike and familiar. This house's glimpsed, secret, individual scenes of torture *are* what constitutes the Dirty War. The fictional house that Gambaro invents in *Foreigners* may have been a construction of imagination in 1974 when the play was written, but it was a prophetic one, since it was later revealed that these kidnappings were a collective pretext to mass murder. As it turned out, the *desaparecida* were never really missing, since to be 'missing' implies that one might be found. Rather, in addition to being missing from their homes, the disappeared were dead. With this hindsight, the house Gambaro posits becomes a tour of a purgatory or a graveyard.

Alaska

The Dirty War ended in 1983 when Gambaro was in her mid-fifties and director Diana Szeinblum was nineteen years old. *Foreigners* takes place inside an actual house. In sharp contrast, *Alaska* unfolds on a rectangle of white dance floor or marley, in itself a symbol of abstraction, producing 'home' nearly exclusively in its offstage spaces. Szeinblum says she called her 2008 play *Alaska* because the name evokes a place that everyone knows, but that most have never visited.[11] By directing her four dancers to use personal memories 'to express with the body all what they couldn't say' at particular traumatic moments in their lives, Szeinblum creates a movement landscape of unspoken individual experiences, reinforcing what Schawb refers to as the simultaneously 'unrelenting' and 'unspeakable' grip of trauma. I read *Alaska* as a collective autobiographical piece that stages the cultural trauma of Argentina's Dirty War (1976–83) and its legacies on the next generation, not because Szeinblum frames the performance in this way (she does not), but because the age and national identity of the artists, in concert with the dance's movement vocabulary, constantly suggest common imageries associated with the war.[12]

Still, Szeinblum does frame her play in terms of domestic space, writing about 'the body as tenant of spaces'. In a programme note, she explains the title, writing that *Alaska* produces 'a supposed interior place, that can be seen as the existence of a last room'. Further, the piece posits the body as a place where trauma is kept at bay, away from consciousness. The body is a 'container of memories where everything that has not been said regarding a personal experience is kept. A place where experiences, sensations, emotions, memories are lodged in a chaotic way'. If the body lodges memories chaotically, then dance attempts to give them order. Szeinblum continues:

> The play will attempt to translate what physical shape had or did not have a real-life situation at the moment of its experience. Four characters desperately inhabit that space. Through an extreme physical language, they seek to arrive at that state of the past. Appealing to the memory of what was lived to find in the body the experience of what has not been revealed. Alaska, a place we all know but nobody ever went to.[13]

Although it is through the theorising and not necessarily the staging, Szeinblum engages the interplay of home and theatre in ways similar to Gambaro, as conversations between the living and Death.

In contrast to the 1974 *Foreigners*, which stages traumas happening simultaneously in hidden rooms and in plain sight, I consider *Alaska* as a response to the national trauma brought on by the war and its aftermaths. Specifically, I consider how Szeinblum's dancers' bodies embody memories of the War on behalf of others, but through the lens of their personal traumatic experiences. As I have noted, Schwab calls for a literature whose very structures are shaped by trauma. I find an answer to Schwab's provocation in Szeinblum's dance, where the repeated transmission of trauma from body to body develops a dialectic of sign systems of torture and dehumanisation that viewers can connect to the Dirty War, to the dancers' onstage bodies, and back to the Dirty War again.

Alaska: a Place that Most have Never Seen

In the first moments of *Alaska*, a barefooted young man (Pablo Lugones) sits in a hard chair; a sign around his neck reads '*Estoy desesperado*'.[14] A young woman stands beside him (Alejandra Ferreyra Ortiz).[15] Knees locked, she swings forward from the waist. She flexes her wrists against her inner thighs, pressing her knuckles hard into her flesh as she swings back up to standing. She stares at the man in the chair. He pays her no attention. She performs this phrase twenty-six times. Another dancer joins (Lucas Condró); he sits on the floor to the other side and behind the seated performer. Legs stretched in front of him, he moves his arms mechanically in a gesture that repeats throughout the piece; while the performer's arms alternatively flap and soar as if flying, the rest of the body remains connected, even bound, to the floor. A fourth dancer enters (Leticia Mazur); she stands at the shoulder of the first woman. Mazur exhales forcefully, rhythmically and repeatedly. She holds one of her hands under her rib cage, as if to display the mechanism of her breathing in a dispassionate, forensic way. The first woman (Ortiz) begins to jump into the air over and over in a frenetic loop of balletic leaps. Now the stage is hosting three dancers who repeat phrases that signify torture, flight and flight/torture while the fourth 'desperate' dancer sits still in a chair, paying them no mind. *Alaska* is built from such brutal repeated movement phrases, most of which fall into one of three types: flight and flying; transforming from person to object and back to person; and disappearance. In addition, each time a dancer enters the space, it is from a position on the edge of the white marley, building a complementary sign system of watching, waiting and witnessing. Together these signs systems of flying, torture, disappearance and witnessing bring to mind the Dirty War without it being expressed in words.

Flying

When interviewed about his role during the Dirty War, sending people to their deaths by dropping them from aeroplanes, Navy Captain Francisco Scilingo uses the language of psychoanalysis, talking of repressed memories, and setting his remembered scenes as if in a dream:

> There are important details but it is difficult for me to talk about them. I think about them and I repress them. They were undressed while being unconscious and when the flight commander gave the order, depending on the location of the plane, the hatch was opened and they were thrown out naked, one by one... As I was quite nervous about the situation, I almost fell and tumbled into the abyss... I stumbled and they grabbed me.[16]

Gestures of aeroplanes and flying connect the dance to the mass murder of Argentinians dropped from planes during the War. These gestures of planes and other machines are found throughout the dance, most notably in a scene that repeats where Condró and Lugones sit side by side, as if pilot and co-pilot. Sitting in chairs, they perform movement phrases in unison, all of which involve dealing with an impediment like a frozen arm or the inability to separate their own clasped hands. It is a dream that Scilingo might have, his repressed memories expressed in a dance of flying an aeroplane against his will – awkwardly flying (like a pilot) while immobilised (like his victims).

In the most free-feeling scene of *Alaska*, all four dancers work in rotating quartets. One dancer runs, the other three pursue. As the first dancer leaps into the sky, the other three catch her or else push her higher up into the clouds. They repeat this score over and over to the underscore of viola and piano. Their poses are athletic, the heights they reach sometimes dangerous. Ortiz freezes, crouched in mid-air. Mazur stands on the outstretched palms of Condró and Lugones. Dance critic Lisa Rinehart's response to *Alaska* as 'a searing trek over emotionally scorched earth' is apt. Making a connection to demons, Rinehart describes the dancers putting themselves 'through some kind of exorcism'. The conflation of the everyday/domestic with the traumatic is best seen through Rinehart's observation that 'clothing is stripped off like skin flayed from a corpse', calling to mind the idea of dead bodies treated in the careless way that Scilingo describes.[17]

Person to Object to Person

Another sign system that develops is that of transforming (animate) people into (inanimate) objects, calling to mind again Scilingo's relationship to his victims during his gruesome killing flights. Dance critic Ryan Tracy of *The Brooklyn Rail* notes of *Alaska* that 'one of Szeinblum's chief tools is her ability, in collaboration with her performers, to turn a person into an object and then back into a person again'.[18] Although framed as an expression of the choreographer and dancers' skill, Tracy's comment is also a testament to the chilling effect of the thin line between 'dead' and 'alive' that the dancers call to mind. In the second section of the dance, Ortiz, Condró and Lugones manipulate Mazur's body, posing her in a reverse plough, her back facing the audience so that she looks like both an abused body

– perhaps a decapitated body – and a guitar. They pose her so many times, regarding her with stony equanimity, that she ceases to seem human. It is the look of a group of curators installing a museum piece. Throughout, the plaintive accompaniment of the piano and viola punctuate each pose, then fade out, the music gaining strength each time Mazur achieves her inanimate pose.

Disappearance

Alaska's many scenes vary among solos and dances for two, three or all four dancers. As one or two dancers dance, another one or two might stand at the edge of the white floor, watching or walking the perimeter, managing to seem disaffected and menacing at the same time. The dancers do not enter a scene so much as they appear; they do not exit so much as they disappear. In the final sequence of *Alaska*, Condró repeats the same simple phrase for six full minutes as the lights occasionally fade, dip, surge, fade out and surge again. The movements that make up the repertoire of this final sequence include lying prostrate; standing while being pulled sidewise from the torso; covering the eyes; and reaching down as if to stroke the head of a child. Just when the sequence starts to induce trance in the viewer, Condró adds another phrase, that of cradling a child in his arms, so briefly that the audience cannot be sure whether they saw it until, of course, he repeats the gesture moments later. Together these gestures mark a child who is/was here/there, but who has disappeared.

The other three dancers witness this solo dance, moving around the space occasionally, watching some parts of it until they too disappear. The dance ends with a light fade so slow that the audience is not sure when the dance is over, or indeed if it is over, as the sound fades out before Condró disappears from view altogether. If, as Herbert Blau has ably shown in his many works about the limits and extremities of theatre, all theatre disappears, then all performance is in some way about disappearance. Blau writes that it is the 'actor's mortality that is the actual subject [of a performance] for he is right there dying in front of [our] eyes'.[19]

Some movements and phrases in *Alaska* clearly signify stress and pain, and some signify rape – stress signified by the repetition of phrases of absurd durations, for example, and specific gestures (such as Ortiz's digging her knuckles into her thighs as if to open them over and over) signifying rape. Other parts of the dance are both more narrative and less physically intense than the opening scenes. Some evoke traumatic memories of failed romance or lost friendship, a narrative response to a prompt for the performers to delve into traumatic memories. In one sequence of two scenes, two of the dancers embrace, a third enters and kisses one of them without the other seeing it. This new pair embraces, leaving the original dancer alone. A scene of betrayal. The scene that follows is a kind of a courtship duet. A shirtless dancer (Lugones) plays the spoons for one of the women (Mazur). He plays for such a long time and on his bare flesh that the audience can see how (literally) painful it is for him. The spoons leave marks. Mazur watches for a while, vaguely interested, then wanders away, leaving him alone, in a reversal of the pattern that no dancer ever joins others on the marley unless she or he first hovers at the end of the dance space, observing.

Signifying Across Generations

Calling on the work of Hannah Arendt and Frantz Fanon, Schwab asserts that 'the collective or communal silencing of violent histories leads to a transgenerational transmission of trauma and the spectre of an involuntary repetition of cycles of violence'.[20] Halfway through *Alaska*, Condró pulls up a chair and sits alone, facing the audience. He takes us in and then announces, 'Now is the part of the performance where you get to ask me personal questions'. It is not an actor's studied attempt at delivering a line. No, Condró is out of breath from his athletic performance when he gasps these words out to us. On the night I attended *Alaska* in Seattle, Washington at On the Boards, an audience member asked Condró: 'What's your idea of the perfect date?' 'Having sex', Condró quickly replied, his response drawing nervous laughter. Another question: 'Is your father proud of you?' 'Yes'. At that point, Condró left the stage. Although the questions vary from night to night, the questions from this night's performance happened to hail the young dancer's father into the stage space, two generations coexisting for just a moment. Using the dramaturgical and kinetic strategies of repetition and disappearance, *Alaska* is a history recounted by and for the next generation.

In the foreword to the 2006 collection *Torture: A Collection*, *Death and the Maiden* playwright Dorfman says that 'terror, the aftermath of torture, once it has burrowed into us, is not conquered in one revelatory flash. It is a slow, zigzag process, just like memory itself'. Dorfman recounts the story of Maria Josepha Ruiz-Tagle, a woman whose father Eugenio Ruiz-Tagle Orrega was killed during the Pinochet regime. Maria Josepha found some letters behind a framed photo of herself as a child. These papers told the truth about her father's death from unrelenting torture, what her mother had always told her was a quick death by firing squad. Dorfman relates that the man who initiated the beatings that eventually killed her father turned out to be Commander of the Chilean air force, and furthermore, that many people knew who he was but did not acknowledge it. In 2000, at a ceremony commemorating the fall of Pinochet, Maria Josepha read a letter that she wrote to her father, saying all the things she wished she could have told him but could not. 'When you bring something out from its hiding place, other things emerge', Dorfman says.[21]

As Pavis would term it, *Alaska* builds its own sign system of domesticity and absence that signifies through a range of stage languages. The rediscovery of semiotics alongside the rediscovery of *mise-en-scène* provides a way to analyse performance in cooperation and in conversation with artists and their dramatic and performed texts. This semiotic analysis of a play performed by Argentinian artists who are one generation removed from the Dirty War engages domestic spaces in hidden ways, reinforcing Szeinblum's insistence that the repressed spaces of memory are closed rooms that are unlocked through performance. Theories of transgenerational trauma combine with the spatial notions of theatre and memory (Sofer) to add a temporal one. In this way, Szeinblum's staging also signals across time to join in the complex history of the *danse macabre*.

Notes

1. It is commonly believed that Chilean exile Dorfman set this play in Chile after the fall of Pinochet, although the country is not named in the play.
2. In the end, Miranda admits his guilt. Referring to the dictatorship, he says, 'I was sorry it ended'.
3. S. Oosterwijk and S. Knöll, 'Introduction', in S. Oosterwijk and S. Knöll (eds), *Mixed Metaphors: The Danse Macabre in Medieval and Early Modern Europe* (Newcastle upon Tyne: Cambridge Scholars Publishing, 2011), p 3.
4. Oosterwijk and Knöll, p. 10.
5. Oosterwijk and Knöll, p. 9.
6. Notably, a piece by Szeinblum's Argentinian contemporary, Lola Arias, *Mi Vida Después*, stages its ensemble members' parents' lives, representing

their parents' bodies by clothing left hollow, on a stage filled with chairs. See Noe Montez, *Memory, Transitional Justice, and Theatre in Postdictatorship Argentina* (Carbondale IL: Southern Illinois University Press, 2018), pp. 116–28.
7. Christopher Balme, *The Cambridge Introduction to Theatre Studies* (Cambridge: Cambridge University Press, 2008), p. 83.
8. Patrice Pavis, *Contemporary* Mise-en-Scène: *Staging Theatre Today* (London: Routledge, 2013).
9. Gabrielle Schwab, *Haunting Legacies: Violent Histories and Transgenerational Trauma* (New York: Columbia University Press, 2010), p. 1.
10. Andrew Sofer, *Dark Matter: Invisibility in Drama, Theater and Performance* (Ann Arbor MI: University of Michigan Press, 2013), p. 119.
11. Although the performance is danced, containing none but a brief segment of audience conversation as text, Szeinblum calls *Alaska* a play, and refers to herself as its director rather than choreographer.
12. With one extreme exception: at a silent moment of the piece, a gigantic dining room table falls from the fly space, breaking into four equal pieces on the floor.
13. Diana Szeinblum's programme note for *Alaska*, On the Boards Seattle, Washington. An archival copy of the performance programme is available on the On the Boards TV website *www.ontheboards.tv*.
14. 'I am desperate'.
15. Director, Diana Szeinblum. Music by Ulises Conti. Performers: Lucas Condró, Leticia Mazur, Alejandra Ferreyra Ortíz, Pablo Lugones. Costumes by Cecilia Alasia. This chapter is based on my viewing of *Alaska* at On the Boards in Seattle, Washington in November 2009, and on subsequent viewings of the archival film available at *ontheboards.tv*.
16. Quoted in A. C. G. M. Robben, 'How Traumatized Societies Remember: The Aftermath of Argentina's Dirty War', *Cultural Critique*, 59 (winter 2005), 120.
17. L. Rinehart, 'Rugged Terrain', 7 February 2008, *danceviewtimes.com*.
18. R. Tracy, 'Dance States of a Theatrical Mind: Diana Szeinblum's *Alaska*', *The Brooklyn Rail*, March 2008, *www.brooklynrail.org*.
19. Herbert Blau, *Blooded Thought: Occasions of Theatre* (New York: Performing Arts Journal Publications, 1982), p. 134.
20. Schwab, *Haunting Legacies*, p. 46.
21. A. Dorfman, 'The Tyranny of Terror: Is Torture Inevitable in Our Century and Beyond?', in S. Levinson (ed.), *Torture: A Collection* (Oxford: Oxford University Press, 2004), pp. 3–18.

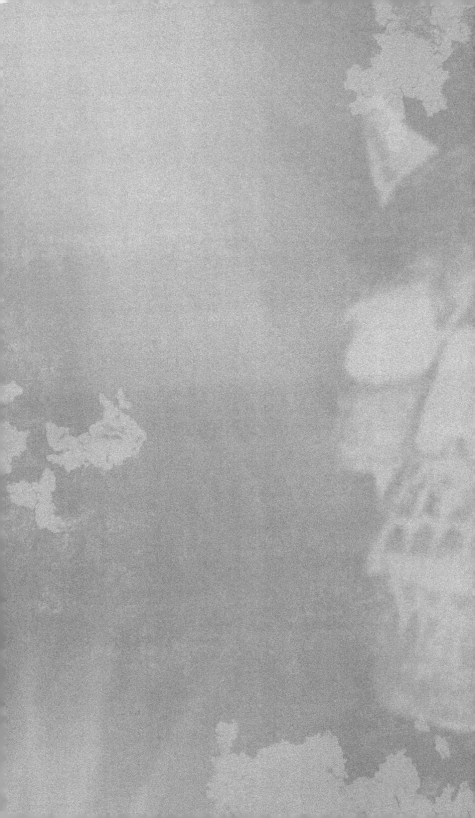

11

'To Die Over and Over Inside My Body'

Three Deaths in Hijikata Tatsumi's *Butoh*

J. Hoay-Fern Ooi

THE FORM OF DANCE known today as *butoh* was first conceived by Hijikata Tatsumi and Ohno Kazuo as *ankoku butoh* ('dance of utter darkness') in the late 1950s. At first glance, the visual elements of *butoh* seemingly echo that of *kabuki* or *noh*. The white body paint used in *kabuki* again appears in *butoh*, and the leaden movements of *butoh* could be said to be drawn from *noh*. It is easy to regard *butoh* as essentially Japanese, a postmodern explosion of its formal and traditional arts, allowing for *ankoku* ('darkness') to erupt on stage, but these links are superficial.[1] Though it would undergo dramatic evolutions, early *butoh* drew heavily from Surrealism, the European *avant garde* and German *Neuer Tanz*.[2] And according to Motofuji Akiko, *butoh*'s adoption of the term *ankoku* actually comes from American film noir, which was then translated as *ankoku eiga*.[3] The significant presence of the West towards and against which *butoh* shaped itself is unsurprising. Japan's 1945 defeat in World War II was preceded by concentrated efforts at modernisation and Westernisation under the Meiji restoration. This was immediately followed by intense but uneasy bouts of political, economic and social change during military occupation by the Allied Powers from 1945 to 1952.[4]

Given both Hijikata[5] and Ohno's[6] wartime experience, there also exists the tendency to conflate the violence of *butoh* with post-war Japanese trauma. Scholars such as Paula Marie Orlando[7] and Owen O'Toole,[8] for example, read in the 'shaking, stumbling' performer, with 'shaved head and a face painted white' the return of the repressed.[9] Adam Broinowski similarly writes of how 'the atomic bombs dropped by the United States ... and the hibakusha (people exposed to the atomic blast) it produced can be seen reflected' in *butoh*.[10]

While I do not disagree with their interpretations, reading *butoh* as stemming primarily from trauma suffered during World War II de-emphasises the other forms of death also manifest in its revolutionary form – by which I mean the ending of past and then-present cultural and aesthetic values. Vicki Sanders links the physical and political devastation suffered by Japan to the explosion of its artists' ties to the traditional arts, but also Western modernism. Sanders makes the claim that Hijikata's *butoh* emerged as 'his country lay in ruins, when there was an opportunity to change a rigid class structure, to throw off the mantle of Westernism, to rediscover and redefine what it meant to be Japanese'.[11] I want to suggest that Hijikata goes further than interrogating post-war Japanese identity; indeed, *butoh* can also be read as an interrogation of subjectivity, the living spirit embodied in the performer. I argue that this third death in *butoh* should be understood as a form of communion, an initiation through the symbolic death of the performer.

Butoh and the Death of the Material Body

Butoh's displacing of pre-war Japanese aesthetics, culture and identity is immediately evident from the beginning of Hijikata's career. Though Hijikata had already been performing a few years prior, the first performance choreographed and staged as *butoh* premiered in 1959 at the All Japan Dance Festival.[12] It borrows its title *Kinjiki* ('*Forbidden Colours*') from Mishima Yukio's novel of the same name.[13] Hijikata played the role of Man and Ohno Yoshito, Ohno's son, played Young Man.[14] Performed in near darkness with barely any accompanying music, *Kinjiki* featured elements of homosexuality, bestiality and sexual assault. The performance begins with Man pursuing Young Man who flees desperately from him. Man then gifts Young Man a chicken, who places it between his legs. Young Man sinks to the ground, suffocating the chicken. Man and Young

Man are then entwined on the ground. Pre-recorded breathing and moaning plays as Man shouts, *'Je t'aime, je t'aime'*. The performance ends in stark silence. Although *Kinjiki* outraged audience members and resulted in Hijikata and Ohno leaving the Association for Contemporary Performing Arts, Hijikata would restage *Kinjiki* later the same year for the *6-nin no Avuangyarudo: 9-gatsu 5-ka 6-ji no Kai* ('*6 Avantgardists: 5 September 6:00 Gathering*').[15]

Kinjiki 2 was structured into two acts, 'Death of Divine' followed by 'Death of the Young Man', each with two scenes. Ohno played the ageing prostitute Divine from Jean Genet's 1943 debut novel *Notre-Dame-des-Fleurs* ('*Our Lady of Flowers*'). Other elements of Genet's novel, including homosexuality, poverty and abjection, also appear. The first scene begins with Divine seated in the audience, slowly rising to the stage. In the second scene, a group of men attack Divine, using feathers as arrows. She writhes about in agony, then falls over and dies. The men carry Divine's body offstage. The first half of the second act repeats *Kinjiki*. In the second scene, ropes lying slack on the stage are snapped taut by a group of boys, hitting Young Man on his chest, back and underarms. The boys then wrap one of the ropes around Young Man's neck. Two boys saw away at the rope as the others taunt Young Man. He falls to the ground and dies; the boys drag him away.

The violence in both performances is physically inflicted upon the performer's body. In *Kinjiki*, the chicken dies, then Man assaults Young Man. In *Kinjiki 2*, two groups assault Divine and Young Man and they both die. Sexual violence is suffered by individuals whose abjection, like their namesakes in *Kinjiki* and *Notre-Dame-des-Fleurs*, is tied to their social identity, that of perceived aberrant sexuality. Following *Kinjiki*, Hijikata would choreograph and perform *Anma* ('*Masseur*') in 1963, *Barairo dansu* ('*Rose-coloured Dance*') in 1965, *Tomato* in 1966, and *Keijijougaku* ('*Emotion in Metaphysics*') in 1967.[16] Similar to *Kinjiki*, these early *butoh* works exhibit weak thematic ties to wartime trauma or violence, serving more as explorations of the body's physicality and its viewing by the audience. As Bruce Baird has pointed out, early *butoh* is a product of its time.[17] Hijikata spent the 1960s working alongside Japanese Neo-Dada and Anti-Art movements. These groups were primarily preoccupied with the contestation of social norms and aesthetic boundaries, and their performances were sexually transgressive and eager to shock.

Hijikata Tatsumi to nihonjin: Nikutai no hanran ('*Hijikata Tatsumi and Japanese People: Rebellion of the Body*') was staged in 1968 and marks the middle phase of the artist's career. Throughout the performance, Hijikata embodied and abandoned a series of personas identifiable only through their accompanying costumes, each dizzying scene similarly clashing and blending into the next. Hijikata's continued experimenting with 'bending joints in the wrong way' would infuse his gestures with a tense instability, mirroring his exploration of shifting social identities.[18] The performance begins with Hijikata in a bridal *kimono* worn backwards, dismounting from a cart. He then disrobes, revealing an erect, golden phallus strapped to his gaunt body. Thrusting his hips violently, he moves about erratically, at some point with his shoulders on the ground and the movement of his feet pushing his body round. Hijikata reappears in the next scene wearing a red gown with black rubber gloves, imitating flamenco gestures. Hijikata's next series of costume changes include a white suit with top hat, then a red T-shirt dress with a girdle and long, ruffled can-can skirt, followed by a girlish, short *kimono* coupled with knee-high socks. His walking, bouncing and squatting movements are all subtly marred by either the over-exerting of force or loss of control over his limbs. The performance ends with stagehands suspending Hijikata above the audience, using ropes tied around each of his arms and both legs. The stagehands then lower Hijikata, who remounts the cart waiting for him, carrying him backstage.

Unlike earlier *butoh* works, *Hijikata Tatsumi to nihonjin* does away with stable character identities and the idea of the docile body. The theme of sexual violence from *Kinjiki* reappears in this performance, but unlike before, where violence was physically inflicted onto individuals by others, sexuality and abjection were stable markers socially imposed onto material bodies, and death was represented by the literal death of the characters played on stage. The new brazen sexuality emanating from *Hijikata Tatsumi to nihonjin* transcends any individual character Hijikata plays, threatening to spill forth and overturn Japanese propriety and tradition. This abjection is doubled through the *Rebellion of the Body*, manifesting in the inelegant and erratic gestures, displacing the conventional image of the dancer, whose body is healthy, beautiful and sane.

In the following years, Hijikata would experiment with methods of forcing *butoh* performers into further relinquishing control, not just of their material bodies but also their subjectivities. Staged in 1972, the series of five performances known collectively as *Shiki no tame no nijunanaban* ('*Twenty-Seven Nights for the Four Seasons*') marks the transition from Hijikata's middle to mature period.[20] Set in rural Japan, memories of his childhood and wartime trauma surface in these performances, 'What Tohoku exports are horses, women, soldiers, and rice'.[21] Most significantly, in contrast to previous *butoh* works, *Hosotan* (*'Story of Smallpox'*), *Susamedama* (*'Dissolute Jewel'*), *Gaishiko* (*'Thoughts of an Insulator'*), *Nadare-ame* (*'Avalanche Candy'*) and *Gibasan* (*'Seaweed Granny'*) were all choreographed using Hijikata's newly developed system.[22]

Hosotan begins with Hijikata alone, dressed in a *kimono* and with wig done up in the style of married women.[23] Hunched over and walking across the stage, his movements are shaky and uncertain. He falls on his back, then returns to his upright position, still crouching. Six naked and tattooed men appear, moving powerfully, if somewhat erratically, across the stage, spinning, falling, doing *karate* chops, front and back flips. In the next scene, a puppet chanter is heard telling the story of *Terakoya* (*'Village School'*) as three women in *kimono* clatter about in wooden *geta*.[24] Seated on the ground, the women touch their *geta* to their faces, then stamp the *geta* on the ground with their hands. Ashikawa Yoko appears then leaps onto the shoulder of fellow dancer Waguri Yukio, who is dressed in a train conductor's hat and sash. Hijikata reappears in the next scene, alone again and on the ground wearing only a loin cloth. His emaciated body is in stark view as he slowly attempts to stand but fails and collapses three times. Thin strands of cotton gauze are wrapped around his body. The women then reappear carrying old futons, now trembling and dressed in rags. Hijikata finally stands, limbs still twisted and crouched over, moving stiffly. His body shudders as he puts each foot down on the ground with too much force. The women sink to the ground, shaking. The performance ends with the dancers standing to bow, then retreating.

All five performances comprising *Shiki no tame no nijunanaban* feature the psychological and physical hardship of life in rural Japan. In *Hosotan*, this strain is made visible through the disease and ugliness inscribed onto the bodies of the peasants, but what makes Hijikata's mature *butoh* so haunting is how this struggle with death is not merely externalised through learned physical gestures, in the frail shaking and stumbling of the performer's limbs, but also internalised through Hijikata's method of instruction. He recognises that 'thinking about the strangeness of our bodies or manipulating them through various training techniques is not enough'.[25] Following *Shiki no tame no nijunanaban*, Hijikata retired from performing, but continued to develop his system of choreographic methodology and notation. He choreographed and directed *Hitogata* (*'Human Shape'*), *Shomen no isho* (*'Costume en Face'*) and *Geisenjo no okugata* (*'Lady on a Whale String*) in 1976 and Ohno's performance *Ra aruhenchina sho* ('*Admiring La Argentina*') in 1977. His last work is Tohoku *Kabuki Keikaku 4* ('*Tohoku Kabuki Plan 4*') in 1985.[26]

Butoh-tai and the Death of Subjectivity

That Hijikata intends for *butoh* to reject the choreographic systematisation of movements is evident. In an interview with Jean Viala and Nourit Masson-Sekine, Hijikata claims how 'in the Stanislavski system or in the techniques of other national dances, it is to a certain degree that such and such an effect can be produced, that the articulation can be categorized', 'thus man finds himself in a narrow and constricted world'.[27] Taking a broader view of things, *butoh* as a genre or family of dance beyond Hijikata has no recognisable style either. It is difficult to categorically determine what is or is not *butoh*, what different *butoh* works have in common and what defines *butoh*. Similar to other postmodern explorations, whether in theatre, dance, art or even literature, *butoh* does not adhere to a standardised set of postures or gestures. There is no official methodology or even vocabulary shared between *butoh* performers of different schools. It is important, however, that *butoh*'s transgression of structured choreography does not itself become structured, that it perpetually contests its own authority, style and method.

Unlike more systematised forms of dance such as waltz or ballet, where choreography for each specific performance must be learned through external instruction and dancers strive to physically depict the figure portrayed in the choreographic notation as closely as possible, *butoh* movements emerge instead from the depths of the performers themselves. As Hijikata stresses, 'in our body history, something is hiding in our subconscious, collected in our unconscious body, which will appear in each detail of our expression'.[28] What lies at the heart of this emergence is not merely the memory of, the performer's act of recalling, but the forceful reanimation of the dead who return to inhabit the body of the performer, necessitating also the surrender of their subjectivity, consciousness or mind. 'I would like to make the dead gestures inside my body die one more time and make the dead themselves dead again', affirms Hijikata.[29]

A key to understanding *butoh* philosophy and how it shapes Hijikata's methodology is the term *butoh-tai*, often translated as '*butoh*-body'.[30] Because *tai* in Japanese connotes the unified mind-body, some have translated *tai* as 'attitude'. I believe the term '*butoh*-being' (as verb and also noun) more accurately captures Hijikata's intentions. He repeatedly stressed against 'expression' in doing *butoh*, which must instead be experienced as a 'convulsion of existence',[31] a form of being and becoming. In performing *Hosotan*, it is not the material body that the *butoh* performer must learn to express and control, conveying weakness through physical sways and minute trembles, but rather their entire being (body and mind) that must be surrendered and given over to death, 'to have a person who has already died over and over inside my body'.[32] For Hata Kanoko, *butoh* movement emerges from within 'an unstandable body that cannot be stood by volition or an uncontrollable body that cannot be operated by intention',[33] Hijikata's *butoh* is 'a dead body standing with his life at risk'.[34]

I base my reading of Hijikata's *butoh*'s methodology on Georges Bataille's notion of inner experience and communication. Inner experience is born from the 'desire to be every thing, to identify with the entirety of universe' by surpassing one's individual boundaries, leading to communication.[35] What Bataille means by communication is not the transmission of ideas from one distinct subjectivity to another, such as the delivery of instruction from choreographer to performer, but a flow 'like a streaming of electricity' that passes through and ruptures any individual, opening into an experience of community.[36] Bataille distinguishes between sovereign communication and 'weak communication', the latter being what Hijikata would term mere 'expression' or figurative mimicry. Sovereign communication must exceed mere destabilisation, the 'subject, is thrown outside of itself, beyond itself' into a shared experience of anguish 'at the limit of nothingness'.[37] To perform Hijikata's *butoh* is to risk possession or even death. The performer embodies *butoh-tai* by communicating, negating their individual body and subjectivity through surrender to external forces: 'We shake hands with the dead, who send us encouragement from beyond our body'.[38]

Butoh-fu and Metamorphosis

For Bataille, laughter, intoxication, religious ecstasy and other instances of when structured thought loses its hold over subjectivity are how an individual arrives at inner experience. He claims it is also possible through language, but only if it 'is less a matter of contemplation than of rupture', through the severing of its chains to rationality and logical knowledge, such as in poetry.[39]

Hijikata utilises a similar method. The rupturing of the performer through *butoh-tai* is mirrored in his *butoh-fu* ('*butoh* choreographic notation'), which consists of two primary components: language (as written or spoken word) and images (in the form of imaginative or material images). The delivery of *butoh* instruction encoded in both language and image is impossible, as Hijikata's rupturing of the notation's form and structure renders its interpretation unstable. And because the performer is unable to literally embody the instructions conveyed in the choreographic notation, understanding of the performance itself and of how to perform *butoh* falls away to reveal a threatening senselessness.

Each performance composed using Hijikata's *butoh-fu* can be divided into scenes, which can then be further broken down into a series of movements. Individual movements may themselves consist of single gestures or a series of gestures. This sequence of actions is then recorded in text, not necessarily by Hijikata himself. In Yamamoto Moe's notes for his role in *Costume en Face*, the scenes in which he appears are listed as:

a. Old Woman
b. Madame Beardsley
c. Bugle Angel
d. Commander (*Kaguya*)
e. White Dress (Tulip)
f. Black Dress
g. Psychology
h. Goldfish (Rainbow Costume)

Of the distinct movements, 337 can be further identified within these eight scenes, with names such as Wings of a Bugler, Order of Sea Lions, Spook of Light, Nullifying a Stuffed Specimen, A Flower of Flesh, A Track of Metallic Flowers, Stagnation of One Hundred Demons.[40] Hijikata's language also consists heavily of made-up words, further problematising the receiving and understanding of these instructions: *ma gusare* ('space-rotting') and *nadare ame* ('candy-dribbling') are two such examples.[41] Unlike a set of textual notations, which aim to secure as close a physical mimicry as possible to a given figure that the performer can embody, Hijikata's instructions work instead to evoke a non-rational state of being in his performers.

Most of Hijikata's movements were derived from images of paintings, photography and other artworks collaged from the art magazines *Mizue* and *Bijutsu techo*. The two publications featured a wide range of works, and his selection in assembling material for each performance is equally as eclectic. In the scrapbook for *Nadare Ame,* Kurt Wurmli identified works by Hans Richter (Dadaism), Christoph Donin (Austrian Expressionism), Koide Narashige (Western-style Japanese Yoga) and Aristide Caillaud (Art Brut), among others.[42] Rather than classification according to nationality, style or temporal era, these images were grouped according to the evocation of textural physicality, in this case, the dribbling of candy. Not all of the materials were literal depictions of either dribbling or candy, in fact, most were not. Likewise, the images in *Hana* ('*Flower*') included works from the Persian Sassanid period (AD 226–651), the Chinese Song Dynasty (AD 960–1279) and late Meiji era painters, such as Ogura Yuki and Maeda Seison.

Because Hijikata's selection of artworks are impossible to figuratively translate to physical positions that the performer can embody, this imagistic chain of instructions 'leads from the known to the unknown'.[44] Rather than reference a specific image or set of actions to be adhered to, Hijikata's rupturing of words and images become liberated from stable 'expression' or 'definition'. The receiving of *butoh* instruction and the possibility of its physical actualisation, meaning the surfacing of the corresponding image through the performer's body, is never singular, never linear, and may not even always be possible, just as how through poetry 'we tear words from these links in a delirium'.[45] Kurihara Nanako describes this process of receiving *butoh* instruction through the exercise *mushikui* ('insect bites').[46] Ashikawa begins by describing to the performers how, 'An insect is crawling from between your index finger and middle finger onto the back of your hand and then on to your lower arm and up to your upper arm'. To aid them, Ashikawa would rub a drumstick across a drum producing a slithering sound, or physically touch specific areas of their bodies, denoting where the insects are. The exercise proceeds with the number of insects increasing one at a time, each occupying a specific site on the performers' bodies, ending only when 'you are eaten by insects who enter through all the pores of your body, and your body becomes hollow like a stuffed animal'.

Similar to the use of evocative images in *butoh* choreographic notation, onomatopoeic language also aids performers in their understanding of 'being' rather than 'expressing'. Unlike English, which phonetically mimics sounds (such as *buzz* for bees), Japanese's use of onomatopoeia is much broader and includes animate and inanimate phonomimes (*goro goro* for thunder), but also non-auditory states of being such as phenomimes (inanimate physical states, such as *pika pika* for shininess) and psychomimes (animate bodily or emotional states, such as *pin pin* for liveliness) that may be silent. When Ashikawa tells performers to embody *jyu jyu*, meaning dampness, they work towards embodying the heavy wetness of a rug, rather than figuratively depict with their bodies what they imagine a rug would look like wet on the floor. In fact, performers who trained at Hijikata's studio frequently covered the mirrors in the lesson room with clothes while practising so as to avoid relying on or grounding themselves in a shallow and purely visual understanding of their bodies. Kurihara stresses the necessity of thoroughly embodying this image and not merely imagining or physically mimicking an idea: 'the condition of the body itself has to be changed'. *Butoh* performers must 'learn to manipulate their own bodies physiologically and psychologically'.[47]

Butoh as Communion

For Mary Wigman, whose influence is evident in Hijikata's early works, any movement could be considered dance if it embodies emotion. Her choreography includes bouncing, vibrating and falling movements.[48] But where Wigman focuses on materialising shifting psychological and emotional states, Hijikata works towards the kaleidoscopic embodying of a series of images instead, comprising people, spirits and animals, living or dead, and even inanimate objects. And as Bataille's being must surrender their individual subjectivities to undergo 'an undefined throng of possible existences' in communication, what *butoh* requires is not simply the surrender of the performer's body and subjectivity so that they may transfigure themselves into another image, but the complete abandonment of all sense of self and being, letting each image surface only momentarily through them before dissipating again.[49] For Nario Goda, Hijikata's butoh 'begins with the abandonment of the self'.[50] To genuinely do *butoh*, performers must learn to surrender to this perpetual metamorphoses, at times rapidly. Such a practice disallows for attachment to any recognisable identity or sense of being in the performers themselves and also in the viewing audience. Susan Klein writes how *butoh* uses this 'continual metamorphosis to confront the audience with the disappearance of the individual subject by refusing to let any dancer remain a single identifiable character'.[51]

Butoh's confrontation is not with the changing of appearance, but with disappearance and the (perpetual) death of being. This relationship with death is not one of rejection (through the compulsive acting out of the traumatic event), acceptance (as in funereal rites that facilitate grieving), or attempted appeasement (such as purification and banishment rituals). All three are external reactions to death, where death is a force to be engaged with momentarily but kept distinct from the performers and their community. I suggest that *butoh* is better understood as a form of communion, where death is willingly internalised.

Theatre or dance as a form of communion is not exclusive to *butoh*. The performing arts share a long history with religious ritual, whether in Ancient Greek, Sanskrit or Japanese theatre. Spiritual communions serve the task of opening a channel of communication to the gods or spirits,[52] and its most extreme form would be the possession of the host's body and subjectivity by spirits. Communions require host performers to enter into an altered, non-rational, non-individual state of consciousness, and are usually induced through the theatrical re-enactment of mythic narratives, accompanied by rhythmic music, dancing, chanting and other ritualistic gestures.[53] Because *butoh* shares many of these performative elements with ritual communions, frequent comparisons have been drawn between *butoh* and *Shinto* invocations. Hijikata however has stressed the absence of religion in his *butoh*, which comes 'not from anything to do with the performing arts of shrines or temples'.[54]

I feel that Michael Sakamoto's reading of *butoh* as a form of shamanistic practice is more apt. Hijikata's plea 'to die over and over'[55] in a body 'not dead but made to be dead'[56] can then be understood as ritual initiation, where 'the initiatory journey to the spirit realm for shaman neophytes is a journey of death'.[57] Just as how the shaman comes to possess 'transformative knowledge gained from literal or figurative life and death experience', Hijikata's performer must likewise undergo a crisis that puts them at risk of death before they are to understand how to metamorphose.[58] The symbolic death of the performer is hence a precursor to *butoh-tai*. Hijikata's *butoh* is a communion with three forms of death: the dying and already departed; the end of Japanese pre-war values and cultural identity; and the transformative dissolution of the performer's being.

Notes

1. B. S. Stein, 'Butoh: 'Twenty Years Ago We Were Crazy, Dirty, and Mad', *The Drama Review*, 30/2 (1986), 111.
2. Sondra Horton Fraleigh, *Dancing into Darkness: Butoh, Zen, and Japan* (Pittsburgh PA: University of Pittsburgh Press, 2010), pp. 31–2.
3. Sondra Horton Fraleigh and Tama Nakamura, *Hijikata Tatsumi and Ohno Kazuo* (New York: Routledge, 2018), p. 23.
4. Fraleigh and Nakamura, *Hijikata Tatsumi and Ohno Kazuo*, pp. 151–3.
5. T. Hijikata, 'Wind Daruma', *The Drama Review*, 44/1 (2000), 76–7.
6. Fraleigh and Nakamura, *Hijikata Tatsumi and Ohno Kazuo*, p. 25.
7. P. M. Orlando, 'Cutting the Surface of the Water: Butoh as Traumatic Awakening', *Social Semiotics*, 11/3 (2001), 308.
8. O. O'Toole, 'Dance of Darkness: A Traveler's Guide to Butoh', *Art Papers*, 24/1 (2000), 20. Quoted in B. Waychoff, 'Butoh, Bodies, and Being', *Kaleidoscope: A Graduate Journal of Qualitative Communication Research*, 8/4 (2009), 45.
9. Fran Lloyd, *Consuming Bodies: Sex and Contemporary Japanese Art* (London: Reaktion Books, 2003), p. 210.
10. A. Broinowski, 'The Atomic Gaze and Ankoku Butoh in Post-War Japan', in N. A. J. Taylor and R. Jacobs (eds), *Reimagining Hiroshima and Nagasaki: Nuclear Humanities in the Post-Cold War* (London and New York: Routledge, 2017), p. 91.
11. V. Sanders, 'Dancing and the Dark Soul of Japan: An Aesthetic Analysis of "Butō"', *Asian Theatre Journal*, 5/2 (1988), 148.
12. N. Kurihara, 'Hijikata Tatsumi Chronology', *The Drama Review*, 44/1 (2000), 29–30.
13. Yukio Mishima and Alfred H. Marks, *Forbidden Colors* (New York: Knopf, 1968).
14. Bruce Baird, *Hijikata Tatsumi and Butoh: Dancing in a Pool of Gray Grits* (Basingstoke: Palgrave Macmillan, 2016), pp. 15–31.
15. The first half of the title, *6-nin no Avuangyarudo* ('*6 Avantgardists*'), refers to the gathering of six *avant garde* performers. Aside from Hijikata, the other five named in the programme include dancer Wakamatsu Miu, filmmaker Donald Richie, scenographer Kanamori Kaoru and music composers Moroi Makoto and Mayuzumi Toshiro. See *www.art-c.keio.ac.jp/old-website/archive/hijikata/portas/performance/RCA_TH_EP1.html*.
16. Kurihara, 'Hijikata Tatsumi Chronology', 30.
17. Baird, *Hijikata Tatsumi and Butoh*, p. 16.

18. Hijikata Tatsumi Archive (ed.), *Hijikata Tatsumi "Butô" shiryôshû dai ippo* (Tokyo: Keio University Research Center for the Arts and Arts Administration, 2004), p. 56. Quoted in Baird, *Hijikata Tatsumi and Butoh*, p. 38.
19. Baird, *Hijikata Tatsumi and Butoh*, pp. 115–21.
20. Kurihara, 'Hijikata Tatsumi Chronology', 30–2.
21. Fraleigh and Nakamura, *Hijikata Tatsumi and Ohno Kazuo*, p. 19.
22. Takashi Morishita, *Hijikata Tatsumi's Notational Butoh: an Innovative Method for Butoh Creation* (Tokyo: Keio University Art Center, 2015), pp. 14, 17.
23. Baird, *Hijikata Tatsumi and Butoh*, pp. 138–54.
24. The play *Sugawara Denju Tenarai Kagami* ('*Sugawara's Secrets of Calligraphy*') was originally written by Takeda Izumo I, Takeda Izumo II, Namiki Sôsuke and Miyoshi Shôraku for *bunraku* ('puppet theatre') and was later adapted for *kabuki*. It is based on the life of Sugawara no Michizane, whose character is named Kan Shojo. The scene *Terakoya* tells the story of Kan Shojo's former retainer, Matsuomaru, who is sent by Fujiwara no Shihei to murder his son, Kan Shusai.
25. Jean Viala and Nourit Masson-Sekine, *Butoh: Shades of Darkness* (Tokyo: Shufunotomo, 1988), p. 185.
26. Kurihara, 'Hijikata Tatsumi Chronology', 32–3.
27. Quoted in Viala and Masson-Sekine, *Butoh: Shades of Darkness*, p. 185.
28. Quoted in Fraleigh and Nakamura, *Hijikata Tatsumi and Ohno Kazuo*, p. 50.
29. Hijikata, 'Wind Daruma', 77.
30. T. Kasai, 'A Note on Butoh Body', *Memoirs of the Hokkaido Institute of Technology*, 28 (2000), 353.
31. Morishita, *Hijikata Tatsumi's Notational Butoh*, p. 7.
32. Hijikata, 'Wind Daruma', 77.
33. Quoted in T. Kasai, 'A Butoh Dance Method for Psychosomatic Exploration', *Memoirs of the Hokkaido Institute of Technology*, 27 (1999), 310.
34. Quoted in S. Yakushiji, 'A revered master is remembered', *Daily Yomiuri*, 6 November 1998. See www.ne.jp/asahi/butoh/itto/hiji/anniv.htm.
35. Bataille, Georges, *Inner Experience* (Albany NY: State University of New York Press, 2014), p. xi.
36. Bataille, *Inner Experience*, p. xv.
37. Bataille, *Inner Experience*, p. 61.
38. Fraleigh and Nakamura, *Hijikata Tatsumi and Ohno Kazuo*, p. 50.
39. Bataille, *Inner Experience*, p. 40.
40. Morishita, *Hijikata Tatsumi's Notational Butoh*, p. 56.
41. N. Kurihara, 'Introduction: Hijikata Tatsumi: The Words of Butoh', *The Drama Review*, 44/1 (2000), 14.

42. K. Wurmli, 'The Power of Image: Hijikata Tatsumi's Scrapbooks and the Art of Butoh' (unpublished PhD thesis: University of Hawai'i at Manoa, 2008), 153–95.
43. Wurmli, 'The Power of Image', 196–8.
44. Bataille, *Inner Experience*, p. 147.
45. Bataille, *Inner Experience*, p. 135.
46. Kurihara, 'The Words of Butoh', 15.
47. Kurihara, 'The Words of Butoh', 16–7.
48. Susan Manning, *Ecstasy and the Demon: The Dances of Mary Wigman* (Minneapolis MN: University of Minnesota Press, 2006), p. 44.
49. Bataille, *Inner Experience*, p. 61.
50. Quoted in Susan Blakeley Klein, *Ankoku Butō the Premodern and Postmodern Influences on the Dance of Utter Darkness* (Ithaca NY: East Asia Program, Cornell University, 1993), p. 34.
51. Klein, *Ankoku Butō*, p. 32.
52. See Eli Rozik, *The Roots of Theatre: Rethinking Ritual and Other Theories of Origin* (Iowa City IA: University of Iowa Press, 2007).
53. See J. Becker, 'Music and trance', *Leonardo Music Journal*, 4/1 (1994), 41–51.
54. Hijikata, 'Wind Daruma', 74.
55. Hijikata, 'Wind Daruma', 77.
56. T. Hijikata, 'To Prison', *The Drama Review*, 44/1 (2000), 46.
57. M. Sakamoto, 'Parallels of Psycho-Physiological and Musical Affect in Trance Ritual and Butoh Performance', *Pacific Review of Ethnomusicology*, 14 (2009).
58. Sakamoto, 'Parallels of Psycho-Physiological and Musical Affect in Trance Ritual and Butoh Performance'.

PART FOUR

THE IMMERSIVE MACABRE

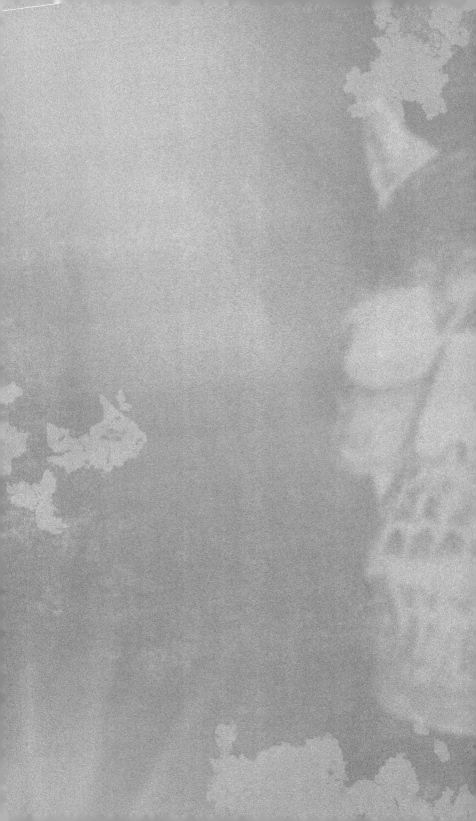

12

'Black and Deep Desires'

Sleep No More and the Immersive Macabre[1]

Dan Venning

MACBETH IS PERHAPS William Shakespeare's most haunted play: it depicts witchcraft, ghostly hauntings, vicious murders and other 'wicked dreams' (II.i.50) and is supposedly subject to a curse that has frightened generations of theatrical artists. The origins of this piece of theatrical folklore – like many stage superstitions from saying 'break a leg' to the supposed origins of the term 'green room' – are murky. Nonetheless, examples of the effects of the supposed curse abound, from the Astor Place Riots (the deadliest riot to its date in Manhattan, in which dozens of citizens were killed and hundreds injured outside of the Astor Place Opera House)[2] to individual disaster-addled productions of *Macbeth* starring Laurence Olivier or Peter O'Toole, or a suicide at the Metropolitan Opera during a performance of Verdi's operatic adaptation of the work. Many practitioners fear that the very mention of the play's name in a theatre will bring bad luck. A recently streamed reading of the play for 'Stars in the House', a bi-weekly online series of remote play readings by star actors over Zoom during the coronavirus pandemic, began with host André De Shields referring to the play by the term 'The Scottish Play', explaining the curse, and promising that as soon as he actually named the play, he would perform an 'antidote' to the curse, commonly known to theatre artists: leave the room, turn around three times, spit, curse and ask forgiveness before being welcomed back into the space.[3] Beyond this historical superstition, *Macbeth* is surely one of the world's most haunted plays in terms of Marvin Carlson's concept of 'ghosting', the process of theatrical intertextuality and remembering. Examining how we often see classic plays repeatedly, or multiple actors in the same role, or different shows in the same theatrical space, Carlson describes how when we watch theatre, echoes and hauntings are often '"bleeding through" the process of reception, the process [he has] called "ghosting"'.[4]

Of course, the plot of *Macbeth* also depicts a world haunted by the forces of evil: both otherworldly malevolence in the form of the witches and all-too-human bloodshed wrought by a 'butcher, and his fiend-like queen' (V.ix.35). The violence that the Macbeths perpetrate is not only limited to a kinsman, guest and liege murdered in his sleep, the swift execution of guiltless patsies, the betrayal of an old friend and an attempted murder of his son as well, the killings of entire families, including children and household servants, and suicide. As the characters of Shakespeare's play articulate, the violence of the Macbeths takes on an epic, allegorical scope, inflicting violence upon the country of Scotland itself. After the murder of King Duncan, the Thane of Ross describes how 'the heavens, as troubled with man's act, / Threatens his bloody stage. By th' clock 'tis day, / And yet dark night strangles the travelling lamp' (II.iv.5–7) and later, as he prepares to depose the tyrant, Malcolm, the son of Duncan, says: 'I think our country sinks beneath the yoke; / It weeps, it bleeds, and each new day a gash / Is added to her wounds' (IV.iii.39–41). More than Shakespeare's English or Roman history plays, which depict the interminable violence of political machinations and civil and international wars, and even more than the Grand Guignol of *Titus Andronicus*, which depicts sexual assault, torture, mutilation and infanticide in addition to numerous more straightforward killings, Shakespeare's *Macbeth* can be described as macabre. The grim otherworldly ghastliness of this medieval Scotland is turned into a metaphorical river of blood in which *Macbeth* is 'Stepped in so far, that should I wade no more, / Returning were as tedious as go o'er' (III.iv.135–6). The murderous king is himself obsessed with blood, uttering the word three times in one line, noting that 'It will have blood they say: blood will have blood' (III.iv.120). Harold Bloom describes the play as one that 'engulfs us in . . . a consistent phantasmagoria of blood' in which 'nature is crime' and the play 'terrifies us partly because that aspect of our own imagination is so frightening: it seems to make us murderers, thieves, usurpers, and rapists'.[5] In other words, Bloom argues that the play itself is immersive macabre, forcing the reader or audience member to internalise the murderous imagination of the title character.

This immersive macabre at the thematic and structural heart of *Macbeth* is literalised within Punchdrunk and Emursive's *Sleep No More*, which is perhaps the most recognisable work of immersive theatre of the past decade. The subject of numerous articles and blogs, many of which are aggregated at 'Behind a White Mask: The Big List of *Sleep No More* Links & Blogs' (*behindawhitemask.tumblr.com*), this ongoing commercial production is a mostly wordless and movement-based immersive adaptation of *Macbeth*, mixed with bits of Daphne du Maurier's *Rebecca*, Alfred Hitchcock's *The 39 Steps*, and more. Following productions in London and Boston, *Sleep No More* ran continuously in New York City in the 'McKittrick Hotel', which is in fact a set of converted warehouses in Manhattan's Chelsea neighbourhood. Since its first performance on 7 March 2011, it ran for over nine years, suspending performances on 12 March 2020 due to the coronavirus pandemic and Governor Andrew Cuomo's executive order suspending theatrical performances for the foreseeable future.

In this chapter, I draw upon numerous published reviews and articles about *Sleep No More*,[6] as well as blogs, theoretical texts and my personal experience in order to demonstrate the ways that this immersive production capitalises on creating what can best be described as an 'immersive macabre', in which nudity and sex, staged violence, drugs and alcohol, fictionalised witchcraft and hauntings, extensive scenography and unbridled capitalism all coalesce into an undeniably compelling grotesquerie, inspired by *Macbeth*. Ostensibly freeing the 'black and deep desires' of an audience by anonymising them through masks and separation from friends, the show encourages a sort of Bakhtinian carnivalesque (or at least carnivalesque-lite) of midnight revelry, which has, in some cases, led to authentically horrific and criminal results, including pickpocketing, labour abuses and sexual assaults.[7]

At its best moments, *Sleep No More* feels less like a theatrical performance and more like a party inside a demented 1930s film noir, brought into vivid colour and three dimensions. After passing nightclub-style bouncers and a coat check, audience members arrive in the jazz-themed Manderley Bar on the building's second floor, to which they can return at any time during the performance to get a drink. In small groups, they are gradually invited into a stairwell, where they are given grey Venetian-style carnival masks and are told to remain silent, but then can otherwise thoroughly explore the five stories in which the show is staged. The top floor of the McKittrick is a lunatic asylum, the 'King James Sanitorium'; this floor also contains a maze, with a bony tree at its centre. There are more than ninety rooms in the four remaining floors, including the fourth-floor town of 'Gallow Green' with a long hallway painted with a sign warmly inviting visitors to the Outer Hebrides of Scotland, a tailor's shop, a candy store or sweet shop (with jars full of real candy), a records office and other functional rooms. Also on this floor is a ghostly cabaret: in one corner a pile of chairs is haphazardly stacked, backlit by a ghostly blue light; on the other side of the room, Hecate frequently holds court. On the third floor is a large dirt-floored cemetery and the Macbeths' residence, a room centred around a large bathtub. The second floor looks like a real hotel lobby, including a bellboy and breakfast room; from this lobby, audience members can return to the bar at any point, remove their masks and order more drinks. The bottom floor is a large ballroom, with a banquet table on a platform and small pine trees circling the room. Throughout all these spaces, Stephen Dobbie's musical score provides a constantly haunting atmosphere.

One could easily spend three hours simply exploring these dimly lit and meticulously crafted spaces: the design, by co-director Felix Barrett as well as Livi Vaughan and Beatrice Minns, is the most extraordinary part of the show. Some audience members do spend their time this way: touching set pieces, eating sweets and candy or trying to discern hidden secrets in notes, letters and charts strewn throughout many of the rooms. But there are dozens of performers in the show, easily distinguishable from fellow audience members because the actors wear no masks. In these many spaces, around and amongst the audience members, the plot of Shakespeare's *Macbeth* plays out several times. Performers, many of whom are trained as dancers, using intensely physical movement and brutally realistic fights choreographed by co-director Maxine Doyle, silently evoke scenes from Shakespeare's play. In the hotel lobby, the witches meet and eagerly await the arrival of Macbeth. In the Macbeths' home, Macbeth and his wife engage in a highly sexual dance/fight as they debate whether to kill Duncan; after the murder, she washes the blood from him. After murdering Banquo, Macbeth hosts a banquet in the ballroom on the bottom floor. As the actors move slowly under shifting lights, the ghost of Banquo appears to haunt Macbeth, who escapes. In a 'black mass' in a ghostly cabaret, which feels much like a rave due to strobe lights and pumping music, the witches present their prophecies to Macbeth: one of the female witches is topless and spills red liquid on her chest under the strobe lights; the male witch is completely naked except for a ram's head mask he wears during this sequence. In the hotel lobby, Macbeth murders the very pregnant Lady Macduff, who appears to be just about to flee the hotel. On the top floor, Lady Macbeth has been committed to the asylum; she tries to wash herself in a bathtub, only for the water in the bath to turn blood-red. Other scenes that not part of Shakespeare's play are also presented: the Porter sends his girlfriend to Hecate, presumably to procure an abortion; Hecate instead collects the girl's tears. *Sleep No More* cycles through *Macbeth* repeatedly, during a single 'performance' most scenes are repeated two or three times. It is as if the audience members have entered a nightmare on a loop. For example, after her scene in the asylum where she 'dies' in the bath of blood, Lady Macbeth dresses and returns to the Macbeths' chamber to find her husband's letter about the witches' prophecy as the plot begins anew. Audience members can try to follow one actor throughout his or her loop, stay in one area and see the different scenes that take place there, or explore the many immaculately detailed spaces. It is almost impossible for any one audience member to see the entire plot of *Macbeth* during a single performance – or even a significant portion of it – since multiple scenes take place at the same time in different spaces far apart in the converted warehouse. The only scene that all audience members are guaranteed to see is the final one: at the end of the show, audience members are herded to the bottom floor, where the banquet scene ends this time with the hanging of Macbeth. Audience members can also be lucky enough to have 'one-on-one' experiences with the cast: pulled swiftly into a room, its door slammed and locked behind them, the performer and viewer alone. The actor may whisper a secret, give a small gift to the audience member, offer a shot of alcohol, or some other moment of intimacy that brings the audience member even deeper into this immersive *Macbeth*: reminding them that they are not just witnesses to, but part of the unfolding horrors. One of these one-on-one moments involves having an audience member help towel-dry the male witch after he showers post-'black mass'; this is only one of several times during the show that audiences can find themselves physically quite close to fully nude performers, such as Macbeth after Duncan's murder, the male witch in the rave sequence or Lady Macbeth in the asylum bathtub.

Prior to the closure of theatres in New York due to the coronavirus crisis, *Sleep No More* had become one of the city's signature theatrical destinations for aficionados and tourists alike. When it opened, New York's leading theatre critics greeted the production with qualified praise. Ben Brantley of the *New York Times* describes the show as 'a voyeur's delight, with all the creepy, shameful pleasures that entails', drawing mostly upon film-noir director Hitchcock's ability to provoke a 'guilty enjoyment' through our own complicity in the 'invasion of private lives and ugly deaths'.[8] In the *New Yorker*, Hilton Als described the immersive nature of *Sleep No More* as playing a 'profound role . . . in altering one's consciousness'; he argues that, as an audience member, 'to see the various characters without masks – or wearing their characters' face – makes our masked faces look and feel more theatrical and fake than the performers'.[9] One of the most positive reviews came from scholar D. J. Hopkins in *Theatre Journal*. Hopkins argues that *Sleep No More*:

> depends not only on obsessively dense scenic design, admirable choreography, and an inventive appropriation of a classic text, but on serious thought given to the role of the audience; it turned us into active voyeurs rather than passive consumers . . . and its strategies of engagement could go a long way towards reviving a theatre scene that seems moribund in comparison to the popularity of film, television, and new media.[10]

The show, originally scheduled for only a limited run, quickly started selling out, with tickets priced almost as expensively as Broadway productions: $75 to $105 for standard tickets; more to go as 'Maximilian's Guest' and skip the queue, and even more for a VIP champagne table at the Manderley Bar before the performance begins.

The online marketing for the show often disguised itself in creative ways. After the show's opening, blogs quickly sprang up, advising audience members of the best places to situate themselves in the space and at what times, in order to receive one of the treasured one-on-one experiences. Many of these blogs are anonymously created Tumblrs, linking to short essays and revealing 'spoilers' and 'Easter eggs' (subtle references throughout the show, from obvious parts of *Macbeth* or *Rebecca* to Werner Herzog's film version of Georg Büchner's *Woyzeck*). The blogs have weird or macabre names such as 'We Can Never Go Back' (*tomanderleyagain.tumblr.com*), 'Back to Manderley' (*paisleysweets.tumblr.com*), 'They Have Scorched the Snake' (*scorchedthesnake.tumblr.com*), 'The Bloody Business' (*thebloodybusiness.tumblr.com*) and 'Blood Will Have Blood, They Say' (*bloodwillhavebloodtheysay.tumblr.com*). These Tumblrs and similar resources are aggregated, as noted earlier, at 'Behind a White Mask', and most have not been updated within the past five or six years. Some have gone offline during the coronavirus crisis. The blogs seem to have been designed to continue building word of mouth for an already successful show; taken together, they suggest that true fans go back to the show again and again, determined to uncover all of its secrets.[11] It is unclear whether these blogs were created by real fans, are the product of marketing firms, or a mixture of both. One of the most creative pieces of online marketing is a false history of the McKittrick Hotel on film location scout Nick Carr's website, 'Scouting New York', which begins with faux old-fashioned photographs and a fake *New York Times* headline, followed by numerous close-up shots of the set of *Sleep No More*.[12]

Even the theatrical programme (which is a memorabilia book, sold after the performance) contributes to the ghastly, immersive spirit of the play. The cover is embossed, featuring a Latin phrase urging violent immersion: 'Ulula cum lupus cum quibus esse cupis' ('howl with the wolves, with whom you wish to be'). Each leaf is in fact uncut, creating a denser feel; cutting the pages reveals a blood-red side to each page, as if the book itself is a living thing that bleeds; in fact, several pages have been augmented with red splotches, as if blood had been dripped onto the programme as it was being printed. The programme includes cast and creator biographies, a synopsis of Shakespeare's *Macbeth*, a 'relationship diagram' of the characters in *Sleep No More*, interviews with and quotations from creators Felix Barrett and Maxine Doyle, and historical dramaturgical material such as the 'Confession of Agnes Sampson', a sermon denouncing witchcraft by Reverend James Hutchison of Killallan, Scotland, which he preached at Paisley on 13 April 1697 amidst a witchcraft scare. But the majority of the memorabilia programme is devoted to macabre images, sometimes in two-page spreads: frogs suspended in jars of formaldehyde, ghostly, uninhabited vistas from the performance space, close ups of creepy writing or a door marked with a chalk 'X'. Each of these plates is labelled '*McKittrick Hotel* PLATE NO.' and followed by a Roman numeral. The first plate is labelled number CCLXXXVIII and the second LXXXVIII, suggesting that we are seeing only a few out of hundreds of such disturbing images. At the centre of the programme is an insert of high-quality colour photographs with ominous captions: a fork and spoon sitting in a pile of salt, with the label 'Due to its purity, salt has long been thought to have the power to repel spiritual and magical evil'; rusted nails and screws of various sizes over the caption 'Pica, a medical condition named for the Latin word for Magpie (Pica Pica)'; taxidermised fowl and rodents over the caption 'All my pretty chickens and their dam at one fell swoop. (MACBETH ACT 4, SC 3)'.[13]

The immersive marketing machine of Punchdrunk, Emursive and the McKittrick Hotel extends well beyond *Sleep No More*. In addition to the roughly 100 meticulously crafted rooms that constitute the space for *Sleep No More* and the production that takes place within them, the warehouses that have been rebranded as the McKittrick Hotel (a reference to Hitchcock's *Vertigo*) also contain a rooftop bar (Gallow Green; named for a Scottish site for executions of women accused of witchcraft) and the Manderley Bar (a reference to the setting of Daphne du Maurier's *Rebecca*). A restaurant within the McKittrick that can be entered separately, The Heath, also serves as a secondary performance venue that has hosted runs of similarly themed shows such as Dave Malloy's *Ghost Quartet* (2015), the National Theatre of Scotland's *The Strange Undoing of Prudencia Hart* (2016–17),[14] and performances by bands or one-off events such as the 2016 benefit fundraiser for The Trevor Project, *A Safe and Special Place*. The show has also spawned a renaissance of immersive performances, from Third Rail Projects' ongoing *Then She Fell* (a take on Lewis Carroll's *Alice in Wonderland* in Brooklyn) to shorter runs like *Seeing You* (2017), an immersive take on World War II produced by Randy Weiner, one of the co-producers of *Sleep No More*. At the curated panel 'Pepys's Progeny: Marvin Carlson's *10,000 Nights: Highlights from 50 Years of Theatre-Going*' at the 2017 meeting of the American Society for Theatre Research in Atlanta, Georgia, celebrating a book in which he had discussed one production per year from 1960 to 2010, one audience member asked Carlson what sorts of production he might have discussed were he to have expanded the book to the next decade. Carlson immediately named *Sleep No More*, suggesting that 'immersive theatre is one of the most significant trends of this decade'.[15]

The immersive aesthetic fostered by *Sleep No More* can certainly be described as 'carnivalesque'. Mikhail Bakhtin theorises the carnivalesque as a 'universal spirit' of discord and rebellion that provides a release valve for pent-up chaos stifled through adherence to the day-to-day regulations of social contracts within ordered societies. Indeed, Bakhtin describes the carnivalesque as immersive: 'carnival does not know footlights, in the sense that it does not acknowledge any distinction between actors and spectators', and within it the spectator/participants can forget their day-to-day lives and responsibilities in the face of an irresistible spirit. 'While carnival lasts, there is no life outside of it', Bakhtin writes.[16] This spirit is encouraged throughout *Sleep No More*, which cultivates the bodily and sexual aesthetics of nightclub culture: an expensive door price with a long queue policed by bouncers, an exotic and meticulously decorated dark space with continuous atmospheric music, lascivious sensuality, strong drinks and late nights out (several weekend performances begin at 11pm and end at 2am). Indeed, during more than one of the performances that I attended, I saw audience members succumbing to this spirit and grinding on one another during the black mass and final scene; partially because of the masks we all wore, it was unclear to me whether these amorous figures had known each other before coming to the performance.

Indeed, some genuinely disturbing (in real life terms) aspects of the show have emerged from this carnivalesque atmosphere. In an echo of the troubling incidents that plagued some 'Happenings' and the experiential theatre of the 1960s, as when performers in The Performance Group's *Dionysus in '69* and The Living Theatre's *Paradise Now* were sexually assaulted by audience members during performances,[17] on 6 February 2018 Amber Jamieson of *BuzzFeed News* broke a story in which eight former performers and staff at *Sleep No More* alleged multiple incidents of groping, harassment or other sexual assaults by masked patrons during performances. Jamieson was able to confirm at least seventeen separate incidents despite non-disclosure agreements and performers fearing being blacklisted.[18] Coming at the beginning of the #MeToo movement, Jamieson's exposé was quickly followed by major entertainment news outlets from the *New York Times* and *The Guardian* to *New York Magazine*'s Vulture cultural section and the feminist blog Jezebel, among others. In such follow-up stories, the producers of *Sleep No More* promised to work harder to ensure the safety of their performers but acknowledged that this was made challenging by the fact that audience members are masked and the space is dark. The news story seems to have ended there: there are no further follow-up stories from later in 2018, 2019 or 2020 at the height of the #MeToo movement. The revelations of sexual assault and the producers' promises to do better to preserve their artists' safety did not seem to have had any real effect on the show's bottom line: *Sleep No More* continued to sell out right up to the day theatres closed due to the coronavirus pandemic, and prices were as expensive as ever.[19] I, personally, have not been back since these revelations, but I have recommended the show to students (especially ones interested in *Macbeth*), friends and family visiting from out of town, among others. The world of the show allows audience members to play at being masked, invisible bystanders only inches from grisly murders and otherworldly witchcraft, but those same carnival masks have allowed some to commit assaults and have turned everyone who buys a ticket or recommends the show into an actual bystander.

Other real-world problems have been financial: Michael Wilson reported for the *New York Times* on a pickpocketing enabled by the anonymity of *Sleep No More*, which the producers dismissed as 'a nonstory'.[20] More notable were the many reports of exploitation of unpaid interns utilised as stage managers, supervisors, props masters, wardrobe supervisors and more, 'juggling backstage tasks that were once performed by paid staff' in what the *International Business Times* describes as 'aggressive violations of the Fair Labor Standards Act'. Following Christopher Zara's original story, former interns reached out anonymously to argue that the 'show's stage-management internship program fosters a pattern of habitual labor and wage violations'.[21] These articles were published in 2013 and seem to have had little effect upon either the ticket sales throughout the rest of the decade or employment practices at *Sleep No More*. The show's management defended their practices, arguing that interns received tangible educational benefits from their unpaid work, and unpaid internships at *Sleep No More* in the wardrobe, costume, stage management and other departments continued to be posted on *Playbill.com* and elsewhere throughout the next six-and-a-half years as ticket prices for this carnivalesque, immersive *Macbeth* continued to gradually rise. Once again, audience members (this time, myself included, since I attended the show twice after Zara published his articles on labour practices) became actually complicit. We paid for tickets to this show staffed by unpaid interns and performed by non-unionised artists, knowing that most of that money went directly into the producers' pockets. The ticket to the carnival that is *Sleep No More* does not, in this sense, immerse audience members in an authentically different world or release them, in a Bakhtinian sense, from day-to-day lives in the world of American capitalism.

In conclusion, then, the most authentically macabre thing that *Sleep No More* does is to immerse everyone in a wholly commercial, capitalist project. Masked audience members are not complicit in the fictional, carefully staged 'deaths' of Duncan, Banquo, Lady Macduff or the Macbeths: those performers are artists who will, momentarily after 'dying', pick themselves up and repeat their loops once more. But the most insidious aspect of the show is that many audience members are perhaps blissfully unaware of the ways in which they are actually complicit in real-world labour abuses or sexual misconduct. *Sleep No More* is a perfect example of what Theodor Adorno called 'the culture industry' that carefully tailors experiences, determining the nature of their consumption and removing any actual rebellious resistance from the seemingly carnivalesque.[22] Those immersed in this culture industry include the audiences who are stripped of as much money as they are willing to pay for tickets, drinks, memorabilia programmes or have stripped from them by pickpockets; the trained artists who have been subject to objectification by some of these paying spectators; and the overworked unpaid interns. Karl Marx begins his *Communist Manifesto* with a reference to a 'spectre' haunting Europe: the spectre of Communism, revivified through the grotesqueries of capitalism, which Marx argues constitutes an insidious oppression whereby the labour of the worker is transformed into capital for the employer. *Sleep No More* gleefully participates in this process: making money hand over fist by releasing everyone's 'black and deep desires' to be immersed in the bloody villainies of *Macbeth*. The show is profoundly self-aware of its capitalist goals – the last page of its programme depicts uncanny faux 1930s advertisements: for furs, taxidermy, corsets and even a detective agency from 'Gallow Green, Galmis, Forfar'. And this capitalist macabre is perhaps the most crucial of the ways in which *Sleep No More* pioneered a profitable new model in the theatrical landscape of the past decade.

Notes

1. The title comes from *Macbeth*, (I.iv.51). Further quotations from *Macbeth* are cited parenthetically.
2. For a detailed description of the Astor Place Riots, its causes and human cost, see the anonymously authored 'Account of the Terrific and Fatal Riot at the New-York Astor Place Opera House', in J. Shapiro (ed.), *Shakespeare in America: An Anthology from the Revolution to Now* (Washington, DC: Library of America, 2016).
3. 'Stars in the House: *Macbeth*', streaming on *www.playbill.com/article/patrick-page-hannah-yelland-donna-bullock-ty-jones-more-read-macbeth-on-stars-in-the-house*, 13–17 June 2020.
4. Marvin Carlson, *The Haunted Stage: The Theatre as Memory Machine* (Ann Arbor MI: University of Michigan Press, 2001), p. 133.
5. Harold Bloom, *Shakespeare: The Invention of the Human* (New York: Riverhead Books, 1998).

6. Two of these are mine: D. Venning, 'Politics and Nightmares: Shakespearean Adaptations in New York', Graduate Center *Advocate* (February 2013), 27–30; and D. Venning, '*Sleep No More* and *Something Rotten!* (dual review)', *Shakespeare Bulletin* 34/1 (spring 2016). Descriptions of the show are drawn from my previous reviews.
7. Although I have serious reservations about the ways in which *Sleep No More* contributes to a corporatisation of artistic practice and administration, as well as about the significant crimes that have been committed during performances, the show itself is hypnotically compelling. I have attended three times; first in 2011, shortly after it opened, again in 2013 when I was reviewing it for the *Advocate*, and a third time in 2015 when I was reviewing it again for *Shakespeare Bulletin*. I thoroughly enjoyed it all three times.
8. B. Brantley, 'Shakespeare Slept Here, Albeit Fitfully', *New York Times* (11 April 2011), www.nytimes.com/2011/04/14/theater/reviews/sleep-no-more-is-a-macbeth-in-a-hotel-review.html.
9. H. Als, 'Shadow and Act: Shakespeare without Words', *New Yorker* (2 May 2011), www.newyorker.com/magazine/2011/05/02/shadow-and-act.
10. D. J. Hopkins, '*Sleep No More* (Performance Review)', *Theatre Journal* 64/2 (May 2012), 271.
11. 'Behind a White Mask: The Big List of *Sleep No More* Links & Blogs', behindawhitemask.tumblr.com.
12. N. Carr, 'Exploring the Abandoned McKittrick Hotel on West 27th Street', *Scouting New York* (4 April 2011), www.scoutingny.com/exploring-new-yorks-abandoned-mckittrick-hotel.
13. T. Maughan and Arkadia & Co., 'The McKittrick Hotel: Open All Year, Established 1939', insert photos by Scott Irvine and Kim Meinelt of Waxenvine, [*Sleep No More* theatrical programme].
14. Both of which were billed as 'immersive'; see www.playbill.com/article/dave-malloys-immersive-ghost-quartet-adds-performances-at-chelseas-mckittrick-hotel-com-342728 and www.playbill.com/article/the-strange-undoing-of-prudencia-hart-extends-for-third-time.
15. M. Carlson, 'Pepys's Progeny: Marvin Carlson's *10,000 Nights: Highlights from 50 Years of Theatre-Going*', American Society for Theatre Research, Atlanta GA, 17 November 2017; and Marvin Carlson, *Ten Thousand Nights: Highlights from 50 Years of Theatre-Going* (Ann Arbor MI: University of Michigan Press, 2017).
16. Mikhail Bakhtin, *Rabelais and His World*, translated by Helene Iswolsky (Bloomington IN: Indiana University Press, 1984), pp. 7–8, 33.

17. J. Penner, 'The Living Theatre and Its Discontents: Excavating the Somatic Utopia of *Paradise Now*', *Ecumenica*, 2/1 (spring 2009).
18. A. Jamieson, 'Performers and Staffers at "*Sleep No More*" Say Audience Members Have Sexually Assaulted Them', *BuzzFeed News* (6 February 2018), *www.buzzfeednews.com/article/amberjamieson/sleep-no-more*.
19. The only demonstrable effect seems to have been on another immersive show, as London's immersive *Wolf of Wall Street* production issued its performers safety alarms after the reports of sexual assaults at *Sleep No More* and *The Great Gatsby* (another London-based immersive production). See L. Bakare, 'Immersive *Wolf of Wall Street* Actors Get Personal Alarm Buttons', *Guardian* (16 September 2019), *www.theguardian.com/stage/2019/sep/16/immersive-wolf-of-wall-street-production-to-introduce-safeguarding*.
20. M. Wilson, 'Spotting a Thief in a Room Full of Masks at "*Sleep No More*"', *New York Times* (1 November 2015), *www.nytimes.com/2015/11/02/nyregion/spotting-a-thief-in-a-room-full-of-masks-at-sleep-no-more.html*.
21. C. Zara, '"*Sleep No More*" Internship Post Flouts Fair Wage Laws: Unpaid Laborers Asked to Work 10-Hour Days', *International Business Times* (3 December 2013), *www.ibtimes.com/sleep-no-more-internship-post-flouts-fair-wage-laws-unpaid-laborers-asked-work-10-hour-days-1493776*; and C. Zara, 'Former "*Sleep No More*" Interns Say Immersive NYC Megahit Offers Little Educational Benefit', *International Business Times* (7 December 2013), *www.ibtimes.com/former-sleep-no-more-interns-say-immersive-nyc-megahit-offers-little-educational-benefit-1499418*.
22. Theodor Adorno, *The Culture Industry: Selected Essays on Mass Culture* (London and New York: Routledge, 1991), pp. 98–9.

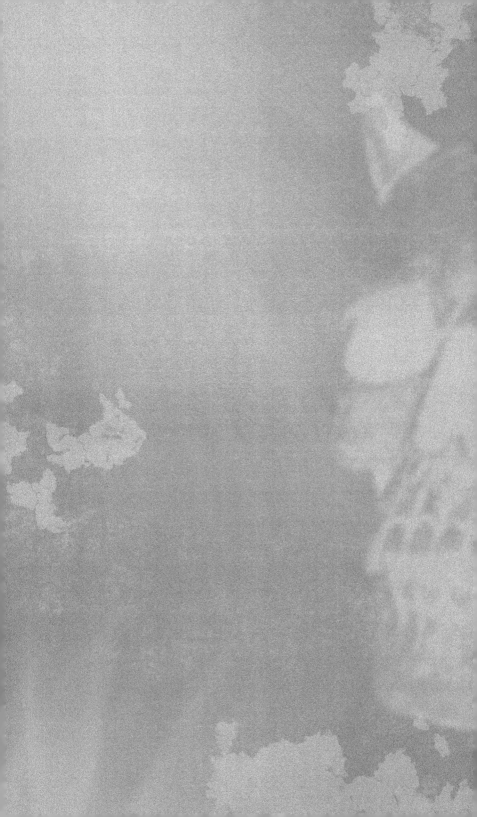

13

The Dark Ride Immersive and the *Danse Macabre*

David Bisaha

TAMI DIXON, PITTSBURGH playwright and co-founder of Bricolage Production Company, received some pointed feedback on the company's immersive work:

> A lot of our audience . . . say that they're scared. 'I'm afraid. I don't want to be put on the spot. I don't want to be touched.' And they think it may be like a haunted house. They have this preconceived notion about what it is, and they don't think that they could be part of an immersive experience. I always say that your life is an immersive experience.[1]

Such an association is not accidental, especially in the United States. Live performance entertainment in fully designed environments is most frequently encountered in popular amusements such as haunted houses, theme parks, ghost tours and historical re-enactments. And now that the current wave of immersive theatre in the United States is just over a decade old – if it is to be dated by its most popular incarnation, Punchdrunk's *Sleep No More* (2011) – it is becoming possible to historicise its beginnings, particularly with relationship to horror themes. Early long-running examples of the genre embraced horror, whether in the occult witchcraft and film-noir vision of *Sleep No More*, period murder thrillers (*Speakeasy Dollhouse: The Bloody Beginning*, 2011) or occult, spooky nightlife circus with *Queen of the Night* (2014) and *Illuminati Ball* (2016).[2] Immersive theatre encompasses much more than *Sleep No More*, and the themes of immersive theatre expand beyond the macabre. Yet, because of the long-running success of some more horror-driven examples, not to mention the over-application of 'immersive' to any manner of thrill attractions, theme park 'fright nights' and escape rooms, the association of dark themes with immersive theatre has endured.

In this chapter I explore some links between two prolific immersive theatre companies and spatial elements of the macabre. Histories of immersive theatre have carefully grounded it in precursors as diverse as the historical European *avant-garde*, environmental performances by the Performance Group and Jerzy Grotowski and a variety of playwright-driven experiments such as Griselda Gambaro's *Information for Foreigners* (1973) and John Krizanc's *Tamara* (1981). British scholar of immersive theatre Josephine Machon identifies additional progenitors in her survey of primarily European examples of the trend: participatory art, live installation art and the 'physical and visual theatres of the 1980s'.[3] I chart two additional inspirations, however, that contribute to immersive theatres of the most recent wave and particularly in the United States.[4] Namely, the amusement park dark ride and the medieval allegory of the *danse macabre* count immersive theatre among their pop culture descendants. Performances created by the Bricolage Production Company and the New York City-based dance/theatre group Third Rail Projects were particularly inspired by these motifs. Both companies' productions emphasise dance, movement and spectacle above text or narrative progression, and they employ a structure in which audience members are led or transported through a series of rooms. After initial successes with productions in 2011 and 2012, they continued to build 'dark ride' immersive experiences as major parts of their company identities. At the same time, they drew on the *danse macabre* as inspiration for their spooky, dance-based content. Together, these companies blended the dark ride structure and the *danse macabre* motif into an influential model for 2010s immersive theatre. This model held because of its ability to prime the participant for individualised exploration of the supernatural.

Space can structure performance in subtle ways. Theatre historian David Wiles has identified several longstanding spatial structures in his work *A Short History of Western Performance Space*. Wiles links the spatial orientations of audience and performers across time. From Greeks to modernism, 'the physical relationship of performer, spectator, and environment determin[e] the communication that takes place'.[5] Among the spaces Wiles explores are processional performances in the street, theatre in sacred architecture, the marketplace and the Platonic cave-like proscenium. Each spatial orientation produces a set of possible meanings, which are primed by the arrangement of performer and audience in space. To Wiles' list of spatial micro-narratives I add the structure of the dark ride: forward motion through an environment with discrete, installation-like scenes or rooms viewed from within a shared vehicular space. This spatial structure is common among theme attractions and includes many haunted houses as well as more traditional dark rides; there is something supernatural and compelling about such movement through space and narrative. This structure, in turn, draws on earlier linkages of inescapable movement to mortality and the supernatural, particularly the musical call of Death as allegorised in the *danse macabre*.

Defining the Dark Ride Immersive

Immersive theatre as a genre connotes an environment that surrounds a spectator. While exact definitions of the term differ by company and theorist, a general sense of the audience member held within the action and afforded some degree of (perceived or actual) interaction persists. Immersive theorist Gareth White notes its relationship to water metaphors: 'to be immersed is to be surrounded, enveloped and potentially annihilated, but it also is to be separate from that which immerses . . . there is a relationship between a work as an exterior thing – for all its dangerous intimacy – and a distinct, swimming subject'.[6] The immersive theatre-focused website No Proscenium agrees: an immersive experience 'physically and (usually) narratively puts the audience in the same place in which the action occurs . . . the audience is a part of the world, even if it is merely as a physical obstacle to the performers'.[7] The spatial arrangement of such work varies. It may involve individual audience members free to roam a large space – so-called 'sandbox' experiences such as *Sleep No More* – or it may involve a more nightclub-like experience in which seated or standing spectators watch action happening in and around them (*The Donkey Show*, 1999; *Here Lies Love*, 2013). But 'dark ride' structure, Noah J. Nelson notes, distinguishes Third Rail's *Then She Fell* and many other performances.

Dark ride immersivity took shape at the amusement park. The first dark rides were built at World's Fairs and were designed as temporary entertainments; only later did they move to permanent amusement wonderlands such as Luna Park in New York City's Coney Island or Pittsburgh's Kennywood. There, dark rides provide the amusement park patrons a kind of momentary escape into literal and figurative darkness. Themes of popular early rides differed, beginning with scenic railways and continuing with 'Old Mill' rides, featuring floating vehicles on a log flume in an enclosed building. Many of these rides took on either fantastical, romantic themes, such as Frederick Thompson's Journey to the Moon, installed at the Buffalo Exposition in 1901, or spooky themes that encouraged lovers to cling to each other in fright. These rides mixed intimacy, immersion, privacy and thrill, allowing fairgoers to encounter macabre and sexual taboos, which could be dispensed with once the ride ended, safely.[8] Joel Zika notes that dark rides became known for their horror elements, particularly after they were reinvented by Disney in the 1960s, but more important to their success was their 'component based way of thinking about a narrative', which left them open for easy re-theming; the Old Mill, in particular, could be quickly re-themed for new romantic or horror themes.[9] In these attractions, it was the narrative function of the rides' forward motion, the complete immersion they offered, and their flexibility that allowed them to succeed as fairground entertainments. For a century this structure has been a powerful container for hidden aspects of human psychology. Such an approach, of horror mixed with intimacy and erotic frisson, was repackaged in the US immersive theatres of the 2010s.

Dark ride immersives, then, to borrow No Proscenium's definition, are 'guided experiences . . . that give you the feeling of having stepped off the track and into the sets of the ride'.[10] And unlike open-world 'sandbox' immersives, dark rides afford the audience limited choice about where to move next. This structuring element allows for the creation of separate 'tracks' per audience member, which may intersect while still ensuring that each audience member has a different set of experiences. By providing a series of related experiences in sequentially organised rooms or locations, the dark ride immersive approximates the forward motion of narrative, through the compulsory movement of the spectator through the performance. Like their structural forebears, the dark ride immersive riffs on ideas from room to room, providing more of an affective experience than a clear narrative. As in the theme park, such affect is transmitted mostly through spectacle and dance, rather than mostly through dialogic text or detailed narratives.

Dark Ride Immersive Companies: Bricolage and Third Rail

Bricolage Production Company was among the first US companies nationally profiled as immersive theatre innovators. Their large immersive production *STRATA* (2012) was featured on the cover of *American Theatre* magazine.[11] Bricolage's work differs from other popular immersives because it emphasises the audience member's sensory experience. Inspired early on by Colombian theatre artist and anthropologist Enrique Vargas' *Teatro de los Sentidos* ('Theatre of the Senses'), Bricolage addresses immersive performance as a series of sensory experiences.[12] Echoing the performance-building methods of companies such as US-based Odyssey Works and the London children's theatre Oily Cart – just some of their professed influences – Bricolage begins with a series of multimodal experiences and builds environments and experiences around those sensations.[13] In this chapter, I will focus on three of Bricolage's larger immersive works: *STRATA*, *Saints Tour Braddock* (2015) and *DODO* (2017).

STRATA consisted of a series of solo experiences, each involving one-on-one contact with an actor in a designed environment. In it, each audience member received numbered cards that tracked a path from room to room, leading them forward on a unique series of widely varying experiences lasting three to five minutes. I recall lying on a bed and listening to a bedtime story while an actor asked me to brush her hair; being forced to shoot hoops while being berated by a high-school gym teacher; dancing with an actor alone at an abandoned high-school prom; and being confronted with a thick manila folder of personal surveillance ('my file') thrown on a desk, while a secretary tried to find a cat hiding under a pile of upended filing cabinets. Each of these experiences, I was told, would lead to my own psychological 'refitnessing', ultimately with the goal of achieving the cheekily named 'iConsciousness'. There was no strong narrative thread, but instead, emphasis was placed on generating sensory, emotional experiences: sadness, nostalgia, anxiety, failure, panic. The spatial logic of this experience echoes the dark ride; while the 'track' differed for each individual, the experiential series of linked, environmentally staged events invites the audience to make a narrative out of that series. By maintaining multiple individual tracks, Bricolage seized the dark ride spatiality and poured it into the architecture of a large gym complex.[14]

Later Bricolage productions continued to use a dark ride structure. Their 2015 production of *Saints Tour* took the format of a walking and bus tour, led by a narrator who spoke of the history of the town (lightly fictionalised) and the yearly emergence of secular 'saints' who left their spirit with the area (mostly fabricated). As the tour walked first on foot, then took a bus through the town, magical pieces of performances emerged, which the narrator glossed as signs of the saints. Mysterious symbols adorned makeshift shrines on the side of the road, or in gardens planted in vacant lots. From bus windows, I witnessed silk aerialists dangle from a tree branch in a graveyard, and as I passed private homes on the bus, community residents would come out and wave, perform on musical instruments, or gesture to the saintly relics left on their fences and doors. Straddling the genres of historic ghost walk and urban bus tour, *Saints Tour* plunged audiences into an otherworldly experience. In Rice's words, 'the purpose is to sort of make the whole neighborhood float a little bit'.[15]

DODO repeated the format. This production took place in the linked Carnegie Museums of Art and Natural History and investigated the philosophy of museum collecting. Upon entering the loading dock, I and five others were interrogated by a guard and then assigned one of several natural history items: a bone, a feather, a shell, an egg, a pinned butterfly, a dried eucalyptus twig. These objects defined our 'tracks', as actors would inspect our items and direct us to the next room. Each audience member was invited to contemplate a painting in a darkened art gallery (itself a dark, eerie experience) before moving into the natural history area for short monologues from characters inspired by the exhibits. An explorer told us of hunting in the Arctic, two actors dressed as birds sang songs from a nest in the attic, and a museum scientist pulled out drawer after drawer of avian specimens and instructed us on the conservation process. The experiences were not narratively linked; rather a constellation of experiences and moments began to solidify into a set of thematic ideas. In this case, what is preserved in a museum? What is worth keeping? Why?[16]

Third Rail Projects focuses their work in New York City, although they have produced elsewhere in the United States and internationally. Their Alice in Wonderland-themed production *Then She Fell* was their flagship production, which ran from 2012–20 at Kingsland Ward, an abandoned hospital in Williamsburg, Brooklyn. Like *STRATA*, *Then She Fell* also moved audiences through a series of rooms for intimate, solo or small group experiences with characters from the Alice stories. Each individual is given a 'track' through a selection of rooms; solo performances with Lewis Carroll, Alice or the Mad Hatter lead to group experiences at a tea party or observing the Red Queen berating Alice. The only spoken text is delivered directly to audience members, in private; in several vignettes, the performers invite audiences to respond by revealing their stories of growing up and keeping secrets. Movement from experience to experience is guided by actors and nurses, and stage management assistants who maintain order. The overall effect is one of childlike wonder, supported by Alice's journey into the 'curiouser and curiouser' world of Wonderland.

Third Rail's 2016 production *The Grand Paradise*, staged in a warehouse transformed into a 1970s tropical resort, saw a family of characters encounter their desires for escape, welcome, intimacy and love. Audience members gathered in a large central plaza area, surrounded by caves and hotel rooms, witnessed as the family checked into the resort and were entertained (in various ways) by the hazy, sexy staff. There were no audience 'tracks' in this performance – we were free to wander a bit more, although invitations and directions were still made – but the same discrete division of space into very different rooms (a hotel, a floor show, a cave, a plaza, a bar) carried some dark ride elements into this piece.[17] Their 2018 production *Ghost Light* took audiences backstage at the Lincoln Center's Claire Tow Theatre. As groups moved from room to room in tracked pathways – no solo experiences here – we met ghosts ranging from ancient historical theatre spectres to tragic Hollywood-era actresses, illicit romances conducted in the wings to a very funny clown routine performed by a theatre janitor and his broom. The performance emphasised its maze-like structure and the unusual vantage points possible when using a proscenium theatre in unexpected ways; several times, the same backstage 'places' calls were given, and watching from different rooms and angles, you could see how the whole clockwork was put together.[18]

The Ride and the Invitation to Dance

Interviews with Bricolage and Third Rail explicitly identify the amusement park ride or thrill attraction as a part of the inspiration for their work. Bricolage artistic director Jeffrey Carpenter began his thinking on immersives with the 'sensory labyrinth' of the Theatre of the Senses but has also fondly recalled childhood memories of kiddie rides:

> Going to the zoo and getting on the train and going around, when you're on the train looking off, and these little scenarios play out. It struck me from a very early age . . . Wow, if we can sort of get back to that.[19]

Third Rail, too, began their immersive dance work with a series of Alice-related projects in 2009 at the *Steampunk Haunted House* at the Abrons Art Center. Over three years of refinement, Third Rail artists transformed their *Then She Fell* from a free-roaming, promenade-style performance (not unlike *Sleep No More*) to one in which audiences were invited and suggested to move in predetermined tracks, further developing the spatial metaphor that they discovered in the haunted house.[20] It is more than a simple moment of inspiration; in turning to the train ride or the haunted house, these artists were tapping into a complex history of rides that blended the immersive, the popular and the spooky into a single cluster.

Dark-ride structure depends on motion, foremost, and some separation of the audience from the environment that surrounds them. The performances in question here began with commitment to audience movement through an environment, rather than a stationary audience and a changing scenic landscape. Whether the motion is on foot or conveyed through a vehicle (the *Saints Tour* bus, for instance) is less crucial than the basic structure of audience mobility and the use of pre-planned tracks rather than improvised audience movement. There may be multiple tracks, and tracks may hold one audience member or several, but the idea of forward motion along the track is the fundamental structuring device. The track idea is so simple as to be obvious, but it is a structure nonetheless; *No Proscenium*'s definition assumes this basic equivalence between physical motion and narrative movement: 'Track: a physical and/or narrative through-line in an experience or event. As in a tracked event, or story tracks'.[21] Every other entailment of the immersive theatre structure – forward motion, surprise created along the way, directed gaze outside the vehicle, a series of sequential themed experiences – derive from the fundamental metaphor of the audience moving forward through the performance in time and space.

The *danse macabre*, a medieval allegory for the universality of death, also incorporated modular structure and visually striking storytelling. The motif consists of death personified as a human skeleton, most often rendered in paintings or carvings on monuments as a *memento mori*. In some versions, Death leads a parade of sinners to the afterlife, with care taken to depict multiple classes and walks of life. From the peasant to the king, Death finds us all, eventually.[22] A series of woodcuts by Hans Holbein the Younger dating from the sixteenth century takes the satire further, depicting the arrival of Death at ironic or inopportune times: a nun sneaking a last look at her lover, a judge about to accept a bribe for a favourable decision. Holbein's work has been read, in particular, as evidence of sectarian unrest during the early Protestant Reformation, as it takes a critical view of sacred and secular power. Yet the allegory both predates Holbein's work and has endured long beyond it.[23] The religious reminder is to embrace piety, as death could happen to anyone, at any moment; however, the smiling motif of the skeletons and the application of 'dance' movements to bodies facing death provide an ironic contrast to the permanency and silence of death. Dances and performances around the subject of death were both performed in some areas of French and German-speaking Europe, and depictions of this dance were published in books (Holbein's woodcuts) and adorned the walls of monuments and churches. Like medieval mystery plays, the performance aspect of the dance permitted deeper learning of the central religious message: at any time, Death may come.

The *danse macabre* motif also centres around a liminal moment and an invitation. The appearance of Death – whether welcome or not – frames the moment of death as a threshold-crossing. Death stretches out a skeletal hand, and the newly deceased person passes from life into the afterlife. Such an invitation is a key moment. Time after time in the immersive performances that I discuss here, I was looked in the eye, offered an outstretched hand or caught by a subtle gesture: 'Come this way!' In writing about immersives, critics (myself included) have struggled to name the feeling of being selected for a one-on-one performance, in particular the change in performance register that emerges when a person in an audience goes from being part of the spectating mass to a willing solo participant. The actor – already in an uncanny position of semi-reality – is both very human and very superhuman in that moment. Such invitations are centrepieces in Bricolage and Third Rail's performances: Alice and the White Rabbit in *Then She Fell* pulled me into closets for interrogations; the resort attendants in *The Grand Paradise* beckoned me to observe their languid affairs; the actors of *STRATA* refitnessed me by placing me in absurd, dreamlike environments; the improvisers of *DODO* posed perplexing questions about my suitability for inclusion in the museum collection. The outstretched hand in immersive performance is an invitation to follow. Acceptance of that invitation – most often as a solo individual, suddenly 'called out' of a larger group – analogically maps onto the *danse macabre*'s vision of Death.

What is more, everyone dances in these performances. Unlike *Sleep No More*, which rewards invested audience members with one-on-ones and novel tasks, Bricolage and Third Rail's work privileges the individual audience member more directly. There is a feeling of radical egalitarianism and individualism in these works. As the *danse macabre* suggests, everyone is touched by the invitation to participate. The universality of the immersive experience and its divergent pathways towards a final conclusion mirror the comic humanism of the *danse macabre*. Although individual audience members went on individual paths within the immersive entertainment, often accepting the actor's invitation to transgress or pass over into another, liminal world, the return to real life often also occurs within some group culminating experience. Often this occurs with some final performance or communal event; *The Grand Paradise* and *Ghost Light* brought together characters into a choreographed finale. *STRATA* ended at the bar, and *Saints Tour* and *DODO* ended with community and food. Having been through the journey, making our way back out of the looking-glass, a kind of temporary death, we return again to the world. Pittsburgh critic Wendy Arons noted this specifically in her final thoughts on *DODO*: 'Each donor takes an individual journey, just as we do in life, although – as in life – we all wind up in the same place in the end. That place . . . is one in which you may experience something akin to a rebirth of consciousness'.[24] Perhaps the immersive experience, then, offers an escape, a chance to experience the dance between the real and the beyond without the usual permanent consequences of such a journey.

The Dark Ride Affective Cluster

My connection of the dark ride and the *danse macabre* to certain immersive theatre productions has been an attempt to describe the feeling of participation, the affective responses of viewing and participating at the same time, and their tendency towards eerie themes, if not outright horror elements. Even those performances that did not engage with the classical elements of the macabre (death, monsters, ghosts, violence) seemed to be inflected with some flavour of the weird. Immersive theatre is, in a way, an arena within which uncanny or supernatural occurrences happen. Magic, ghost stories, historical murder thrillers, circuses, museums and the glamour of pop culture nostalgia are all widely represented in 2010s immersives. By connecting this cluster of feeling to earlier technological representations of the odd and the taboo, I venture an explanation for the feeling of immersivity itself: touching the weird, walking into the abyss.

Writing about *The Grand Paradise*, Zay Amsbury found that 'the characters, setting, and events are all pointing to something else, some mystery, some set of ideas, some haunting or yearning or lustful or murderous force, something like death, lurking behind everything you can see and experience'.[25] *Grand Paradise* did stage some version of ghostliness, as the resort attendants emerged out of the dark, dancing to woozy tropical steel guitars. In fact, Amsbury's feeling of surprise, apprehension and a nostalgic or erotic thrill is behind each of the performances detailed here. Ghosts are explicitly depicted in *Saints Tour* and *Ghost Light*, and implicitly invoked as museum figures come to life in *DODO*, or as Wonderland characters that materialise in the corner of a Victorian hospital room. Importantly, neither Bricolage nor Third Rail overdetermine their stories or their mythology; plenty of questions are left unanswered. Such flexibility is aided by the performances' reliance on visual spectacle, dance and music.

Speaking of immersive work in general, Ben Brantley acknowledged the 'delicate line' that Bricolage and Third Rail walk: 'You want people to be just uncomfortable enough so that they feel disoriented, but you don't want them to freak out, either. There has to be some feeling in the back of your mind that you're in good hands.'[26] Like the dark ride, immersives provide the popular thrill, the near-miss with horror. But such a structure places these works' genealogy squarely in the amusement park. A part of what makes works like *Then She Fell* or even *Sleep No More* so long-running is their gestures towards familiar popular entertainment forms: the nightclub, the amusement park, the haunted ride. They harken back to earlier immersive entertainments and macabre images, from medieval death allegories to the hokey comedy of Disney attractions. Perhaps to medieval eyes and ears, performances and representations of the *danse macabre* had a similar immersive effect, allowing the play of fantasy and working-through of death anxiety. But the haunted house, the Old Mill ride and the invitation to dance with death also lie subtly underneath the immersive theatre structure. And even if Bricolage's audience members are not subjected to bloody tableaux or jump scares, they might still encounter something of the macabre in Bricolage's immersive performances. It is not a haunted house, but it is not not one, either.

Notes

1. Steve Cuden, interview with Tami Dixon and Jeffrey Carpenter, *Storybeat: The Podcast for the Creative Mind*, podcast audio, 24 January 2019, www.storybeat.net/tami-dixon-jeffrey-carpenter/.
2. D. Tran, 'The Walls Come Tumbling Down: In Immersive Theatre, Audiences Are Breaking the Rules – Moving Around, Talking with the Actors and Molding the Action', *American Theatre*, 30/6 (July 2013), 30.
3. Arnold Aronson et al., *The History and Theory of Environmental Scenography: Second Edition* (London, New York: Methuen Drama, 2018); Josephine Machon, *Immersive Theatres: Intimacy and Immediacy in Contemporary Performance* (London: Palgrave Macmillan, 2013), p. xv.
4. Among early twentieth-century dark rides, 'American audiences preferred darker more fearful adventures whilst UK audiences preferred less dramatic destinations', often based in exotic tourism. J. Zika, 'The Dawn of the Dark Ride at the Amusement Park', *IE2014: Proceedings of the 2014 Conference on Interactive Entertainment* (December 2014), https://doi.org/10.1145/2677758.2677775.
5. David Wiles, *A Short History of Western Performance Space* (New York: Cambridge University Press, 2003), p. 19.
6. G. White, 'On Immersive Theatre', *Theatre Research International*, 37/3 (2012), 228.
7. N. J. Nelson, 'The No Proscenium Glossary', *No Proscenium*, updated 14 September 2019, https://noproscenium.com/the-no-proscenium-glossary-for-audiences-c1597d510268.
8. 'The dark ride inherited the art and technology of the Chambers of Horror but bested them by transporting its audience both mentally and physically, sending them on a journey through graphic scenes and surprises before safely delivering them into the open air again.' B. Kwaitek, 'The Dark Ride', (unpublished MA thesis: Western Kentucky University, 1995) http://digitalcommons.wku.edu/theses/914.
9. 'The darkness or "spooky" quality of these rides is not necessarily the most important but it has become their legacy . . . it is not simply the act of committing one's body to a track or a path, it is the much deeper concept of traveling through a space in order to immersive oneself in some form of narrative.' Zika, 'The Dawn of the Dark Ride'.
10. Nelson, 'The No Proscenium Glossary'.
11. Tran, 'The Walls Come Tumbling Down'.
12. Artistic director Jeffrey Carpenter: 'When I worked with Enrique Vargas and Teatro de los Sentidos out of Barcelona on the U.S. premiere of Echo of the

Shadow, that work began to crystalize and inform all our creative direction . . . audience members were individual "travelers" embarking on a journey through a series of dream-like chambers in search of their shadow, which they had lost, ultimately a metaphor for our deeper unconscious selves.'; K. Yu, 'The Immersive 5 with Bricolage's Jeffrey Carpenter and Tami Dixon', *No Proscenium*, 16 May 2018, *https://noproscenium.com/the-immersive-5-with-bricolages-artistic-director-jeffrey-carpenter-and-producing-artistic-70ca91371a4d*.

13. Bricolage's work has further developed sensory immersion, including *OjO* (2014), a travel performance performed for blindfolded audiences, and *The Forest of Everywhere* (2018), a sensory-friendly piece for autism-spectrum audiences.

14. See B. Mueller, 'Bricolage's "Strata" Offers Layers of Oddity', *Pittsburgh Post-Gazette*, 12 August 2012; and linked reviews on Bricolage's website, *www.bricolagepgh.org/press/in-the-media/strata/*.

15. Rice quoted in B. O'Driscoll, 'When the Saints Go Marching in a Mill Town', *American Theatre* (May 2015), *www.americantheatre.org/2015/04/29/when-the-saints-go-marching-in-a-mill-town*. See also S. Eberson, 'A Tour of Braddock Will Discover Compassionate and Talented Performers', *Pittsburgh Post-Gazette*, 20 May 2015; and W. Arons, 'Braddock Saints Tour', *The Pittsburgh Tatler*, 31 May 2015, *https://wendyarons.wordpress.com/2015/05/31/braddock-saints-tour-a-bricolage-and-realtime-interventions-co-production/*.

16. A. Knell, '"DODO" is a Dream: Bricolage Breathes Life into Carnegie Museums', *No Proscenium*, 31 October 2017, *https://noproscenium.com/dodo-is-a-dream-bricolage-breathes-life-into-carnegie-museums-the-nopro-review-cde-051ba6189*; S. Brewster, '*Dodo* by Jeffrey Carpenter et al.', *Theatre Journal*, 70/4 (December 2018), 544–5; and W. Arons, '"*DODO*" at Bricolage Production Company', *The Pittsburgh Tatler*, 21 October 2017, *https://wendyarons.wordpress.com/2017/10/21/dodo-at-bricolage-production-company/*.

17. D. Tran, 'You Can Go Your Own Way', *New York Times*, 27 December 2015; B. Shaefer, 'Welcome to Paradise', *Dance Magazine*, 89/2 (December 2015); E. Hefner, 'The New Immersive Theater', *Hudson Review*, 69/1 (spring 2016), 108–14.

18. 'What are the ways we can move the audience through the space in unexpected ways . . . can we find ways to create a maze inside this theatre?' asks Third Rail co-Artistic Director Zach Morris. J. Chandler, 'Backstage at Lincoln Center Theater's "Ghost Light"', *NBC 4 New York*, *www.nbcnewyork.com/news/local/backstage-at-lincoln-center-theater_s-_ghost-light__new-york/210827/*. See also M. S. Eddy, 'Managing the Ephemeral', *Stage Directions* (October 2017), 8–9;

and D. Bisaha, 'Ghost Light by Zach Morris', *Theatre Journal*, 70/2 (June 2018), 238–40.
19. Cuden, interview with Tami Dixon and Jeffrey Carpenter, *Storybeat*.
20. J. Ritter, 'Dance and Immersive Performance: A Multicase Study of Three International Immersive Productions' (unpublished PhD Dissertation: Texas Woman's University, 2016), 121–36.
21. Nelson, 'The No Proscenium Glossary'.
22. Sophie Oosterwijk and Stefanie Knöll (eds), *Mixed Metaphors: The* Danse Macabre *in Medieval and Early Modern Europe* (Newcastle upon Tyne: Cambridge Scholars Publishing, 2011), and B. Corriveau Gotschall, 'A Brief History of the *"Danse Macabre"'*, *Atlas Obscura*, 11 October 2017, s*www.atlasobscura.com/articles/danse-macabre-david-pumpkins-art-history*.
23. J. P. Mackenbach and R. P. Dreier, 'Dances of Death: Macabre Mirrors of an Unequal Society', *International Journal of Public Health*, 57 (2012), 915.
24. W. Arons, 'DODO at Bricolage Production Company'.
25. Z. Amsbury, 'Getting to Paradise: The Grand Paradise by Third Rail Projects', *No Proscenium*, 10 February 2016, https://noproscenium.com/getting-to-paradise-the-grand-paradise-by-third-rail-projects-810904ae59c4.
26. Interviewed in *Between Yourself and Me*, Dance Films Association in collaboration with Third Rail Projects, producer, New York, 2017.

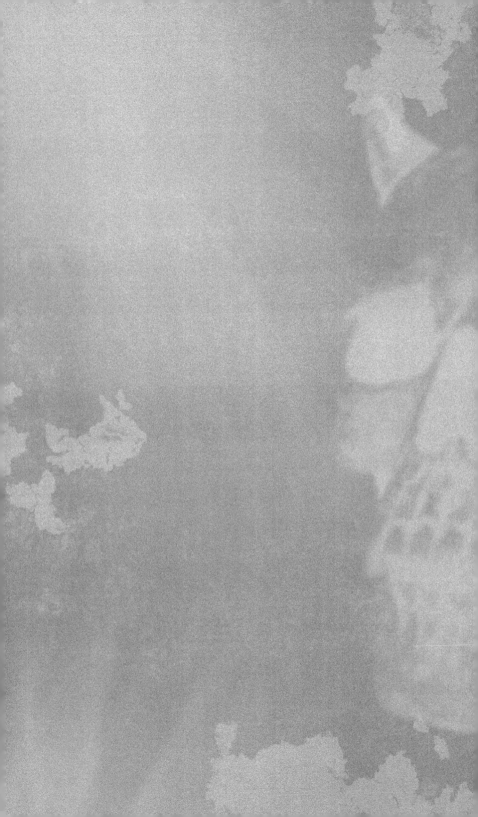

14

Liveness and Aliveness

Chasing the Uncanny in the Contemporary Haunt Industry

David Norris

IN HER ESSAY on the use of dolls and object vivification within Gothic film, Joana Rita Ramalho proposes a 'taxonomy of inanimate bodies',[1] in which a collective branch of non-person, inanimate objects is split into two subcategories: 'human-like objects' and 'dead bodies'. Across these classifications exist figures common to horror including dolls, mannequins, dummies, automata, ghosts, vampires and zombies. While Ramalho's essay addresses film, this chapter centres upon the non-person, inanimate objects that human actors embody in immersive scare attractions. In particular, I will analyse the character of the doll, gauging the extent to which it sparks an affective uncanny response in scare attraction visitors. Drawing upon my own ten years of experience in the haunt industry along with case studies from high-profile European and American scream parks, I will consider the ways in which the performer-embodied doll figure disorientates and manipulates spectators' perceptions of liveness. I argue that it is the relative vagueness of the doll as a horror trope that makes it distinctly useful in the scare entertainment industry, where producers are generally aiming at a broad market with a range of expectations.

Scare attractions are a subset of immersive theatre, sitting within the definition provided by Adam Alston of 'theatre that surrounds audiences within an aesthetic space in which they are frequently . . . free to move and/or participate'.[2] Scholars of this form often emphasise the spectator's increased agency and control,[3] or extend 'the participatory nature of audiencing'[4] in these formats compared to the relatively more passive spectatorship contexts of book, film and observational theatre. A satisfying rendering of the uncanny in a live environment requires a relative abdication of control by the creator whereby the audience member's imagination generates potential threats that are not stated outright. A resulting collaboration occurs between the creation and the audience member's creative imagination and their own body (which is less mediated), thus promoting a more 'visceral understanding and experience of performance' that may be felt as an authentic moment of uncanny fear.[5] Thus, effective characters within relatively passive media forms may operate differently in immersive environments, where a lack of fixed offstage space, a less controllable soundscape and a more unpredictable spectator-actor relationship shape the uncanny's materialisation.

The Terrain of the Haunt Industry

Scholars of horror and performance have increasingly turned their attention to the haunt industry's dynamic entertainments, with Madelon Hoedt defining the scare attraction as 'a venue designed to frighten its audience. The term does not apply to sites that claim to be haunted by actual ghosts. Instead, the venues have a basis in fiction or "horrible history"'.[6] She identifies scare attractions as site-specific performances featuring live actors, custom sets, animatronics and sound and lighting effects. Though Hoedt's definition is sound, I would contest that frightening the guests is not the only possible positive audience response, with some haunts using tropes associated with horror and horror franchises to elicit other responses. Humour factors into 2018's *Revenge of Chucky* 'ScareZone' from Universal Studios Hollywood's *Halloween Horror Nights 28*, which featured a wisecracking interactive version of the eponymous film-series character surrounded by large-scale grotesque versions of popular board games.[7] Furthermore, I will differentiate between the terms 'scare attraction', 'scream park' and 'scare maze'. Theme parks will often operate a series of indoor walkthrough events in autumn under titles like Universal Studios Theme Parks' *Halloween Horror Nights*; *Knott's Scary Farm* at Knott's Berry Farm in Buena Park, California; and *Alton Towers Scarefest* at Alton

Towers, Staffordshire, England. Seasonal events also take place annually on converted farmland or in farm parks, including *Tulley's Shocktoberfest* in West Sussex, England; *Farmageddon* in Ormskirk, England; and *NetherWorld Haunted House* in Atlanta, Georgia. Each of these events features multiple, separately themed walkthrough areas. The term 'scream park', therefore, refers to events with multiple components, while the term 'scare maze' refers to individually themed components within the larger parks. The somewhat counter-intuitive word 'maze' is non-literal here and is an industry-standard term for any single continuous walkthrough regardless of whether there is a labyrinthine component.

One metaphor that I often use when describing commercial scare attractions is that of a bread sampling plate with an array of accompanying dips. A restaurateur cannot dictate to a customer which bread to put into which dip, and certainly cannot predict with total accuracy the preferences of any individual guest, owing to a natural variation in personal tastes, cultural expectations or other dynamics. What can be done is to identify the combinations that most customers have responded well to and make recommendations based on those responses, while still leaving opportunities for choice and individual agency. Likewise, scare attraction marketers take standard horror tropes, characters and scenarios and deploy them in a range of contexts. Universal Studios Hollywood's *Revenge of Chucky* was a humorous zoned area that centred on the infamous killer doll, while Universal Studios Orlando, also under the *Halloween Horror Nights* brand, used the doll archetype far differently four years earlier in the *Dollhouse of the Damned* scare maze. With little scholarly research focused on the haunt attraction industry and commercial interests as a major driver, approaches to scare attractions evolve primarily through trial and error. Over time, attraction designers build industry knowledge on the most effective guest-terrorising techniques, all the while recognising that audience responses, including fear-based reactions, are inherently variable and challenging to assess.

Scare attraction designers seek to balance and juxtapose an atmosphere of collective celebration and tension-release with attempts to activate individual spectators' self-reflexive horror responses. This tension can be seen in the scare attraction's use of crowd-pleasing jump scares and elements that trigger the uncanny. A jump scare, in which a build-up of tension precedes a sudden, adrenaline-releasing surprise, is perhaps the simplest tool in the horror creator's arsenal. Describing the aural jump scare within film, Valerio Sbravatti addresses the 'startle response, that is, the instinctive defensive reaction that occurs when humans . . . are exposed to a sudden and intense auditory stimulus'.[8] Scare attraction jump scares operate on the same principles. Hoedt observes similar dynamics within scare attractions: 'the most basic examples of [breaking the feeling of control in audience members] are simple shock effects, with actors or animatronics suddenly jumping out at you'.[9] In most instances, it matters very little whether the actor or animatronic is dressed as a doll, a vampire, a zombie, an axe murderer or an average joe: if the attraction successfully builds tension in between jump scares, the startle's specific trigger is of little importance. The jump scare is both the haunt industry's bread and butter and something of a *bête noir*. As with films, scare attractions perceived to rely exclusively on jump scares are often criticised as 'an end in themselves',[10] with the implication that they are simplistic, one-dimensional and creatively lazy. While these critiques are perhaps short-sighted, the most adept of scare attraction designers combine fragmentary jump scares with attempts to build a more sustained fear response. One of the most popular ways to do this is through engaging the uncanny.

The Theoretical Uncanny

Foundational to contemporary understandings of the uncanny are Ernst Jentsch's 'On the Psychology of the Uncanny' (1906)[11] and Sigmund Freud's 'The Uncanny' (1919).[12] Most theorists, including Freud himself, have treated the latter as an extension of the former, with Freud explicitly crediting Jentsch as originating the theory. However, as Carol Leader observes, the two essays' treatment of the idea are ontologically different, especially in their approach to the case study text, E. T. A. Hoffman's 'The Sandman' (1818).[13] Both essays use the Sandman character as an example of the uncanny, but while Freud's definition of the *unheimlich* ('uncanny') focuses on the sensations of the 'familiar yet unhomely' triggered within the spectator, Jentsch is more concerned with how an alien object is living or inanimate. Another way of framing this is that Freud's definition of the affective response revolves around the spectator's relationship with themselves and their worldview, while Jentsch's definition is preoccupied with the spectator's relationship with a viewed object that represents a direct threat. The affective uncanny response, therefore, has been tied directly to human survival.[14] The implication of this Jentschian definition (and subsequent empirical findings of the uncanny as a potential form of survival response) is that the live encounter creates and strengthens the affective uncanny response beyond what is possible in literary and filmic mediums. There is, however, another consideration: live encounters with the uncanny demand a different level of belief suspension and credibility. For live manifestations of the uncanny to truly affect the audience, scare attraction designers must override the dissonance of bearing witness to what they know are inanimate objects coming to life alongside the suspension of disbelief that knows this is both impossible and manipulative.

In addition to empathy, Michael Parsons identifies the 'sum of past experience', or individuals' personal histories, encounters or exposures to particular character types, as being central to their affective uncanny responses.[15] Masahiro Mori's notion of the 'uncanny valley', adapted as a name from his own Japanese term '*Shinwakan*' (anglicised), also affirms the impact of individual and cultural expectations.[16] Together, these theorists suggest that there may be a 'shelf-life' to the efficacy of uncanny characters based on cultural exposure. As Roxana Stuart remarks, 'When we think of the vampire today, we are more likely to snicker than to shudder. We know everything'.[17]

In *The Uncanny* (2003), Nicholas Royle invokes not a sense of externality, but a sense of the self-reflexive, arguing that 'The uncanny involves feelings of uncertainty, in particular regarding the reality of who one is and what is being experienced. Suddenly one's sense of oneself . . . seems strangely questionable'.[18] This emphasis frames the uncanny as a sensation that centres the individual spectator and is derived internally by a kind of crisis of self, rather than the seen object itself directly conveying the uncanny response. Royle's suppositions are aligned with Freud, who suggests that the uncanny emerges in the following sequence: an object is viewed; the perceiver has a strange affective response to the viewed object; and the perceiver experiences discomfort from their own initial response to the viewed object. Jentsch offers a different chain of events, which aligns with Parsons' survival model: a strange object is viewed, and the perceiver experiences an uncomfortable affective response.

Identifying manifestations of the uncanny does not stop with these two chains. Mori's understanding of *Shinwakan*, for example, recognises that while human-like behaviour in artificial intelligence (AI) elicits positive responses from perceivers, there is a level of AI human-likeness that inspires intense discomfort.[19] For Mori, humans experience unease when interacting with a machine or automaton that behaves mostly, but not entirely, like a human. James Hamilton describes this phenomenon as 'a combination, perhaps a blending, of repulsion and attraction . . . felt in the presence of fixtures whose visually apparent features are very close to, but not exactly like, those of a healthy human being'.[20] '*Shinwakan*' has no simple English definition and is best translated as a combination of the phrases 'mutually be friendly' and '"the sense of" hybridized as a negative sensation'.[21] Unsurprisingly, robotics researchers, social scientists and humanities scholars often return to Mori's uncanny valley to theorise how humans respond to human-like entities. Such encounters can inspire fear, disgust, shock and nervousness, suggesting that 'the uncanny valley may not be a single phenomenon to be explained by a single theory but rather a nexus of phenomena with disparate causes'.[22] This is encouraging for scare attraction designers seeking to employ the uncanny as a dynamic; the more varied phenomena available, the more possible collaborations between performers and participants.

An individual's propensity for empathy also contours Mori's uncanny valley, as researchers determined from comparing spectators' scores on a Davis (1980, 1983) Interpersonal Reactivity Index (a measurement of innate empathetic behaviours) against the responses to base and uncanny versions of cartoon animal characters.[23] These observations have two implications for scare attraction designers. First, the designers can most effectively serve a broad audience by embracing a variety of human-like characters, the better to trigger spectators' uncanny responses. Second, as spectators have naturally varying levels of empathy, it perhaps follows that they have varying tendencies in collaborating, consciously or unconsciously, with an actor's attempt to elicit an uncanny response. Thus, while both the *unheimlich* and the uncanny valley have at times been treated as representing a single, overlapping affective dynamic, these notions are better understood as incorporating multiple sensations, all of which are subject to individual variety.

The Human-like Object in the Commercial Haunt Industry: the Doll as a Case Study

In representing the undead, an actor is tasked with performing their own dead body brought back to life. The spectator is subsequently asked to understand this intention and, in a horror environment, be afraid of it. However, in the instance of Ramalho's human-like entities, including the doll, the human actor is being tasked with performing something 'other'.

Something less than human. Something empty. A doll is neither alive nor dead; it is an inanimate object that we imbue with animation: the living-unliving. And scholars have long linked the doll to strong uncanny responses.[24]

In a live environment, the presentation of a human-like entity like the doll does not require a visible weapon or detailed backstory to generate a threat for the spectator. The spectator is often left instead to make such active choices of their own regarding what 'possible' threats they might provide. However, unlike the undead in popular culture, which come back to animated life, the doll is partially uncanny because of its lack of motion, or its implied potential motion.[25] The doll has the potential both to be 'weird' and 'eerie', two aspects of the uncanny as proposed by Mark Fisher. Fisher describes the weird as 'so strange that it should not exist here. Yet if the entity or object is here, then the categories which we have up until now used to make sense of the world cannot be valid'.[26] This evokes both the 'categorisational uncertainty' model, which Christopher Ramey argues is at heart of Mori's uncanny valley,[27] and the 'categorical interstitiality' proposed by Noël Carroll when describing the doll's sinister effect.[28] In the case of the live actor embodying a doll, two qualities are being endowed to the doll that 'should not exist here' – namely the ability to move and the presence of a mind. Ramalho, who presents these two qualities as the locus of a doll's uncanniness, claims that dolls 'always seem to be on the verge of moving and revealing agency'.[29] Not only might dolls create weird sensations, but also eerie ones, 'either when there is something present where there should be nothing, or there is nothing present when there should be something'.[30] In the case of the doll and other human-like inanimate objects, the absence of movement and a brain is the void where that 'nothing' exists – the things that are repurposed when the doll becomes animate. This might in theory have the potential to negate any possible uncanny sensation with the potential 'nothing' filled in, but not if the movement and brain are not perfectly aligned with human behaviour. If the actor executes movement of a non-human quality, then both eerie and weird sensations may materialise. Likewise, the mind projected by the animate doll is of a somewhat alien nature, as it is subject to both the imaginative whims of the spectator and an important component: the mask. The doll character's mask may be relatively neutral or grotesque, generally failing to convey the doll's attitude. As such, the scare attraction doll may have 'a' brain; to the susceptible spectator, however, it is an unclear, ambiguous, non-human brain. Under these circumstances there is the possibility of human mirroring – the self-reflective dynamic of Freud's *unheimlich* that allows the spectator to be confronted with their own object-ness, a challenging of identity. A thing that is defined by being-looked-at is now doing-the-looking-at; subject becomes object and vice versa. This dynamic, along with the scare attraction's already optimal conditions for generating the uncanny, allows a doll to become perhaps the most frightening character type in scare attractions.

In the summer of 2012, I was part of the production team working for AtmosFEAR! Scare Entertainment on the show *Horror Camp Live!*, billed as the first overnight scare attraction in Europe. With a high price point, the event catered to small audiences of just thirty-six spectators and was located on the site of the *Scare Kingdom* seasonal Halloween event. *Horror Camp Live!* used a pre-existing scare maze structure (known as 'Blood Bath' during Halloween) as part of its setting, in addition to a camping area and a room that operated as a bar during the Halloween season. For *Horror Camp Live!*, however, a quiet, empty scare maze bordered the area in which the visitors congregated.

Horror Camp Live! incorporated standard horror characters, one of which was a living porcelain doll named 'Domina'. Domina was conceived by director Jason Karl as a character that would interact with audiences in a manner not possible in conventional scare mazes since her relationship to them would develop over the course of the evening. Domina was introduced to the spectators early in the evening, with a group of twelve sent to 'retrieve' her from her location at the farm's far end. Once found, Domina would follow the group and, arriving at the base, disappear into the body of the 'Blood Bath' attraction. From this moment on, Domina would materialise and sporadically take individual guests into 'Blood Bath' for an unspecified time. The performer playing Domina had free reign to do what she wanted in response to the guest's fear level: she would walk hand-in-hand with the guest in the pitch dark, sit the guest in a chair to abandon them, use a torch to create jump scares, dance with or for the guest and make ambiguous gestures and hand movements, among other discomforting activities. Many guests found their encounter to be extremely frightening, frequently using the given safe-word to end the experience; there were multiple instances of guests bursting into tears.

The case of Domina is taken from a niche attraction and is not the industry norm. It does, however, show the potency of dolls to generate the uncanny response in a live environment. Domina's performer operated in optimum conditions (e.g., low audience numbers and extended time availability) and thus was gifted many opportunities to generate frightening scenarios. These optimum conditions are, however, outside the constraints of most Halloween scare mazes that require greater guest throughput and subsequently have less exposure time and more environmental controls. (Few scare attractions operate in an environment that can be silent or that can isolate guests away from larger groups.) *Horror Camp Live!* was a high-cost event that, through its small audience sizes, curtailed undesirable audience behaviours and encouraged collaboration.

Major US scare attractions have profited from featuring performer-embodied dolls within disorientating mazes. In 2014, *Halloween Horror Nights* showcased the Orlando maze *Dollhouse of the Damned*, while *Knotts Scary Farm* hosted *The Doll Factory* annually from 2007 to 2011. Both mazes depended heavily on jump scares, but they also generated a greater range of potential frights than comparative attractions. Indeed, they thematically demonstrated opposing approaches to the doll's inherent uncanniness. *Dollhouse of the Damned* presented the dolls as weird objects: grotesque and oversized.[31] The maze intermixed live performers with an unusually proportioned baby doll, headless mannequins and ballerinas with impossibly contorted bodies. Conversely, the long-running *The Doll Factory* staged the slow loss of humanity as an industrial unit turned human beings into dolls, which visitors encountered throughout the attraction.[32] This arguably invokes Ramalho's 'dollifying', or the 'recurring tendency towards abjection, self-hate and destruction', which she suggests is a source of the doll's uncanniness (and reinforces the self-crisis in Freud's *unheimlich*).[33] *The Doll Factory*'s embodied dolls still executed jump scares, but within this narrative audiences also were prompted through the attraction's varied collaborations to experience self-reflexive uncanny responses.

Concluding Thoughts: a Difficult Balance with Some Untapped Potential

In terms of the eliciting of an uncanny response, it may be expected that producers of scare attractions would be prone to use predominantly undead character types such as the vampire or zombie in their attractions – animated corpse monsters. These tropes are indeed used regularly within the industry when creating non-uncanny responses such as jump scares. However, scare attraction producers will more often use actors playing inanimate human-like entities such as dolls when aiming to stimulate the uncanny response when compared to their use of undead characters. In this chapter I have indicated some of the reasons why this is the case:

1. Audience overfamiliarity with undead character types that lessens the characters' ability to prompt uncanny responses.
2. The double dissonance inherent in live actors, playing undead roles, who are present in the same shared space as the spectator. The spectator is asked to suspend disbelief by reading a living body that is viscerally present in their space as a corpse-object, and simultaneously suspend disbelief in a different way by reading a corpse-object as animate. This asks for high levels of conscious collaboration from the audience to be sustained for any length of time.
3. The human-like entity's status, especially in the case of the doll, is potentially both a weird and eerie object when played by actors. This allows for a greater range of affective opportunities and provides more ways of being discomforted within a genre that is affected considerably by individual preference.
4. The doll is more easily sprinkled in as a component part of a wider aesthetic or narrative within scare mazes, whereas undead characters often demand exclusive focus. Dolls can be intermingled semi-formally with other horror tropes more readily than, for instance, a vampire.

As Andy Lavender claims, 'we have moved from a society of the spectacle to a society of involved spectation; in turn, we experience ourselves having an experience'.[34] This evokes the Freudian *unheimlich* chain and multiple models of Mori's *Shinwakan*. It has been claimed that the current performance environment is one where audiences seek 'a greater range of choices', in order to '[perform] a larger array of actions'.[35] I propose that within scare attractions there is a multiplicity of invitations provided by designers, of which the uncanny is a potentially useful, but simultaneously problematic one. In the case of the human-like object there are fewer obstacles, and scare attractions are usually designed, at least potentially, to offer the spectator an uncanny response. However, offers of the uncanny response are compromised by the mechanical aspects of the scare attraction industry, especially during the high-volume Halloween season, and cannot be solely relied upon. It is often blended with other spectatorial offerings such as jump scares, humour and pop-culture references, in order to produce an experience that attendees rate as having high-satisfaction. *Horror Camp Live!* indicates the considerable potential of live actors playing dolls for instilling the uncanny, while *The Doll Factory* demonstrates how this dynamic may be partially maintained while also incorporated into the standard industry model. Therefore, exploring the range and scope of human-like objects offers extremely fertile ground in live performance for generating uneasy and uncomfortable responses in a wide range of audiences. While our cinema and television screens may be prone to fill with creatures that emanate from the graveyard or crypt, the immersive environments of live horror are less likely to threaten us with fangs and more likely to stare at us blankly from plastic eyeballs, indicating nothing and letting us suspect anything.

Notes

1. J. R. Ramalho, 'The Uncanny Afterlife of Dolls: Reconfiguring Personhood through Object Vivification in Gothic Film', *Studies in Gothic Fiction*, 6/2 (2020), 29.
2. A. Alston, 'Audience Participation and Neoliberal Value: Risk, Agency and Responsibility in Immersive Theatre', *Performance Research*, 18/2 (2013), 129.
3. Josephine Machon, *Immersive Theatres: Intimacy and Immediacy in Contemporary Performance* (London: Palgrave Macmillan, 2013).
4. James Frieze (ed.), *Reframing Immersive Theatre: The Politics and Pragmatics of Participatory Performance* (London: Palgrave Macmillan, 2016), p. 6.
5. Daniel Schulze, *Authenticity in Contemporary Theatre and Performance* (London: Methuen, 2017), p. 37.
6. M. Hoedt, 'Keeping a Distance: The Joy of Haunted Attractions', *The Irish Journal of Gothic and Horror Studies*, 7 (2009), 36.
7. AllCentralFlorida *Revenge of Chucky – Halloween Horror Nights Orlando 2018* (2018), *www.youtube.com/watch?v=LIbbh1Nlei8&t=1163s*.
8. V. Sbravatti, 'Acoustic Startles in Horror Films: A Neurofilmological Approach', *Projections*, 13/1 (2019), 46.
9. Hoedt, 'Keeping a Distance', 39.
10. A. Landsberg, 'Horror Vérité: Politics and History in Jordan Peele's Get Out', *Continuum*, 32/5 (2018), 635.
11. E. Jentsch, 'On the Psychology of the Uncanny', translated by R. Sellars, *Angelaki: Journal of the Theoretical Humanities*, 2/1 (1995), 16.

12. S. Freud, 'The Uncanny', in James Stackey (ed.), *The Standard Edition of the Complete Psychological Works of Sigmund Freud* (London: The Hogarth Press, 1961/1919).
13. C. Leader, 'Supervising the Uncanny: The Play within the Play', *Journal of Analytical Psychology*, 60/5 (2015); E. T. A. Hoffman, 'The Sandman', translated by John Oxenford, in R. Godwin-Jones (ed.), *19th Century German Stories* (1994), *http://germanstories.vcu.edu*.
14. Michael Parsons, *Living Psychoanalysis: From Theory to Experience* (London: Karnac, 2014), pp. 8–9.
15. Parsons, *Living Psychoanalysis*, p. 9.
16. C. Bartneck, T. Kanda, H. Ishiguro and N. Hagita, 'Is the uncanny valley an uncanny cliff?', Proceedings of the 16th Institute of Electrical and Electronics Engineers International Symposium on Robot and Human Interactive Communication, RO-MAN, Jeju, Korea (2007), pp. 368–73.
17. Roxana Stuart, *Stage Blood: Vampires of the 19th Century Stage* (Bowling Green OH: Bowling Green State University Popular Press, 1994), p. 256.
18. Nicholas Royle, *The Uncanny* (Manchester: Manchester University Press, 2003), p. 1.
19. M. Mori, 'The Uncanny Valley', translated by K. F. MacDorman and T. Minato, *Energy*, 7 (1970/2005), 33–5.
20. J. Hamilton, 'The "Uncanny Valley" and Spectating Animated Objects', *Performance Research*, 20/2 (2015), 60–1.
21. S. Wang, S. Lilienfeld and P. Rochat, 'The Uncanny Valley: Existence and Explanations', *Review of General Psychology*, 19/4 (2015), 398.
22. C. Ho, K. MacDorman and Z. Pramano, 'Human emotion and the uncanny valley: A GLM, MDS, and Isomap analysis of robot video ratings', in Proceedings of the 3rd ACM/IEEE International Conference on Human Robot Interaction, HRI '08 (2008).
23. K. Smirnov and J. Pracejus, 'Empathy Drivers in the Uncanny Valley', *Advances in Consumer Research*, 38 (2011), 807.
24. R. Ballestriedo, 'From the Contortion of Reality to the Sinister: The Uncomfortable Hyperrealism of Mannequins, Dolls, Effigies and Wax figures', *Revista de Investigación sobre lo Fantástico*, 4/2 (2016), 93; H. Király, 'An Uncanny Cinema, a Cinema of the Uncanny: The Trope of the Doll in the Films of Manoel de Oliveira', *Acta Universitatis Sapientiae Film and Media Studies*, 15/1 (2018), 33; S. Y. Sencidiver, 'The Doll's Uncanny Soul', in L. Pinatti-Farnell and M. Beville (eds), *The Gothic and the Everyday: Living Gothic* (London: Palgrave Macmillan, 2014), p. 103.
25. Király, 'An Uncanny Cinema', p. 36.

26. Mark Fisher, *The Weird and the Eerie* (London: Repeater, 2016), p. 15.
27. C. H. Ramey, 'An Inventory of Reported Characteristics for Home Computers, Robots, and Human Beings: Applications for Android Science and the Uncanny Valley', in The Proceedings of the ICCS/CogSci-2006 Long Symposium 'Towards Social Mechanisms of Android Science', Vancouver, Canada, 2006. Quoted in Wang, Lilienfeld, S. and P. Rochat, 'The Uncanny Valley: Existence and Explanations'.
28. N. Carroll, 'The Nature of Horror', *The Journal of Aesthetics and Art Criticism*, 46/1 (1987), 55.
29. Ramalho, 'The Uncanny Afterlife of Dolls', 29.
30. Fisher, *The Weird and the Eerie*, p. 61.
31. Behind the Thrills, 'Dollhouse of the Damned at HHN 24 Full Walkthrough' (2014), *www.youtube.com/watch?v=YFtLGKs-rks&t=15s*.
32. ThemeParkAdventure, 'Knott's Scary Farm's THE DOLL FACTORY 2011 Maze Flow-Through', *www.youtube.com/watch?v=Efp8numQaA4*.
33. Ramalho, 'The Uncanny Afterlife of Dolls', 35.
34. Andy Lavender, *Performance in the Twenty-First Century* (London: Routledge, 2016), pp. 29–30.
35. Lavender, *Performance in the Twenty-First Century*, p. 29.

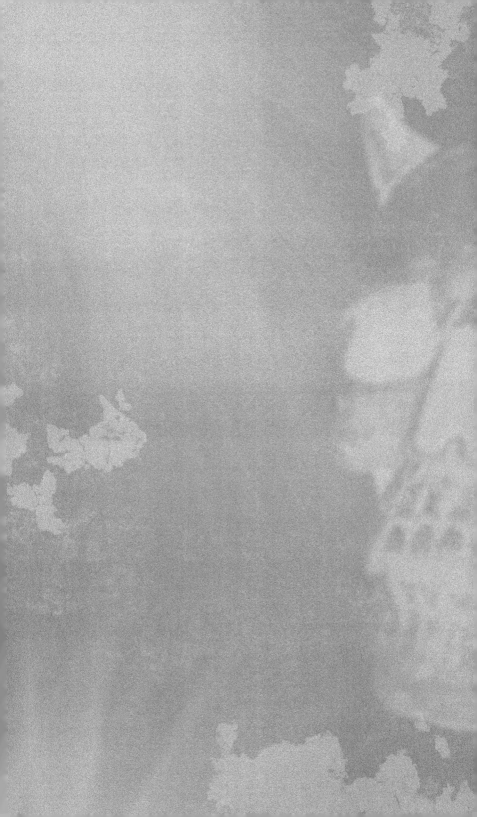

15

American Hells

Hell Houses, Abortion Frames and Unsexed Women

Robyn Lee Horn

IT WAS UNSEASONABLY COLD for Halloween in East Texas, but a queue of people stood shivering outside Clawson Assembly, an Assemblies of God Church, waiting for their turn to enter 2019's *Hell House: Present Darkness* (*HHPD*). I asked the woman running a snack table in the car park if she was involved in the production. 'No, but my granddaughter is', she beamed, handing me my hot chocolate. 'She'll be one of the girls in a cage in hell!' Noting my widening eyes, she let out a small laugh and said, 'I guess that sounds pretty strange, huh? Y'all ever been to a hell house before?'[1] *HHPD* was my first live experience, but I had a clear set of expectations going in. After immersing myself in the media coverage and scholarship on this conservative Christian performance phenomenon and watching hours of shaky mobile-phone footage taken by visitors to hell houses across the United States, I was prepared for blood, gore and shocking violence. I had travelled from New York specifically to see the bloody centrepiece of these horror performances: the hell house abortion scene.

Hell houses are a product of evangelical Christianity, which is an umbrella term for several conservative Protestant denominations that share defining characteristics: a literal interpretation of the Bible as God's revelation to humanity, the centralisation of a spiritual awakening or being 'born again', and a mandate to evangelise and convert others to the faith.[2] Evangelicals are also the lifeblood of the Christian Right, an increasingly powerful US political movement that helped propel Donald Trump to the presidency. Just as evangelicals are far from a monolith, the Christian Right is not an official political party. As such, they have no sanctioned political platform, but their ability to unify around talking points is a core strength of the movement. Perhaps no single issue has done more to coalesce evangelicals and engage them as political actors than abortion.

This chapter aims to uncover what hell houses can teach us about the field of theatre and performance, not to track the machinations of the Christian Right. However, because I will investigate how theatre can both advance and undermine the discursive strategies of activist groups, an overview of past and present anti-abortion tactics and rhetoric is salient to this research. For scholars interested in contemporary religious performance, hell houses have proven a rich site of enquiry. As a genre, hell houses are part haunted house, part B-movie slasher flick, part medieval morality play. They were a form of immersive theatre before *Sleep No More* infiltrated the consciousness of theatregoers everywhere.[3] They are amateur performances, primarily created by and for teenagers. Brian Jackson situates hell houses historiographically within a religious tradition that persuades by 'appealing to fear'.[4] Hank Willenbrink theorises the 'salvific performative' in hell houses, or the moment of narrative completion where rhetoric becomes real; these performances, Willenbrink posits, achieve actual transformation in their audience in the form of religious conversion (an enviable feat for theatre-makers). Both Anne Pellegrini and John Fletcher focus less on conversion; instead, they analyse hell houses as activist performance. Pellegrini deploys Raymond Williams' term 'structures of feeling' to describe how hell houses work upon an emerging ideology that is felt but not yet articulated.[5] In his landmark 2013 book, *Preaching to Convert: Outreach and Performance Activism in a Secular Age*, Fletcher positions hell houses within a tradition of activist theatre, although as a form that is more a utopian tool for shoring up the base than a mode for converting non-believers. As Fletcher describes it, hell houses are 'preaching to the converted'.[6] He rightly argues that while hell houses may be gruesome, teenage demons are not actually very frightening – certainly not enough to shift the mindset of one who is not already primed with eschatological terror.[7] Building on the premise that hell houses are activist theatre, I contend that embodiment carries the power to disrupt and contradict the rhetoric that activist theatre purports to advance. After describing hell houses' form and structure, I will detail the new rhetorical political strategy that underpins the dramaturgy of *HHPD* and the implicit dramaturgies of that work in opposition to theological and rhetorical themes.

Around Halloween, evangelical congregations in the United States, particularly in Texas, Florida and other parts of the South, stage hell houses as a conservative Christian alternative to secular haunted houses. Hell houses advertise their parallels to haunted houses through similar alliterative names and late-October performance dates. Both use horror techniques and graphic depictions of violence to entertain and instill fear in visitors, but they do so through different means and to achieve different ends. A visitor to a typical haunted house might be spooked by cackling witches, axe murderers and ghosts; in a hell house, the audience is witness to sinful transgressions with eternal consequences, a moral message that is amplified through repetition. In a series of hell house rooms, the audience watches disconnected scenes, each featuring a protagonist who struggles against temptation, relents to sin and then suffers retribution. The reiterative structure builds on itself, making each misstep seem overdetermined. Set against human predictability is the inspired cruelty of the punishments, which, in contrast, are startlingly varied and creative. Hell house dramaturgies teach that people cannot outmanoeuvre the devil, and even the smallest transgression is enough to open the door for evil to enter.

In addition to the obvious divergence in purpose between hell houses and haunted houses, the spectator experience is fundamentally different. Jump scares and grabby ghouls encourage participants to run and scream their way through haunted houses and come out the other side victorious. Hell houses slow down the experience considerably. Like medieval liturgical dramas that included 'dramatic representations of violence as a means of coercing theatre audiences into accepting the various truths "enacted dialectically"', hell houses encourage audiences to engage dialectic truths more contemplatively.[8] Robed demonic guides lead groups in an orderly fashion from room to room, verbally enforcing obedience and compliance along the way. This processional style allows the audience to see the stories as connected and progressively leading down a path towards one of life's inevitable conclusions: infinite reward or agonising punishment. Despite the audience's physical proximity to the players, the watchful death monitors and the delineated actor/audience division foreclose impulses to intervene physically or verbally. Like Augusto Boal's spect-actors, these audiences 'rehearse' other outcomes; however, hell house visitors cannot act. This creates dramatic irony akin to watching a horror film and wanting to yell at the screen: 'Don't go upstairs!' The construction results in hell house spectators focusing not on the monster, as they would in a haunted house, but instead on the protagonist. The monster's existence and appetites are inevitable; an individual's fate is sealed because of a fatal flaw in human judgement.[9]

Hell houses do not stage epic battles between personifications of God and the devil. In *HHPD*, Satan worked through the material trappings of a wicked world – mobile phones, marijuana, social media and music. While the dominant dramaturgical strategy of *HHPD* was to warn teenagers against worldly things, the embodied nature of theatre revealed hidden dramaturgies. I argue that the display and positioning of women – and the places where women are absent – put the ideological position of hell house creators on exhibit and highlight contradictions between ideology and chosen strategy. The conservative Christian stance on women's rights has undergone a series of careful revisions since the 1970s. Before these revisions were dramatised in hell houses, they were reflected in strategic shifts in anti-abortion rhetoric.

Although abortion is now central to evangelical identity and political advocacy, evangelicals did not share a unified opinion on abortion, much less a coherent strategy, until several years after the passage of *Roe v Wade*, the 1973 Supreme Court decision that legalised abortion in the United States. Early evangelicals who decried abortion framed it as emblematic of the breakdown of 'traditional' patriarchal family structures caused by feminism, the Equal Rights Amendment and sexual liberation.[10] Jerry Falwell, who founded the Christian Right political organisation 'The Moral Majority' in 1979, was one of several charismatic and media-savvy evangelical leaders who recognised abortion as the issue capable of coalescing evangelicals as powerful political actors. Co-opting rights and equality arguments from the secular left, the new Christian Right deployed a central strategy of 'fetal animation',[11] which put a visualised foetus as the victim at the debate's centre. The foetal-centric narrative served as a counterpoint to rights-based arguments from advocates for legal abortion by assigning rights to the foetus while neutralising charges of sexism by effectively erasing women from the debate. The National Right to Life Committee's print advertisement library is visual evidence of female erasure and the primacy of the foetus; of twelve approved advertisements, only one includes a woman, while close-up foetal images dominate eight advertisements.[12] The foetal-centric strategy not only deflected opposition arguments, but also mobilised an evangelical base through graphic descriptions of abortions and bloody images of aborted foetuses. In her research on evangelical rhetoric, Susan Harding argues that these images resonate with Christians, 'not automatically, but as an outcome of preacherly rhetoric, as sinful sacrifice, as ritual action that defiles and destroys the relationship between persona and God'.[13] In the rhetoric and imagery of the anti-abortion movement, the foetus plays a Jesus-like, sacrificial role of slaughtered purity. Without the foetus as actor in hell house abortion scenes, the 'abortion girls' become stand-ins for lost innocent lives. In hell houses abortion scenes, the young woman is having an abortion and is also being aborted, as her body and purity are destroyed.

Before visiting *HHPD*, I viewed four recordings of hell houses on YouTube as well as the 2001 documentary film *Hell House*, which followed the auditions, rehearsals and performances of *Hell House X: The Walking Dead* at Cedar Hill Church in Texas. In each case, the abortion scene was the performance's bloody centrepiece, employing the most dramatic special effects, violence and enactments of suffering. One scene in the film shows the teenage actors gathered around the cast list to see who would receive the coveted role of 'abortion girl'. In an interview for National Public Radio's *This American Life*, George Ratliff, director of the documentary *Hell House*, explained, 'The girls always want to be the suicide girl or the abortion girl, because those are the scenes where you get to scream and cry and emote the most'. In every hell house that I watched on video, the 'abortion girl' was the recipient of the most gruesome torture. As one ex-evangelical woman described in a 2018 interview with *New York Magazine*:

> I went to so many Hell Houses, year after year, and there was always an abortion scene. It was always a girl in a hospital bed, with the sheets soaked in blood. It was so graphic. Blood everywhere. Everywhere. So, so bloody. You as the audience starts [*sic*] to understand that she's had an abortion, and it was not done correctly. And she's crying, and she was very pale, and clearly about to die.[15]

In the YouTube recording of *Hell House 2013* by Greater Works Delivery Ministries, the abortion scene has the singular distinction of being preceded by a 'Graphic Content' disclaimer, although it immediately follows a school shooting scene in which ten students are 'executed' at close range with a realistic-looking handgun.[16] While other hell house scenes seek to portray violence realistically, the abortion scenes are a horror show filled with brutality and gore. Bloodstained walls, oversized medical instruments and stringy bits of meat meant to suggest an aborted foetus are the backdrop for an extravagant enactment of suffering, as the 'abortion girl' becomes a surrogate for the foetus.

When I attended *HHPD* in 2019, the theatrical tradition of hell houses appeared to be on the cusp of change. There are three major hell houses in the region of east Texas that I visited, Trinity Church (featured in the documentary *Hell House*), Tyler Metro Church and Clawson Assembly. Trinity Church and Tyler Metro Church told me that, while they customarily feature an abortion scene, they were not offering it in 2019. Clawson Assembly's hell house addressed abortion, but there was no bloody portrayal of the act. Instead, abortion was given only cursory consideration during the closing scene in a 'too liberal' church service. After the pastor told his congregation, 'It doesn't matter what you do. Just know that God loves you, as long as it makes you happy', we heard the inner thoughts of congregation members, including a young woman who said, 'See? "Whatever makes you happy". My body, my choice, so I'm going to the clinic tomorrow'. I wondered if the missing abortion scenes might reflect a mainstreaming of what Fletcher calls the 'in-yer-face' evangelism of hell houses, or if it was evidence of progressive values reaching evangelical congregations.[17] If hell houses are an activist theatre branch of the Christian Right political movement, then the abrupt change in a thirty-year theatrical tradition that formally centralised abortion perhaps denotes a deliberate shift in anti-abortion strategy.

While the anti-abortion movement continues to rely upon foetal-centric Christian morality, an emergent discursive strategy has been slowly gaining prominence: the pro-woman, or 'Post-abortion Syndrome' frame. Anti-abortion activist David Reardon, founder of the Elliot Institute for Social Science Research and author of several books, has been a leading voice in this movement. Although his academic credentials are dubious – he holds a PhD from a non-accredited, online university – he has partnered with several researchers to publish findings in nationally recognised scientific journals about the psychological effects of abortion on women.[18] In these studies, he claims that abortion results in sleep disorders,[19] generalised anxiety[20] and substance abuse[21] to support a broader claim of abortion as a trigger of post-traumatic stress.[22] Reardon's 1996 book *Making Abortion Rare: A Healing Strategy for a Divided Nation* is a playbook for winning over the 'middle majority' who consider themselves personally pro-life but politically pro-choice because they are reluctant to impose their moral views on women. Reardon asserts that the only winning anti-abortion strategy is to shift the movement's frame from protecting the foetus to protecting women from the dangers of abortion.[23] His book even includes an appendix of 'ProWoman/Pro-life Soundbites', effectively scripting the movement.

Reardon and his 'pro-women' position have received attention in the popular press[24] and from scholars,[25] but Reardon's strategy largely failed to take hold in the United States. In her 2006 article 'Pro-Life, Pro-Woman', Melody Rose suggests that Reardon's emergent strategy might backfire because 'the 2006 and 2008 elections may reveal a nation weary of pseudo-science and yearning for evidence-based policy'.[26] Rose could not have anticipated that the Trump era and the normalisation of 'alternative facts' would create the perfect conditions for Reardon's strategy to flourish.[27] In 2020, the Trump administration made several political moves indicating that the administration was adopting the pro-woman strategy. Trump posthumously pardoned Susan B. Anthony, a figure embraced by the anti-abortion movement, and featured anti-abortion activist and former Planned Parenthood employee Abby Johnson as a speaker for the Republican political convention. Johnson played the role of the repentant and reformed woman, mirroring the regretful woman narrative.[28] This reframing is perhaps connected to the ultimate pro-woman/pro-life manoeuvre: installing Amy Coney Barrett, a Christian woman who has expressed anti-abortion views, to the Supreme Court.[29]

Hell house abortion rooms exemplify the anti-abortion movement's foetal-centric rhetorical frame, and their sudden absence belies the pro-woman frame, but hell house performances also expose the persistence of the anti-feminist, patriarchal 'morality' frame that motivated early anti-abortion activists. The anti-feminist frame leaves the Christian Right open to being labelled a party of misogynists, a charge that the foetal-centric and pro-woman frames have attempted to deflect by erasing or championing women. Hell houses are full of teenage demons, who seduce and sneer in their ghoulish makeup, but I contend that the implicit villains of hell houses are archetypal female characters whom I call 'unsexed women'. Unsexed women embody the nightmarish ends of feminism as imagined by proponents of patriarchal gender roles. In each of the abortion scenes I watched on video, the doctor performing the abortion was played by a woman who rushed through formalities and offered rote platitudes to the frightened and uncertain 'abortion girl'. As the stage blood accumulated and the abortion girl's screams reached fever pitch, it was clear that the procedure had gone terribly wrong, but rather than offering a maternal response of comfort and care, the female doctor told the abortion girl to 'calm down' and 'shut up'.[30] Like Lady Macbeth, who sheds her femininity to commit heinous acts, these doctors were unsexed.[31]

Although the abortion scene was absent, *HHPD* presented several iterations of the unsexed woman. One scene begins with a father talking to his young son Chris (the only named character) while folding laundry on the living room couch. Suddenly, his wife flies through the door, bearing the unsexed markers of a business suit and strident impatience, and begins complaining, 'I've been up since six o'clock this morning. I've worked all day. I should be able to come home to my own house and have somewhere to sit'. As his son looks on, the henpecked and cowering father apologises, 'I'm sorry. I'll move it. I've been trying to get all his laundry done. I started dinner because I knew you'd be home soon'. The demon narrator stops the scene and gestures to the child, saying 'Let's check on Chris twenty years later and see what he's learned'. In the following scene, the lights come up on a now-grown-up Chris, drinking beer with his feet up, when a weary-looking young woman enters and begins to press him to help support their family by getting a job. Chris suddenly flies from his chair and, in a realistic-looking bit of stage combat, wraps his hands around his wife's throat and slams her against the refrigerator, choking her. The implied causal link was that Chris's misogyny and violence results directly from his parents' transposed gender roles.

A sex trafficking scene reinforces patriarchal ideology less directly, but actions taken by women bring about the scene's horrific outcomes. Like the abortion scenes in earlier hell house performances, men are almost entirely absent from this narrative. The lights come up on Sarah, a thirteen-year-old girl sitting alone in her bedroom. Strewn across Sarah's bed are stuffed animals and teen magazines, marking the girl as existing in the liminal space between childhood and adolescence. A chime, recognisable as an incoming text-message alert, comes through the speaker. As Sarah begins to type on her phone, the text-message exchange is projected on a screen and is narrated by two youthful, pre-recorded female voices. The conversation reveals that Sarah's mother is not at home because she is working late. Although this unsexed woman never appears on stage, she has an outsized presence. Due to her unmaternal absence, she cannot intervene as her daughter opens a Snapchat account, flirts with someone she thinks is a boy from her school and sneaks out to meet him. The only man in the scene appears just long enough to drag Sarah screaming offstage. Next, a black curtain is drawn back to reveal six dog kennels, each containing an adolescent girl on her hands and knees while an older teen, dressed in a tight black dress and fishnet thigh-high stockings looks on, smiling. In shades of black, grey and crimson, her ghoulish makeup indicates that she is one of the demons. There are many demons or female friends in hell house performances who persuade the protagonists to go to the party, drink alcohol, get abortions or, in this case, open a social media account. These characters are simultaneously the serpent in the garden and Eve; they embody both temptation and dangerous female desire. While these sirens facilitate the passage down the pathway to evil, they are not the root cause of evil – that role is reserved for unsexed women.

The perils of female independence are reinforced by a siren-demon who describes the alleged mistake or failing that leads to each child's downfall. While pointing to one girl, the demon says, 'She just wanted to make more money. Guess she didn't know what that could cost her, did she?' Pointing to another weeping child who looks no older than ten, the demon sneers, 'she just wanted to be loved and accepted. She's accepted now. Over fifteen times a day' (*HHPD*). While the scene purports to warn girls about the dangers of social media, the embedded dramaturgy of patriarchy stages the belief that women, even children, who are victims of male-perpetrated sexual or physical violence are architects of their own destructions, a distortion of Jesus's teaching, 'For whatsoever a man soweth, that shall he also reap'.[32]

At the time of writing in the autumn of 2020, it remains to be seen whether the women-protective anti-abortion strategy seemingly at play in US politics will shift American opinions about abortion. Because we are in the midst of a pandemic, most hell houses have not been in operation so we do not yet know how these activist performances will embody the new rhetorical strategy. However, at least one hell house began staging this rhetoric in 2018. On the blog 'Haunting', which describes various fear-based immersive theatre experiences, Elliot Bessette describes the abortion scene in the 2018 Tyler Church Hell House. It begins with a woman in a rocking chair:

> She has dark circles under her eyes and coos insanely as she rocks nothing in her arms. The demon in this room explains that the woman aborted her fetus and is now poisoned with guilt for the rest of her life. I scan the room and see, on the floor next to a hospital bed, a disgusting spillage of blood and viscera from the abortion.[33]

This description indicates a performance in transition from a foetal-centric to a women-protective or pro-woman framing. While graphic evidence of the abortion is still visible, the focus is primarily on the woman and her emotional trauma, indicating that a shift towards the pro-woman strategy was already gaining traction in 2018. In the public sphere, pro-woman framing was prominently featured at the 2020 'March for Life', the world's largest annual anti-abortion demonstration, which gathered under the banner, 'Life Empowers: Pro-Life is Pro-Woman'.[34] Despite careful anti-abortion framing by the Christian Right, scholars can look to hell houses to understand the movement's hidden ideology. Hell house performances use fear to frighten audiences away from secular temptation, but the embodiment of female characters reveals that feminism still has the Christian Right running scared.

Notes

1. Discussion with snack-bar worker, Clawson Assembly, Pollok, Texas, 31 October 2019.
2. Matthew Avery Sutton, *American Apocalypse* (Cambridge MA: Harvard University Press, 2014), p. x.
3. See Dan Venning's chapter in this volume.
4. H. Willenbrink, 'The Act of Being Saved: Hell House and the Salvific Performative', *Theatre Journal*, 66/1 (2014), 75.
5. A. Pellegrini, '"Signaling through the Flames": Hell House Performance and Structures of Religious Feeling', *American Quarterly*, 59/3 (2007), 911.
6. John Fletcher, *Preaching to Convert: Evangelical Outreach and Performance Activism in a Secular Age* (Ann Arbor MI: The University of Michigan Press, 2013), p. 163.
7. Fletcher, *Preaching to Convert*, p. 163.
8. Jody Enders, *The Medieval Theater of Cruelty: Rhetoric, Memory, Violence* (Ithaca NY: Cornell University Press, 2002), p. x.
9. Of course, staging a protagonist's journey towards peripeteia makes for compelling drama, but it also exemplifies a defining element of evangelical hermeneutics: personal salvation.
10. Andrew R. Lewis, *The Rights Turn in Conservative Christian Politics: How Abortion Transformed the Culture Wars* (Cambridge: Cambridge University Press, 2017), p. 22.
11. M. Rose, 'Pro-Life, Pro-Woman? Frame Extension in the American Antiabortion Movement', *Journal of Women, Politics and Policy*, 32/1 (2011), 7.

12. See *www.nrlc.org/communications/printads/*.
13. Susan Harding, *The Book of Jerry Falwell: Fundamentalist Language and Politics* (Princeton NJ: Princeton University Press, 2001), p. 197.
14. I. Glass, 'The Devil on My Shoulder', *This American Life*, 24 May 2002.
15. M. Dahl, '4 Ex-Evangelical Women on their Memories of Hell Houses', *New York Magazine*, 31 October 2018, *www.thecut.com*.
16. *Hell House 2013*, Greater Works Deliverance Ministries, (YouTube) 28 January 2017, *www.youtube.com/watch?v=TVgjUD2xRL4*.
17. Fletcher, *Preaching to Convert*, p. 160.
18. Paul Saurette and K. Gordon, *The Changing Voice of the Anti-abortion Movement: The Rise of 'Pro-Woman' Rhetoric in Canada and the United States* (Toronto: University of Toronto Press, 2016), p. 300.
19. D. C. Reardon and P. K. Coleman, 'Relative treatment rates for sleep disorders and sleep disturbances following abortion and childbirth: a prospective record-based study', *Sleep*, 29/1 (2006), 105–6.
20. J. R. Cougle, D. C. Reardon and P. K. Coleman, 'Generalized anxiety following unintended pregnancies resolved through childbirth and abortion: a cohort study of the 1995 National Survey of Family Growth', *Journal of Anxiety Disorders*, 19/1 (2005), 137–42.
21. P. K. Coleman, D. C. Reardon, V. M. Rue and J. Cougle, 'A history of induced abortion in relation to substance use during subsequent pregnancies carried to term', *American Journal of Obstetrics and Gynecology*, 187/6 (2002), 1673–7.
22. V. M. Rue, P. K. Coleman, J. J. Rue and D.C. Reardon, 'Induced abortion and traumatic stress: a preliminary comparison of American and Russian women', *Medical Science Monitor*, 10/10 (2004), SR5–SR16.
23. Reardon claims that the majority of women who terminate a pregnancy are coerced or pressured to do so, but his numbers fluctuate throughout the book: 55 per cent (213), 60 per cent (58) and 80 per cent (82).
24. See E. Bazelon, 'Is There a Post-Abortion Syndrome?', *New York Times*, 21 January 2007, *www.nytimes.com/2007/01/21/magazine/21abortion.t.html*.
25. See Rose, 'Pro-Life, Pro-Woman?'; and P. Saurette and K. Gordon, *The Changing Voice of the Anti-abortion Movement*.
26. Rose, 'Pro-Life, Pro Woman', 19.
27. E. Bradner, 'Conway: Trump White House Offered "Alternative Facts" on Crowd Size', CNN, 23 January 2017, *www.cnn.com/2017/01/22/politics/kellyanne-conway-alternative-facts/index.html*.
28. Although Reardon frames abortion providers as coercive and unscrupulous, he also claims that they are victims by saying, 'abortionists may enjoy the easy wealth of their trade, but they often feel like hired executioners. This feeling

that they are being exploited often creates callous or resentful feelings towards the very women they are supposed to be trying to help', 40.

29. On 30 September 2020, *The National Review* reported that in 2006, Barrett signed her name to a Right to Life advertisement and on 9 October 2020, *CNN* reported that Barrett failed to disclose two speaking engagements with anti-abortion student groups.

30. *Hell House Trinity 27*, Trinity Church, 21 October 2017; and *Hell House*, King's Chapel Oahu, 31 October 2010.

31. There are echoes of *Macbeth* in anti-abortion rhetoric from the Christian Right. One of Donald Trump's favorite anti-abortion rhetorical flourishes is to describe a 'baby ripped from the mother's womb' (used in the 2016 Democratic Debate and after the 2019 passage of New York's Reproductive Health Care Act), similar language to (V.viii.15–16) 'Macduff was from his mother's womb / Untimely ripp'd' (in reference to caesarean delivery). Lady Macbeth claims she would kill her baby before defaulting on a promise: 'I would, while it was smiling in my face, / Have plucked my nipple from his boneless gums / And dashed the brains out, had I so sworn as you / Have done to this' (I.v.55–58).

32. *Galatians* 6:7 (New Revised Standard Version).

33. E. Bessette, 'Hell Houses: A Journey Through Evangelical Christian Haunts', *Haunting*, 30 March 2018, *www.haunting.net/hell-houses/*.

34. R. Ponnuru, 'Barrett, in 2006, Supported the Right to Life', *National Review*, 2 October 2020, *www.nationalreview.com/corner/amy-coney-barrett-in-2006-supported-the-right-to-life/*.

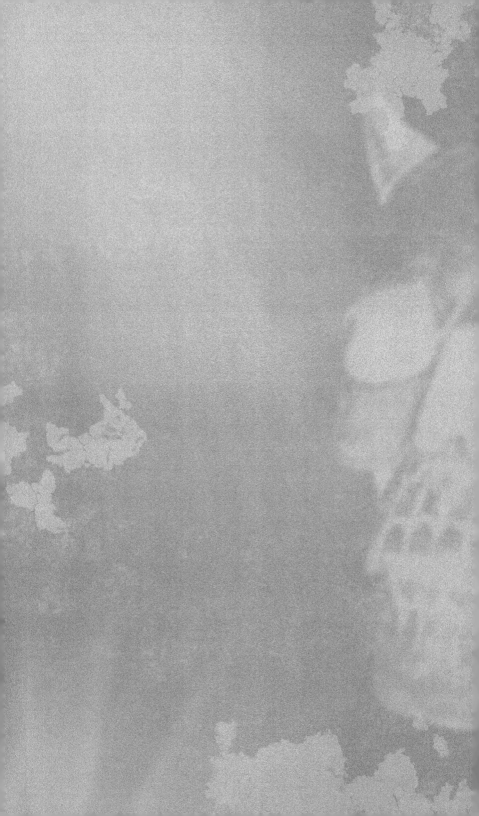

16

Haunting the Stage

Macabre Tourism, *Lieux de Mémoire* and the Immortal Death of Abraham Lincoln at Ford's Theatre

Meredith Conti

THE SOUNDS OF WASHINGTON DC's frenetic morning rush hour are audible but unobtrusive on a block of Tenth Street, where an orderly queue is forming on the red-brick sidewalk. A spring rain falls, enough to necessitate hats and jackets but too little for deploying umbrellas. Circulating convivially among those waiting in line are several costumed re-enactors, crinolines rustling and military boots clunking. Nearby, a historian of expert knowledge but unknown credentials ticks off dates and facts on his fingers for a rapt pair of pre-teen boys. At the historian's mentions of 'bullet', 'brain matter' and 'blood clot', the boys glance conspiratorially at each other, relishing the gruesome details. More than half of those waiting are white men, middle-aged or older, a number of them sporting sweatshirts, t-shirts and caps with patriotic slogans or Civil War battlefield logos. Diversifying the queue in gender, colour and age are a number of families with women and children, a few small school groups, and me: a historian of nineteenth-century theatre and culture, intent on revisiting Ford's Theatre on the sesquicentennial of Abraham Lincoln's assassination. As the doors open and the queue moves into the theatre's lobby space, the re-enactors progress down the street, bowing and curtsying to arriving visitors.

Lincoln himself greets the entrants to Ford's Theatre, peering down placidly from the prominent donor wall opposite the main door. The words 'With malice toward none; with charity for all' scroll along the wall's upper border in cursive writing. Directly under the word 'charity' begins the list of donors; fossil fuel giants Exxon Mobil and BP America are the first two names listed, predictable corporate donors in the neoliberal landscape and yet inconvenient companions to Lincoln's altruistic words. Behind the donor wall awaits one of the site's two gift shops, where Lincoln-themed shirts, keyrings and candy tempt visitors. My entry ticket scanned, I follow the crowd to the theatre for a performance of *One Destiny*, a play about the assassination told from the perspective of Harry Ford, the theatre's co-owner, and actor Harry Hawk. *En route* to the auditorium, a sign to the left of the hallway draws my attention: the image of a handgun crossed by a diagonal line is accompanied by the words 'Warning: Firearms Prohibited'. Of course, the sign's messaging exceeds its practical usage and even its conspicuous irony. It indexes the past, where an explosive moment of gun violence shattered the theatre's (not entirely earned) reputation as a space of innocuous fantasy, of 'danger' drained of repercussions. It also engages directly with the present, where American guns are ubiquitous and federal gun-control laws are lax. And, through its mere presence, the sign acknowledges the powerful, ever-evolving narrative that connects the past, present and future: that of US gun culture.

My intellectual foray into gun studies as part of a developing monograph has also been a physical foray into spaces defined or changed by guns: from Greenville, Ohio, the birthplace and burial site of Annie Oakley (and the location of the Annie Oakley Center museum), to the rifle-lined barn of Daniel Fish's Broadway revival of *Oklahoma!*, to the Buffalo Bill Center of the West's Cody Firearms Museum in Wyoming. In this chapter, I consider the touristic experiences arranged and produced by one such site, Ford's Theatre, which I have visited on three different occasions: on a weekend date with my spouse in 2012; on my solo trip on the anniversary of Lincoln's death in 2015; and with my spouse and children in September 2019, when we spent several days in DC participating in climate strikes, political protests, museum visits and ghost tours. As my visits to 'gun sites' have increased (and spanned two political climates), I have grown deliberate in assessing my hybrid role of historian-tourist. In a reflection of this orientation, what follows will move between autoethnographic and historiographical methodologies.

Ford's Theatre both typifies and complicates French historian Pierre Nora's notion of *lieu de mémoire* ('site of memory'). Indeed, Ford's Theatre contains several interlocking *lieux de mémoire* – a cluster of historic buildings, a multi-phase museum installation and a working theatre – all of which continuously reconstruct the site's legendary past while keeping time with the ever-evolving present. With a schedule that includes theatre productions about the assassination, unguided or audio-guided tours, ranger talks, K-12 educational programmes and historic walking tours, Ford's Theatre operates as a classroom, a pilgrimage site and an entertainment venue. Simultaneously, it also traffics in dark tourism, an abundantly theatrical transaction between purveyors and visitors that animates tourist destinations and experiences from historic battlefields to true-crime walking tours. At Ford's, the sacred coexists with the grisly: artefacts of Lincoln's violent death are on display, including assassin John Wilkes Booth's pistol and one of several bloodstained pillows used to cradle the dying president's head. Visitors can also walk to the nearby Petersen House, where the president succumbed to his gunshot wound in the morning hours of 15 April 1865. Drawing upon dark tourism and museum studies scholarship, as well as works by Nora, Marvin Carlson and Silke Arnold-de-Simine that analyse the relationship of place, memory and identity, I consider the various macabre encounters that haunt Ford's Theatre as it recounts Lincoln's presidency, the assassination and its aftermath. A *lieu de mémoire* and a multimodal theatre of the macabre, Ford's Theatre continuously represents Lincoln's death and by doing so guarantees his immortality.

Dark Tourism, Macabre Tourism

Of course, Ford's Theatre lured mourners and the morbidly curious to its doors long before it opened as a National Historic Site. Mere minutes after␃Lincoln's shooting, crowds converged on Tenth Street. 'Most of those who had been in the theater [during the assassination] remained in the neighborhood', wrote the *Evening Star*'s James Waldo Fawcett in 1931, when restorations to Ford's Theatre were underway as part of a planned Lincoln Museum. 'Their numbers were augmented by hundreds who, hearing the news, hastened to the scene. Late the next day trains were still bringing people from distant cities – people who, perhaps unreasonably, felt drawn by the tragedy.'[1] In the days and months following his death, many gathered to gaze at the shuttered theatre and visit, stay in or seize death relics from Petersen's boarding house.[2] These embodied rituals, in which America's citizen-mourners roamed the spaces redefined by Lincoln's violent martyrdom, served commemorative and divertive functions and marked Ford's Theatre as a dark tourism destination.

In 2000, John Lennon and Malcolm Foley subsumed a range of touristic experiences dealing directly or tangentially with 'death, disaster and atrocity' under one conceptual umbrella with an evocative name: dark tourism.[3] As a practice and a product, dark tourism harkens subtly back to pre-modern pilgrimages, in which visiting and revisiting sites of death and suffering served as 'acts of remembrances'.[4] It is also possible, writes Glenn Hooper, to relate the spectatorial desires motivating present-day dark tourism devotees with those of ancient audiences witnessing Roman gladiators fight to the death or nineteenth-century curiosity seekers visiting the inmates of Bedlam.[5] However, Lennon and Foley argue that dark tourism should be conceived as 'an intimation of post-modernity' that exploits 'global communication technologies' and 'introduce[s] anxiety and doubt about the project of modernity'.[6] Since the publication of Lennon and Foley's book, a blooming catalogue of scholarship has legitimised dark tourism as a subject of interdisciplinary academic enquiry. 'Dark tourism' remains the most enduring and employed term to describe experiences variously named by scholars as 'negative sightseeing' (Dean MacCannell), 'Black Spot tourism' (Chris Rojek), 'thanatourism' (Tony Seaton), 'fright tourism' (Robert S. Bristol and Mirela Newman), 'morbid tourism' (Thomas Blom) and 'trauma tourism' (Laurie Beth Clark), among others.[7]

As this abbreviated list of terms suggests, a crucial challenge in theorising dark tourism is that it encompasses a startling array of experiential phenomena, within permanent or temporary sites, and generated by for-profit and non-profit entities. Because of dark tourism's conceptual broadness, writes Richard Sharpley, 'the meaning of the term has become increasingly diluted and fuzzy'.[8] Indeed, most scholars would agree that, despite their obvious differences, Hawai'i's Pearl Harbor National Memorial, Cambodia's Tuol Sleng Museum of Genocide, The London Dungeon and Ukraine's Chernobyl Nuclear Power Plant are all dark tourism sites. In order to make distinctions, dark tourism experts plot such experiences on spectrums of intensity (pale versus dark), categorise them into types or distinguish between their business practices.[9] Still, Philip R. Stone's description provides some useful boundaries for the present project:

[Dark tourism,] the commodification of death for popular touristic consumption, whether in the guise of memorials and museums, visitor attractions, special events and exhibitions, or specific tours, has become a focus of mainstream tourist providers. Dark tourism is concerned with tourist encounters with spaces of death or calamity that have perturbed the public consciousness, whereby actual and recreated places of the deceased, horror, atrocity, or depravity, are consumed through visitor experiences.[10]

In experimenting with the term 'macabre tourism', in the midst of this already swelling terminology, I am attempting to carve out – for myself and others – a particular segment of dark tourism that is not necessary predicated on postmodern attitudes and technologies, as Lennon and Foley argue, but embraces the macabre as an enticement to tourists to engage in historical and cultural remembering without activating feelings of shame, guilt or vicarious trauma that accompany darker forms of tourism. Indeed, I wish to differentiate between tourist experiences inspired by distant or semi-distant atrocities and those that coalesce around recent events of death and suffering. Makeshift shrines honouring mass-shooting victims, for example, are saturated with darkness in ways that the Tower of London's execution yard will perhaps never be. Furthermore, macabre tourism is adaptable to both the formal, dispassionate exhibiting of dark subjects by traditional museums and the lucrative 'kitschification' of memorial sites, the latter due to what Hooper describes as 'a growing acceptance of the appeal of fear, anxiety and fun, of a clearly identified lighter side of dark tourism'.[11] Such kitschified experiences indulge tourists' inclinations to delight in the morbid while pursuing, however superficially, some measure of historical or cultural edification. Finally, I see macabre tourism as a category of experience that (partly) dodges many of the ethics-based critiques of dark tourism through their design, placement, implementation and marketing strategies.

As with those queuing outside Ford's Theatre on 14 April 2015, the primary progenitors of dark tourism scholarship have been white men, and even as the community of contributors grows more diverse, the studies and observations of male scholars remain somewhat centralised, venerated and generally unchallenged.[12] Moreover, despite the field's earnest intentions and rich, interdisciplinary research outputs, the oft-cited foundational literature casts the dark tourist as a sort of universal figure of transposable goals, experiences and opinions. This purportedly race-less, gender-less tourist is, of course, implicitly raced (white) and gendered (male), having been granted unrestricted access to dark tourism experiences both real and hypothetical. However, crucial questions of how race, gender, class, religion, age and ability affect both the supply and demand sides of dark tourism are being raised by an increasingly heterogenous cadre of scholars, including performance scholar Emma Willis, whose 2014 book investigates the tangled ethics of dark tourism spectatorship, and historian Tiya Miles, who explores as a Black tourist the exploiting and commodifying of slave stories in US Southern tourism.[13] While this chapter does not directly interrogate notions of identity, representation and inclusivity in dark tourism scholarship and patronage, I will offer my own impressions of being a white American woman visiting Ford's Theatre National Historic Site.

Collecting, Curating and Spectating the Macabre: Ford's Theatre, Washington DC

On a typical day, visitors to Ford's Theatre enter the building and descend a staircase to the basement, a dimly lit room partitioned into a warren of exhibit spaces. The museum first surveys the years immediately preceding Lincoln's assassination, depicting in quick but effective brushstrokes a host of consequential topics: the Civil War; chattel slavery in the American South; the politics of 1860s Washington; life in the Lincoln White House; and the president's affinity with theatre. Directing visitors through the exhibits are curated walls of images and text, display cases and interactive placards that slide to reveal first-person accounts of the period, while looping History Channel videos play in small screening rooms or in designated corners. Blocking one potential passage into the central exhibit space is an installation of (almost) life-sized plaster figures depicting men seeking appointments to Lincoln's cabinet. (The irony of this obstructionist wall of aspiring white male politicians was not lost on me.)

The last third of the basement museum focuses on the assassination itself. Glass cases display a macabre assortment of assassination artefacts: the interior door to the private box in which John Wilkes Booth bore a peephole; the bit of music stand that Booth used to wedge the box's outer door closed; theatre tickets to the 14 April production of *Our American Cousin*; witness and stabbing victim Henry Rathbone's bloody gloves; and Lincoln's death mask, among other things. The Deringer pistol used to kill the president hovers in its own three-sided glass case, mounted away from

Figure 3. John Wilkes Booth's Deringer pistol. Ford's Theatre, 21 September 2019. Author's photograph.

the wall so that visitors may step directly in front of the tiny gun's barrel or behind its handle, trying on both the victim's and villain's roles (see Figure 3). Nearby a three-dimensional facsimile of the gun and a touch-screen monitor invite visitors to feel the weapon's curves and etchings, to rotate and enlarge its digital replica for closer examination. In all three of my visits to Ford's, the macabre object displays created bottlenecks in the museum's traffic flow.

A staircase leads up from the underground museum space to a ramped hallway of Union blue and Rebel grey. The sound of a clock ticks steadily as images on either side of the hall provide duelling timelines of Lincoln and Booth's actions on 14 April 1865. The men's days progress as visitors progress down the hall, and yet within the overarching timeline of events that begin in the basement museum, we have rewound a bit, to before the play began, before the Deringer was fired, before pillows were bloodied. The hallway, then, seems both in and out of time, linking the traditional museum space (and the 'clean', linear narrative that it constructs) to the theatre itself (a temporally supple space, as all theatres are, and yet exceptional in its consolidating of a notorious past and a workaday present). In operating as a physical and narrative bridge, the hallway offers a discrete example of what scholars Laura Hourston Hanks, Jonathan Hale and Suzanne MacLeod together describe as the 'gaps' inherent in museums that storytelling helps span:

> The museum as a space with so much narrative potential is, so to speak, inherently full of voids: temporal gaps between some other past and our own present; geographical gaps between remote locations; cultural gaps between opposing world-views; societal gaps between different groups of visitors; professional gaps between the various occupations involved in museum fabrication; and physical gaps, between the diverse media employed in the museum. Narrative is so pervasive and promising as a mediating strategy precisely because it allows us to bridge these gaps – persuasively and with immediacy in the embodied medium of museum space.[15]

Although there are a number of more explicitly theatrical spaces in Ford's Theatre – including the stage itself – the hallway is perhaps the most knowingly dramaturgical. That is, it builds anticipatory tension by counting the hours and minutes before the climactic shooting, which is then reinforced by the ramp's upward trajectory, an architectural echoing of the

Figure 4. The Presidential Box. Ford's Theatre, 21 September 2019. Author's photograph.

Figure 5. The Petersen House, 21 September 2019. Author's photograph.

Aristotelian plot structure's rising action. It isolates protagonist and antagonist on opposite walls, going about their day's business, only one cognisant of what will unfold that night. And because the site's visitors have already confronted the assassination's material artefacts in the basement museum (and presumably studied US history some point in their lives) they are not unlike audiences of *Romeo and Juliet*, who learn of the young lovers' deaths in the play's prologue before witnessing their last living days.

The hallway delivers visitors into the auditorium's dress circle. Park rangers wait to answer questions as tourists perambulate, snapping photos of the presidential box (see Figure 4) and the stage, some prowling near the antechamber door that led Booth to Lincoln.

The theatre's post-assassination history, marked by years of vacancy, disrepair and repurposing, is rigorously denied by its restored 1865 appearance, although rangers relay to morbidly curious tourists another human tragedy that haunts Ford's: a ceiling collapse that killed twenty-two office clerks in 1893. Visitors next track the path of Lincoln's unconscious body as it was carried across Tenth Street into the house of William and Anna Petersen, also restored to its 1865 appearance (see Figure 5). Here tourists walk through the parlour that a distraught Mary Todd Lincoln occupied during Lincoln's final hours before proceeding to the bedroom, where a replica of Lincoln's too-short deathbed stands behind a low wall of protective Plexiglas.

The final leg of the tour begins when an elevator ferries tourists to the top of the rowhouse adjacent to the Petersen House, where three floors of museum space recount the assassination's consequences: Lincoln's funeral train and the mourning of a nation; the twelve-day manhunt for the assassin and his death in a Virginia barn; the trials and sentencing of Booth's co-conspirators; and the tragedies suffered by the Lincoln family. Visitors walk along a faux dirt alleyway dotted with 'muddy' footprints, hoofprints and wagon-wheel tracks, with posters and newspaper headlines decrying the assassination plastered on the brick walls. They can enter a replica of the casket-bearing funeral car, its windows framed by black satin curtains, or spy a mannequin of Booth hiding behind a barn door, armed and waiting. The spiral staircase that connects the museum floors encircles an impressive four-story cylindrical book tower of Lincoln-inspired publications; an enlarged photograph of the hanging executions of several co-conspirators covers the entire upper wall, visible from each floor. After an exhibit highlighting the new 'Lincolns', a diverse and multi-generational collection of present-day activists, philanthropists and politicians, visitors arrive at the ground level. Darkness – as an intentional curatorial ambience and a mode of touring – recedes as visitors descend the levels, countering the ascending and increasingly macabre path that the first portion of the museum takes, from the underground museum to the theatre's balcony. The experience ends as it begins – with a gift shop.

The Memory Museum and the Macabre

How might we understand the cultural work of Ford's Theatre? Like many historic tourist spots in the United States and beyond, Ford's Theatre operates as a memory museum, one that draws validity from its powerful sitedness as well as the prominence of Abraham Lincoln within the American imagination. 'To live is to leave traces', as Walter Benjamin famously said, and some leave larger traces than others. In *The Haunted Stage: The Theatre as Memory Machine*, Marvin Carlson writes:

> Theories of tourism have often noted that physical locations, like individual human beings, can by the operations of frame be so deeply implanted in the consciousness of a culture that individuals in that culture, actually encountering them for the first time, inevitably find that experience already haunted by the cultural construction of these persons and places.[16]

To be clear, the sixteenth president of the United States haunts Ford's Theatre, and not (just) in the way that ghost hunters or dark tourists would wish. Lincoln's celebrity – which was secured by his graphic death and subsequent martyrdom as much as by his extraordinary political career – is the defining character of Ford's. Lincoln's assassin lurks in the shadows, outshone, confined to his role as antagonist, while the story of America's sundering and (ongoing) re-knitting, a far more complex and messy narrative than Lincoln's Aristotelian fall or Booth's melodramatic villainy, largely fulfils an expository function.

For Pierre Nora, *lieux de mémoire* exist because *milieux de mémoire* ('real environments of memory') no longer do. Due to the disappearance of *milieux de mémoire*, memory scholar Astrid Erll notes of Nora's theory, 'sites of memory function as a sort of artificial placeholder for the no longer existent, natural collective memory'.[17] Operating along three dimensions – the material (as 'cultural objectivations'), the functional (in that they fulfil a societal function) and the symbolic, Nora's sites of memory could include 'geographical locations, buildings, monuments and works of art as well as historical persons, memorial days, philosophical and scientific texts, or symbolic actions'.[18] While I disagree with Nora's insistence that history and memory are detached entities, each a repository for what the other cannot capture, his claim that *lieux de mémoire* are manufactured to supply communities with places to perform remembering is instructive. 'It is [the] very push and pull [of history and memory] that produces *lieux de mémoire*', he offers, 'moments of history torn away from the movement of history, then returned; no longer quite life, not yet death, like shells on the shore when the sea of living memory has receded'.[19]

Visitors to Ford's are surrounded by Victorian-era *memento mori*: symbols of mourning and invitations to remember. Black fabric adorns not just the funeral car, but a portrait of Willie Lincoln, who died at age eleven. Commemorative objects sold after Lincoln's death, from ribbons to sheet music, populate the display cases. In the Petersen House, placards read 'What would you have said to comfort Mary Lincoln?' and 'What was the first national tragedy you personally remember?' According to cultural memory scholar Silke Arnold-de-Simine, memory museums 'encourage visitors to empathise and identify with individual sufferers and victims, as if "reliving" their experience, in order to thus develop more personal and immediate forms of engagement'.[20] The site's representative mourners are largely women, a curatorial decision that supports what historian Erik R. Seeman describes as 'women's deep involvement in grief work . . . in the nineteenth century'.[21] And yet, because Lincoln's assassination is a historical event dominated by male actants, from the victim and villain to the vast majority of the co-conspirators, doctors, politicians, police officers and judges, women are generally restricted within the museum's overarching narrative to bereaving, nurturing and commemorating: *Our American Cousin* actress Laura Keene cradled Lincoln's bloody head, Mary Todd succumbed to despair and Columbia mourned for a nation.

Similarly, Ford's inclusion of Black perspectives, particularly in the basement museum, feels somewhat limited. Images and testimonials of free and enslaved Black Americans appear alongside those of white Northerners and Southerners, while a looping film attends to Black orator and abolitionist Frederick Douglass's complex relationship with the 'Great Emancipator'. Unlike the considered and unflinching 'Slavery and Freedom' exhibit at the nearby Smithsonian National Museum of African American History and Culture, Ford's Theatre fails to manifest for visitors the true horrors of slavery. Instead, perhaps expectedly, the horrors of assassination loom larger. Black knowledge production about Lincoln's life and sociopolitical legacy materialises more perceptibly through Ford's productions of Black-written plays and in the Center for Education and Leadership, where the aftermath exhibits are located. Yet whiteness remains an implicit node to which much of the Ford's Theatre experience affixes.

Befitting its National Historic Site status, Ford's Theatre boasts no jump scares or harrowing reenactments, although the uncanny dances about the edges in the form of nearly life-sized figures dotted throughout the site. Rather, its immersive techniques are physically and aesthetically tame, encouraging in visitors a quiet, at times reverent contemplation. It makes no bones, however, about embracing the macabre as an instrument of pedagogical and theatrical value, one that engages visitors in cultural remembering through visual and aural cuing and tactile activities. Rather than dismissing Ford's use of the macabre as somehow antithetical to its 'serious' work as a *lieu de mémoire*, I see it as an invigorating device of the *lieu de mémoire*.

Notes

1. J. W. Fawcett, 'Ford's Theater to be Lincoln Museum', *Evening Star*, 6 December 1931, 13.
2. Large collections of Lincolnalia were amassed by Union soldier Osborn H. Oldroyd, hotel proprietor George Rector and contemporary Lincoln scholar Harold Holzer. A number of the artefacts displayed at Ford's Theatre are from Oldroyd's collection. Fred Petersen, son of the boarding house's owner William Petersen, had held onto the bloodied pillowcases and quilt from Lincoln's deathbed, but eventually sold them. The collecting of Lincoln assassination memorabilia and relics is a macabre hobby most prevalent among white men of privilege and education. In a *Smithsonian Magazine* article in March 2015, Lincoln historian and author of *Manhunt: The 12-Day Chase for Lincoln's Killer*, James L. Swanson, labels himself a 'crazed collector who happens to write books'. Swanson also describes his yearly 14 April visits to Ford's, where he sits outside of the theatre at 10pm to observe the anniversary of Lincoln's shooting, as 'pilgrimages'. J. C. Hemphill, 'Deathbed Relics Here Tell of Lincoln Tragedy', *New York Times*, 9 February 1913; and J. L. Swanson, 'The Blood Relic from the Lincoln Assassination', *Smithsonian Magazine* (March 2015).

3. John Lennon and Malcolm Foley, *Dark Tourism: The Attraction of Death and Disaster* (London: Continuum, 2000), p. 3.
4. Lennon and Foley, *Dark Tourism*, p. 3.
5. G. Hooper, 'Introduction', in G. Hooper and J. J. Lennon (eds), *Dark Tourism: Practice and Interpretation* (Abingdon: Routledge, 2017), p. 3.
6. Lennon and Foley, *Dark Tourism*, p. 11.
7. Dean MacCannell, *The Tourist: A New Theory of the Leisure Class* (Berkeley CA: University of California Press, 2013); Chris Rojek, *Ways of Escape* (Basingstoke: Palgrave Macmillan Ltd, 1993); A. V. Seaton, 'War and Thanatourism: Waterloo 1815–1914', *Annals of Tourism Research*, 26/1 (1999); R. S. Bristol and M. Newman, 'Myth vs. Fact: An Exploration of Fright Tourism', in K. Bricker and S. J. Millington (eds), *Proceedings of the 2004 Northeastern Recreation Research Symposium* (Newtown Square PA: USDA Forest Service, Northeastern Research Station General Technical Report NE-326, 2005); T. Blom, 'Morbid Tourism: A Postmodern Market Niche with an Example from Althorp', *Norwegian Journal of Geography*, 54/1 (May 2000); L. B. Clark, 'Ruined Landscapes and Residual Architecture: Affect and Palimpsest in Trauma Tourism', *Performance Research*, 20/3 (May 2015). See also Hooper and Lennon (eds), *Dark Tourism: Practice and Interpretation*; P. R. Stone et al. (eds), *The Palgrave Handbook of Dark Tourism Studies* (Basingstoke: Palgrave Macmillan, 2018); L. White and E. Frew (eds), *Dark Tourism and Place Identity: Managing and Interpreting Dark Places* (London: Routledge, 2013).
8. R. Sharpley, 'Shedding Light on Dark Tourism: An Introduction', in R. Sharpley and P. R. Stone (eds), *The Darker Side of Tourism: The Theory and Practice of Dark Tourism* (Bristol and Buffalo NY: Channel Publications, 2009), p. 6.
9. See Sharpley, 'Shedding Light on Dark Tourism', pp. 15–21 for a summary of these distinctions.
10. Quoted in Derek Dalton, *Dark Tourism and Crime* (London: Routledge, 2015), p. 2.
11. Hooper, 'Introduction', *Dark Tourism*, p. 3.
12. Men comprise the entire list of contributors in Sharpley and Stone's 2009 edited volume *The Darker Side of Tourism*, for example.
13. See Emma Willis, *Theatricality, Dark Tourism and Ethical Spectatorship: Absent Others* (Basingstoke: Palgrave Macmillian, 2014); and Tiya Miles, *Tales from the Haunted South: Dark Tourism and Memories of Slavery from the Civil War Era* (Chapel Hill NC: University of North Carolina Press, 2015).
14. Allison Hartley, a former intern in Ford's education department, reported that in her early months working at the historic site, she often directed visitors to

the pistol in the basement museum, 'thinking it should top their "must-see" list. But their reactions surprised me', Hartley continues, 'most people would ask to see Lincoln's suit before the gun, and I engaged in more conversations with visitors about Lincoln's personal effects in the back of the museum than I had expected'. A. Hartley, 'Eccentricities from Our Archives: The Man Who Collected Lincoln', *fords.org*.

15. Suzanne MacLeod, Laura Hourston Hanks and Jonathan Hale, *Museum Making: Narratives, Architectures, Exhibitions* (London: Routledge, 2012), p. xxiii.
16. Marvin Carlson, *The Haunted Stage: The Theatre as Memory Machine* (Ann Arbor MI: University of Michigan Press, 2006), p. 135.
17. Astrid Erll, *Memory in Culture*, translated by Sara B. Young (New York: Palgrave Macmillan, 2011), p. 23.
18. Eril, *Memory in Culture*, p. 24.
19. P. Nora, 'Between Memory and History: Les Lieux de Mémoire', *Representations*, 26 (spring 1989), 12.
20. S. Arnold-de-Simine, quoted in Dalton, *Dark Tourism and Crime* (Abingdon: Routledge, 2015), pp. 6–7.
21. Erik R. Seeman, *Speaking with the Dead in Early America* (Philadelphia PA: University of Pennsylvania Press, 2019), p. 8.

Bibliography

Adorno, Theodor, *The Culture Industry: Selected Essays on Mass Culture* (London and New York: Routledge, 1991).

Als, H., 'Shadow and Act: Shakespeare without Words', *New Yorker*, 2 May 2011, www.newyorker.com/magazine/2011/05/02/shadow-and-act (accessed 16 September 2020).

Alston, A., 'Audience Participation and Neoliberal Value: Risk, agency and responsibility in immersive theatre', *Performance Research*, 18/2 (2013), 128–38.

Altick, Richard, *The Shows of London: A Panoramic History of Exhibitions* (Cambridge MA: Harvard University Press, 1978).

Amsbury, Z., 'Getting to Paradise: The Grand Paradise by Third Rail Projects', *No Proscenium*, 10 February 2016, https://noproscenium.com/getting-to-paradise-the-grand-paradise-by-third-rail-projects-810904ae59c4 (accessed 22 May 2020).

Archibald, William, *The Innocents: A New Play* (London: Samuel French, 1950).

Armitage, H., 'Political Language, Uses and Abuses: How the Term "Partial Birth" Changed the Abortion Debate in the United States', *Australasian Journal of American Studies*, 29/1 (2010), 15–35.

Arndt, J., J. Allen and J. Greenberg, 'Traces of Terror: Subliminal Death Primes and Facial Electromyographic Indices of Affect', *Motivation and Emotion*, 25 (2001), 253–77.

Arndt, J. and M. Vess, 'Tales from Existential Oceans: Terror Management Theory', *Social and Personality Psychology Compass*, 2 (2008), 909–28.

Arons, W., 'Braddock Saints Tour', *The Pittsburgh Tatler*, 31 May 2015, https://wendyarons.wordpress.com/2015/05/31/braddock-saints-tour-a-bricolage-and-realtime-interventions-co-production/ (accessed 28 May 2020).

— '"DODO" at Bricolage Production Company', *The Pittsburgh Tatler*, 21 October 2017, *https://wendyarons.wordpress.com/2017/10/21/dodo-at-bricolage-production-company/* (accessed 25 May 2020).

Aronson, Arnold, et al., *The History and Theory of Environmental Scenography: Second Edition* (London and New York: Methuen Drama, 2018).

Augustine, *City of God* (New York: Doubleday, 1972).

Bachelard, Gaston, *The Poetics of Space: The Classic Look at How We Experience Intimate Places*, translated by M. Jolas (Boston MA: Beacon Press, 1994).

Bai, Y. et al., 'Awe, the Diminished Self, and Collective Engagement: Universals and Cultural Variations in the Small Self', *Attitudes and Social Cognition*, 113/2 (2017), 185–209.

Baird, Bruce, *Hijikata Tatsumi and Butoh: Dancing in a Pool of Gray Grits* (Basingstoke: Palgrave Macmillan, 2016).

Bakare, L., 'Immersive *Wolf of Wall Street* Actors Get Personal Alarm Buttons', *Guardian*, 16 September 2019, *www.theguardian.com/stage/2019/sep/16/immersive-wolf-of-wall-street-production-to-introduce-safeguarding* (accessed 16 September 2020).

Bakhtin, Mikhail, *Rabelais and His World*, translated by H. Iswolsky (Bloomington IN: Indiana University Press, 1984).

Balanzategui, Jennifer, *The Uncanny Child in Transnational Cinema: Ghosts of Futurity at the Turn of the Twenty-First Century* (Amsterdam: Amsterdam University Press, 2018).

Ballestriedo, R., 'From the Contortion of Reality to the Sinister: The Uncomfortable Hyperrealism of Mannequins, Dolls, Effigies and Wax Figures', *Revista de Investigación sobre lo Fantástico*, 4/2 (2016), 93–115.

Balme, Christopher, *The Cambridge Introduction to Theatre Studies* (Cambridge: Cambridge University Press, 2008).

Barnum, P. T., *The Life of P. T. Barnum, Written by Himself* (New York: Redfield, 1855).

Bartneck, C., T. Kanda, H. Ishiguro and N. Hagita, 'Is the uncanny valley an uncanny cliff?', Proceedings of the 16th Institute of Electrical and Electronics Engineers International Symposium on Robot and Human Interactive Communication, RO-MAN, Jeju, Korea (2007).

Bataille, Georges, *Inner Experience* (Albany NY: State University of New York Press, 2014).

Baudelaire, Charles, *Les Fleurs du mal* (Boston MA: Godine, 1983).

Baudrillard, Jean, *Simulacra and Simulation* (Ann Arbor MI: University of Michigan Press, 1994).

Bazelon, E., 'Is There a Post-Abortion Syndrome?', *New York Times*, 21 January 2007, *www.nytimes.com/2007/01/21/magazine/21abortion.t.html*.

Bechdel, Alison, *Fun Home: A Family Tragicomic* (New York: First Mariner Books, 2004).
Becker, Ernest, *The Denial of Death* (New York: Free Press, 1973).
Becker, J., 'Music and trance', *Leonardo Music Journal*, 4/1 (1994), 41–51.
'Behind a White Mask: The Big List of *Sleep No More* Links & Blogs', *behindawhitemask.tumblr.com* (accessed 16 September 2020).
Benjamin, Walter, *Illuminations* (New York: Schocken, 1968).
— *The Origin of German Tragic Drama* (New York: Verso, 1998).
— *Reflections* (New York: Schocken, 1978).
— *The Writer of Modern Life: Essays on Charles Baudelaire*, M. W. Jennings (ed.) (Cambridge MA: Harvard University Press, 2006).
Berger Cardany, A., 'Mitigating Death Anxiety: Identifying Music's Role in Terror Management', *Psychology of Music*, 46/1 (2018), 3–17.
Bessette, E., 'Hell Houses: A Journey Through Evangelical Christian Haunts', *Haunting*, 30 March 2018, *www.haunting.net/hell-houses/* (accessed 9 October 2020).
Betzien, Angela, *The Dark Room* (Brisbane: Playlab, 2009).
— *Mortido* (Sydney: Currency Press, 2015).
— *The Hanging* (Sydney: Currency Press, 2016).
Beyes, T. and C. Steyaert, 'Strangely familiar: The uncanny and unsiting organisational analysis', *Organization Studies*, 34/10 (2013), 1445–65.
Biernoff, Suzannah, 'The Rhetoric of Disfigurement in First World War Britain', *Social History of Medicine*, 24/3 (2011), 666–85.
— *Portraits of Violence: War and the Aesthetics of Disfigurement* (Ann Arbor MI: University of Michigan Press, 2017).
Bisaha, D., 'Ghost Light by Zach Morris', *Theatre Journal*, 70/2 (June 2018), 238–40.
Blake, E., 'Belvoir braces for controversy over child actors in Colin Friels' drug drama *Mortido*', *Sydney Morning Herald*, 11 November 2015.
Blau, Herbert, *Blooded Thought: Occasions of Theatre* (New York: Performing Arts Journal Publications, 1982).
Blom, T., 'Morbid Tourism: A Postmodern Market Niche with an Example from Althorp', *Norwegian Journal of Geography*, 54/1 (May 2000), 29–36.
Bloom, Harold, *Shakespeare: The Invention of the Human* (New York: Riverhead Books, 1998).
Borowitz, A. I., 'Under Sentence of Death', *American Bar Association Journal*, 64/8 (1978), 1259–65.
Borowski, Wiesław, *Tadeusz Kantor* (Warszawa: Wydawnictwa Artystyczne I Filmowe, 1982).

Bourke, Joanna, *Dismembering the Male: Men's Bodies, Britain and the Great War* (London: Reaktion, 1999).

Bradner, E., 'Conway: Trump White House Offered "Alternative Facts" on Crowd Size', *CNN*, 23 January 2017, *www.cnn.com/2017/01/22/politics/kelly-anne-conway-alternative-facts/index.html* (accessed 9 October 2020).

Branach-Kallas, A. and P. Sadkowski (eds), *Comparing Grief in French, British and Canadian Great War Fiction (1977–2014)* (Leiden: Brill, 2018).

Brantley, B., 'Shakespeare Slept Here, Albeit Fitfully', *New York Times*, 11 April 2011, *www.nytimes.com/2011/04/14/theater/reviews/sleep-no-more-is-a-macbeth-in-a-hotel-review.html* (accessed 16 September 2020).

Brewster, S., '*Dodo* by Jeffrey Carpenter et al.', *Theatre Journal*, 70/4 (December 2018), 544–5.

Bristol, R. S. and M. Newman, 'Myth vs. Fact: An Exploration of Fright Tourism', in K. Bricker and S. J. Millington (eds), *Proceedings of the 2004 Northeastern Recreation Research Symposium* (Newtown Square PA: USDA Forest Service, Northeastern Research Station General Technical Report NE–326: 2005), pp. 215–21.

Broinowski, A., 'The Atomic Gaze and Ankoku Butoh in Post-War Japan', in N. A. J. Taylor and R. Jacobs (eds), *Reimagining Hiroshima and Nagasaki: Nuclear Humanities in the Post-Cold War* (Routledge, 2017), pp. 91–107.

Brown, M., 'When you could catch the underground to see a hanging', *The Londonist*, 6 September 2018, *https://londonist.com/london/undergroundtoapublic hanging*.

Brooks, Kinitra D., *Searching for Sycorax: Black Women's Hauntings in Contemporary Horror* (New Brunswick NJ: Rutgers University Press, 2017).

Buck-Morss, Susan, *The Dialectics of Seeing: Walter Benjamin and the Arcades Project* (Cambridge MA: The MIT Press, 1989).

Burdekin, R., 'Pepper's Ghost at the Opera', *Theatre Notebook: A Journal of the History and Technique of the British Theatre*, 69/3 (2015), 152–64.

Burke, B. et al., 'Two Decades of Terror Management Theory: A Meta-Analysis of Mortality Salience Research', *Personality and Social Psychology Review*, 14 (2010), 155–95.

Cameron, C., 'Trump Repeats a False Claim That Doctors "Execute" Newborns', *New York Times*, 28 April 2019, *www.nytimes.com/2019/04/28/us/politics/trump-abortion-fact-check.html* (accessed 9 October 2020).

Carlson, Marvin, *The Haunted Stage: The Theatre as Memory Machine* (Ann Arbor MI: University of Michigan Press, 2006).

— *Ten Thousand Nights: Highlights from Fifty Years of Theatre-Going* (Ann Arbor MI: The University of Michigan Press, 2017).

Carr, N., 'Exploring the Abandoned McKittrick Hotel on West 27th Street', *Scouting New York*, 4 April 2011, *www.scoutingny.com/exploring-new-york's-abandoned-mckittrick-hotel/* (accessed 16 September 2020).
Carroll, N., 'The Nature of Horror', *The Journal of Aesthetics and Art Criticism*, 46/1 (1987), 51–9.
—— *The Philosophy of Horror, or Paradoxes of the Heart* (London and New York: Routledge, 1990).
—— 'Horror and Humor', *The Journal of Aesthetics and Criticism*, 57/2 (spring 1999), 145–60.
Cave, D., 'Behind the Scenes: Picturing Fetal Remains', *New York Times*, 9 October 2009, *https://lens.blogs.nytimes.com/2009/10/09/behind-19/* (accessed 9 September 2020).
Chandler, J., 'Backstage at Lincoln Center Theater's "Ghost Light"', *NBC 4 New York*, *www.nbcnewyork.com/news/local/backstage-at-lincoln-center-theater_s-_ghost-light__new-york/210827/*.
Chemers, Michael M., *Staging Stigma: A Critical Examination of the American Freak Show* (New York: Palgrave MacMillan, 2007).
—— *Ghost Light: An Introductory Handbook for Dramaturgy* (Carbondale IL: Southern Illinois University Press, 2010).
—— *The Monster in Theatre History: This Thing of Darkness* (Abingdon: Routledge, 2018).
Cherry, Brigid, *Horror* (London and New York: Routledge, 2009).
Clark, L. B., 'Ruined Landscapes and Residual Architecture: Affect and Palimpsest in Trauma Tourism', *Performance Research*, 20/3 (May 2015), 83–93.
Clement, O., 'The Strange Undoing of Prudencia Hart Extends for a Third Time', *Playbill*, 16 November 2016, *www.playbill.com/article/the-strange-undoing-of-prudencia-hart-extends-for-third-time* (accessed 16 September 2020).
Cohen, F. et al., 'Finding Ever-land: Flight Fantasies and the Desire to Transcend Mortality', *Journal of Experimental Social Psychology*, 47 (2009), 88–102.
Cohen, J., 'Monster Culture: Seven Theses', in J. J. Cohen (ed.), *Monster Theory: Reading Culture* (Minneapolis MN: University of Minnesota Press, 1996), pp. 3–25.
Colbert, Soyica Diggs, *The African American Theatrical Body: Reception, Performance, and the Stage* (Cambridge: Cambridge University Press, 2011).
Coleman, P., D. Reardon, V. Rue and J. Cougle, 'A History of Induced Abortion in Relation to Substance Use During Subsequent Pregnancies Carried to Term', *American Journal of Obstetrics and Gynecology*, 187/6 (2002), 1673–7.
Connor, Steven, *Samuel Beckett: Repetition, Theory and Text* (Oxford: Oxford University Press, 1988).

Cook, Jr, James W., 'Of Men, Missing Links, and Nondescripts: The Strange Career of P. T. Barnum's "What is It?" Exhibition', in R. G. Thomson (ed.), *Freakery: The Cultural Spectacle of the Extraordinary Body* (New York: New York University Press, 1996), pp. 137–57.

—— *The Art of Deception: Playing with Fraud in the Age of Barnum* (Cambridge MA: Harvard University Press, 2001).

Cougle, J., D. Reardon and P. Coleman, 'Generalized Anxiety following unintended pregnancies resolved through childbirth and abortion: a cohort study of the 1995 national survey of family growth', *Journal of Anxiety Disorders*, 19/1 (2005), 137–42.

Creed, B., 'Horror and the Monstrous Feminine: An Imaginary Abjection', in M. Jancovich (ed.) *Horror: The Film Reader* (London: Routledge, 2001), pp. 67–76.

—— *The Monstrous-Feminine: Film, Feminism, Psychoanalysis* (London: Routledge, 2007).

Cuden, S., interview with T. Dixon and J. Carpenter, *Storybeat: The Podcast for the Creative Mind*, podcast audio, 24 January 2019, www.storybeat.net/tami-dixon-jeffrey-carpenter/ (accessed 30 May 2020).

Curtin, Adrian, *Death in Modern Theatre: Stages of Mortality* (Manchester: Manchester University Press, 2019).

Dahl, M., '4 Ex-Evangelical Women on their Memories of Hell Houses', *New York Magazine*, 31 October 2018, www.thecut.com (accessed 3 November 2020).

Dalton, Derek, *Dark Tourism and Crime* (London: Routledge, 2015).

D'Arcy, G., 'The Corsican trap: its mechanism and reception', *Theatre Notebook*, 65/1 (2011), https://tinyurl.com/y7pa2str.

Davis, C., 'Hauntology, spectres and phantoms', *French Studies*, 59/3 (2005), 373–9.

Davis, Janet M., *Circus Age: Culture and Society Under the American Big Top* (Chapel Hill NC: University of North Carolina Press, 2002).

Dawidoff, R., 'Foreword', in Paul K. Longmore, *Why I Burned My Book and Other Essays on Disability* (Philadelphia PA: Temple University Press, 2003), pp. vii–ix.

Delaporte, Sophie, *Les Gueules Cassées: Les blesses de la face de la Grande Guerre* (Paris: Éd. Noêsis, 1996).

Dean, J., 'Review of *The Theatre of Martin McDonagh: A World of Savage Stories* by Eamonn Jordan and Lilian Chambers', *New Theatre Quarterly*, 23/3 (2007), 286–7.

Dear, Nick, *Plays 1* (London: Faber and Faber, 1999).

Dimitrijevic, Selma, *Dr Frankenstein* (London: Oberon, 2017).

Dissanayake, Ellen, *Homo Aestheticus: Where Art Comes From and Why* (Seattle WA: University of Washington Press, 1992).

Dorfman, A., 'The Tyranny of Terror: Is Torture Inevitable in Our Century and Beyond?', in S. Levinson (ed.), *Torture: A Collection* (Oxford: Oxford University Press, 2004), pp. 3–18.

Eberson, S., 'A Tour of Braddock Will Discover Compassionate and Talented Performers', *Pittsburgh Post-Gazette*, 20 May 2015.

Eddy, M. S., 'Managing the Ephemeral', *Stage Directions* (October 2017), 8–9.

Elliott, A., 'The Rise of Indigenous Horror: How a Fiction Genre is Confronting a Monstrous Reality', *CBC*, 17 October 2019.

Enders, Jody, *The Medieval Theater of Cruelty: Rhetoric, Memory, Violence* (Ithaca NY: Cornell University Press, 2002).

Engel, Howard, *Lord High Executioner: An Unashamed Look at Hangmen, Headsmen, and Their Kind* (Buffalo NY: Firefly, 1996).

Erll, Astrid, *Memory in Culture*, translated by S. B. Young (New York: Palgrave Macmillan, 2011).

Evans, Robert Alan, *The Woods* (London: Faber and Faber, 2018).

Fahy, T., (ed.), *The Philosophy of Horror* (Lexington KY: University Press of Kentucky, 2010).

Fawcett, J. W., 'Ford's Theater to be Lincoln Museum', *Evening Star*, 6 December 1931.

Fisher, Mark, *The Weird and the Eerie* (London: Repeater, 2016).

Finuacane, R. C., *Ghosts: Appearances of the Dead and Cultural Transformation* (New York: Prometheus, 1996).

Fletcher, John, 'Tasteless as Hell: Community Performance, Distinction, and Countertaste in Hell House', *Theatre Survey*, 48/2 (2007), 313–30.

— *Preaching to Convert: Evangelical Outreach and Performance Activism in a Secular Age* (Ann Arbor MI: The University of Michigan Press, 2013).

Foucault, Michel, *Discipline and Punish: The Birth of the Prison* (New York: Vintage Books, 1995).

Fraleigh, Sondra Horton, *Dancing into Darkness: Butoh, Zen, and Japan* (Pittsburgh PA: University of Pittsburgh Press, 2010).

Fraleigh, Sondra Horton and Tama Nakamura, *Hijikata Tatsumi and Ohno Kazuo* (New York: Routledge, 2018).

Francus, Marilyn, *Monstrous Motherhood: Eighteenth-Century Culture and the Ideology of Domesticity* (Baltimore MD: Johns Hopkins Press, 2012).

Freeland, Cynthia A., *The Naked and the Undead: Evil and the Appeal of Horror* (London and New York: Routledge, 2018).

Freud, Sigmund, *Beyond the Pleasure Principle* (New York: Bantam, 1959).

— 'The Uncanny', in James Stackey (ed.), *The Standard Edition of the Complete Psychological Works of Sigmund Freud* (London: The Hogarth Press, 1961/1919), pp. 217–56.

— 'The Uncanny', *Collected Works of Sigmund Freud* (New York: W. W. Norton, 1976), pp. 219–33.

— *Mourning and Melancholia* (New York: Norton, 1978).

Friedlander, E., 'On the Musical Gathering of Echoes of the Voice: Walter Benjamin on Opera and the *Trauerspiel*', *The Opera Quarterly*, 21/4 (autumn 2005), 631–46.

Frieze, James, (ed.), *Reframing Immersive Theatre: The Politics and Pragmatics of Participatory Performance* (London: Palgrave Macmillan, 2016).

Gambaro, Griselda, *Information for Foreigners: Three Plays by Griselda Gambaro* (Evanston IL: Northwestern University Press, 1992).

Gehrhardt, M., 'Gueules Cassées: The Men Behind the Masks', *Journal of War and Culture Studies*, 6/4 (2013), 267–81.

Georgieva, M., 'The Political Child', in *The Gothic Child* (London, Palgrave Macmillan, 2013), pp. 121–67.

Gioia, M. and A. Gans, 'Dave Malloy's Immersive *Ghost Quartet* Adds Performances at Chelsea's McKittrick Hotel', *Playbill*, 26 February 2015, www.playbill.com/article/dave-malloys-immersive-ghost-quartet-adds-performances-at-chelseas-mckittrick-hotel-com-342728 (accessed 16 September 2020).

Girard, René, *Violence and the Sacred* (Baltimore MD: Johns Hopkins University Press, 1977).

— *Scapegoat* (Baltimore MD: Johns Hopkins University Press, 1985).

Glass, I., 'Devil on My Shoulder', *This American Life*, 12 May 2002.

Goethe, Johann Wolfgang von and Friedrich Schiller, *Correspondence between Goethe and Schiller, 1794–1805* (New York: Lang, 1994).

Goldenberg, J. L., 'Ambivalence Toward the Body: Death, Neuroticism, and the Flight from Physical Sensation', *Personality and Social Psychology Bulletin*, 32 (2006), 1264–77.

Goldenberg, J. L. et al., 'The Appeal of Tragedy: A Terror Management Perspective', *Media Psychology*, 1 (1999), 313–29.

Goodall, Jane R., *Performance and Evolution in the Age of Darwin: Out of the Natural Order* (London: Routledge, 2002).

Gordon, Mel, *Theatre of Fear and Horror: The Grisly Spectacle of the Grand Guignol of Paris, 1897–1962* (Port Townsend WA: Feral House, 2016).

Gotschall, B., 'A Brief History of the "Danse Macabre"', *Atlas Obscura*, 11 October 2017, www.atlasobscura.com/articles/danse-macabre-david-pumpkins-art-history (accessed 7 April 2020).

Gregory, Adrian, *The Silence of Memory: Armistice Day, 1919–1946* (London and New York: Bloomsbury, 1994).

Griffiths, Jay, *Pip Pip: A Sideways Look at Time* (London: Flamingo, 1999).

Gritzner, Karoline (ed.), *Eroticism and Death in Theatre and Performance* (Hatfield: University of Hertfordshire Press, 2010).
Grixti, Joseph, *Terrors of Uncertainty: The Cultural Contexts of Horror Fiction* (London and New York: Routledge, 1989).
Haberman, M. and K. Rogers, 'On Centennial of 19th Amendment, Trump Pardons Susan B. Anthony and Targets 2020 Election', *New York Times*, 18 August 2020, *www.nytimes.com/2020/08/18/us/politics/trump-susan-b-anthony-pardon.html* (accessed 9 October 2020).
Hackney, C., 'The Effect of Mortality Salience on the Evaluation of Humorous Material', *The Journal of Social Psychology*, 151/1 (2011), 51–62.
Hamilton, J., 'The "Uncanny Valley" and spectating animated objects', *Performance Research*, 20/2 (2015), 60–9.
Hand, Richard J. and Michael Wilson, *Grand-Guignol: The French Theatre of Horror* (Exeter: University of Exeter Press, 2002).
—— *Performing Grand-Guignol: Playing the Theatre of Horror* (Exeter: University of Exeter Press, 2016).
Harding, Susan, *The Book of Jerry Falwell: Fundamentalist Language and Politics* (Princeton NJ: Princeton University Press, 2001).
Harris, M., 'The Hologram of Tupac at Coachella and saints: the value of relics for devotees', *Celebrity Studies*, 4/2 (2013), 238–40.
Hart, E., 'Education: Kabuki Props', *Props*, 21 February 2011, *www.props.erichart.com/education/kabuki-props/* (accessed 13 December 2019).
Hartley, A., 'Eccentricities from Our Archives: The Man Who Collected Lincoln', *fords.org*.
Hefner, E., 'The New Immersive Theater', *Hudson Review*, 69/1 (spring 2016), 108–14.
Hemphill, J. C., 'Deathbed Relics Here Tell of Lincoln Tragedy', *New York Times*, 9 February 1913.
Hijikata, T., 'From Being Jealous of a Dog's Vein', *The Drama Review*, 44/1 (2000), 56–9.
—— 'To Prison', *The Drama Review*, 44/1 (2000) 43–8.
—— 'Wind Daruma', *The Drama Review*, 44/1 (2000) 71–9.
Hirrel, M. J., 'Severed heads on the Elizabethan stage', *The Review of English Studies*, 15 March 2015, *https://blog.oup.com/2015/03/severed-heads-elizabethan-plays/* (accessed 13 December 2019).
Ho, C., K. MacDorman and Z. Pramano, 'Human emotion and the uncanny valley: A GLM, MDS, and Isomap analysis of robot video ratings', in Proceedings of the 3rd ACM/IEEE International Conference on Human Robot Interaction, HRI '08 (2008).

Hoedt, M., 'Keeping a Distance: The Joy of Haunted Attractions', *The Irish Journal of Gothic and Horror Studies*, 7 (2009), 34–46.

Hoffman, E. T. A., 'The Sandman', translated by J. Oxenford, in R. Godwin-Jones (ed.), *19th Century German Stories*, (1994), http://germanstories.vcu.edu.

Hooper, G. and J. J. Lennon (eds), *Dark Tourism: Practice and Interpretation* (Abingdon: Routledge, 2017).

Hopkins, D. J., '*Sleep No More* (Performance Review)', *Theatre Journal*, 64/2 (May 2012), 269–71.

Jackson, B., 'Jonathan Edwards Goes to Hell (House): Fear Appeals in American Evangelism', *Rhetoric Review*, 26/1 (2007), 42–59.

James, P., 'Interview: Author Peter James talks The House on Cold Hill', *Frankly My Dear*, 18 April 2019, https://tinyurl.com/y8s7dhrs.

Jamieson, A., 'Performers and Staffers at "*Sleep No More*" Say Audience Members Have Sexually Assaulted Them', *BuzzFeed News*, 6 February 2018, www.buzzfeednews.com/article/amberjamieson/sleep-no-more (accessed 16 September 2020).

Janes, Regina, *Losing Our Heads: Beheadings in Literature and Culture* (New York: New York University Press, 2005).

Jentsch, E., 'On the Psychology of the Uncanny', translated by R. Sellars, Angelaki: *Journal of the Theoretical Humanities*, 2/1 (1906/1995), 7–21.

Jonas, E., J. Schimel, J. Greenberg and T. Pyszczynski, 'The Scrooge Effect: Evidence that mortality salience increases prosocial attitudes and behavior', *Personality and Social Psychology Bulletin*, 28 (2002), 1342–53.

Jones, K., B. Poore and R. Dean (eds), *Contemporary Gothic Drama: Attraction, Consummation and Consumption on the Modern British Stage* (London: Palgrave Macmillan, 2018).

Jones, Jr, S. (ed. and translator), *Sugawara and the Secrets of Calligraphy* (New York: Columbia University Press, 1985).

Jordan, E., 'A Grand-Guignol legacy: Martin McDonagh's *A Behanding in Spokane*', *Irish Studies Review*, 20/4 (2012), 447–61.

Kantor, Tadeusz, *The Manifesto of the Theatre of Death* (unpublished Cricoteka manuscripts), in Michal Kobialka (ed. and translator), *A Journey through Other Spaces: Essays and Manifestos, 1944–1990* (Berkeley CA: University of California Press, 1993), pp. 106–17.

Kasai, T., 'A Butoh Dance Method for Psychosomatic Exploration', *Memoirs of the Hokkaido Institute of Technology*, 27 (1999), 309–16.

— 'A Note on Butoh Body', *Memoirs of the Hokkaido Institute of Technology*, 28 (2000), 353–60.

Kastenmuller, A. et al., 'Disaster Threat and Justice Sensitivity: A Terror Management Perspective', *Journal of Applied Social Psychology*, 43/10 (2013), 2100–6.
Kattelman, B. A., 'Magic, Monsters, and Movies: America's Midnight Ghost Shows', *Theatre Journal*, 62/1 (2010), 23–39.
Kelly, S. and K. Riach, 'Halloween, Organisation, and the Ethics of Uncanny Celebration', *Journal of Business Ethics*, 161/1 (2020), 103–14.
Kesebir, P., 'A Quiet Ego Quiets Death Anxiety: Humility as an Existential Anxiety Buffer', *Journal of Personality and Social Psychology*, 104/4 (2014), 610–23.
King, Stephen, *Danse Macabre* (New York: Simon & Schuster Inc., 2010).
Király, H., 'An Uncanny Cinema, a Cinema of the Uncanny: The Trope of the Doll in the Films of Manoel de Oliveira', *Acta Universitatis Sapientiae Film and Media Studies*, 15/1 (2018), 33–51.
Klein, Susan Blakeley, *Ankoku Butō the Premodern and Postmodern Influences on the Dance of Utter Darkness* (Ithaca NY: East Asia Program, Cornell University, 1993).
Kneer, J. and D. Rieger, 'The Memory Remains: How Heavy Metal Fans Buffer Against the Fear of Death', *Psychology of Popular Media Culture* (2015), 1–15.
Knell, A., '"DODO" is a Dream: Bricolage Breathes Life into Carnegie Museums', *No Proscenium*, 31 October 2017, *https://noproscenium.com/dodo-is-a-dream-bricolage-breathes-life-into-carnegie-museums-the-nopro-review-cde051ba6189* (accessed 22 May 2020).
Koger, A. (ed.), 'The Adelphi Theatre; Calendar for 1837–1838', *The Adelphi Calendar Project*, A. L. Nelson and G. B. Cross, general editors, *www.umass.edu/AdelphiTheatreCalendar/m37d.htm* (accessed 10 July 2020).
Komporaly, J., 'Making a Spectacle: Motherhood in Contemporary British Theatre and Performance', *Theatre History Studies*, 35 (2016), 161–78.
Kristeva, Julia, *Strangers to Ourselves* (New York: Columbia University Press, 1994).
— *The Severed Head: Capital Visions*, translated by J. Gladding (New York: Columbia University Press, 2012).
Kron, Lisa and Jeanine Tesori, *Fun Home* (New York: Samuel French, 2014).
Kurihara, N., 'Hijikata Tatsumi Chronology', *The Drama Review*, 44/1 (2000), 29–33.
— 'Introduction: Hijikata Tatsumi: The Words of Butoh', *The Drama Review*, 44/1 (2000), 10–28.
Kwaitek, B., 'The Dark Ride' (unpublished MA thesis: Western Kentucky University, 1995).
Lacan, Jacques, 'The Mirror Stage', in *Écrits: A Selection* (New York: Norton, 1977), pp. 1–7.
— *The Ethics of Psychoanalysis, Seminar VII* (New York: Norton, 1992).

Lakoff, George and Mark Johnson, *Metaphors We Live By* (Chicago IL: University of Chicago Press, 1980).

Landsberg, A., 'Horror vérité: politics and history in Jordan Peele's Get Out', *Continuum*, 32/5 (2018), 629–42.

Lavender, Andy, *Performance in the Twenty-First Century* (London: Routledge, 2016).

Lavendier, D., 'The More things Change, the More they Stay the Same: Tupac Shakur's "hologram," Victorian Death Customs, and American Voyeurism', *Relevant Rhetoric: A New Journal of Rhetorical Studies*, 11 (2020), 1–14.

Leader, C., 'Supervising the Uncanny: The play within the play', *Journal of Analytical Psychology*, 60/5 (2015), 657–78.

Leiter, S., 'The Depiction of Violence on the Kabuki Stage', *Educational Theatre Journal*, 21/2 (May 1969), 147–55.

Lennon, John and Malcolm Foley, *Dark Tourism: The Attraction of Death and Disaster* (London: Continuum, 2000).

Levy, A., 'March for Life Unveils Its 2020 Theme – Life Empowers: Pro-Life Is Pro-Woman', *March for Life*, 10 December 2019, https://marchforlife.org/march-for-life-unveils-its-2020-theme-life-empowers-pro-life-is-pro-woman/ (accessed 4 October 2020).

Lewis, Andrew R., *The Rights Turn in Conservative Christian Politics: How Abortion Transformed the Culture Wars* (Cambridge: Cambridge University Press, 2017).

Lindsay, Joan, *Picnic at Hanging Rock* (Melbourne: F. W. Cheshire, 1967).

Lloyd, Fran, *Consuming Bodies: Sex and Contemporary Japanese Art* (London: Reaktion Books, 2003).

Lonergan, Patrick, *The Theatre and Films of Martin McDonagh* (London: Bloomsbury Methuen Drama, 2013).

Long, C. and D. Greenwood, 'Joking in the face of death: A terror management approach to humor production', *International Journal of Humor Research* (2013), 493–509.

MacCannell, Dean, *The Tourist: A New Theory of the Leisure Class* (Berkeley CA: University of California Press, 2013).

MacCarthy, D., 'The Grand Guignol Company', *The New Statesman*, 5/115 (19 June 2015), 255–6.

Machon, Josephine, *Immersive Theatres: Intimacy and Immediacy in Contemporary Performance* (London: Palgrave Macmillan, 2013).

Machon, Josephine with Punchdrunk, *The Punchdrunk Encyclopaedia* (London: Routledge, 2019).

Mackenbach, J. P. and R. P. Dreier, 'Dances of Death: Macabre Mirrors of an Unequal Society', *International Journal of Public Health*, 57 (2012), 915–24.

MacLeod, Suzanne, Laura Hourston Hanks and Jonathan Hale, *Museum Making: Narratives, Architectures, Exhibitions* (London: Routledge, 2012).

Manning, Susan, *Ecstasy and the Demon: The Dances of Mary Wigman* (Minneapolis MN: University of Minnesota Press, 2006).

Martin, F., '"O die a rare example": Beheading the Body on the Jacobean Stage', *Early Modern Literary Studies*, 19 (2009), 1–24.

Maughan, T. and Arkadia & Co. 'The McKittrick Hotel: Open All Year, Established 1939' [*Sleep No More* theatrical programme].

Mayhew, Henry, *London Labour and the London Poor*, 3 (1851), ebook at *Project Gutenberg*, 2018, *www.gutenberg.org/files/57060/57060-h/57060-h.htm*.

McDonagh, Martin, *Hangmen* (London: Faber and Faber, 2015).

McEvoy, Emma, 'Gothic and the Romantics', in C. Spooner and E. McEvoy (eds), *The Routledge Companion to Gothic* (Abingdon: Routledge, 2007), 19–28.

— *Gothic Tourism* (London: Palgrave Macmillan, 2016).

McPherson, Conor, *Plays: Three* (London: Nick Hern Books, 2013).

Miles, Tiya, *Tales from the Haunted South: Dark Tourism and Memories of Slavery from the Civil War Era* (Chapel Hill NC: University of North Carolina Press, 2015).

Miklaszewski, Krzysztof, *Encounters with Tadeusz Kantor*, translated by George M. Hyde (New York: Routledge, 2002).

Mishima, Yukio and Alfred H. Marks, *Forbidden Colors* (New York: Knopf, 1968).

Montez, Noe, *Memory, Transitional Justice, and Theatre in Postdictatorship Argentina* (Carbondale IL: University of Carbondale Press, 2018).

Morgan, F., 'Review: *The Woods*', *The Stage*, 13 September 2018, *www.thestage.co.uk/reviews/the-woods-review-at-royal-court-london--harrowing-and-hallucinatory* (accessed 31 May 2020).

Mori, M., 'The Uncanny Valley', translated by K. F. MacDorman and T. Minato, *Energy*, 7 (1970/2005), 33–5.

Morishita, Takashi, *Hijikata Tatsumi's Notational Butoh: an Innovational Method for Butoh Creation* (Tokyo: Keio University Art Center, 2015).

Mueller, B., 'Bricolage's "Strata" Offers Layers of Oddity', *Pittsburgh Post-Gazette*, 12 August 2012.

Muir, Ward, *The Happy Hospital* (London: Simkin Marshall, 1918).

Murray, C., 'The Supernatural in Conor McPherson's *The Seafarer* and *The Birds*', in L. Chambers and E. Jordan (eds), *The Theatre of Conor McPherson: Right Beside the Beyond* (Dublin: Carysfort Press, 2012), pp. 197–213.

Nägele, Rainer, *Theatre, Theory, Speculation* (Baltimore MD: Johns Hopkins University Press, 1991).

Nelson, N., 'The No Proscenium Glossary', *No Proscenium*, 14 September 2019, *https://noproscenium.com/the-no-proscenium-glossary-for-audiences-c1597d510268* (accessed 7 April 2020).

Niemec, C. et al., 'Being Present in the Face of Existential Threat: The Role of Trait Mindfulness in Reducing Defensive Responses to Mortality Salience', *Journal of Personality and Social Psychology*, 99/2 (2010), 344–65.

Niziołek, Grzegorz, *The Polish Theatre of the Holocaust*, translated by Ursula Phillips (London: Methuen Drama, 2019).

Nora, P., 'Between Memory and History: Les Lieux de Mémoire', *Representations*, 26 (spring 1989), 7–24.

O'Driscoll, B., 'When the Saints Go Marching in a Mill Town', *American Theatre* (May 2015), *www.americantheatre.org/2015/04/29/when-the-saints-go-marching-in-a-mill-town/* (accessed 28 May 2020).

O'Hagan, S., 'Martin McDonagh Interview: "Theatre is never going to be edgy the way I want it to be"', *Guardian*, 13 September 2015, *www.theguardian.com/culture/2015/sep/11/martin-mcdonagh-theatre-never-going-to-be-edgy-hangmen-interview*.

Oosterwijk, S., '"Fro Paris to Inglond?": The *Danse Macabre* in Image and Text in Late-Medieval England' (unpublished PhD thesis: Leiden University, 2009).

Oosterwijk, S. and S. Knöll (eds), *Mixed Metaphors: The* Danse Macabre *in Medieval and Early Modern Europe* (Newcastle upon Tyne: Cambridge Scholars Publishing, 2011).

Orlando, P. M., 'Cutting the Surface of the Water: Butoh as Traumatic Awakening', *Social Semiotics*, 11/3 (2001), 307–24.

O'Toole, O., 'Dance of Darkness: A Traveler's Guide to Butoh', *Art Papers*, 24/1 (2000), 20–5.

Parsons, Michael, *Living Psychoanalysis: from Theory to Experience* (London: Karnac, 2014).

Pavis, Patrice, *Contemporary* Mise-en-Scène*: Staging Theatre Today* (London: Routledge, 2013).

Peele, George, *The Battle of Alcazar*, in C. Edelman (ed.), *The Stukeley Plays* (Manchester: Manchester University Press, 2005), 59–128.

Pellegrini, A., '"Signaling through the Flames": Hell House Performance and Structures of Religious Feeling', *American Quarterly*, 59/3 (2007), 911–35.

Penner, J., 'The Living Theatre and Its Discontents: Excavating the Somatic Utopia of *Paradise Now*', *Ecumenica*, 2/1 (spring 2009), 17–36.

Pensky, Max, *Melancholy Dialectics: Walter Benjamin and the Play of Mourning* (Amherst MA: University of Massachusetts Press, 1993).

'Pepys's Progeny: Marvin Carlson's *10,000 Nights: Highlights from 50 Years of Theatre-Going*' (17 November 2017), Panel at American Society for Theatre Research, Atlanta GA.

Picton, Tom, *Fun and Fancy in Old New York: Reminiscences of a Man About Town* (New York: Borgo, 2007).

Pierce, Peter, *The Country of Lost Children: An Australian Anxiety* (Cambridge: Cambridge University Press, 1999).

Pilbeam, Pamela, *Madame Tussaud and the History of Waxworks* (London: Hambeldon Continuum, 2003).

Pineau, E., 'Haunted by Ghosts: Collaborating with Absent Others', *International Review of Qualitative Research*, 5/4 (2012), 459–65.

Plato, *The Republic* (New York: Quality Paperback Books, 1999).

Pilný, O., 'Martin McDonagh: Parody? Satire? Complacency?', *Irish Studies Review*, 12/2 (2004), 225–32.

Ponnuru, R., 'Barrett, in 2006, Supported the Right to Life', *National Review* (2 October 2020), *www.nationalreview.com/corner/amy-coney-barrett-in-2006-supported-the-right-to-life/* (accessed 9 October 2020).

Pyszczynski, T. et al., 'Whistling in the Dark: Exaggerated Consensus Estimates in Response to Incidental Reminders of Mortality', *Psychological Science*, 7 (1996), 332–6.

Rabey, David Ian, *Theatre, Time and Temporality: Melting Clocks and Snapped Elastics* (Bristol: Intellect, 2016).

Ralph, M., A. Beliso-De Jesús and S. Palmié, 'SAINT TUPAC', *Transforming Anthropology*, 25/2 (2017), 90–100.

Ramalho, J. R., 'The Uncanny Afterlife of Dolls: Reconfiguring Personhood through Object Vivification in Gothic Film', *Studies in Gothic Fiction*, 6/2 (2020), 27–38.

Ratliff, George, *Hell House*, dir. George Ratcliff, Texas, March 2001.

Reardon, D. and P. Coleman, 'Relative treatment rates for sleep disorders and sleep disturbances following abortion and childbirth: a prospective record-based study', *Sleep*, 29/1 (2006), 105–6.

Reardon, D. and P. Ney, 'Abortion and subsequent substance abuse', *The American Journal of Drug and Alcohol Abuse*, 26/1 (2000), 61–75.

Ridout, Nicholas, *Stage Fright, Animals, and Other Theatrical Problems* (Cambridge: Cambridge University Press, 2006).

Rinehart, L., 'Rugged Terrain', 7 February 2008, *danceviewtimes.com*.

Ritter, J., 'Dance and Immersive Performance: A Multicase Study of Three International Immersive Productions' (unpublished PhD thesis: Texas Woman's University, 2016).

Robben, A. C. G. M., 'How Traumatized Societies Remember: The Aftermath of Argentina's Dirty War', *Cultural Critique*, 59 (winter 2005), 120–64.

Rojek, Chris, *Ways of Escape* (Basingstoke: Palgrave Macmillan, 1993).

Rose, M., 'Pro-life, Pro-Woman? Frame Extension in the American Antiabortion Movement', *Journal of Women, Politics and Policy*, 32/1 (2011), 1–27.

Routledge, C. et al., 'The Life and Death of Creativity: The Effects of Mortality Salience on Self Versus Social-Directed Creative Expression', *Motivation and Emotion*, 32 (2008), 331–8.

Royle, Nicholas, *The Uncanny* (Manchester: Manchester University Press, 2003).

Rozik, Eli, *The Roots of Theatre: Rethinking Ritual and Other Theories of Origin* (Iowa City IA: University of Iowa Press, 2007).

Rudolph, Valerie C., *Nineteenth-Century British Drama, Encyclopedia of Literature* (Amenia NY: Salem Press, 2019).

Rue, V., P. Coleman, J. Rue and D. Reardon, 'Induced abortion and traumatic stress: a preliminary comparison of American and Russian women', *Medical Science Monitor*, 10/10 (2004), SR5–SR16.

Saglia, D., '"The frighted stage": the sensational proliferation of ghost melodrama in the 1820s', *Studies in Romanticism*, 54/2 (2015), 269–93.

Sakamoto, M., 'Parallels of Psycho-Physiological and Musical Affect in Trance Ritual and Butoh Performance', *Pacific Review of Ethnomusicology*, 14 (2009), https://ethnomusicologyreview.ucla.edu/journal/volume/14/piece/485 (accessed 1 June 2020).

Sanders, V., 'Dancing and the Dark Soul of Japan: An Aesthetic Analysis of "Butō"', *Asian Theatre Journal*, 5/2 (1988), 148–63.

Santana, Analola, *Freak Performances: Dissidence in Latin American Theater* (Ann Arbor MI: University of Michigan Press, 2018).

Saurette, Paul and K. Gordon, *The Changing Voice of the Anti-abortion Movement: The Rise of 'Pro-Woman' Rhetoric in Canada and the United States* (Toronto: University of Toronto Press, 2016).

Saxon, A. H., *Selected Letters of P. T. Barnum* (New York: Columbia University Press, 1983).

Sbravatti, V., 'Acoustic Startles in Horror Films: A Neurofilmological Approach', *Projections*, 13/1 (2009), 45–66.

Schulze, Daniel, *Authenticity in Contemporary Theatre and Performance* (London: Methuen, 2017).

Schwab, Gabrielle, *Haunting Legacies: Violent Histories and Transgenerational Trauma* (New York: Columbia University Press, 2010).

Seaton, A. V., 'War and Thanatourism: Waterloo 1815–1914', *Annals of Tourism Research*, 26/1 (1999), 130–58.

Seeman, Erik R., *Speaking with the Dead in Early America* (Philadelphia PA: University of Pennsylvania Press, 2019).
Sencidiver, S. Y., 'The Doll's Uncanny Soul', in L. Pinatti-Farnell and M. Beville (eds), *The Gothic and the Everyday: Living Gothic* (London: Palgrave Macmillan, 2014), pp. 103–30.
Shaefer, B., 'Welcome to Paradise', *Dance Magazine*, 89/2 (December 2015), 64–7.
Shakespeare, William, *Complete Works*, J. Bate and E. Rasmussen (eds) (New York: The Modern Library, 2007).
Shapiro, J. (ed.), *Shakespeare in America: An Anthology from the Revolution to Now* (Washington, DC: Library of America, 2016).
Sharpley, R. and P. R. Stone (eds), *The Darker Side of Tourism: The Theory and Practice of Dark Tourism* (Bristol and Buffalo NY: Channel Publications, 2009).
Šimić, L. and E. U. Lee, 'Editorial', *Performance Research*, 22 (June 2017), 1–4.
Smirnov, K. and J. Pracejus, 'Empathy Drivers in the Uncanny Valley', *Advances in Consumer Research*, 38 (2011), 807–9.
Smith, J., 'The Adventures of the Human Fly, 1830–1930', *Early Popular Visual Culture*, 6 (2008), 51–66.
Smith, K., 'Daggers Drawn', *The New Criterion*, 36/7 (2018), 37–40.
Sofer, Andrew, *Dark Matter: Invisibility in Drama, Theater and Performance* (Ann Arbor MI: University of Michigan Press, 2014).
— *The Stage Life of Props* (Ann Arbor MI: University of Michigan Press, 2003).
Solomon, S. et al., 'Teach These Souls to Fly: Supernatural as Human Adaptation', in M. Schaller et al. (eds), *Evolution, Culture and the Human Mind* (New York: Taylor and Francis Group, 2012), pp. 99–118.
Solomon, S., J. Greenberg and T. Pyszczynski, *The Worm at the Core: On the Role of Death in Life* (New York: Random House, 2015).
Solomon, S. and M. J. Landau, 'Little Murders: Cultural Animals in an Existential Age', in D. Sullivan and J. Greenberg (eds), *Death in Classic and Contemporary Film* (New York: Palgrave Macmillan, 2013), 55–71.
'Stars in the House: *Macbeth*', 13–17 June 2020, streaming on *www.playbill.com/article/patrick-page-hannah-yelland-donna-bullock-ty-jones-more-read-macbeth-on-stars-in-the-house* (accessed 16 June 2020).
Stein, B. S., 'Butoh: "Twenty Years Ago We Were Crazy, Dirty, and Mad"', *The Drama Review*, 30/2 (1986), 107–26.
Steinberg, M., 'Benjamin and the Critique of Allegorical Reason', in *Walter Benjamin and the Demands of History* (Ithaca NY: Cornell University Press, 1996), pp. 1–24.
Stone, P. R. et al. (eds), *The Palgrave Handbook of Dark Tourism Studies* (Basingstoke: Palgrave Macmillan, 2018).

Stone, Simon, *Yerma* (London: Oberon, 2017).
Stuart, Roxana, *Stage Blood: Vampires of the 19th-Century Stage* (Bowling Green OH: Bowling Green State University Popular Press, 1994).
Strube, H., 'White Crocodile, Black Skirt: Theatre for Young People and Cultural Memory', *Australasian Drama Studies*, 47 (October 2005), 55–72.
Sullivan, D. et al., 'Toward a New Understanding of Two Films from the Dark Side: Terror Management Theory Applied to *Rosemary's Baby* and *Straw Dogs*', *Journal of Popular Film and Television*, 37 (2010), 42–51.
Sutton, Matthew Avery, *American Apocalypse* (Cambridge MA: Harvard University Press, 2014).
Swain, M., 'Tar-black gallows humour galore in Martin McDonagh's triumphant return', *Arts Desk.com*, 8 December 2015, https://theartsdesk.com/theatre/hangmen-wyndhams-theatre.
Swanson, J. L., 'The Blood Relic from the Lincoln Assassination', *Smithsonian Magazine* (March 2005), https://www.smithsonianmag.com/history/the-blood-relics-from-the-lincoln-assassination-180954331/ (accessed 17 July 2020).
Taylor, L., 'Death and Television: Terror Management Theory and Themes of Law and Justice on Television', *Death Studies*, 36 (2012), 340–59.
Tompkins, J., 'Space and the Geographies of Theatre: An Introduction', *Modern Drama*, 46/4 (2003), 537–41.
Thomson, Rosemary Garland, *Extraordinary Bodies: Figuring Physical Disability in American Culture and Literature* (New York: Columbia University Press, 1996).
Torok, M., 'The Illness of Mourning and the Fantasy of the Exquisite Corpse', in N. T. Rand (ed.), *The Shell and the Kernel: Renewals of Psychoanalysis* (Chicago IL: University of Chicago Press, 1994), pp. 107–24.
Torok, M. and N. Abraham, '"The Lost Object – Me": Notes on Endocryptic Identification', in N. T. Rand (ed.), *The Shell and the Kernel: Renewals of Psychoanalysis* (Chicago IL: University of Chicago Press, 1994), pp. 139–56.
Tracy, R., 'Dance States of a Theatrical Mind: Diana Szeinblum's Alaska', *The Brooklyn Rail*, March 2008, www.brooklynrail.org.
Tran, D., 'The Walls Come Tumbling Down: In Immersive Theatre, Audiences Are Breaking the Rules – Moving Around, Talking with the Actors and Molding the Action', *American Theatre*, 30/6 (July 2013), 30–5.
— 'You Can Go Your Own Way', *New York Times*, 27 December 2015.
Trigg, Dylan, *The Memory of Place: The Phenomenology of the Uncanny* (Athens OH: Ohio University Press, 2012).
Tudor, A., 'Why Horror? The Peculiar Pleasures of a Popular Genre', in Mark Jancovich (ed.), *Horror: The Film Reader* (New York: Routledge, 2002), pp. 47–55.

Twitchin, Mischa, *The Theatre of Death – The Uncanny in Mimesis* (New York: Palgrave Macmillan, 2016).
Vail, K. E. et al., 'The Aftermath of Destruction: Images of Destroyed Buildings Increase Support for War, Dogmatism, and Death Thought Accessibility', *Journal of Experimental Social Psychology*, 48 (2012), 1069–81.
Vedantam, S., 'Reminders of Mortality Bring Out the Charitable Side', *Washington Post*, 24 December 2007.
Venning, D., 'Politics and Nightmares: Shakespearean Adaptations in New York', *Graduate Center Advocate* (February 2013), 27–30.
— '*Sleep No More* and *Something Rotten!* (dual review)', *Shakespeare Bulletin*, 34/1 (spring 2016), 157–65.
Viala, Jean and Nourit Masson-Sekine, *Butoh: Shades of Darkness* (Tokyo: Shufunotomo, 1988).
Wang, S., S. Lilienfeld and P. Rochat, 'The Uncanny Valley: Existence and Explanations', *Review of General Psychology*, 19/4 (2015), 393–407.
Waychoff, B., 'Butoh, Bodies, and Being', *Kaleidoscope: A Graduate Journal of Qualitative Communication Research*, 8/4 (2009), 37–53.
West, Arthur Graeme, *The Diary of a Dead Officer, being the posthumous papers of Arthur Graeme West* (London: George Allen and Unwin, 1918).
White, G., 'On Immersive Theatre', *Theatre Research International*, 37/3 (2012), 221–35.
White, L. and E. Frew (eds), *Dark Tourism and Place Identity: Managing and Interpreting Dark Places* (London: Routledge, 2013).
Wilde, Oscar, *The Plays of Oscar Wilde* (New York: Vintage, 1988).
Wiles, David, *A Short History of Western Performance Space* (New York: Cambridge University Press, 2003).
— *Theatre and Time* (Basingstoke: Palgrave, 2014).
Willenbrink, H., 'The Act of Being Saved: Hell House and the Salvific Performative', *Theatre Journal*, 66/1 (2014), 73–92.
Willis, Emma, *Theatricality, Dark Tourism and Ethical Spectatorship: Absent Others* (Basingstoke: Palgrave Macmillan, 2014).
Wilson, M., 'Spotting a Thief in a Room Full of Masks at "*Sleep No More*"', *New York Times*, 1 November 2015, *www.nytimes.com/2015/11/02/nyregion/spotting-a-thief-in-a-room-full-of-masks-at-sleep-no-more.html* (accessed 16 September 2020).
Wurmli, K., 'The Power of Image: Hijikata Tatsumi's Scrapbooks and the Art of Butoh' (unpublished PhD thesis: University of Hawai'i at Manoa, 2008).
Wynne, Catherine, *Bram Stoker, Dracula and the Victorian Gothic Stage* (Basingstoke: Palgrave Macmillan, 2013).

Yu, K., 'The Immersive 5 with Bricolage's Jeffrey Carpenter and Tami Dixon', *No Proscenium*, 16 May 2018, https://noproscenium.com/the-immersive-5-with-bricolages-artistic-director-jeffrey-carpenter-and-producing-artistic-70ca91371a4d (accessed 18 May 2020).

Zara, C., '"*Sleep No More*" Internship Post Flouts Fair Wage Laws: Unpaid Laborers Asked to Work 10-Hour Days', *International Business Times*, 3 December 2013, www.ibtimes.com/sleep-no-more-internship-post-flouts-fair-wage-laws-unpaid-laborers-asked-work-10-hour-days-1493776 (accessed 16 September 2020).

— 'Former "*Sleep No More*" Interns Say Immersive NYC Megahit Offers Little Educational Benefit', *International Business Times*, 7 December 2013, www.ibtimes.com/former-sleep-no-more-interns-say-immersive-nyc-megahit-offers-little-educational-benefit-1499418 (accessed 16 September 2020).

Zika, J., 'The Dawn of the Dark Ride at the Amusement Park', *IE2014: Proceedings of the 2014 Conference on Interactive Entertainment* (December 2014), https://doi.org/10.1145/2677758.2677775.

Zinn, Jeff, *The Existential Actor: Life and Death Onstage and Off* (Hanover: Smith and Kraus, 2015).

Žižek, Slavoj, *The Sublime Object of Ideology* (London: Verso, 1989).

Index

39 Steps, The 195

Abbott and Costello Meet Frankenstein 20
abjection 48, 64, 146, 177, 178, 231
abortion 8, 106, 237–8, 240–6
Alien 72
Alleyn, Edward 150
Alton Towers 224–5
Ankoku butoh 7, 175–85
Anthony, Susan B. 243
Archibald, William 50, 51
  The Innocents 50, 51, 52, 55

Baartman, Sarah 4
Bakhtin's carnivalesque 7, 195, 200–2
Barrett, Amy Coney 243
Baudelaire, Charles 81
Beagan, Tara 5
Beardsley, Aubrey 155
Becker, Ernest 129
  The Denial of Death 129
Bechdel, Alison 127, 128, 131, 132, 133

Benjamin, Walter 5, 79–83, 86–7, 89–90, 262
Benkei Jōshi 151
Bergson, Henri 21
Berton, René 156
  L'Homme qui a tué la mort 156–7
Betzien, Angela 6, 95–108
  The Dark Room 6, 96, 98, 103–6, 107, 108
  The Hanging 6, 96, 99–1, 103, 105, 106
  Mortido 6, 95, 96, 98, 101–3, 105, 107, 108
Black Death 1
Bond, Edward 65
  Saved 65
Bonis–Charancle, Marc 48
  La Maison hantée 48
Booth, John Wilkes 253, 256, 257
Boucicault, Dion 53
  The Corsican Brothers 53
Box Tale Soup 52
Bricolage Production Company 207, 211–17

Bride of Frankenstein 26, 63, 69, 73–5
Büchner, Georg 198
  Woyzeck 198
bunraku 151–3, 158, 187
Bush, George W. 147
Butoh *see* ankoku butoh

Cedar Hill Church 241
Christie, Agatha 55
  The Mousetrap 55
Churchill, Caryl 65
  Top Girls 66
coronavirus/Covid-19 45, 57, 193, 195, 197, 199, 201

danse macabre 1–2, 4, 6, 7, 8, 162, 163, 172, 208, 209, 213, 215, 216, 217
dark ride 7, 207–18
dark tourism 8, 251, 253–6
Dear, Nick 52
Dekker, Thomas 150
de Lorde, Andre 156
Devereux, Robert 148
día de los Muertos 4
Dickens, Charles 55
  The Haunted Man and the Ghost's Bargain 55
Dimitrijevic, Selma 6, 63, 69, 73–5
  Dr Frankenstein 5, 63, 69, 73–5
Dionysus in '69 201
Dirty War 6, 162–8, 172
disability 13, 14, 23–5
disfigurement 5, 30, 33–5
dismemberment 5, 79, 81, 85, 87–8
Disney theme parks 56, 210
Dixon, Tami 207
DODO 212, 216, 217

Doll Factory, The 231
Dollhouse of the Damned 225, 231
dolls 223, 229, 230, 231–3
Donkey Show, The 209
Dorfman, Ariel 161, 163
  Death and the Maiden 161, 163, 166
Drury, Jackie Sibblies 4
Du Maurier, Daphne 200
  Rebecca 198, 200

Elliott, Alicia 4
Emursive (theatre company) 7, 195, 200
Euripides 3
evangelicals 2, 8, 237, 238–42
Evans, Robert Alan 5, 63, 69–71
  The Woods 5, 63, 69–71
execution 6, 7, 83, 84, 87, 114, 115, 116, 119, 147, 148, 154, 155, 156, 200, 255, 261

Falwell, Jerry 240
Farmageddon 225
Flaubert, Gustav 155
Fletcher, John 150
freak shows 2, 14, 16, 24
Ford's Theatre 8, 251–64
Frankenstein 3, 6, 20, 23
Freud, Sigmund 6, 21, 50, 85, 86, 87, 115, 226, 227, 230, 231, 232
  Mourning and Melancholia 86
  'The Uncanny' 21, 226, 231
Fun Home 6, 127–138

Gambaro, Griselda 163, 165, 166, 208
  Information for Foreigners 163, 165–6, 167, 208

Game of Thrones 147, 148
Genet, Jean 177
ghosts 5, 19, 21, 24, 45–57, 65, 68, 105–8, 193, 194, 196, 199, 200, 207, 213, 216–17, 223, 239, 251, 262
ghost light 45, 46, 57, 213
Ghost Light (play) 213, 216, 217
The Gnome Fly 16, 18
Goethe, Johann Wolfgang von 81
Gothic 2, 5, 47, 48, 50, 53, 54, 55, 63–8, 72, 73, 75, 97–8, 104, 120, 223
Grand Guignol 2, 5, 29–40, 47–9, 53, 116, 118, 147, 155–6
Grand Paradise, The 213, 215, 216
Greenidge, Kirsten 4
Griffin, Kathy 148
Grotowski, Jerzy 208
guillotine 147, 154, 155, 156

Halloween Horror Nights 224, 231
haunt industry 7, 56, 223–6, 228, 230–2
hauntology 46, 56
Hell House (film) 241
Hell House 2013 241
Hell House: Present Darkness (HHPD) 237, 239, 240, 241, 242, 244–5
Hell House X: The Walking Dead 241
hell houses 2, 8, 237–46
Hemingway, Ernest 131
Henry VIII 148
Here Lies Love 209
Herzog, Werner 198
Hijikata Tastsumi 7, 175–84
Hill, Susan 50, 66
Hitchcock, Alfred 63, 198, 200

Hoffman, E.T.A. 226
'The Sandman' 226
horror 3, 4, 29–40, 51, 63, 64, 66, 86, 97, 153, 210, 216, 217, 223, 224–5, 228, 230, 232, 239
cinematic 33, 240
as genre 3, 4, 13, 29, 30, 48, 207, 208
and gender 3, 4, 64
and humour 13–14, 16–20, 23
and race 4, 264
and sexuality 21, 210
Horror Camp Live! 230–1, 233
House of Frankenstein 20
humour 5, 13–14, 16, 20–4, 115, 118, 128, 131, 133, 137, 224, 233

Ichijō Ōkura Monogatari 151
Ichi-no-Tani Futaba Gunki 153
Illuminati Ball 208
immersive theatre 7, 47, 57, 193, 195–200, 202, 205, 207–17, 223, 224, 233, 238, 245, 264
The Innocents (film) 52
Irving, Henry 53–4

James, Henry 50
The Turn of the Screw 50, 52
James, Peter 54
The House on Cold Hill (play) 54–5
Johnson, Boris 147

kabuki 147, 151–3, 175, 180, 187
King, Stephen 8, 36, 63
Knott's Berry Farm 224, 231
Krizanc, John 208
Tamara 208

Kron, Lisa 6, 127
Kumagai Jinya 153

La Veillée de Jean Rémy 39–40
Lacan, Jaques 6, 83, 85, 88
Law and Order 130
Le Baiser dans la Nuit 30, 33–6, 37, 39
Leach, Harvey 5, 13–25
Lenkiewicz, Rebecca 52
Lewis, Leopold 53
   The Bells 53
Lewis, Matthew 'Monk' 65
   The Castle Spectre 65
Lincoln, Abraham 8, 251–64
Lincoln, Mary Todd 261, 263
Lincoln, Willie 263
Living Theatre 201
Lopez, Rodrigo 148
Lorca, Federico García 5, 63, 71
   Yerma 5, 63
Luscombe, Tim 52

macabre tourism *see* dark tourism
Mallatratt, Stephen 50, 66
   The Woman in Black 50, 52, 54, 55, 66
Malloy, Dave 200
   The Ghost Quartet 200
Marlowe, Christopher 67
   Doctor Faustus 67
Markham, Geruase 150
Marston, John 150
   The Insatiate Countess 150
Massinger, Philip 150
Maturin, Charles 65
   Bertram 65
McDonagh, Martin 6, 113–23
   A Behanding in Spokane 6, 114
   Hangmen 6, 113–23

The Pillowman 6, 114
A Skull in Connemara 6
A Very Very Very Dark Matter 6
McKenna, Shaun 54
McPherson, Conor 48–50
   Shining City 48–9
   The Weir 49–50
memento mori 6, 87, 146, 151, 214, 263
Merrick, Joseph 4
Mishima Yukio 176
   Kinjiki 176, 177
modernism/modernity 79, 80, 176, 209, 254
monster theory 21
monstrous maternal 4, 63, 74, 244
Moreau, Gustav 155
Moritsuna Jinya 153
Moses, Daniel David 5

NetherWorld Haunted House 225
No Proscenium 209, 210, 214

Oakley, Annie 252
Ohno Kazuo 175, 176, 177, 180
Oklahoma! 252
Olivier, Laurence 193
Ômi Genji Senjin Yakata 153
One Destiny 252
O'Toole, Peter 193
Our American Cousin 256

Paradise Now 201
Peele, George 150
   The Battle of Alcazar 150
Pepper's Ghost 55, 56, 57
Performance Group 201
Petersen, Anna 253, 254, 260, 261, 263

Petersen, William 253, 254, 260, 261, 263, 264
phantasmagoria 4, 194
Pierrepoint, Albert 122
Psycho 63
Punchdrunk 7, 47, 195, 200, 207
   Clod and Pebble 47
puppets 52, 80, 84, 85, 113, 154, 158

Queen of the Night 208

Radcliffe, Ann 65
   The Sicilian Romance; or the Apparition of the Cliffs 65
Reardon, David 242–3
   Making Abortion Rare: A Healing Strategy for a Divided Nation 242–3
Redon, Odilon 155
Renard, Maurice 48, 50
   L'Amant de la mort 48, 50
Revenge of Chucky 224, 225
Rilke, Rainer Maria 82
Roe v. Wade 240

Saints Tour 211, 214, 216, 217
Sampson, William 150
Sanson, Charles-Henri 154
semiotics 163–4, 172
Shakespeare, William 2, 7, 64, 65, 70, 149–50, 165, 193, 194, 196, 197, 199
   Cymbeline 149
   Hamlet 145–6, 150–1
   Henry VI, Part Two 149
   Macbeth 7, 63, 65, 146, 149, 150, 193–203, 244, 248
   Measure for Measure 149
   Romeo and Juliet 261

   The Tempest 4
   Titus Andronicus 64, 194
Shakur, Tupac 56
Shibaraku 152
Shinwakan 227, 232
slasher films 4
Sleep No More 7, 193–203, 207–8, 209, 214, 217, 238
Slowthai 148
Sous La Lumiére Rouge 30, 33, 36–9
Speakeasy Dollhouse: The Bloody Beginning 208
Stenham, Polly 66
   That Face 66
Stone, Simon 5, 63, 69, 71, 72
   Yerma 5, 63, 69, 71–3
Strange Undoing of Prudencia Hart, The 200
Sugawara Denju Tenarai Kagami 152
Szeinblum, Diane 6, 163–72
   Alaska 6, 163–72

ta'ziyeh 4
Teatro de los Sentidos 211
terror management theory 6, 128, 129, 131, 133, 134, 136, 137, 138, 139
Tesori, Jeanine 6, 127
Then She Fell 200, 209, 214, 215, 217
Third Rail 200, 209, 211, 212–17
trauerspiel 6, 79–90
trauma 5, 6, 7, 30, 49, 50, 57, 69, 83, 97, 98, 128, 163–7, 169, 171, 172, 176, 177, 179, 185, 242, 246, 254, 255
Trevor Project 200
Tulley's Shocktoberfest 225
Tussaud, Marie 154

uncanny 3, 7, 21, 47, 50, 51, 53, 54, 55, 56, 57, 82, 85, 87, 90, 96, 98, 100, 105, 106, 115, 146, 203, 215, 216, 223–33, 264
Universal Studios 224, 225, 231

vampire 21, 68, 223, 226, 227, 231, 232

Walpole, Horace 65
   The Mysterious Mother 65
Webster, John 4, 145
Wilde, Oscar 155
   Salome 155
Wilson, August 2, 47
   The Piano Lesson 47
World War I 5, 29, 30, 31, 34, 35, 37
World War II 147, 175, 176, 200

also in series

Lindsey Decker, *Transnationalism and Genre Hybridity in New British Horror Cinema* (2021)

Stacey Abbott and Lorna Jowett (eds), *Global TV Horror* (2021)

Michael J. Blouin, *Stephen King and American Politics* (2021)

Eddie Falvey, Joe Hickinbottom and Jonathan Wroot (eds), *New Blood: Critical Approaches to Contemporary Horror* (2020)

Darren Elliott-Smith and John Edgar Browning (eds), *New Queer Horror Film and Television* (2020)

Jonathan Newell, *A Century of Weird Fiction, 1832–1937* (2020)

Alexandra Heller-Nicholas, *Masks in Horror Cinema: Eyes Without Faces* (2019)

Eleanor Beal and Jonathan Greenaway (eds), *Horror and Religion: New literary approaches to Theology, Race and Sexuality* (2019)

Dawn Stobbart, *Videogames and Horror: From Amnesia to Zombies, Run!* (2019)

David Annwn Jones, *Re-envisaging the First Age of Cinematic Horror, 1896–1934: Quanta of Fear* (2018)